THE CROOK AND FLAIL

THE SHE-KING: BOOK TWO

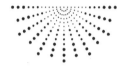

LIBBIE HAWKER

RUNNING RABBIT PRESS

Cover design: Running Rabbit Press

ALSO BY LIBBIE HAWKER

The She-King Series:

The Sekhmet Bed - Book 1

Sovereign of Stars - Book 3

The Bull of Min - Book 4

House of Rejoicing

Storm in the Sky

Eater of Hearts

White Lotus

Persian Rose

Blood Hemlock

Daughter of Sand and Stone

Tidewater

Mercer Girls

Madam

When I was firm upon the throne of Re, I was ennobled until the two periods of years. I came as the One Horus, flaming against my enemies.

-Inscription from Djeser-Djeseru, mortuary temple of Hatshepsut, fifth king of the Eighteenth Dynasty.

PART I
SON OF THE GOD

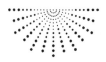

1486 B.C.E.

CHAPTER ONE

H ATSHEPSUT'S FINGERS ACHED FROM THE harp
strings, but she had played better today than ever before.
Her music tutor, a pinched and dour old woman named Mut-
tuy, had even raised an eyebrow and nodded at the performance. From Mut-tuy, this was as good as resounding acclaim.
She suspected she would find a few blisters on her fingertips by
supper time, but Hatshepsut was well pleased. She drifted
unhurried through the halls of the House of Women, rustling
faintly in her bright blue gown of a hundred pleats. To either
side, her guardsmen hulked as solid as river barges. They passed
the sunlight of a courtyard in full flower where a group of
women sat gossiping over chilled beer and cheese. The daggers
at her guards' belts glimmered in the afternoon glare. She was
not pleased that she must have an armed escort even in the
harem palace. She had grown up here, as was customary for a
king's daughter. Here the most common kitchen servants' faces
were as familiar to Hatshepsut as her own. But this was what
her mother Ahmose had commanded six years ago, when
Hatshepsut's father the Pharaoh died, when she was but a girl of
eight. What the Lady Regent ordered was not to be questioned.

When they reached her private apartment Hatshepsut dismissed the guards to her door. In the courtyard outside her room slender lotus pillars rose up beside women's private porches. The courtyard was heavily planted with sweet flowers and broad-leaved climbing vines, which cast an inviting green shade on the paving stones. The odors of perfume and the incense of offerings drifted from the halls of the palace. It was a pleasant afternoon. A swim in the harem's lotus pond would be welcome, but there were lessons yet today. Judging by the sun, her tutor was likely already waiting. She smiled.

Inside her dressing room, Hatshepsut's servants stood ready: Sitre-In, her sweet-tempered old nurse with the soft green eyes; Ita and Tem, the two chatty women who tended her bath and brought her meals; and – there he was – Senenmut, the tall, quiet tutor-priest with his solemn face and expressive hands.

At the sight of him she chased the smile from her face, though it fought to remain. His services had been gifted her by the Temple of Amun when she was only ten years old, but he was no slave. Senenmut chose to serve the Temple and the throne of his own free will. Whether he did it out of loyalty to the royal family or simply to advance his own well-being mattered not a whit to Hatshepsut. He was an exceptional teacher, though he was young – perhaps twenty-two or -three, if that. Under his guidance, she had refined her reading and writing until she was as capable as any scribe in the Two Lands. He had coached her in all the tongues a Great Royal Wife would need: the language of Retjenu from the north and east; Phoenician for dealing with tradesmen; sharp and brutal Heqa-Khasewet; the language of Kush. She had enjoyed his daily presence in her life from the start of his service. Senenmut took her seriously, even as a young girl; he answered all her questions without the usual patronizing air most adults reserved for children. And now that her womanhood was near she enjoyed his presence even more.

"Bring me a fresh kilt," she said to her maids, "and help me out of these sandals." She was weary after all. Mut-tuy was a demanding harp-mistress. She sank onto the stool at her dressing table with a sigh, rotating her wrists to work the ache from her hands. Ita knelt to untie the laces of her sandals. Hatshepsut flexed her toes, causing the bones of her feet to crackle.

She glanced up at Senenmut, who stood patiently waiting her pleasure. When he met her eye, he said, "I have brought scrolls for you, Great Lady: all the histories I could find on the station of God's Wife of Amun."

Hatshepsut's mouth went dry. There was no more putting it off. Though she still had not begun to bleed, she was fourteen years old – well into marriageable age – and her half-brother Thutmose was nearly eleven. He was old enough now to take the throne, and probably would as soon as Hatshepsut became a woman. It was not for the daughter of a Pharaoh to pick and choose among suitors, as common women may. She had no sisters left living who might take her place and spare her a life-time of Thutmose.

Well, if she must resign herself to a sour fate as Thutmose's wife, she would at least perform her duty with dedication, and do honor to her dead father's memory. She would learn the station of God's Wife so well that she would be beyond reproach. She would be the greatest God's Wife of them all. To achieve such a thing – ah, it would have made her father's face light with approval.

Maat is all, Hatet. She had heard him say it so many times that his voice still sounded in her heart, long after he had left the living world for the Field of Reeds. *If Egypt does not have its righteous order, then Egypt has nothing. Let maat be your guide in all things, and you will never place a foot wrong.* Marriage to Thut-mose was maat – the righteous way, the fundamental what-must-be that kept the world in working order. And that was that.

"Thank you, Senenmut. I will begin reading them tomorrow. What of our lesson this afternoon?"

"I thought I might discuss with you how the southern outposts fare, and what Egypt's presence in Kush means to the throne."

Boring, drier than old bones. But it would have to be done. A Great Royal Wife must know – a God's Wife must know. She nodded, inspected her braided sidelock in her electrum mirror, passed a hand over the stubble that powdered her scalp. It was a boy's hairstyle she wore, one thick lock of black hair worked into a braid over her ear, the rest shaved bald as an old man's pate. But it suited her, the sharpness of her nose, the steady black glare of her eyes. She had her father's features; she liked to stress them. She had been going about with a boy's hairstyle since she was a baby, to hear Sitre-In tell it, and she had no plans to change her ways now. But her scalp did need a pass of the razor. Time enough for that when Senenmut's lesson was finished.

Hatshepsut slipped the rings off her fingers, dropped them one by one into the ebony box Ita held. She removed the bangles from her wrists – all but one, a golden band set with a double row of tiny lapis scarabs. It was her favorite. She twisted its coolness against her skin as Ita and Tem removed a broad, heavy collar of golden leaves from her shoulders, laid it in its case, and helped her out of her gown.

As always when she undressed in his presence, Senenmut turned tactfully away, gazing out through the door of her chamber to the warm sunlit glow of the garden, predictably immaculate in his manners. She wished he would at least try to glimpse her bare flesh. She would not have punished him for that particular impudence.

Tem wound a short white boy's kilt around Hatshepsut's

hips, fastened it with an ivory pin in the likeness of Sekhmet, the warrior she-lion. For modesty's sake, Hatshepsut chose a drape of hundreds of strings of tiny beads to hang around her neck, covering her small new breasts. What she wouldn't give to be able to run once more bare-chested in boy's clothing, with her boy's hair, unfettered through the gardens. Too much was changing, and too fast, now that she was nearly a woman.

"Let's forgo the lesson, Senenmut. Walk with me in the garden," she commanded, and he turned back to her, his long face flustered. "Don't look so put out. There will be time enough to teach me all about Kushite politics tomorrow. Or the day after. Or in a year."

Senenmut smiled. "*Tomorrow*, then."

They strolled out together into the afternoon heat. Clouds of gnats shimmered white and silver above the most fragrant of the flowers. Brown darts of birds dived among the flies, snatching supper on the wing. Sitre-In and the maids wandered in their wake, far enough away to afford privacy of conversation but not so far as to let the king's daughter out of sight with her tutor.

Senenmut walked with hands clasped behind his back, his long, straight nose tilted toward the ground, immersed in the depth of his thoughts. He was inscrutable at times like these, turned inward and waiting for a word from her, a question, a challenge, to pull him into reality again, to make him blink like a man shaking off a magician's spell, draw a sudden breath, a swimmer breaking the surface of an unknowable water. She allowed a smile, but only when her face was turned away from her women, so Sitre-In would not grow suspicious.

"I am to be God's Wife soon."

And there was the blink, the breath. "Soon or late, it is bound to happen. You are nearly a woman."

"And that means I will soon be married."

"This troubles you, Great Lady?"

7

"Thutmose is weak-spirited and ill-tempered. I do not look forward to calling him my husband."

"He is young," Senenmut said gently. "With time, he will grow to be a better man."

On that count, Hatshepsut had her doubts. "Meanwhile, I must marry the whining, pouting boy, and not the better man."

"Who knows? Your womanhood may be far off yet. Perhaps by the time you marry he will have matured into a respectable king. You share a father. Thutmose the First was the greatest Pharaoh in living memory. Surely the son will take after the father."

In a misery, Hatshepsut longed for her sister, and not for the first time. Neferubity had died when she was still but a babe on the breast, barely old enough to walk and babble her half-formed words in her sweet, lisping way. It was not inconceivable that a younger daughter of the Pharaoh might be chosen as Great Royal Wife. It had happened to Ahmose; she had been set above her elder sister, wedded to the new king when she was only thirteen years old.

"In any case," Senenmut went on, breaking into her bleak musings, "you will enjoy learning the stations of God's Wife. There are many ceremonies you will perform, many rites you will be expected to know. And you must learn all the histories of the station, of course, and the locations of all the temples in the Two Lands, the names of all the High Priests, the incantations. If I know my student, she will relish the pursuit of this knowledge."

She nodded, but said nothing.

"You are so quiet. If I may be so bold as to question you, Great Lady, why does the prospect of marriage trouble you so? Ever since you were a small child you have known you will be wed to Thutmose. You have always understood what it means to be the king's daughter. This is no surprise."

"Knowing the name of the spice does not make a foul dish

THE CROOK AND FLAIL

more palatable. Come, tell a story to cheer me. Something of when you were my age – when you were an apprentice in the Temple."

The light in the garden slanted, deepening toward evening's orange-red glow. Hatshepsut slapped insects from her arms and her bare waist, waiting for Senenmut to begin.

"All right," he said. "Here is a true story from my days as an apprentice at the Temple of Amun.

"We had a boy in the temple, an apprentice who did not want to be there. He had other plans for his life, and being a priest of Amun was no part of his desires. Even though he got his bread and beer every day and had a comfortable enough place to sleep each night, he dreamed of freedom from his duties. He was forever trying to sneak out of the temple. One time the boy tried to drug the apprentice-master's beer, to put the man to sleep long enough that the boy could run away. But he used the wrong herb, so the apprentice-master's bowels ran for two days and the discontented boy was chosen to attend the master's privy. Another time, he stirred up a fight between five different boys, and they all began brawling in the courtyard. When the priests' attention was on the fight, he tried to sneak out through the temple gate, but one of the fighting boys threw a rock. It missed its intended target and knocked the boy senseless well before he could reach the road.

"Finally, one night after a festival when everybody was sleepy from eating too much, the boy, who had eaten sparingly and was alert, found a secret route out of the temple. He wrapped up his few belongings in his blanket and slung it onto his back. He walked right out into the fields and headed for Waset, where he thought he might work his way onto a barge crew and sail downriver, far from the Temple of Amun.

"It was just after the season of emergence, when the flood waters retreat. He decided to travel closer to the river, where the land was flat and clear, the going easier. But he did not know that a herd of deby had moved into the area. He heard a great bellow in the darkness and suddenly he was running for his life from a very cross river horse. He was forced to drop his bundle, which the deby trampled into the mud, and in turn forced to climb a very thin and scraggly tree – and there the creature kept him until sunrise.

"After the beast gave up and returned to the river, the boy was obliged to walk back to the Temple of Amun and confess what had happened. The other apprentices had a good laugh over it, and the priests gave him all the most disgusting chores for a month.

"But he learned that we are all given our burdens to bear, and the gods put us right where they want us to be. For although he never included priesthood in his dreams of the future, the priesthood eventually led him to honored service to the throne – as tutor to the king's daughter."

She laughed. "I knew the tale was about you."

"Clever as always, Great Lady. Yes, I was the boy who passed a night treed by a deby. In those days I would have given anything to shirk my duty. Now, though, I am blessed by all the gods to be where I am. I am glad I turned my whole heart to the task I was given."

"But what was it you dreamed of, Senenmut? What tempted you away from Amun? Why did you want to sail downriver?"

He shook his head. His face was all cool colors in the sycamore shadow, pale violet and blue, solemn. "Great Lady, I find it useless to speak of what might have been."

"All the same, I would know."

"Please. I do not delight in talking of what will never come to pass. And I take great pride in my service to you. I would not change my life now."

He would; Hatshepsut could see that plainly. He said what his station compelled him to say, and any nobleman might have accepted Senenmut at his word, so cool and quick was his speech. But the girl knew her tutor as well as he knew her. Some part of Senenmut still longed for that far-off dream. She slipped the scarab bracelet from her wrist and pressed it into his hand. "A gift for you, if you will only tell me what you once dreamed of."

Senenmut chuckled, tried to push the bracelet back. "Great Lady, do you think you must bribe me? It is not for the king's daughter to bribe any man, but especially not her most devoted servant."

"It is my favorite bracelet, and I make it a gift to you because it pleases me to do so. I *command* you to tell me what you dreamed of because I am the king's daughter. And because you are my most devoted servant, you will not disobey me."

Senenmut hung his head as if in chastisement, but he smiled broadly. "No, I never will disobey, Great Lady; do not fear that. Very well. I dreamed of becoming an architect. A great one, too – I wanted to create the most beautiful buildings in all the world."

"A far cry from tutoring a Pharaoh's daughter."

"Or from tending Amun's shrine, counting up the god's tallies of gold and grain and cattle. Ah, my life is different from what I had hoped for, but the gods have blessed me all the same. I am not unhappy. I have found peace and pride in accepting the burden the gods wish me to bear. And you will find pride, too, as Great Royal Wife."

"How much happier would you be if you had taken up the burden you wished for yourself?"

Senenmut turned Hatshepsut's bracelet over in his hands. It caught and reflected the glow of sunset. The inlaid scarabs shimmered. At length he said, "I will confess that the beauty of architecture still does sing to me. Palaces, temples, monuments to the gods – they all touch my spirit in ways that other men seem not to feel. I find a particular joy in the strength of walls, the elegance of pillars, and when I stand in their shadows, admiration for the men who can create such works fills my heart to bursting. But the gods have set my path. I am not unhappy."

She led him back to the pillared porch at her garden door. "My mother and aunt are coming to the House of Women this evening for a feast," she said. "I must prepare."

Senenmut raised his palms to her, a precise, correct bow.

"Make sure the history scrolls are ready in my chamber. I will begin accepting my burden when the sun rises. It will not take a deby to drive me toward the gods' will, I promise you."

He smiled at her words, his face as long and wise as ever, and barely touched by sadness. When he turned away, she saw how carefully he tucked her gift into the edge of his kilt, how his elegant hand lingered on the hoop of gold, which might, she thought, still hold the heat of her skin.

CHAPTER TWO

S UPPER WAS LAID OUT ON clusters of tables in the vast communal garden of the House of Women. The summer evening was welcoming, soft, stirred gently by a breeze from the river. The air smelled of moving water, of spice and warmth, of honey-sweet blossoms just closing before the advance of the mild valley night. The tail end of the day's light graded to dense green shadows among the flower beds.

Servants, sturdily attractive in their simple white frocks, carried jars of wine from the kitchens or stood near the tables waving flies away from platters with fans of pliant feathers on long, slender stems. Hatshepsut stood in the grass watching the servants scurry through the garden under burdens of roasted meat, great sloshing tureens of steaming soups, armfuls of fine light bread. Among so much plain white linen she longed for her own boy's kilt, but such an informality would be an insult to her mother the regent. Instead she had selected from her great standing chest a loose-woven crimson gown. It displayed through its light fabric the shape of her developing breasts, the breadth of her hips. It would please Ahmose, she thought, to see how her daughter progressed toward womanhood, even if her blood still refused to flow. Sitre-In had hauled a wide, flat box from some niche or other and produced from it an intricate collar of shocking blue faience bars joined with links of gold. "Very fashionable just now, I hear," Sitre-In had said as she hefted the collar to Hatshepsut's shoulders. It had taken two women to hold it in place and fasten the links at her nape. The collar immediately brought a nagging ache to her neck and shoulders, but her women cooed so over its bright color and elegant lines that she was determined to endure it for the night. Perhaps Ahmose would be pleased by this, too – by seeing Hatshepsut pay a care for what was popular among the women of Waset's royal court.

A ripple of soft laughter drifted from the pillars of the harem house – controlled, light, feminine laughter, not too loud, dainty hands held over delicate mouths. The former Pharaoh's harem emerged from the darkened House of Women like bright boats from a river mist. They moved in a muted rustle of linen of every color, every weave, the sheer open weave that displayed the charms of the female body, the tight, liquid weave that flowed and rippled like water in moonlight. Here and there faience collars as bright as Hatshepsut's own gleamed in the final traces of evening light. Dark wigs swung with beaded, banded braids. The women's voices, petal-soft, rose with the gleaming, languid drifts of winged insects to float, lulling and hazy, above the grass.

The women parted, fanning out into the gentle evening in twos and threes. At the heart of the harem, the two queens of Egypt walked arm in arm.

Ahmose, the shorter and thinner of the two, looked straight ahead as she stepped onto the grass. She was still smiling lightly at whatever jest had set the harem women to laughing, but her black eyes were far distant, serene. Her fine, small feet, shining in silver-threaded sandals, rippled the pleats of her immaculate white gown. Dozens of malachite bracelets ringed her arms; a collar of shining green leaves lay across her narrow shoulders. The gold cobra of the Great Royal Wife circled her head, reared above her brow, as aloof and poised as the regent herself.

Mutnofret, second wife of the departed Pharaoh, was startling in the force of her beauty. Even Hatshepsut, young as she was, sensed the strength of her aunt's appeal, saw how brightly Mutnofret outshone her younger sister. The second wife had borne four sons, though only Thutmose still lived. The soft roundness of her belly pressed against the pleats of her blue gown; her breasts lay heavy on her chest; yet her beauty was not diminished. These frank reminders of fertility only ripened her allure. Her face was angled, cat-like, her wide eyes set at an intriguing cant, her broad mouth curved into a slow, confident smile. The easy grace of her movements, the way her elbow crooked lightly around Ahmose's hand, made Hatshepsut flush with admiration. Mutnofret was not one hair lesser a queen than Ahmose, whatever her official rank might suggest. Both women flashed in the retiring sunlight, gold and electrum lighting each elegant finger of each careful hand. Their belts and wig ornaments sparkled with fine polished stones. There was nothing to choose between them. It was only official decree that gave Ahmose higher standing than Mutnofret. Even attending a mere garden feast, the second wife was as formidable as the first.

Hatshepsut stepped forward to greet them. She bowed, palms out, properly demure.

"Well," Ahmose said, her voice carrying a precise measure of amusement. "I half expected to see you in a kilt, Hatet. Last time your aunt and I held a feast at the House of Women, you were bare-chested and dressed like a boy. I am pleased that you are a lady this evening."

"A pity no one can get her to wear her hair like a lady," Mutnofret said. "Shaving it all off like some filthy market boy. Imagine."

"Yes, Aunt Mutnofret." Hatshepsut could think of nothing acceptable to add. She shuffled her feet in the grass, eyes downcast.

"Thutmose," Mutnofret called over her shoulder. "Come greet your sister."

Hatshepsut bit her lips together to fight off a groan. She had hoped her half-brother would not attend the supper party, but should have known that hope was futile. Thutmose went wherever Mutnofret went, trailing behind his mother with arrogance rolling from him the way body odor trailed gardeners on a hot day, a miasma of self-satisfaction. He had been allowed to go on living in the royal palace even though he was more than old enough to move to the House of Women for his schooling, as was proper for any prince. This privilege made him smugger by the day, plumping his opinion of his own royal person as a goose grows fat in its pen.

Prince Thutmose edged from the shadow of a pillar. He was dressed in a formal white kilt, an imitation of a grown man's fine pleated garment. It fell not to his knees but all the way to the ground, and he kicked carelessly at the hem as he walked.

Mutnofret reached out as her son drew near, laid her hand protectively on his shoulder and pulled him close to her side. "Greet your sister properly."

Thutmose gave off a petulant sigh. Mutnofret's hand tightened on his shoulder; he squirmed, then said flatly, "Hello, Hatshepsut. You look well."

She pursed her lips, glanced at Ahmose; the regent's brows furrowed in warning, and Hatshepsut said quickly, "And you, brother. I am pleased to see you. Won't you sit with me at the feast? I would..." she glanced at her mother again, who nodded almost imperceptibly, "I would be honored by your company." The words burned her throat, but Ahmose raised her chin in mute approval.

The royal children had their own small table beneath the

spreading boughs of a sycamore, set apart from the gossiping women. The tree was alive with mobile, whispering leaves, fresh and green. As the sun sank lower and the garden darkened in shades of violet, bats snicked through the boughs overhead. Servants poured oil into the bowls of bronze lamps, set the wicks ablaze. Pools of lamplight spread between tables; moths spun in pale whirlwinds about the flames, sizzled now and then when one drew too near and perished.

Hatshepsut sat across the table from Thutmose – a small mercy, that she was not forced any nearer. He slouched in his seat. A surly arrogance colored his every gesture. She did her best to ignore him, gazing up at the bats and the sycamore leaves. Servants ladled rich spicy gravy into bowls, cut fine and tender portions from roasted joints of meat. Hatshepsut pretended Thutmose did not exist, concentrating on her supper in contented silence. When the servants brought bowls of honeyed milk and fruit, Thutmose spoke at last. "Aren't you going to entertain me? If you're to be my wife some day, you'd better be more interesting than you are tonight."

Hatshepsut's bare scalp prickled. "This feast is for the entertainment of the harem women, not for *your* highness. With no Pharaoh on the throne, my mother must be sure the women of the king's house feel their expectations of luxury are well met; otherwise political alliances may be lost."

Thutmose snorted. "Did you memorize that speech, O Great Orator? You talk like a wooden doll."

Hatshepsut's face flushed hot. She had, in fact, memorized the words Ahmose had spoken that morning, when she had informed Hatshepsut of the feast. She had liked the sound of them, liked the way Ahmose had laden a simple supper party with such import using only a few well-chosen words. Now she felt like a fool. She glowered at Thutmose. "If you should care to take your proper place in the House of Women, Thutmose, then you might reasonably expect some entertainment tonight. I did not memorize that speech, Mighty Lord of the Two Lands, but perhaps you ought to."

"Don't get short with me, fat-head. Your head looks like a big ugly melon. And you shave it like a boy. You don't even know if you're a boy or a girl."

"Is this entertaining enough for you, Tiny Horus?" She opened her mouth, showing him a mess of half-chewed fruit.

"You're disgusting," Thutmose turned his face away with fastidious delicacy. "No wonder your mother sent you off to the harem instead of keeping you in the palace."

It took a great effort to swallow the fruit; a sudden and painful lump obstructed Hatshepsut's throat. "You don't know anything about it. You follow your mother around like a halfwit duckling. You probably don't even see the regent at all. You're too busy hiding behind Mutnofret's skirt."

Thutmose would not be goaded. He stared flatly at Hatshepsut, his eyes long and slanted like his mother's. "I don't need to see the regent, Lady Bald-Head. My mother has given me the finest tutors and priests in the empire to teach me how to be a king. What could I learn about ruling Egypt from a woman?"

It took the greatest effort for Hatshepsut to bite her tongue. Ahmose did this petulant donkey's-rump of a boy a great favor by acting as his regent.

Thutmose went on: "I'm glad I don't have to live here with the rest of the boys and girls. What do you learn from your tutors? Sums and reading and writing? I know all *that*. I know how to rule the kingdom. I'm going to be Pharaoh some day, and then you'll have to do what I say."

"Is that what you think?"

"You will. I'll be Pharaoh, and I'll marry you, and you'll have to do everything I say, because I'll be the king and your husband!"

Like a cobra, rage reared up in Hatshepsut's heart. She abandoned all pretense of ladylike behavior. If Thutmose wished to drag her onto a battle field, she would oblige him with a fight. "Piss on your throne! I'll never marry you, ever! And without marriage to me, you can never be king. I'll go off and start my own country and invade Egypt and throw you in a crocodile pool."

"That's a marvelous idea. You can go off into the Red Land and rule the sand dunes. You can be the ruler of beetles and desert rats. I'll be the king of Egypt."

"Do you think you can be king without me? You, the son of a second wife? You may as well be the son of a harem girl! I am the blood of the Pharaoh and the Great Royal Wife; without me by your side, you are nothing." All at once she was on her feet, swaying under the weight of her collar. "You won't have any throne unless I consent to marry you, so you'd best start treating me with respect. And anyway, I'd be a better king than you. At least I can make decisions for myself without tugging on my mawat's skirt and whimpering. I'm surprised Mutnofret let you out of your swaddling long enough to attend the feast!"

Thutmose, unflappable, rolled his eyes. "You can't be the king, stupid. You're a girl. You're an ugly girl with a shaved head, who nobody would ever want to marry, even if it was the only way for a man to take the throne."

Hatshepsut hurled her dish of fruit straight into Thutmose's face. It bounced off his head and disappeared in the shadows beyond the sycamore trunk. Honeyed milk washed down his face and chest; at once he began to bawl like a weaning calf. A hand took Hatshepsut by the upper arm. She did not dare look around. She could tell by the ferocity of the grip that it was Ahmose who held her.

"What in Amun's name is happening here?" When Hatshepsut said nothing, Ahmose shook her hard. "Speak up when the regent asks you a question!"

"He – he mocked me. He said I'm ugly."

"She is ugly!" Servants with ewers of water appeared to flock around Thutmose. Two stood by with fresh towels as Thutmose rinsed his chest and arms clean. "She's ugly and stupid and acts improperly!"

"Be quiet, Thutmose," Ahmose snapped. "I gave you no leave to speak."

The prince gaped at his regent as if he had been slapped. Then his face crumpled, his chin wobbled, and fresh tears rolled down his cheeks. Mutnofret laid a clean towel on the grass beside him and sank to her knees, stroking his head, dabbing at his chest with a damp cloth. "Hush, little one," she murmured.

Hatshepsut snorted. *Little one.*

"She can't talk to me that way," Thutmose wailed, pointing at Ahmose. "Mawat, tell her she has to be nice to me!"

Mutnofret made a frustrated noise, half growl, half sigh. "Thutmose, my sweet prince, Ahmose is the regent, and we are to do as she commands." Mutnofret's voice was patient and gentle, but Hatshepsut saw the resentment shining in the second wife's eyes as she cut her glance toward Ahmose. She saw the way Mutnofret's arm held strong and steady around her son's shoulders. *We must do as she commands for now, until you sit the throne.* Those were Mutnofret's true words, the words she said with her eyes, her posture. Senenmut had taught Hatshepsut how to watch courtiers' faces, to discern the truth behind their artful speech. She watched Mutnofret comfort the prince through narrowed eyes.

A crowd of servants and harem women flocked about the children's table. Ahmose marched Hatshepsut away from the bluster of bodies.

"I told your nurse to enjoy an evening off because I thought you were old enough to conduct yourself with some measure of dignity. Mut's sake, Hatshepsut, you are the king's daughter! And you are fourteen years old. I was already Great Royal Wife when I was fully a year younger than you. I had hoped that living in the House of Women might teach you how to be a proper lady. What am I to do with you if you will not behave?"

"So you did send me away from the palace to make me be a lady – to teach me how to wear dresses and dance and sing."

Ahmose's face softened. "No. I misspoke. I moved you to the harem because all royal children must grow up in the harem. It is maat – the righteous way. A palace is too busy, far too dangerous a place for growing young people. In the House of Women you may learn all the arts that will make you…"

"Thutmose doesn't have to live here. He gets to stay in the palace and learn how to rule the country. If I am to be his Great Royal Wife someday, I must know how to rule, too." She pulled away from Ahmose's grip, dashed her fists against her thighs in a helpless fury. "This makes no sense!"

"Hatet, Hatet. How can I make you understand?" Ahmose rubbed at her forehead, smoothed the lines she wore beneath the cobra crown. "It is not for Thutmose's sake that I've allowed him to stay in the palace. It is for Mutnofret's sake."

"Why should Mutnofret care whether her revolting son lives in the palace or the harem?"

Ahmose looked away, out across the blue shadows of the garden. An expression of great pain crossed her face, then fled again, replaced by the studied calm of the Great Royal Wife. Hatshepsut waited a long time, hands clasped and eyes down like a properly contrite daughter, and at last Ahmose spoke. "Hatet, you are no ordinary girl."

I know, she wanted to say. But she kept her peace, and let her mother speak on in a voice that broke often, yet was still clear.

"I have kept things from you…important things…not because I do not care for you – never think that, my love. You have always been the light of my heart. There are some stories we are not strong enough to know as children…but you are almost a woman now. You are old enough to know the way of the world, my daughter. My son."

Hatshepsut's head came up sharply. Her eyes, wide, disbelieving, held the regent's. She had not heard correctly. That was it – she had not heard correctly.

"We will go to your room now," Ahmose said, "And I will tell you everything."

CHAPTER THREE

THEY SAT TOGETHER ON HATSHEPSUT'S bed, mirroring one another's posture: rigid, straight-backed, cold hands folded in laps, mouths in tight pale lines. Ita and Tem had tidied the room and set oil alight in the lamps. The braziers glowed orange and fragrant, reflecting their light off mirror-polished bronze discs. Streamers of dark smoke reached up to the high ceiling, escaped outside past the bars of the wind-catcher to the deep blue evening sky. In the dim light, Ahmose's face was lined and darkened, all harsh angles and deep shadows. Finally she spoke.

"What I tell you now must remain between us. It is not for any other soul to know. You must never tell anyone; not even your nurse or your tutor."

Hatshepsut nodded.

"Swear it," Ahmose said.

She was a stern woman, serious in her duties, but even so, Hatshepsut had never known her mother to be this grave. The quiet force of her voice raised the hairs on Hatshepsut's arms.

"Swear it on the goddess."

"I swear by Mut's wings," Hatshepsut whispered.

"Good. And I swear by Mut that what I tell you is true."

The pressure of silence squeezed all around. Hatshepsut's eyelid twitched again and again, but she did not dare break the stillness to rub the twitch away.

"You are not what you seem to be, Hatet. You are not just a girl. And you are not only the daughter of the Pharaoh.

"When I was close to your age – when I had barely begun to bleed – my father, King Amunhotep, died. He had no royal sons and had appointed no heir. The sons of his concubines were no more than infants. Egypt was on the verge of invasion by the Heqa-Khasewet in the north and the Kushites in the south. The country was in great danger."

Hatshepsut nodded, bridling her impatience. She knew all this; Senenmut had told her this story before.

"Rather than risk the land to the rule of an infant, my mother and grandmother, both wise queens, chose a man for the Horus Throne. A man of common blood – a rekhet – but also a great soldier, a tactician and battle leader who could not be beaten on the field."

"Father," Hatshepsut said.

"Yes, your father. And they were right to choose him. I believe still that no other man could have kept Egypt safe from the jackals waiting to tear the land apart. Thutmose the general – he was the gods' own choice for the throne. But my mother and grandmother worried, you see, that because he was rekhet-born others may not recognize his right to be the king.

"The Amun priesthood, Hatshepsut: it is very powerful. It controls much of the wealth of the land, and more importantly, it has great influence over the hearts of all men, noble and rekhet. My mother feared the priests of Amun would reject a rekhet king. She feared they would turn the people's hearts against your father. She needed a token to back her chosen king – a pawn, like a game piece on a senet board."

"You were her pawn." Hatshepsut had never thought to question why Ahmose was the Great Royal Wife rather than Mutnofret, who was the elder of the sisters. "But why you?"

"Do you know what it means to be god-chosen, Hatet?"

"I have heard such a thing mentioned before, at the Temple. But I don't know precisely...."

"The god-chosen are rare people, touched by the divine. Sometimes they hear the gods' voices, or fall into trances to speak with the voice of a god. Sometimes they know the meanings of dreams, or read omens, or see the future. I am god-chosen – a dream-reader, though in your lifetime I have mostly kept the skill to myself. It is demanding enough work ruling Egypt without the added toil of interpreting dreams. But when I was your age, everyone in Waset knew of my gift, even the priests. My mother reasoned – not incorrectly, I think – that if I was the Great Royal Wife, no priest would dare to speak against your father for fear of the gods' wrath.

"But Mutnofret is my elder, of course, and she was first in line for the title of Great Royal Wife. She had always expected to be the new king's chief wife when our father went on to the Field of Reeds. When our family set me ahead of her, Mutnofret was savage with hate. She never forgave me for taking her birthright, though the gods know it was not my doing. And soon she and I were locked in a battle to give the Pharaoh sons.

"Mutnofret had..." Ahmose's voice faltered. She breathed steadily for a moment, as if stilling a sickness in her stomach, and at last went on. "Mutnofret had three sons. Beautiful boys; I loved them, despite the war she and I fought. They were, after all, my own blood, and the children of the sister I had once loved beyond life."

Hatshepsut said their names quietly. "Wadjmose, Amunmose, and Ramose." She knew of them. Sitre-In had told many stories of her long-gone brothers. Sometimes Hatshepsut thought she could recall their faces.

"Yes. They were good boys. You played often with them, and

they were kind to you. We all loved them – Mutnofret, of course, and I, and your father. But your father would not name any of them heir."

"Why?"

Ahmose stared at her hands in her lap. Her thick lashes, matted with kohl, obscured her eyes. "He'd had a dream, Hatet, a dream that had visited him many times, even before he was called to the throne. In this dream, he saw the child who would succeed him as Pharaoh, and it was none of Mutnofret's boys."

A deep, shocking chill covered her, penetrated all her skin at once, as if she had been thrown into the cold, fierce river. *There is nothing to fear; it's just a story*, she told herself. But a sharp, painful certainty dug at her ribs, pounded there with the beat of her heart. Was this what it felt like, to be touched by a god, to hear a god's voice? Reluctantly, Hatshepsut asked the question, though she already knew the answer. "Who was the child in Father's dream?"

"You."

Hatshepsut could find no words. *I am female. I cannot be Pharaoh.*

Ahmose continued the tale. "You were not yet born, of course. Your father knew only that he would have his heir from my body. And I knew with the certainty of the god-chosen that I would never bear a son. It was a source of great strife between us. His insistence that his Great Royal Wife produce his heir only soured poor Mutnofret all the more; she and I were at odds all the time. I kept trying to make him name one of the boys as his successor, just to pacify my sister, but he refused, and the tragedy and strain of her fate began to tear at Mutnofret's heart. Soon she was seeing threats everywhere. She accused me of trying to steal Wadjmose, the eldest, to raise him as my own child."

Ahmose fell silent. She lifted her face, gazing up at Hatshepsut's painted walls. Even in the dim light, the walls were bright with the images of the goddesses. Ahmose rose, graceful and straight. She walked to the nearest mural, reached out a finger to trace the form of Mut, the mother-goddess, with pure white wings outstretched. Hatshepsut wanted to hear how the story ended – needed to hear it now, now that she knew about her father's dream, about her own part in it. But the darkness in Ahmose's silence forbade questions. Hatshepsut sat quietly, working her fingers into knots, pressing her nails into the palms of her hands.

After a long time, Ahmose turned away from Mut's image. She faced Hatshepsut once more. "I had a terrible fight with your aunt, Hatet, one day when her suspicion and rage had pushed me beyond the limits of my endurance. I threw her to the ground and beat her with a stick, as if she were a disobedient slave."

Hatshepsut stared hard at her mother, eyes wide. *Beat her? Mutnofret?* Impossible. Ahmose was a small woman – smaller than Mutnofret, certainly – and the second wife wore a compelling, hypnotic allure all about her, as tangible as a priest's leopard-skin mantle. No woman or man could beat the second wife. Hatshepsut was sure of it.

"I was in anguish over what I had done. Not only to Mutnofret, but to Egypt. I was young, you see, and inexperienced, and your father was too often away at war. By this time, I was afraid for my station in life, afraid Mutnofret would take all I had. So I...I did things that...I angered the gods, Hatshepsut. It is my greatest shame. In my fear and isolation, I took a lover – my own steward – and I usurped the title of God's Wife of Amun from my grandmother, who was too old and weak to stop me."

Ahmose's voice quavered with shame, but Hatshepsut hardly noticed, flung as she was into a state far beyond excitement. This was better than any adventure story, better than she had imagined! She gaped at her mother, thrilled and impressed. "You took a *lover*? And you are the God's Wife?"

"It is no longer my title," Ahmose said quickly, her voice stern. "I was never truly God's Wife, though if you look at court records dating back fifteen or sixteen years, I am referred to by the title. But it was never mine to take. It was a lie – a dreadful, despicable lie – one for which I will be sorry until my dying day, and after, too. I was young, but that is no good excuse. The gods turned their faces from Egypt because of my irresponsibility. The river failed; Egypt came very near to famine. All because of me, because I was too weak to deal with Mutnofret without scheming like a louse."

Ahmose faltered. Her face pinched, and just for a moment her chin quivered as if she might cry. She drew a long, shaking breath. Then she said, so quietly, "And even that is not entirely true. I want to deny what I did. I want to deny that I was ever the God's Wife, because I came to the title in such a terrible, cruel, unfair way, and knowing I was ever capable of such wickedness burns my heart. And because your father made me renounce all claim to the title once he learned what I had one. But I *was* the God's Wife, after all."

"I don't understand, Mawat."

"We do as the gods will us, Hatet. You and I, the king, all the people of Egypt. Whatever our plans, in the end we do as they will.

"The god Amun wanted a son. And so he chose me – I will never understand why – but he chose me, and he took me; brought me to his side and to his bed, though the path that led me there nearly destroyed me. It nearly destroyed our family, and Egypt, too. He made me his wife, the same as any man makes any woman his wife. I could not escape my fate.

"This last great fight I had with Mutnofret…. I felt so guilty, so soiled, that I fled to the Temple of Amun and begged the god to forgive me. I sought forgiveness for everything – taking the title from my grandmother, taking a lover, hurting Mutnofret. I pleaded with all the gods for redemption. Straight into the night I prayed. And they heard my prayers."

Ahmose returned to the bed. She sat close; in the brief space between them, Hatshepsut could feel the vulnerable, human warmth of her mother's skin.

"The gods sent me a vision, Hatet. The strongest and greatest vision I have ever received. They would give me my redemption, an amendment for all my wrongs: a son, the heir to the Horus Throne. A Pharaoh unlike any other, who would heal the river, restore maat, and bring glory to Egypt. A child of Amun, half god, with nine souls, nine great and fearless kas.

"And on that same night, Amun came to me in your father's body, and made me the God's Wife in the flesh. On that night, the Pharaoh and I made you – our prince."

Because she could not look at her mother, Hatshepsut watched the flame in the nearest brazier. It bent, flickered as if it might snuff itself out. Then it found some well of strength and leapt up higher, brighter than it had burned before. "But I'm a girl," she said, her lips and hands tingling.

"On the outside. One of your nine kas is female, and it has dictated the form of your body. But you have eight more; every one of them is male."

Hatshepsut said nothing. Her ears seemed to hear a distant pounding, drums far off. Then she remembered Thutmose, and Mutnofret, and saw that there was still more to Ahmose's story.

"Although you were born a girl, I knew you for the prince you are from the moment they laid you at my breast. I tried to convince your father. He thought I was mad. I warned him that you were Amun's son, and that if he did not name you his heir, the gods would be angry. But he worried over what the people would think: a girl, heir to the throne. And I understood his worries. I do not blame him."

"Blame him for what?"

Ahmose would not speak, or could not.

Hatshepsut's heart filled with dread, a terrible cold pressure that stole her breath. "Blame him for what, Mawat?"

"For the deaths of Mutnofret's boys. I knew, if he failed to raise you as heir, that the gods would break him to their will. But your father was always so stubborn, so certain I would bear another son – one male of body, not only male of ka. And because he would not do the work the gods gave him, because he would not acknowledge you as a prince, the gods took away his other sons one by one."

Tears welled in Hatshepsut's eyes. She blinked them away without raising her hands to wipe them. In a way, then, it was her fault the boys had died.

"Prince Thutmose was born on the same day Wadjmose died. The death of her eldest son broke Mutnofret, and she stayed broken for many years – my poor, poor sister. But the new baby kept her heart from fleeing entirely into darkness. Thutmose was her only joy, her only reason for living. She nursed him herself, and would let no other woman care for him, not even for a moment. Not until he was much older did she finally assign a nurse to see to some of his needs; but even now, it is Mutnofret who is, without question, the prince's only mawat.

"And so you see, Hatet, I could not bear to send the prince to the harem when his sixth year came. I feared it might shatter Mutnofret completely, to take the prince away from her. There have been times in my life when I have hated Mutnofret, may the gods curse me, but I love my sister now. I love her and I pity her. Her life has been one great sorrow, and to take away her son might destroy her.

"And now do you understand?"

Numb, stunned, Hatshepsut nodded. Then a wild thought flared in her breast, a whisper that she tried to ignore. She shook her head to deny it, but it licked up, bright and dancing, a flame. "Mother, Prince Thutmose – he is still alive. The gods spared him. Why, when Mutnofret's other sons all died?"

"Because," Ahmose said, and raised her hand to caress Hatshepsut's cheek, to lift her chin so their eyes met and held, "in the end, your father did the task the gods gave him. He proclaimed you his heir at Annu, the sacred city of the north. As your regent, I have kept the throne for you until you come of age to claim it as the rightful king."

But all of Egypt believed Thutmose was the heir. "You are Thutmose's regent."

"No. I have never called him the heir, nor called myself the regent of Thutmose. I have always been careful, in every dealing and proclamation, to name myself only the regent of *the* heir, and to name Thutmose only the prince, never the inheritor. The people of Egypt may not be ready yet to accept you as their rightful ruler – the people and the priests of Amun. But by the gods, it shall be as your father commanded. I swear, Hatshepsut, I will see you crowned king. You are the rightful lord of the Two Lands. The crook and flail are yours."

CHAPTER FOUR

SENENMUT KNEW HE BLUSHED TOO easily. It was a habit unbecoming a man, but try as he might, he seemed unable to control the unfortunate reflex. Hatshepsut, observant as always, seemed to have made a game of his blushes. Every evening now she took her lessons in the garden, walking through a gathering blue dusk or sitting with Senenmut on the carved bench beneath the sycamore. Always her nurse and handmaids remained at a distance, and Hatshepsut was free to pose the questions that brought the color to his cheeks. They were simple enough questions, in truth, about the nature of men and women. Senenmut was bound by his service to answer as directly as he dared. Had his charge been a prince, he would have found no difficulty. Somehow the fact of her rough, emerging femininity added a disorienting dimension, so that he picked through his words with ostentatious care, and a word or two into his response his face would heat, his throat would dry, and he would catch Hatshepsut peering at him from the corner of her eye, though her face was always turned, aloof with chin raised, to stare impassively into the depths of the garden.

For all her mischief, she was a dedicated student. They spoke often enough of serious matters that Senenmut felt secure in his achievements as tutor to the king's daughter. On a peaceful evening redolent with the water-green scent of lotus, he sat beside her on the bench while she furrowed her brow and volleyed at him a string of questions concerning the various works of her father Thutmose. Of late she had been drifting into quiet, pensive distances. No doubt her impending marriage had left some trouble on her heart.

"And what do you know of my father's early expeditions?" Hatshepsut's fingers tangled and clicked in the beads strung about her neck.

"Quite a lot; it is recent history. Is there a particular expedition you wish to learn of?"

"His trek to Annu."

"Annu?" Senenmut paused, considering. "I cannot say that I know of any of your father's doings in Annu. It's an important city, of course, full of very old temples with many powerful priesthoods still practicing their work. He must have visited Annu for political reasons – ah, probably several times. But if there is any special visit he made to Annu, I have not read of it yet."

"Political reasons," she repeated in a faint, distracted sort of way, and fell into one of her musing silences. Into the pause, Ita and Tem laughed over their spindles, but Hatshepsut's eyes remained unfocused on the shade-and-sunlight of the garden path. "If my father had ever made an important proclamation at Annu, it would be in the histories, would it not?"

"I suppose that depends on how important the proclamation was, and to whom it was made, and what was its purpose. Some directives are relevant only in the moment – for a year or a month, or for merely a day. If no record is known to exist, that does not mean a proclamation never was issued."

"This proclamation would be extremely important. To everybody, and for more than a day."

"What exactly are you hunting, Lady? If it is a particular history you seek I can help you find it."

"I cannot speak of it," she said, suddenly agitated. "I took a vow. No doubt if anyone could find this particular record, you could, Senenmut. You know the scrolls better than any man. And so I can be certain that no record exists."

Her brusque reply left him at a loss for words. He tilted his head at her, quizzical, hoping to coax out by gesture something more to go by.

Hatshepsut smiled in spite of her strange preoccupation. "Don't worry yourself. If a record no longer exists, that indicates nothing, as you say. It is not so easy to erase history. The past cannot be scratched out just by tearing up scrolls or defacing a few carvings. History lives in the minds of men, too – you have said as much. One day I will have the truth of Annu. If the gods will it, I will have the truth."

"You grow wiser every day, Great Lady, and more like a Great Royal Wife."

Ordinarily his words would have made her beam, exposing the large front teeth she had inherited from her father, the slender dark gap between that made her smiles so unaccountably riveting. But she frowned.

"What do you know of the time my father proclaimed Thutmose his heir?"

"It happened here in Waset, at the Temple of Amun, seven years ago."

"And records exist?"

"Oh, yes, Lady. Many. I could bring them to you, if you wish to read them."

She pursed her lips, an expression that pinched her already rather unrefined face. He knew the look well. The prospect of reading the scrolls did not please her.

"Bring me everything you can find."

"Great Lady? Did I say something wrong?"

"No," she said, smoothing her face and her short kilt. She even put on a little smile for him. "I was only lost in thought."

"What sort of thought, if I may ask?"

She shrugged and toyed again with the thick drape of beads. Just as she drew a slow breath to make an answer, a clamor erupted at the far end of the garden. Hatshepsut leaped to her feet. Startled out of all self-possession, Senenmut sprang in front of her, shielding her with an out-thrust arm, from what he did not know. In a heartbeat they both realized that the dreadful noise was only two cats battling. Senenmut laughed, and this time he did not mind when the heat of embarrassment rose to his face.

"Oh, bother those beasts!" Ita shuffled off toward the racket, waving her hands fiercely to scatter the cats apart. She disappeared into a flower bed, and on the instant shrieked like a bird in a net. Tem and Sitre-In went laughing into the dusk to remove the clawing cat from Ita's skirt.

"Senenmut," Hatshepsut said, commanding.

He turned to look at her. And she stepped forward, laid her hands on his chest, pressed her lips to his. The kiss lasted only a moment. He jerked back.

"Hush," she said, to forestall his protests.

Alone with my charge, he thought in a panic, glancing around for the nurse, the handmaids. They were still preoccupied, giggling and squealing in the bushes. Hatshepsut's little game made a queasy sort of sense to him now. She had been testing him, probing at his feelings for her, an oarsman finding the depth of muddied water. And she had misread his flustered responses as...*love?*

The women came struggling from the flower bed, Ita wailing over her shredded skirt. Hatshepsut turned triumphant eyes on him.

"That's enough tutoring for today," he said.

"You may go then."

35

Senenmut fled the garden as quickly as propriety would allow.

It was a testament to Hatshepsut's stubbornness that she was able to kiss him once more, when rare privacy presented itself. Tutor and princess were seldom alone for more than a moment; Senenmut made sure of it, calling a woman to fetch him water for his dry throat or a fan to keep the flies away, though in this season flies were scarce and seldom a bother. He drew Hatshepsut's servants toward him constantly as he worked, like a fisherman drawing in one net, then casting it out only to draw immediately upon another. But Hatshepsut was more practiced than he at managing servants. Smoothly attending to her history lesson with bright, keen eyes and pertinent questions, she sent her servants on a series of urgent errands in a display of juggling that would have made a court acrobat sick with envy, and soon Senenmut found himself without a witness. For the briefest moment there was no one to observe them, and in the middle of a somber question about the defeat of the Heqa-Khasewet, Hatshepsut stopped speaking and leaned forward to press her lips to Senenmut's. Gently, he laid his hands on her shoulders and pushed her away.

"Great Lady, I am your humblest servant and it is not for me to deny you. However, this is highly improper and should not continue."

"Why?"

"You are still a girl, and I am a grown man. Beyond even that consideration, you are the king's daughter. I am a common man, and your servant. Kissing games between two children may be natural enough, but this is not maat."

Hatshepsut narrowed her black eyes.

"Do not be angry with me, Great Lady, I beg you. It is my place as your tutor and priest to advise you, to guide you toward wiser actions. Aside from all that, it could be dangerous for me. What if one of your maids sees? Do you suppose Ahmose will believe it was all your idea? Certainly not; she will assume that this man who was trusted to educate you has taken advantage of his station to impose himself upon an innocent girl. I would be punished, and quite harshly, I imagine."

She slumped. "All right. You have made your point, Senenmut. I see that you are correct."

She was a lioness of a girl, fierce and arrogant. But he had known her all these years. Beneath her poise there was, he knew, the same tender heart all girls possessed. For its sake, he did not allow his relief to show on his face. He smiled tenuously and took up the lesson where he had left off. When he had finished his day's duty he begged her leave to go. She hesitated, more distracted than she had been for days, with a sorrow in her eyes that cut Senenmut's throat and belly with guilty knives. But at last she nodded and waved him away.

He said, "Until tomorrow, Great Lady," and bowed at her door.

Hatshepsut made no reply. She turned away from him, a curt dismissal, and Senenmut was arrested by the flash of an unfamiliar expression: eyes gazing inward at some raw, tender truth, mouth pale and quivering. It was the first time he had ever seen doubt on his young mistress's face.

CHAPTER FIVE

THE SEASON OF AKHET, THE inundation, drew near. The morning air was close and damp, opulent with the scent of the flood. Frogs, anticipating the great stretches of still water that would rise along the banks of the Iteru, woke from their underground chambers to rattle the evenings with song. To their choruses, the flood itself arrived, first turning the harvested fields black with dampness, then seeping up to break furrows with lines of reflected sky, at last ascending until every house and road on hillock or causeway stood clear of a vast, sparkling plane of green water. Rekhet opened the sluices in irrigation ditches; their farmland slumbered beneath the water while farmers traveled to construction sites in city and hills to build the tombs of noble men until the season of Peret arrived. When the flood receded they would resume the farming life, planting their fields, tending their crops and cattle, and Egypt would burgeon with its green and growing riches.

Hatshepsut waited for her blood to arrive, hopeful and anxious. But as the flood brought fertility to the land, she remained a girl.

She told no one of her failed attempt to make Senenmut her

lover. His refusal had humiliated her. As much as the rejection shamed her, though, she was far more ashamed that she had not seen the situation clearly, that her thinking had been clouded by desire. How unlike her. Senenmut was right, of course. Such an involvement with the king's daughter could be dangerous for him, possibly fatal, and however like a woman she may feel, her bloodless months proclaimed her a child. Senenmut would be unnatural if he desired a child. She burned with mortification whenever she thought of her attempts to seduce him. *Childish,* she told herself. *How could you have been so childish?*

In her lessons she was all focus and composure, applying herself to Senenmut's teachings even more completely than before. He never mentioned the slip of her graces. Hatshepsut still felt a surge of desire whenever she looked at him, though, still cried sometimes at night when her maids had retired. She may weep alone, but a fact was a fact: his heart did not burn as hers did.

For his part, Senenmut remained dutiful as always. He worked eagerly at Hatshepsut's request for her family's histories. He had found more than a dozen scrolls on Thutmose's heirship, and brought every one to his pupil's chambers. When lessons and feasts did not occupy her, Hatshepsut combed through the scrolls, searching for some answer to the puzzle. Why had her father named her the heir at Annu, and three years later also named Thutmose heir in Waset? For all the scrolls agreed on one point: he had proclaimed Thutmose during the season of the emergence seven years ago, in a gathering of high priests and other powerful men at the Temple of Amun.

Sitre-In noticed Hatshepsut's pensive mood. She did all she could to bring Hatshepsut around: soothing music during meals, a dance instructor to teach her all the most popular steps. But Hatshepsut was rather coarse and graceless despite her age, and she gave up dance quickly, too discouraged by her lack of natural talent to apply herself. Finally, at her wits' end, Sitre-In alerted the regent that her daughter was caught up in a black mood, and Ahmose herself visited the House of Women to see to the king's daughter on her own terms.

Hatshepsut dressed in her finest blue gown to greet her mother, angrily aware of how blocky her body was, how unfeminine. The fine fabric slumped about her shoulders and hips rather than falling like water, the way it did over the supple bodies of the harem women. If only she were a woman herself, she might have won Senenmut's heart. But even the most beautiful clothing could not make her look the part. When Ahmose arrived, Hatshepsut bowed in greeting and tried to conceal her unhappiness behind an emotionless face. It did not work.

"Whatever has come over you?" Ahmose stood, hand on hip, eying her daughter critically.

Hatshepsut wilted a little more beneath the stare.

"Have you nothing at all to say?"

"Perhaps it is the change of seasons."

"Boredom, like a rekhet child? Shall I send you off barefoot to run errands for some tomb builder?"

The prospect sounded like an improvement over another day of lessons with Senenmut, where she must act as if her foolish attempt at seduction had never happened. But it would never do to admit such a thing to Ahmose. "Please sit with me," Hatshepsut said, struggling to recall some semblance of courtly manners. She waved toward the cushioned chairs surrounding her senet board. Ahmose took her seat with a natural, casual grace that even Hatshepsut's simplest gestures lacked.

"Wine and honey cakes," Ahmose called to Tem, who bowed low and hurried from the room with an energy she never showed for Hatshepsut's commands. "Sitre-In certainly had it right. You are moping. No, I don't want to know why; I can guess the reason. I was a girl once, too, you know. All I will say to you is that you had better come out of it, and quickly, too. Young Thutmose is growing older and more confident all the

time, and the nobles of the city have begun to question why I
have not yet given him the throne. He is ten years old now, old
enough to at least sit upon the Horus Seat, if not to rule from it.
Time forces my hand sooner than I would like, but we must
make our move. I have sent to Annu to summon the priests who
were present when your father declared you the heir. As soon as
they reach Waset I will present you to the Temple of Amun as
your father's successor."

All thoughts of Senenmut left her in a rush. She gaped at
Ahmose, gripping the arms of her chair to steady her body.

"Well, that brightened your eyes," Ahmose said. "But don't
leap ahead of yourself. The priests from Annu are not here yet,
and even with their support it will be difficult to convince the
servants of Amun. They will be the first obstacle in your path,
but not the only one. The nobles of the city will need convinc-
ing, too. And Mutnofret knows them well. Many are loyal to her
and to Thutmose. You will need the priesthood and the wealth
of the nobles behind you if you are to claim your birthright.
This is not merely a decision between two sons with an equal
claim, Hatshepsut. They will see only your physical form, not
your kas. To them you are a female, and fit only for the office of
Great Royal Wife."

"Then what shall I do to help?"

Tem returned with a tray of cakes and cups of wine. She laid
the tray on Hatshepsut's senet table and backed away, bowing.
Ahmose plucked up a cake between thumb and forefinger,
nibbled delicately. "Keep up with your studies, for now. The
more intelligent and capable you look when set beside your lout
of a brother, the more inclined they may be to support you. You
must be strong and confident, a woman ready to make decisions
and give orders. No more of this moodiness."

Hatshepsut nodded. "I will do my best."

"Undoubtedly." Her face softened. "Just as your father always
did his best. You are your father's daughter. You even look like

41

him, while Thutmose favors his mother. Perhaps that, too, will work in your favor."

"But will I be as good a king as he was?"

"Time will tell. For now, you will be wise to listen to what I say, and allow me to make the political decisions for you. Remember that I have been the regent all these years. The court and the priests trust me, for the most part, and will listen to my counsel."

There was the faintest whisper of unspoken words in Ahmose's voice. *I hope.*

Hatshepsut's stomach clenched. "Yes, Mother."

"And concentrate on presenting a face of maturity to the court. If they are to believe you are the one to sit the Horus Throne, they must see you as a woman, not as a child."

LATE THAT AFTERNOON, AS HATSHEPSUT BENT OVER HER HARP IN AN attempt to play away her eager tension, Ita admitted a strange man into the chamber, flanked by two of Hatshepsut's guards. The man had the uncovered, shaven scalp and the red sash of an apprentice priest of Amun. He bowed deeply to Hatshepsut, reached into a neat leather pouch hung about his waist, and offered her a thick papyrus scroll. "From Senenmut, Great Lady," the priest said.

She dismissed the man with a distracted, wondering wave of the hand. Her guards hustled him away. She let her harp drop to the floor, too keen on the scroll even to set it in its stand. Ita tutted and whisked the instrument away.

Hatshepsut settled onto a stack of bright cushions. Wrapped around the outside of the scroll was a curl of papyrus, penned in Senenmut's well-formed and angular hand.

Great Lady,

I have found one last scroll pertaining to the proclamation of your brother. It was written by the hand of Waser-hat, a priest known for his meticulous attention to detail. We at the Temple consider Waser-hat's recordings to be among the finest and most useful. His reputation for accuracy is unsurpassed.

I trust I have pleased you in my duties.

Always your faithful servant,

Senenmut

Breathless, Hatshepsut unrolled the scroll. It was several sheets thick, and the papyrus had crinkled with age. She smoothed the pages carefully on the floor in front of her.

It is the first day of the month of Taab, in the season of the emergence. I, Waser-hat, having been summoned to the Temple of Amun to bear witness to a proclamation of the king, Aah-keper-ka-ra, Thutmose, the Mighty Bull and the Body of Horus, do report faithfully all that came to pass on this day, by my sacred honor as a priest and by my hope for a glorious afterlife.

An hour after dawn on this day, the king gathered his followers into the forecourt of the Temple of Amun of Waset, the greatest city in the Two Lands. In attendance were Setnakhte, the High Priest; and with him, his priest-attendants, Sikhepre and Meryra...

She skimmed the next pages – endless accounts of all in attendance and their relation to the throne, the priesthood, and to the noble houses. Dull stuff, of no use to her, but it seemed here at last was the detail she had longed for. Her heart pounded as she scanned the pages.

The Pharaoh stood before the assemblage in his holy leopard cloak. Beside him stood the child Thutmose the Second, aged about three

*years, and the child's mother, the second wife Mutnofret. With the
voice of a god the king said, so that all might hear:*

*"Behold, let it be known that I have proclaimed my eldest living
son as the heir to Egypt, to take the throne upon my death. My son is
of the blood of the gods. The throne will be his, may he live!"*

Waser-hat went on to detail the feast that followed, every
dish and entertainer. *Meticulous indeed.* She glanced over the
latter portion, but could see nothing there to enlighten her.

But she read her father's proclamation once more, and again,
and again, keen-eyed, quivering with excitement. Pharaoh
Thutmose had indeed made a proclamation about the heirship
seven years ago. But if Waser-hat could be trusted – and his
obsession with specifics was indeed impressive; exhaustive,
tedious, even – then her father had never spoken young Thutmose's name. The boy was present, and the party gathered to
hear the Pharaoh's address no doubt believed their king spoke
of that same boy. But if Hatshepsut's many kas were mostly
male, then the gods recognized *her* at the Pharaoh's eldest son.
The Pharaoh had spoken truthfully before the court. For the
sake of political harmony, he had allowed Waset's priests to
believe what they would. But he had not undone the proclamation at Annu that had named Hatshepsut heir – rather, he had
reaffirmed it. Before the eyes of the gods, his address at Annu
stood.

CHAPTER SIX

HATSHEPSUT LEFT HER BODYGUARDS AT the door. She walked alone into the small audience chamber of Waset's great palace. The room was small only by comparison with the great hall: a space so vast, so magnificent in its appointments that *great* seemed an insufficient word to describe it. The small chamber stretched a good seventy paces from end to end. Its high ceiling was held aloft by a row of pillars along either wall. Paintings on the pillars depicted, as one walked the length of the room, the history of the land from the time of Hatshepsut's great-grandfather, the Pharaoh Ahmose, who had driven the Heqa-Khasewet from Egyptian soil and restored the Two Lands to the rightful rule of the gods.

At the far end of the chamber stood a low red-granite dais, not nearly so grand as the one at the head of the great hall. This one was but a step above the floor, and narrow. It held a single throne, small but gleaming in the morning light that spilled down from the nearest windcatchers. She stepped up beside the throne, ran her hands along its back, its cool, gilded arms. It would be hers soon. She sank slowly upon the seat, holding her breath. The feel of the throne beneath her body set her skin tingling. The tingling increased the longer she sat; soon she was filled with the uncomfortable sensation of being watched from behind. She turned quickly on the throne, and came face to face with the image of her father.

She had been in the small chamber often, but the painting of Pharaoh Thutmose had never struck her with the import of its presence – not like it did now. He stood taller than he had in life, a golden-brown, fit young body striding, confident and strong, toward a glorious future. To either side of the king, Amun and Horus lifted their hands, and from their palms poured great arcing streams of ankhs, so that the Pharaoh was showered in unending life. Hatshepsut rose from her seat and drew near the image, hugging her body with her thin arms, rocking on her heels. At least she reached out a tentative finger to touch the painting. She trailed her hand along her father's arm from shoulder to wrist. Her fingers lingered on his hand, and she fell into reluctant memory.

The guardsmen at her father's chamber wore drawn faces; their eyes were sunk deep in shadows. When Hatshepsut and her nurse approached, the guards threw open the chamber doors, each holding up a palm in solemn salute. She passed them by without a second glance. The cloying odor of holy incense and the rote, resigned chanting of priests summoned up a dark, sharp memory: the last desperate moments of her baby sister's life, sweet little Neferubity, lost to a fever. Just as at Neferubity's bedside, there was no timbre of urgency in these prayers. The priests and physicians had given up. Pharaoh Thutmose would not live.

Hatshepsut pulled at the strong grip of her nurse's hand, could not get free, jerked like a creature in a trap, and stumbled as Sitre-In suddenly let her go. The nurse whispered her name, a note of warning in her voice.

Hatshepsut flew to her father's bedside. She shoved between the royal physicians who flanked the king, and stopped abruptly at the sight of him. She had been told – Sitre-In had sat her down solemnly to tell her that the king had come home early from his southern campaign. His chariot had overturned, hurting him badly. The injuries were serious; he might not live. The gods may choose to take him to the Field of Reeds at any time. She had been told, but telling could not prepare her.

When the Pharaoh had left for the land of Kush, he had been a strong man – reaching his twilight years, yes, but still with the strength of a great bull. He had seemed so mighty and unmovable that day when Hatshepsut and little Thutmose had watched him leave. She remembered how he'd looked, waving to them from the prow of his great blue-hulled ship, Falcon's Wing. *The ship itself had seemed to stare back with its painted eye-of-Horus, watching the royal children with the untouchable confidence that belongs to those who have never known defeat. She had stood on the wall of the quay and waved until* Falcon's Wing *was out of sight, lost in a white-blue morning haze with the rest of the war fleet. That had been only a few weeks before. How could the Pharaoh have returned in such a state?*

Thutmose's face was sunken and dry, as if he already lay beneath the salts that would preserve his body for eternity. The familiar long, sharp arch of his nose and the prominent jut of his upper teeth were accentuated by his sickly state, rough and pronounced as the first tries of a portrait carver's chisel. His chest, once firm and flat with muscle, now caved slightly at its center. His ribs showed plain. Arms that had been like a fisherman's knots were softened by weakness. And from beneath the cloth that covered his hips, a putrid smell rose to assert itself over the hysterical sweetness of the incense. A deep black bruise rose from that place, too, staining the Pharaoh's skin halfway up his side.

"Amun's eyes," *Hatshepsut swore.*

Sitre-In hissed at the impiety.

The king's lips twitched. On the other side of his bed, a sudden movement: Ahmose raised her hand in one imperious gesture. The chanting ceased at once. The king spoke again.

"Hatet."

"I am here, Father."

He lifted a hand, frail-looking, a weak old man's claw, not the gentle, strong hand she had often held, the hand that had guided hers on the chariot reins and the bow, the hand that held her heart. She took it all the same and squeezed it with an eight-year-old's strength, so he would know she was truly at his side.

"Gods have mercy," he whispered. "My son."

"Your son is here as well," said Aunt Mutnofret from her place just behind Ahmose's shoulder. Mutnofret's voice was musical as always, smoky, conspicuously ungrieved. At the sound of her words, the king waved his free hand as if chasing away a fly, and Mutnofret's eyes squinted like a cat's in the sun. She stooped, picked up her boychild who whined a complaint, and swept from the room.

"The gods have mercy on me. Hatshepsut."

She did not know what to say. It was as if he sought some solace from her in particular, though he was surrounded by the finest priests and physicians in all Egypt. What could Hatshepsut say of the gods' mercy? She was only a child. But she understood that her father was frightened; or if not exactly frightened, then seeking some comfort that only she could give before he journeyed to the underworld to lay his heart upon Anupu's scale.

"They will have mercy on you, Father. I know it. Don't be afraid. You'll see Neferubity in the Field of Reeds."

He gave her a wincing smile. His eyes streamed with water. "Neferubity, yes. She was a good little girl. A good daughter. I loved her. I love all my children, all of them. I love you, Hatet. Never doubt that."

Hatshepsut looked down at the tiled floor, at her toes poking out from her gilded sandals. There was still dirt under her toenails. She had been playing in the garden, dressed in a boy's kilt as was her custom, when her nurse had rushed her inside and dressed her up like *a girl to come to the king's bedside. She had known by Sitre-In's crimped face and fast, ungentle hands that the visit would not be a good one, but she had not expected this. Tears fell from her eyes to darken the tiles near her toes.*

"I will never doubt it, Father. I swear."

"Gods have mercy." His voice was a pale breath.

"You were a good king," she said, desperate to soothe him. Her mother made a small sound, a sigh or a sob. "Anupu will find your heart light. You were an obedient king. You always did what the gods told you."

Had she said something wrong? Ahmose shifted, tensed; the Pharaoh's hand tightened with a sudden, desperate strength.

"Annu," Thutmose whispered. "Gods forgive me. Hatet, forgive me."

His hand went slack in her grip. The fingers curled like a dry leaf. All at once there was a stillness to the king so complete that even a young girl could not mistake it. It was the same stillness that had fallen over Neferubity when Anupu had come for her ka.

Gentle fingers pried her from the Pharaoh's still, cooling grip. She turned, wordless, to bury her face against Sitre-In's hip, but she cried silently, so none of the priests might hear.

"Come, Hatshepsut." It was Ahmose. Hatshepsut turned away from the comfort of her nurse, squared her shoulders to face her mother. The Great Royal Wife leaned down until her face was level with Hatshepsut's own. Her cool, fine hands took Hatshepsut by the shoulders, pinioned her firmly. She said, "Now is not the time to cry, dear one. Time enough for crying when you are back in your chambers, when no one can see. We have a struggle ahead of us. We must be strong now, you and I."

Outside the Pharaoh's dark chamber, in the halls of the palace, a clamor went up: the priestesses' holy sesheshet rattled, announcing the Pharaoh's death to man and god alike. The shrill voices of servant women and concubines rose in a quavering cry.

"Be strong," Ahmose said. "Remember who your father was: Thutmose, the greatest of all kings."

49

The chamber doors swung open. Backlit by the bright glare of the hallway's lamps, Mutnofret returned, her wig in perfect plaits framing a beautiful, unperturbed face. A handful of body servants and her son's nurse shuffled behind her. The nurse carried the boy Thutmose. At four years of age he was old enough to walk about the palace on his own two feet. Hatshepsut frowned to see him riding pudgy and satisfied in his nurse's arms, unaware that their father had just departed the world of the living. Aunt Mutnofret had tied about Thutmose's head the Nemes crown, the cloth head-dress of the king. It was far too big for a child of his age. The blue-and-white striped linen sagged about his ears and flopped over his naked shoulders in an undignified manner. The sight would have made Hatshepsut laugh, had this been a time for laughter.

"Sister. Why is your son wearing the Pharaoh's crown?" Ahmose's voice was dangerously calm.

"My son was the heir and is now the king," Mutnofret said. "Did you forget, sister, that he was proclaimed before the royal court last year?"

"Did you forget about Annu, second wife?"

Mutnofret glared. "Are you mad? The people will never accept such an absurdity. You manipulated our husband to do your twisted bidding while he lived, but now that he is gone I will see the righteousness of maat upheld. Thutmose is the rightful heir. Thutmose shall be king."

Ahmose held out one hand. She spoke no command, nor did she glance around – her eyes, cold and hard, never left Mutnofret's – but a steward scurried forward to place a scroll in her hand. She paced across the floor and thrust it at Mutnofret, who gestured to one of her maids to unroll it near a lighted brazier so that she might read. Mutnofret's eyes grew angrier as they moved over the words.

"You, Ahmose, regent?"

Ahmose said nothing.

"I do not accept this. Thutmose will be ready to take the throne in

seventy days, as soon as our husband is in his tomb. My son needs no regent; he will have the finest advisors in all of Egypt."

"It does not matter whether you accept it or not," Ahmose said. "It is the king's decree, carried even now by messengers to every sepat in the Two Lands. Our husband wished me to rule in the heir's place until the heir comes of age. All of Egypt backs my regency. Who will stand against me? Your four-year-old boy?"

Mutnofret's smile was tight. She turned it on Hatshepsut, and inwardly the girl quailed at the glint of hatred in her aunt's eye. But she was determined to show no fear, as her mother had admonished. She stared back solemnly at Mutnofret until the second wife turned away, gave a crisp command to her women, and bustled from the king's chamber.

"Come, Hatet," Sitre-In said. "You have had a long night. Let us get you into your bath and then to bed."

Dutifully, Hatshepsut followed her nurse from the chamber. Outside the darkened room, surrounded by walls painted bright with scenes of the king's victories, she shivered – with relief at being in the light again, in the fresh air away from her father's sickbed – and with sorrow, for the one she loved most in all the world was gone.

The palace rang with the sound of mourning, a constant piercing din. Hatshepsut longed to cry out with the mourners, but here too many could see her face. She firmed herself; she donned a mask of calm, as she had so often seen her mother do. Now that her father was dead, Hatshepsut would eventually succeed her mother as Great Royal Wife. Sooner or later, when Thutmose came of age, Hatshepsut must marry him. That thought made her almost as sorrowful as her father's death.

She followed Sitre-In through the maze of the palace's halls to the courtyard where their two-seated litter waited. Wordless, she climbed into her chair beside Sitre-In and waited in a show of perfect peace as the guards drew heavy linen curtains. As the litter was lifted feather-smooth onto the shoulders of its bearers, Hatshepsut realized that now only her nurse could see her face. Yet still she would not allow herself to grieve. A Great Royal Wife would not cry until she was truly alone, without any servant, however trusted, for witness. All the way back to the House of Women, Hatshepsut wore her mask and did not cry.

❀

HATSHEPSUT JERKED HER FINGERS BACK FROM THE IMAGE OF HER father. She wiped the tears from her cheeks with a quick, smooth motion. No one was near enough to see her weeping, not even the guards she had left back on the door, but still she despised herself for this loss of control. She must have full rein of her emotions, she knew. A struggle lay ahead of her, as it had on that terrible day six years ago when the Pharaoh had left the world of the living.

It had taken fourteen days for two priests of Annu to arrive. They came at Ahmose's summons to offer Hatshepsut their respect and support. She had received them gravely the night before from her small princess's throne in the great hall while Ahmose, seated on the king's gilded chair in the regent's rightful place, looked on with silent approval.

They were very old men, wrinkled as disused water skins, weathered as frayed rope. Their bodies bent under their priestly mantles. They had been fit and fine and in the prime of their careers when Hatshepsut was declared the heir, but that was ten years past. Now they hobbled, weak and half-blind, grizzled and knobby old goats. Two more priests still lived, they told her, who had borne witness to the Pharaoh's proclamation that his daughter would be the heir. The others had sent along letters voicing their support, but they were too weak with age to make the long trek from Annu to Waset. No other witnesses to the Pharaoh's proclamation remained in the world of the living.

Once the old priests had been given their due welcome and seen off to their quarters, Hatshepsut and Ahmose departed for the regent's own rich rooms. Ahmose had dismissed her servants tersely. When they were alone, she had said, "I hoped there would be more than two who would come in person, but if it pleases Amun to preserve only two witnesses to his son's power, then so be it. Two shall be all we require. It is the gods' will."

"Two old men and you, Mother, against Mutnofret and all the men she commands? I fear it will not be enough to convince anyone."

"I have every faith in the gods, Hatet. And so should you."

Hatshepsut had not failed to notice the distance in her mother's eyes, the shimmer of doubt. But she said nothing, only nodded in what she hoped was a confident way.

"Now go back to the House of Women and make ready. You will feast your witnesses tomorrow night in the small audience hall; there is much to prepare. The following day we shall present you at Ipet-Isut – the Temple of Amun – for the god's blessing. I have consulted with my magicians; it will be the most auspicious day of the month to seek Amun's approval."

She had done as her mother commanded her, enlisting the help of her women to plan all the details of a private feast meant to solidify her ties to Annu's revered priesthood, such as it was. The whole while a fierce and unfamiliar sensation had gnawed at her heart, weakening her joints and furrowing her brow. When the last of her servants had scurried away to see to the preparation of the feast, Hatshepsut had wandered into her garden and picked leaves off a flowering bush, folding and crushing them until her fingers were sticky with green, fragrant sap. She wondered at the darkness that plagued her, seeking in vain for a name to put to the quailing of her kas.

At last she found it: doubt. The simplicity of the word had struck her in the act of reaching for another leaf, and she stood frozen with hand outstretched. She had never doubted herself before. As the word settled into her heart she closed her eyes against its presence, and saw in the solitude of memory the look on Senenmut's face when he pushed her gently away, refusing her kiss.

It was Senenmut who made me doubt. If not for him I would be strong now, able to face Mutnofret without fear. She had ripped at the bush's leaves, tearing a dozen away in one angry pass, and the sudden overwhelming smell of sap assaulted her nostrils.

In the quiet of the small audience chamber, Hatshepsut gazed from Thutmose's face to Amun's. *Father, guide me. Clarify my heart. Set me feet upon the path of maat. Take away my doubt.* She did not know whether she implored Thutmose or the god.

CHAPTER SEVEN

W HEN THE TABLE WAS LAID to her liking, when the
braziers burned bright and steady on their pedestals
along the wall, when the musicians were well into their subdued
melody (using her mother's steward – a frantic, bird-like man –
as her mouthpiece, she had corrected the volume and tempo of
the music several times), Hatshepsut at last turned to the door-
guard and nodded. The man was broad-backed, imposing in his
height, with an earth-dark complexion that proved him to be of
Medjay descent. The guard bowed at once and spun on a
sandaled foot; she noted how even the lines of his ankle and
heel were thick and sturdy, bull-strong. The presence of this
man seemed to her an uplifting sign. This small feast to
welcome her supporters from Annu was her first act of state. In
her frantic planning – Ahmose had insisted Hatshepsut handle
the entire affair herself – she had not thought to request a
specific guard, but had only sent for one as an afterthought. And
here the gods had provided her with a fearsome great hulk of a
man to stand at her door. He would set the tone, all right.
*Hatshepsut, who will be your king, commands the greatest strength of
the land, even at her supper parties.* The gods had done her a good

turn. The next morning she would load her servants with baskets of meat and bread and honey, and offer it all in gratitude to Amun and Mut.

The guard pushed open the double doors. They sighed on their hinges, and as they swung wide, the gilt of their carved scarabs caught the glow of her braziers and she blinked at the flash, her heart quailing for one uncertain beat. *No*, she told herself sternly. *You will not fear. This is your night. These are your priests, come to affirm your birthright. It is all yours; the whole of the Two Lands.* She breathed deep. The small audience hall was rich with the scent of myrrh, spicy and warm. The walls of the room glowed golden in the lamplight, slashed by a band of silver where the full moon shone through the bars of a windcatcher. The beam of the moon fell upon the painted image of Pharaoh Thutmose. She hoped this echo of her father's presence would fill her priests with surety. She must rely on them to bring the priests of Waset, her own city, to her side.

The guard stood clear, rigidly at attention. Beyond, in the cool night-time dimness of the palace, Ahmose walked slowly between the bent and shuffling forms of the two old priests. The regent moved with a poise that seemed contrary to her small, delicate frame, her fingers clasped above a hip-belt of shining sun discs which held in place the white pleats of her gown so they flowed, precise and even, to the floor. Her mouth moved in unheard conversation. Her lips were still full and colorful, even in the face of her advancing age; her head inclined gracefully first this way, then that, as she spoke softly to each priest in turn. The old men smiled, bent their stiff necks, clearly taken with Ahmose's feminine charm.

Hatshepsut wondered whether she had miscalculated. In her agony of worry, struggling to make every detail of tonight's feast exactly right, she had torn through her chests of gowns, discarding every garment in turn, declaring them all to be wrong, all wrong. She had left a trail of bright dresses across her room, trampling them as she paced, searching for the perfect garment, until Ita shrieked in frustration and Tem begged her to be gentle with her gowns or her poor servants would spend an entire season washing and mending. At last Hatshepsut had settled, in considerable despair, on the only clothing that ever made her feel like herself: the kilt of a boy. She had allowed her women to press fine pleats into the kilt and to choose for her a selection of jewels, including a womanly belt of faience scarabs as bright and blue as the afternoon sky, and a broad collar of golden flowers, the center of each one glimmering with a tiny carnelian or turquoise stone.

The effect, she had thought, was perfect: an exact balance of female and male. Now, though, as Ahmose halted in the doorway and lowered her eyelids to take in the sight of her daughter, Hatshepsut's heart was buffeted by doubt. Perhaps after all it would have been better to come before the priests as the expected girl, robed and painted. She, too, could charm them and win their hearts; she felt certain she could, despite the Senenmut debacle. But in another moment Ahmose lifted her chin and smiled slightly, then cut her eyes toward the kilt and gave the merest wry twist to her mouth, amused, approving.

"King's Daughter and Great Lady of the Two Lands," Ahmose spoke formally, "Son of Thutmose, Son of Amun, Hatshepsut: I present the priests of Annu, Messuway and Nakht."

Hatshepsut would not have thought it possible that two such stooped old grandfathers could bow low, and yet they did, extending their palms to her in a show of supplication. Their hands were knobbed with age, brown and dry as cedar branches.

Messuway spoke in a whispery voice. "It has been ten years since I last saw you, Great Lady, and when you came to Annu you were only a very small thing. But I remember how your father presented you to us at the Annu Temple. I recall how

Amun made my heart tremble when I looked upon your face. For as long as I live I shall remember it. We are here to do the bidding of the king – yes, and of the god. You have the backing of Annu, such as it is – whatever the support of two old men far from their temple may be worth."

Hatshepsut took Messuway's hand with both her own. His was cool, trembling, the skin as thin and wrinkled as an over-read scroll, but she clutched it as if the old priest were as beloved to her as her own mother. "Your support is worth more than riches," she said. "I know of the magic of Annu. It is a place that has long been sacred to the gods – far longer than has my own city. If the priests of Annu back my claim to the throne, then surely no other priesthood will fail to do the same. Come – we will all dine together, and you must tell me of your journey from Annu. I have not made such a long trip since the last time you saw me. I would hear of everything."

The musicians softly played through a selection of northern ballads, chosen to put the old men at their ease. Servants brought fish roasted in grape leaves, onions in tart black vinegar, the musky small boats of tender lettuce leaves filled with shreds of spiced ox-flesh. Their bread was especially fine, even for the palace kitchens, flecked with aromatic herbs, drizzled in olive oil so pure it must have come from the temple's own stores. Hatshepsut, as she smiled and hummed politely in accompaniment to the priests' stories, felt a warm glow of pride reflect from Ahmose as the sacred lake reflects the sun.

"And tell me of the pyramids," Hatshepsut said. "I recall seeing them from the rail of my father's ship, as we sailed north to Annu. But it was so many years ago; tell me how they look today."

Nakht chuckled. "They look as they have always looked, Great Lady, impossible and inspiring. They rise up from the land as a bird rises in flight, up into the highest reaches of the sky to touch the sun. No doubt you will see them again, when you claim your throne and make your progression..."

A gruff sound interrupted him, a startled grunt, a wooden bump. She looked around to see the Medjay guard holding tight to the doors' rings. The muscles in his arms tensed as he held the doors closed; they tilted fractionally outward, giving to whoever was tugging at the outside before the guard pulled them securely shut again.

"Here; what's this?"

The door-guard glanced over his shoulder. His face conveyed and equal measure of apology and anger. "Your pardons, Great Lady, Lady Regent, my good priests. Someone is trying to enter."

Hatshepsut and Ahmose shared an uneasy look. There were more guards down the hall, of course. A brigand in the palace would have been killed already, and an alarm would certainly have been raised. No, only one person could breeze through the palace at will without inciting suspicion.

Hatshepsut stood. "Let my aunt Mutnofret enter."

The door-guard managed a semblance of a bow and stepped back, a ready hand gripping the hilt of his sword. The doors jerked wide to reveal Mutnofret, smiling sweetly, radiant with victory. She was flanked by two strong servants, their hands still upon the door rings. Hatshepsut could feel Ahmose tense beside her, but the regent remained seated, poised and silent, waiting.

"Mutnofret," Hatshepsut said. She was keenly aware of the priests' eyes on her naked back – of her mother's eyes, too. She would not shrink before her aunt like a courtier, like some kicked dog. A princess, still immature, ought to greet the second wife with a graceful bow, palms out. But a king would not bow before his wife. Hatshepsut raised her chin. The air of the room all but crackled; a tingle of danger ran beneath her skin.

"You are having a little feast with my niece," Mutnofret said. "How nice. Isn't she a charming girl?" The second wife came into the audience chamber like a breeze through a sycamore, light, rustling, sweet-scented. She brushed past Hatshepsut without a glance and stood over Ahmose; the regent raised a golden cup to her lips as if to disguise her frown.

Nakht and Messuway rose from their chairs, made their creaky bows. "And you are the second wife, of course," Nakht said. Surely the priests sensed the tension among the women. "What a delight to meet you at last."

"At last," said Mutnofret. "Sister, there has been some mistake. Should not the heir and his mother have been present to greet our guests? Annu is an important city, esteemed by the gods." Her words flowed so smoothly that Hatshepsut could not tell whether Mutnofret was sincere, or whether she subtly mocked the priests of Annu. "Certainly these men wish to see the heir to the Horus Throne. Why else should they travel so far?"

This plays before me like a spectacle at a feast, exactly as it played the night my father died. She was eight years old once more, small and helpless, staring down at her dirty toes.

Hatshepsut turned to her mother, an involuntary response, and immediately cringed at the impulse. Ahmose set her cup upon the table, gazed across the hall at the painting of Amun and the Pharaoh as if the second wife were nothing – a bird crying in the garden, a pestering fly. "They have seen the heir. I am sure they are satisfied."

There was silence for one ragged heartbeat while Mutnofret digested Ahmose's cool words. Anger flitted across Mutnofret's face, tense the corners of her mouth, narrowed her dark-rimmed eyes. Then she drew in a breath through her nostrils, sharp and noisy, just as an overworked nurse might when dealing with an unruly child. She laughed lightly. "Oh, my sister. I can see you are still cherishing that old dream of yours. It is the fantasy of every woman in the harem to be called Mother of the King, I know, but you have no sons. It is simply not what the gods intend for you. Leave it be."

Hatshepsut had fretted over the smallest details of this supper. Now Messuway and Nakht stood gaping from one queen to the other, their discomfort evident. The serving woman who had carried in the sweet course whispered in the ear of the wine-bearer, eyes wide. Even the musicians had stopped playing. Mutnofret's jealousy had spoiled Hatshepsut's first act of statecraft. She clenched her teeth, but the pressure of her own jaws seemed only to further inflame her anger. She advanced on Mutnofret. "The Great Royal Wife is no mere harem woman. You will not speak to her so crudely."

Mutnofret blinked. She seemed startled to find Hatshepsut in possession of a tongue.

"There was no mistake tonight. You were not invited because you were not needed. These good priests have come to Waset to back my claim to the throne. You have imposed yourself, and I am not pleased."

"Who," said Mutnofret, her voice pitched high, trembling on the verge of a shriek, "is this *child* who dares insult me?" Her face flushed. The tendons in her neck stood out sharp and hard above the colorful bars of a jeweled collar.

Hatshepsut stepped closer, so close she could feel the warmth of the second wife's body. Mutnofret gave ground reluctantly, sliding her feet back just enough to maintain some distance between them. Her sandals hissed across the tiles. "This is the child of the king. The son of the king. The eldest, the heir. This child will soon be your king, and you would be wise not to cross her."

Mutnofret spun, shoulders square, with an air that indicated any reply was far beneath her dignity. She drifted toward the doors where her guards waited under the glower of the Medjay soldier. For a moment Hatshepsut thought she would leave, and allowed herself to sink back on her heels with relief. Then

Mutnofret whirled to face the room once more. She took them all in with her burning eyes – the priests, the regent, even the musicians huddled in their dim corner, clutching their harps and horns – but she stared most fiercely at Hatshepsut. "Before you may take your throne, son of the king, you must receive Amun's blessing. Do you imagine the god or his priests will suffer that mockery, to see a girl brought before them in the place of a man? I can think of no greater affront to maat than to try Amun so boldly. Be wary, *son of the king*. Ask the Lady Regent what happens when we set our own hearts above maat."

And she was gone, merciful gods, striding away into the dark of the palace. Hatshepsut's blood pounded along her limbs. She felt wobbly and wild, fierce enough to tear the very bricks from the walls, frightened enough to climb into her mother's lap and cry.

Calm, said a quiet, admonishing voice deep in her racing heart. It was Senenmut's – one of his lessons in the garden. *The ability to stay calm cannot be overstated. It is perhaps the greatest skill a Great Royal Wife can possess.*

"A Pharaoh," she replied aloud, though Senenmut could not hear her.

The Medjay guard chuckled. His laugh was deep and hoarse, a voice used to shouting. She stared at him, affronted.

"Er – apologies, Great Lady," he said quickly, and snapped to attention. But his lips quivered with the effort of fighting a smile.

"Insolent!" Hatshepsut called him. He grinned. She found his familiarity somehow gratifying. "Speak freely."

"I beg your pardon. I know it is not proper for a guard to show such amusement. But to watch you rout the second wife...you, young as you are, with your side-lock and all...." He gave another rasping chuckle. "Like a hound pup snapping at the whiskers of some lady's pampered cat! I fought under your father's command, and I have eyes to see. By the gods, here stands Thutmose's true heir, and no mistake."

Hatshepsut smiled. But when she turned back to her mother and the priests, Ahmose's face was grave, and the smile fled from Hatshepsut's lips.

CHAPTER EIGHT

SHE RACED THE SUN AS it climbed the vault of the sky. Amun awaited: her god, her father – the only father she had left. Waset dwindled behind her chariot, and the pale, imposing walls of Ipet-Isut, its lofty pylons impassable and stern, grew ever larger, ever more real between the sleek heads of the two horses who bore her.

The Medjay guardsman handled the chariot as a scribe handles his brush, with an unthinking, faultless skill, movements reflexive, instinctive, assured. His name was Nehesi. When Ahmose's steward had arrived at dawn to instruct Hatshepsut to wait on her mother's word, for Mutnofret had raised her opposition and gathered her men to protest at the Temple of Amun, Hatshepsut had sent Tem to the palace to find the man who had guarded her door at supper. In the fury of the moment she had had no clear plan for the guard. She only remembered that the man had appreciated her strength in facing Mutnofret down. Somehow, the thought of him was a comfort to her then, and she wished for his presence. But by the time Tem had returned to Hatshepsut's apartment with the great bull of a man on her heels, she saw clearly what she must do.

"You are a strong man," she had said to him, and he had nodded his frank, unhumble acceptance. "I am to go into a den of leopards this morning. I would have you at my back."

"The hound pup takes on more cats, is that the way of it?"

"Be wary, soldier. This hound pup knows how to bite, and she does not take well to teasing."

The man had bowed at once, instantly contrite and yielding. "My apologies, Great Lady. I meant no disrespect. As you command, I will be at your back. But what is the nature of the work, if I may ask? Nehesi never goes into battle unprepared."

Hatshepsut's mouth had twisted, a weak imitation of a wry smile. "Apparently Mutnofret has rallied her men at the Temple of Amun. They intend to bar my entry to the god's presence. They think to prevent me from seeking the holy blessing."

"And you want me to cut a way through."

She had considered the several knives sheathed along his worn leather belt, the handle of his curved bronze sword. "Perhaps not *cut*. But make me a way, yes."

Sitre-In had come in from the garden as Hatshepsut was speaking. She often spent her early mornings there, tending the flower beds, although the House of Women employed several gardeners. Working amongst the beds seemed to bring the woman peace. But when she heard Hatshepsut's words a look of panic had come over Sitre-In's face.

"Oh, no," she had said, "you are to stay put until we have word from your mother!"

"The gods take me if I wait. I will stand before Amun today as planned, or I will be cursed by Set. Mutnofret cannot be allowed to stop me. I will not permit it."

Sitre-In had lunged for her, but she had dodged behind Nehesi, made a quick egress from her chamber and Sitre-In's furious glower. "I'll tell your mother," her nurse had shrieked as she led Nehesi briskly from the House of Women. "I'll tell Senenmut!"

Now the outer pylons of Ipet-Isut stretched above their heads. They passed into the cool shadows of the complex; the horses tossed their heads, spraying foam from their mouths. Hatshepsut could see the crowd in the forecourt of Amun's great temple. The number surprised her: more than she had expected, perhaps fifty in all, milling and shouting while, on the steps of the temple itself, a handful of red-belted priests gestured, demanding order or arguing amongst themselves. Never had she dreamed Mutnofret commanded the hearts of so many nobles. And how many of the Amun priests had already been swayed to her aunt's side? Hatshepsut's mouth tightened with a feeling that was half fear, half annoyance. At the sound of her horses' hooves on the hard-packed roadway, several of the men looked around. She watched their mouths open in angry shouts. She could not hear their words over the pounding in her ears. *Is it the hooves I hear, or my own heart?*

Nehesi drew rein. At once the crowd surged toward them. "Stand back," her guard shouted, and leaped from the chariot. His hand clutched the hilt of his knife, ready and eager to draw.

Calm. The greatest...the greatest skill... Senenmut's words faltered in her heart. She thought she could hear her tutor laughing at her, or perhaps it was a nobleman in the crowd. Astonishing herself with her own composed air, she stepped lightly from the chariot and stood near to Nehesi's side, back straight, eyes on the temple, haughty and self-possessed.

Nehesi's blades were not needed. The mere sight of him, hulking and bristling, was enough to part the crowd as she moved toward the temple's mouth. On the steps the priests clustered together then fluttered apart like a flock of ibis disturbed, their red sashes flapping.

"They have been whipped into a frenzy," Nehesi muttered behind her. "They are dogs eager for a fight. Religious fervor is the last thing I like to see in a crowd, even in a small crowd. Anything may happen when the gods are involved."

Hatshepsut did not reply. It was too late now to withdraw. She must go on to stand before Amun, whatever may come of it.

She gained the steps and sketched a slight bow to the High Priest, barely bending at the waist, the measured, courtly respect a king must show to Amun's chief servant. Then, breathing deep, hoping she did not shake, she turned to face the crowd. "Good noblemen of Egypt," she said. The crowd had ceased its milling, ceased its murmuring. All eyes turned upon her. She felt the force of those stares, suspicious and hard. "The gods bless you for coming to the temple on this most auspicious day, the day when I shall present myself to the god and receive his blessing as heir to the Horus Throne."

There was the smallest ripple among the crowd as heads turned to seek out some brave volunteer who might speak for all. At last an older man stepped forward, deep lines long-formed around his eyes and mouth. His short-cropped wig was slightly askew. She knew him from court: a kindly grandfather, patron of a wealthy house, and a long-time friend to her family. Senenmut had once told her how the old man's house had been staunch supporters of her father, even in the earliest days when he was nothing but a common soldier seeking to find his feet in Waset's fierce political currents. She was saddened to see her father's supporter here, standing against her own claim. But she made herself smile down at him, as delighted as though he had taken her hand at a festival. "Harwa. I am glad to find you here. You have always been a friend to Thutmose, and to all his house."

"Er...." Harwa lowered his eyes. "Great Lady, we mean you no personal affront, you must understand. It is maat that brings us here."

"Maat!" someone shouted from the edges of the crowd, a shrill and wild call.

"Maat has ever been my first and greatest concern," she said, loudly so all might hear. "My father Thutmose taught me to revere it above all else. As your king, I will guard maat as keenly as the falcon guards her nest. You have nothing to fear."

The crowd gave off a muffled groan, the sound of an ox moaning under its burden.

"We fear, Great Lady, that a woman – a *girl* on the throne would itself be an offense to maat. When maat is disrupted, all manner of evil may fall upon Egypt."

Harwa's words were too much like Mutnofret's threat the night before. Hatshepsut could not stop her eyes narrowing. More men found their bravery and shouted at her with the words of the second wife.

"There is a son! The king left a son as heir!"

"I saw young Thutmose proclaimed the heir myself, here at the temple!"

"I will have no king who has not undergone the rites."

At this last, Hatshepsut raised a hand for silence. It did not come, and she was obliged to shout back: "What rites? What rites do you demand? Only tell me, and I will give my people what they require."

"Circumcision," a young man replied, boldly raising one fist into the air. His response was immediate and far too determined. Frustration stabbed at her heart; Mutnofret had set this up, no doubt – had put the thought of circumcision into these men's hearts, then set them loose upon the temple. It was a rite any fourteen-year-old prince would be expected to endure, to prove his bravery and strength. But Hatshepsut had no manhood to cut! *A plot to discredit me, to make me look foolish. Beyond foolish – helpless, inadequate. Female.* And in her anger and haste, Hatshepsut had walked obligingly into Mutnofret's snare. What answer could she give to such a demand?

She stared at the young man, helpless to save face, while he rhythmically waved his fist. Soon the men nearest him took up his chant. *The rite! The rite!* She did not know the man. He had the shaved, wigless pate of a priest, and though his kilt was unadorned, as befitted a servant of Amun, it was made of especially fine linen. The crowd seemed to esteem him; men thumped him on the back and smiled confidently into his face as his clenched fist led their chanting. When their cries died away, the young man shouted, "We all bled for Egypt, to show our strength and fearlessness, to prove we were worthy men of the Two Lands. We will not have any king who cannot do the same!"

"The king must bleed," someone cried. "Bleed as we bled! Or maat will not stand!"

Hatshepsut shouted over the din. "You speak foolishness. What flesh would you have me cut? I will hear no more of this."

Nehesi growled a warning. The crowd surged toward the steps, clamoring. Led by the fine-kilted priest, several men ran up the steps themselves, giving Hatshepsut and her guard a wide berth. They stayed well beyond the reach of Nehesi's sword, but when they reached the temple doorway they linked arms to bar her entry.

"Move aside," Nehesi commanded the nearest man, "or I'll cut a door through your guts."

Hatshepsut's heart raced. To kill on the steps of the temple – that would offend maat, with certainty. She laid a hand on Nehesi's arm to restrain him, but the fire of battle burned in him. Unaware, he twitched free of her touch as though her hand was a gnat on his skin.

Quickly, she stepped in front of her guard and faced the men who blocked the way herself. "Stand aside. Do you know better than Amun? If he wills that I take the throne, then I shall, no matter what you say or do. If he wills that my brother should be king, then Amun will surely tell me now. Stand aside, and allow me to commune with my god."

The High Priest, quivering and pale, moved to her side. He

addressed the brash young priest with a dry whisper of a voice. "The king's daughter speaks with great wisdom, Nebseny. There is no harm in consulting the god. If she is not meant for the throne, then Amun shall make his truth known to us all. Let the girl pass."

"Never," a rough voice shouted from the courtyard. "Stand your ground, Nebseny!"

Hatshepsut did not dare look behind her. She could feel Mutnofret's little fire fanning itself into a conflagration at her back. These men were like horses racing with bits in their teeth, wild, unthinking, headlong. And she had thrown herself into their path.

"There must be a circumcision!"

"No king who does not bleed!"

"As we bled, ah, for Egypt!"

"Amun's eyes," Hatshepsut spat, and the High Priest gulped at her curse. She snatched a dagger from Nehesi's belt; he grunted in surprise.

A brazier stood beside the blocked temple doorway, crackling as it consumed nuggets of myrrh, raising a column of blue smoke to the sky. As she approached it with the dagger held before her, the men nearest the brazier drew back, pressing into their companions' sides, but still they did not give way. Hatshepsut thrust the dagger into the flame. The smoke made her eyes burn, and she blinked, furious, unwilling to let the crowd see tears in her eyes. A hollow clatter of hooves rang in the forecourt; she looked up in time to see Senenmut fling himself from a chariot while the two old priests of Annu struggled to take hold of the loose reins.

Hatshepsut spun to face the crowd, the knife blackened and smoking in her hand. The Amun priests drew back, retreated down the steps; the crowd at last fell silent.

"Princess," Nehesi said, low and warning.

Hatshepsut fumbled one-handed at the knot of her kilt. It

dropped at last. She stood before them unclothed, sunlight shimmering on the sweat of excitement that dampened her skin. A wordless shout came from somewhere in the distance; the courtyard and its crowd were unaccountably receding, drawing out to the end of a dark tunnel so that she stood isolated and powerful, the only living thing to feel Re's glorious light, alone in the world as Atum was alone on his hill at the birth of all things. *Senenmut*, murmured a voice in her heart, and she saw with her distant eyes the tutor pushing his way through the crowd, fighting to reach her, his mouth shouting her name, though she did not hear his voice.

Hatshepsut lowered the knife, drew it slowly across the crux of her thighs. She felt a stinging cold that in her far-off state did not register as pain, but as a surge of power coursing along her limbs, making her tremble with the force of her own might, with Amun's might. And then a wash of heat down her legs as the blood flowed to pool beneath her feet.

"Gods' mercy," a voice whispered, or shouted – Hatshepsut's ears were full of the sound of the river, a frantic rushing. She could not say who had spoken.

A gentle hand pried the knife from her fingers. Senenmut was there with her – Senenmut, drawing her awareness to a great pain lancing upward from her loins, tracing a path of fire through her belly; to the astonished faces of the nobles, the pale silence of the priests.

"Give me your hands," he said quietly. His voice carried deep into the heart of the transfixed crowd, though it had never been a powerful voice. "I am the one who comes to be among you. I am the blood that falls from the root of Re, who cuts his own flesh to bring forth the ancestral gods. I am Re, the sun; I am Hu, the word of power; I am Sia, the all-knowing. We who are one follow Atum, the father-sun, in the course of every day."

No one spoke. No one moved. Hatshepsut's eyes widened with the pain; her nostrils flared, but she she did not cry out.

Messuway and Nakht mounted the steps to stand beside her. Their priestly robes were disheveled. "Here before you stands the heir to the Horus Throne, Hatshepsut, daughter of the king." Messuway waved his arm toward her, his flesh loose and swinging. She quivered, bracing herself against the burning in her groin, refusing to show her pain on her face.

"As it was proclaimed before us in Annu," Nakht intoned, "so be it here. Amun himself has sired her. Let no man doubt the god."

At the foot of the steps, a handful of the Amun priests knelt, palms toward her. And a scattering of nobles, too, sank to their knees in the courtyard. Nebseny half-crouched, seemingly torn between supplication and disgust. Many who had been clamoring moments before, priests and nobles alike, now hastened away, fleeing from the blood, the strangeness, the disorder.

Nehesi shouted after those who fled. "Who among you held the knife in his own hand when he was cut? And she did not cry out – not once!"

"Let them go," Senenmut said. "Let them carry the story back to Waset. Let them leave now. It is better that they don't see."

Don't see what? Hatshepsut tried to say, but her head was light and silly, and when she opened her mouth to speak only a pained gasp emerged. Her knees had gone unaccountably weak. She swayed.

In an instant Nehesi's arms were there, lifting her as gently as a nurse lifts a babe, for all their great strength and hardness.

She heard Senenmut shout for his chariot.

Hatshepsut closed her eyes.

CHAPTER NINE

W HEN SHE ROUSED, SHE WAS lying in her own soft bed in the House of Women. Sitre-In, facing away from where Hatshepsut lay beneath a wool blanket, drifted between the cosmetics box on its ebony table and the great painted chest full of gowns and kilts. Hatshepsut watched her nurse move through a hazy blur and blinked to clear the film from her eyes. Somewhere – outside – the garden – she heard Tem's voice, rising into the range of Hatshepsut's hearing and falling away again, distant as a thin red haze on the horizon. "On the very steps of the temple...the whole crowd...then that tutor of hers quoted the holy texts...."

That tutor. She looked around for Senenmut, but he was not there.

The blanket was too hot. She raised one leg to kick it away, and hissed in pain as cats' claws dug into her groin.

Sitre-In turned at the sound. "Oh!"

"Get it off. Hot."

"There, there." Sitre-In peeled the blanket back.

Cool air fell across her naked skin like a blessing from Mut. She looked down to the cut across her bare hillock. Someone had stitched it up with horses' hairs; a thick translucent paste, sharp-scented, covered the length of the wound.

"That great hulk of a guard carried you all the way back in his arms while your tutor drove the horses like a demon wind. You fainted clean away from loss of blood. Or from pain; the physicians aren't sure which." She paused a moment, fussed with a length of linen in her hands. "I feared for you."

"I'm all right, Mawat." She moved again, slowly. So long as she was careful the pain was not too great.

"You will have a scar," Sitre-In said, mournful. "And right there, too...oh, Hatshepsut!"

"Good. It will remind my people that I bled for Egypt, just like any prince." She tried to lever herself but fell back, weak as a newborn. Her arms shook; her bones had lost all their solidity.

"You just lie there and rest. The physicians said you will get better with the proper spells and with the right foods, but you are still much too pale. It will take time."

"I haven't got time. Mutnofret raised fifty nobles and Amun knows how many priests. With every hour that passes she may be adding more to her tally." A terrible thought occurred to her. "How long have I been here? Not days. Oh, tell me it has not been days!"

"No, no. Look at the sun, you foolish girl. It has been only hours. But you are not going anywhere," Sitre-In added quickly. "You must rest. I won't have you endangering yourself again."

The door to her apartment swung wide. Through it Hatshepsut could see her door guard bowing low; two harem ladies, chattering as they passed, halted mid-step, bowing likewise.

"Oh, no."

"Did I forget to mention?" Sitre-In said, all airy unconcern. "Your mother is coming to see you. I imagine she is not best pleased."

Hatshepsut could do nothing but lie still and naked as

Ahmose swung into her room, angry and swift like water from a burst dam. Hatshepsut thought for a moment Ahmose might storm right over the bed, trampling her as she passed, but the regent halted at her bedside. Ahmose spared a glance at the stitched wound across Hatshepsut's loins. "I hope your little drama was worth a disfiguring scar. You've quite possibly ruined more than just your body. Tales go fast as gazelles through a city. Half of Waset thinks you are mad. Well? Have you nothing to say for yourself?"

"The other half of Waset thinks I am a god."

"Oh, Set take you! You played right into Mutnofret's hands. I may have convinced a council of nobles, with the help of your priests, that your father wanted only you as his heir. Now they will all have heard that you are impulsive, and that you like to play with knives!"

"And that I am fearless, and confident, and willing to make any sacrifice for my people."

Ahmose's voice fell to a dangerous, slow growl. "If you weren't so weak from loss of blood, I would slap you until your face swelled."

"They would not let me stand before Amun to receive his blessing, nor even to commune with him, to ask him whether I ought to take the throne. They demanded a circumcision."

"And so you sliced your body? What did that prove?"

"That I won't be denied just because I am female. That Mutnofret cannot stop me. She only put the idea of circumcision into their heads because it would force me to confront, before the court and the priests - before the gods! - the fact that I haven't got a couple of figs hanging between my legs. Well, they saw what I have, all right. They saw me make the cut with my own hand. Tales go fast as gazelles? Then you've heard already that I did not cry out, did not fall before them. Mutnofret tried to make me less than a prince. I made myself more."

Ahmose's mouth tightened, but she said nothing. Then her chest and shoulders lurched. Hatshepsut blinked, wondering if some fit had fallen over her mother, wondering whether Ahmose would strike her, until at last she realized that the regent was choking back reluctant laughter. "Figs," Ahmose muttered.

"Well, what do we do now?" Hatshepsut pushing herself up again, noting with fierce pleasure that this time she was not so weak as before. Sitre-In scurried forward to prop a cushion behind her back.

"We give you one day to regain your strength. One day only. On the morrow we meet with a council of priests and nobles, and we convince them to see sense. We do it the right way."

Hatshepsut nodded. "I will be ready."

"If you go against my word a second time, Hatshepsut, I cannot save you. You are not the Pharaoh yet. You would do well to remember. Sitre-In, send to the kitchens for ox-blood broth and bread with honey. This daughter of mine must have all her strength restored to her, the gods help us all."

Hatshepsut scowled. She hated the taste of ox-blood broth.

Ahmose swept for the door, but halted on the threshold. She turned back to regard Hatshepsut, unspeaking for a long moment. Hatshepsut would not allow herself to break her mother's stare. "Pray that your gazelle can outrun Mutnofret's," she said. She turned her head with regal purpose, and in a flutter of linen she was gone.

CHAPTER TEN

THEY MET ONCE MORE IN the small audience chamber. For all its beauty, its god-painted pillars crowned with lotuses, its sweet scent of incense and northern wine, Hatshepsut had come to regard the hall as a place of torment. When she had arrived at the palace that morning, Ahmose had already seemed tired, harried, worn around the edges, and Hatshepsut, recognizing the strain of futility on her mother's face, had quailed inside, dreading the meeting to come. But even knowing that Ahmose was less than confident, Hatshepsut was not prepared for the blunt force of Mutnofret's presence. The second wife was a terror of surety, moving and speaking with a cool, powerful grace. She had brought seven priests of Amun to stand against Hatshepsut's two old men, and eight nobles as well, unafraid to show their opposition to the regent in the plain light of day. That did not bode well, Hatshepsut knew. When men as small as mere nobles saw no danger in standing against Egypt's crowned ruler, the likelihood of a victory was meager at best.

The room was set with two rows of tables, running the length of the chamber with a space between where servants moved, pouring wine and refreshing bowls of olives and dates, visibly cringing at the tension vibrating through the room. Ahmose sat stiffly on one side, gazing across the narrow gap as though peering over a great abyss. Her face was pale with the knowledge of the struggle to come. She had managed to bring only two priests of Amun from the local temple to support Hatshepsut's claim, and three nobles. Their seven looked a paltry, ragged handful against Mutnofret's fifteen.

Hatshepsut drank very little wine, though the warmth of it would have soothed the pain from her wound. *I must keep my mind sharp.* Now and then she moved in her seat, and her sutures stung beneath her kilt – the boy's kilt that, for once, Ahmose had specifically instructed her to wear. "We will use everything in our power to make them see you as a prince."

Nebseny was there, he of the fine kilt and the chanting voice, seated thin and elegant on Mutnofret's side of the room. He toyed with his golden wine cup, rolling it between his hands as he spoke. "Far be it from me to nay-say our departed king Thutmose. Surely the Pharaoh had his reasons for taking the princess to Annu. And with all respect to our good priests of that city, you understand, all respect – but when has Egypt ever seated a woman upon the king's throne?"

"Netikerty," one of Ahmose's nobles volleyed back.

"Bah!" Nebseny gave the man a scornful laugh. "A legend, seven hundred years gone. There was no King Netikerty; talk sense."

"Sobeknefru, then."

"She was never king, but a lone queen, and pressed into rule at that, with Egypt in despair. And she brought the Two Lands to ultimate disaster! No one called her Pharaoh, but in any case, there – Sobeknefru is your answer. A woman ruling Egypt alone, in the place rightfully belonging to a man, leads to naught but ruin."

"They called her Pharaoh; indeed they did."

Nebseny rolled his eyes. "So say you."

"And it was not she who brought Egypt to disaster, but the Heqa-Khasewet invaders."

"And," Nebseny said, amused and condescending, "it was Sobeknefru who failed to stop their invasion. Why are we even discussing this? The very idea is not only absurd, but dangerous."

"You must understand," said another of Mutnofret's nobles, "it's for maat we fear. There is no doubt that the young princess is brave and fierce. I wish my own sons had as strong a will as the Great Lady's. But to set her over us as king? This disrupts order. This is not maat. If maat goes from the world, what follows? I think we are better off not discovering the answer to that question, eh?"

Ahmose stepped into the somber, musing pause. "You all know that I am god-chosen. Your wives came to me before I was regent, that I might read their dreams. I ask you to be sensible. Who knows the desires of the gods better than the god-chosen, unless it is the High Priests?"

"And where is our ancient High Priest of Amun?" Nebseny said. "No doubt huddled over his chamber pot with a flux. He is old and failing, but I grant you, his opinion on the matter would as good as decide us."

"Would it truly?" Ahmose countered. "I wonder. You will not listen to the words of a god-chosen queen who has led Egypt wisely and fairly all these years, and now you mock your own High Priest..."

"Mm," Mutnofret interjected. "I doubt very much whether all would agree that you have been a *wise* ruler, Ahmose. None of us has forgotten that the floods failed for two years running when you were raised to Great Royal Wife. What did you do, I wonder, to anger the gods? And what greater anger could we expect if we put your daughter on the Horus Throne? The gods will not be mocked. One needn't be god-chosen to know that much. Not only is she female, but Hatshepsut is unpredictable and rash. Yesterday's display on the temple steps showed us all that much. Why, we are lucky the gods have not inflicted us already. Imagine, a girl making a mockery of the circumcision rites, at Amun's sacred doorstep."

Hatshepsut glanced at her mother – at her clenched jaw, her tense eyes – and kept her mouth shut.

"She does mock us," one of Mutnofret's priests said. "She even wears the garb of a boy, and shaves her head. She is unnatural. The gods will not suffer her insolence."

"Do you presume to speak for the High Priest?" Ahmose snapped.

"Never, Great Lady. My voice is my own. I am a man of Egypt as surely as I am a priest. Does Egypt's voice mean so little to the throne?"

They argued on, late into the morning, while Hatshepsut grew more miserable and uncertain. Fifteen to seven, the High Priest declining to show, and one of her supporters invoking a child's bed-time story as evidence for her claim. She stared in desperation at the painting of her father, standing proud before Amun who poured the blessings of the ankh over his head. *My father breathed the breath of life from Amun's own hand, but I am withered and winded.* Faced with Mutnofret's erudite, cool-tempered contingent, she was ashamed of her rashness at the temple. She should have listened to Ahmose, should have waited until the time was right, until the High Priest could be moved, until some sign, some miracle arrived from Amun that would leave no one in doubt. *Have I failed you, father, or did you fail me?* She half expected Thutmose's image to turn its face toward her, to speak to her from the bricks of the chamber. The dead king said nothing, and the voices of Egypt clamored back and forth, back and forth, growing more fierce, more insistent, more sharply divided with each word.

I was wrong. I was wrong to think I knew Amun's will. I was

*wrong about Waser-hat's history. The king did proclaim my brother
his heir, and undid my own proclamation. What else is maat, but a
male heir, a prince in body and in ka?*

The assembly had escalated to a shouting match. Ahmose
and Mutnofret discarded their regal bearings; they raised their
voices along with the men.

"And what of the Heqa-Khasewet?" one man cried. "They
have not forgotten that they held Egypt for their own, make no
mistake! It was not so long ago. They wait for our weakness.
They thirst for our blood. They will be back to impose their
blasphemies on our land and our people the moment we waver
from the gods' will. Have you forgotten how Egypt suffered
under their lash, Lady Regent?"

Ahmose stood, and the shouting subsided. "It was my own
grandfather who routed the Heqa-Khasewet from the Two
Lands. Maat flows in my very blood. I forget nothing. But I tell
you truthfully: I will not defy the gods in this. I would sooner
tear Egypt apart with my own hands and give it to the Heqa-
Khasewet brick by brick than see the false heir on the throne."

Mutnofret pounded her table, shrieking. "You see how little
she cares for our land!" Her men roared along with her.

Ahmose trembled.

It's my fault she's so worn down, Hatshepsut told herself. *She
feared for me after I cut myself, and now we are all paying for my
folly.*

The priest Nakht rose from his table, gesturing for silence. It
was long in coming, but at last the room settled. "We are all
greatly taxed in our hearts. The morning has been long. My
friends, we are making no progress, shouting like a lot of sailors
at their oars. Let us adjourn for an hour. We will all benefit by
taking fresh air."

"A sensible suggestion." Ahmose, too, rose. "We meet again in
an hour. Hatshepsut, come."

CHAPTER ELEVEN

SENENMUT SQUATTED ON HIS HEELS several paces from the chamber's door. The man Nehesi loitered beside him, leaning one great, muscular shoulder against a the finely painted palace wall. The guards on the door narrowed their eyes at Nehesi's casual presumption, but the Medjay guardsman only lifted his chin and leaned harder, his arms folded below his scarred chest. Senenmut could not quite decide whether he liked Nehesi or despised him. The man was coarse in manner and mind, lacking in courtly refinement as soldiers often are. But he seemed eminently pleased with the favor the princess had bestowed upon him, and his regard for the safety of her person could not be questioned. Nehesi had held the crowd at the Temple of Amun at bay, and Senenmut had witnessed how tenderly Nehesi carried Hatshepsut to her bed in the House of Women, how he'd laid her pale form down and stood over her until the physicians arrived with their copper needles and their salves, watchful as a father over his sleeping daughter. Whatever faults Senenmut may find in a man who made his living with the sword, he could not fault Nehesi in loyalty to his lady.

They had waited outside the audience chamber for at least

three hours, first standing at attention, then pacing, finally falling to idle talk while Senenmut slumped on the floor. He was about to make some half-hearted attempt to raise a conversation again when he became aware of a strange, muted buzz coming from the chamber doors. It rose in pitch, and he scrambled to his feet, recognizing the collective thrum of many angry voices. His knees protested as he straightened; he shook each leg in turn, and heard Nehesi grunt as he levered himself away from the wall.

The door opened; the guards started, snapped more fully to attention, pointing their spears exactly upright. Hatshepsut was among the first to emerge, following close behind Lady Regent Ahmose. The girl caught Senenmut's eye, and something like relief filled her narrow, harsh features. He tried a tentative smile, but she shook her head, the braided side-lock swinging. Senenmut bowed low as the princess and the regent approached.

"An adjournment only," Hatshepsut told him quietly as men streamed from the audience hall. "No one has been swayed to my side yet. To tell the truth, we may have lost some of the few we brought into that chamber with us."

The frown on Ahmose's face deepened, darkened. "Good men, accompany my daughter into the garden. She and I both need time to collect our thoughts, and I must be alone to pray." She turned and swept down the hallway, raising and turning her shoulders to avoid brushing against any of Mutnofret's men. She did not move in the direction of her royal apartments, but heading for the garden, no doubt to seek the comfort of the shade trees or the raised edge of the great rectangular lake.

"Shall we go?" Nehesi said.

"No." Hatshepsut gazed after her mother with a curious, detached sadness. Senenmut held himself very still, and watched in her eyes an intricate play of remorse, anger, guilt, resolution. "Come with me."

She led them through halls he did not know, past open courtyards where men and women, dressed in bright finery, gathered to entertain emissaries of far-off lands, past the doors to humble offices where scribes worked endlessly, recording the words and works of the regent, composing letters to foreign kings, tallying the wealth of Egypt. As tutor to the king's daughter, his services had seldom been required at the palace; most of his work was confined to the House of Women. It took him some time to realize where Hatshepsut led them, but once he knew, he reached out to touch her wrist, trying to restrain her. She shook off his touch with a peremptory twitch.

Two guards, dressed in the blue-and-white kilts of royal protectors, stood attentive before Lady Regent Ahmose's private rooms. Hatshepsut halted a little way down the hall, evidently struck by sudden uncertainty. Senenmut felt a wash of relief; the guards would not allow even the king's daughter inside without Ahmose's permission.

Nehesi saw the dilemma and, ducking his head in a brief, apologetic bow, stepped ahead of Hatshepsut.

"Good day, my brothers."

The two men eyed him, murmured a tentative greeting.

"Have you heard the news from the barracks? Our new bows have arrived from Mehu."

One guard glanced at the other, his eyebrows raised.

"I've heard they can shoot from here to the Delta," Nehesi said.

The second guard looked back at his mate, paused, and at last shrugged. "Who's to take over?" he asked of Nehesi.

"I am. Be gone quick; I haven't anything else for you. You will need to find out the rest when you get back to the barracks."

"Right." The men trotted away, their striped kilts rippling.

Hatshepsut took Senenmut by the hand and pulled him toward the queen's chamber. Somehow the gesture soothed his heart after the way she had shaken him off moments before. He had not even realized her avoidance of his touch had wounded him. *And how silly that it should. You are her tutor, man, and she is still a girl.* His heart, his thoughts were like the ruffled feathers of a bird, disorganized and rattling, obscuring all shape and form and sense. He tried to sort through these disorienting emotions as Hatshepsut dragged him across the queen's threshold. He could see but one idea clearly: that something in his young lady's manner, something in the very air today, spoke of sudden change – catastrophic, perhaps, but definitely momentous. It made him wild to cling to the here-and-now, and he stared at Hatshepsut desperately, as if he had only moments to memorize her face, her manners, before a god or a demon spirited her far away forever.

Inside the chamber, Hatshepsut barred the door, then beamed at Nehesi. "Good man! Those were secret words you spoke, weren't they?"

"New bows, Mehu, the Delta. The three together tell any man in the royal guard, 'Disregard your previous order. A new one has been given.'" He paused, rolled his lower lip into his mouth. "I took a risk, Great Lady, for you. I can never go back to the guard. I have falsified an order from a commander. It could mean my death."

"Say no more. You entered this chamber a palace guard, but you will leave my personal servant. I claim you for my own. No one will question the king's daughter in this matter."

Senenmut sucked in a cold breath, but she forestalled his protest with one quick, brown hand. "Now there is no time to waste. Help me, both of you."

Despite his fear and his strange sense of floating detachment, Senenmut could not help but gape at the luxury of Ahmose's apartments. She lived in great resplendence, from the sweep of her tiled floor – bright faience pieces forming an image of the goddess Mut that stretched the whole long span of the room – to the tall electrum mirror framed by a pair of carved ebony-wood goddesses, to the senet board perched on her little game-table, its squares and pawns fashioned from precious stones and polished to a deep, rich luster. Wind-catchers near the ceiling let in a rising mid-day breeze that smelled of high water and sweet herbs; the breeze stirred tapestries of the lightest, finest linen so that the goddesses painted upon them swayed in a languid dance.

Hatshepsut surely had visited her mother here before. Indeed, she had spent most of her earliest days in these apartments, until she reached the age of six and was sent off to the harem to be educated. She led the men confidently across the expanse of the anteroom, past a finely made table where Ahmose received her visitors, past a gold-ribbed harp, its strings sparkling in a column of sunbeams admitted past the windcatcher's bars. She took them directly to a great door carved with the image of the sun-scarab and into Ahmose's own bed chamber.

The chamber was a stunning work of architecture. Through his dizzy rush, Senenmut checked and stared at the wonder of the room. The wall opposite the door was not solid, but a series of flat, rectangular columns, with spaces between perhaps two hands wide, so that one saw straight out into Ahmose's private garden as if peeking through fingers held over the eyes, or through a grove of saplings. The columns stretched from floor to ceiling, the entire soaring height of the palace, and high up where the smoke from the queen's night-braziers had darkened the sandstone, huge, heavy bolts of woolen fabric hung rolled, ready to be loosed to cover the miraculous wall against winter's chill and damp. In the center of the wall, dividing the widest of the columns, a door afforded access to the walled garden.

The whole place was lit up with an intense, bright white light, the brilliance of the sun at its zenith. It fell across Ahmose's bed, a huge and opulent thing piled with bright linens,

THE CROOK AND FLAIL

crowned by a curved ivory headrest. The light fell, too, on a
bank of wardrobes and jewelry boxes. Hatshepsut crossed to
one of these, a chest so large Nehesi could have stood inside of
it comfortably. It smelled strongly of oiled wood, and faintly of
sweet myrrh and lavender. Hatshepsut tugged open its doors.
The sweet scent intensified, overwhelming the room.
Hatshepsut paused, suddenly shaken in her strange, headlong
determination. Senenmut said tentatively, "Great Lady?"

"My mother's favorite perfume," she said. Her eyes were
locked on nothing, on some memory playing out before her
own private heart. She shuddered and squeezed her eyes shut,
drew in a breath as if savoring Ahmose's scent, as if this would
be the last time she would ever breathe it in.

She reached into the wardrobe and pulled out a gown, thin-
woven red linen so fine Senenmut could see her hands through
it; a veil, little more. She handed it to him, sorted through her
mother's belts and sashes, settled on one particularly fine belt of
lapis scarabs rolling golden balls, linked one after the other. In
another chest she located fine sandals, braided and wrapped
with cool golden wire, beaded with turquoise. "My feet are
larger than Ahmose's, but I need not wear these for long."

She tugged the knot of her boy's kilt loose. Senenmut and
Nehesi both turned away from her nakedness, but she said,
"Don't be fools. We have no time for modesty. Help me into the
gown."

"Great Lady," Senenmut turned back at her command and
looked away, looked anywhere but at her bare flesh. She had
often undressed before him; the fact of it had never flustered
him before. Now he felt out of his depth, swimming against a
hot current of desire and regret and fear. He stammered, "I
don't know how to dress a woman."

"I can't tie these knots myself." She snatched the gown from
his hands and threw it over her shoulder, fussed with its drape
about her waist.

"Sake of Sobek," Nehesi hissed at Senenmut. "I can do it. The gods know I've helped enough women back into their frocks before their husbands came home. You've led a boring life, tutor." Hatshepsut raised her eyebrows, gave her guard a sharp stare. "Begging your pardon, Great Lady."

"Only tie this thing so it stays on me, and I will pardon you anything."

Nehesi bent over her shoulder, knotting the delicate fabric with fingers surprisingly deft for their thickness. She fastened the belt herself, then sent Nehesi to choose the finest jewels from Ahmose's casks.

She settled onto the stool at Ahmose's mirror-table. She stared at herself sternly in the round, bright mirror. "The razor, Senenmut."

He moved toward her on reluctant, numb feet, as slowly as a man entranced. He took up the regent's delicate copper razor; it was ivory-handled, cleverly curved. Then he stopped, uncertain. "Er – Lady?"

"Shave off my lock."

Senenmut held her eye in the mirror. He knew now what she intended. "Lady, you have not begun to bleed." His voice was hardly more than a whisper. He would not shame her in front of Nehesi. "You cannot do this thing. Not until…."

"I will do it all the same. Surely you two heard the council from the palace halls. If I do not do something now then Egypt will rip itself in two, starting with my mother and Mutnofret. Do you believe strife will stop with them? Of course it will not. It will spread like a disease until the whole land is broken. I will not allow that, Senenmut. It is not maat, this fighting. Shave off my lock."

He hesitated only a moment longer. This was where his regret came from. *A grown woman has no need of a tutor.* This was the last he would ever serve her. The knowledge, now named, now identified, filled him with a poignant sorrow. He gripped the handle of the razor until the skin of his his knuckles stung.

There was no time to whip salt and oil together into a soothing froth. He shaved her head dry, scraping carefully at the root of her side-lock until the last vestige of her childhood hung by a few dark hairs, pulling at her tender skin so that she screwed her face up in a girlish wince. Senenmut made one more pass, and the side-lock parted from her head with the razor's faint hiss. The braid fell onto the ground, still as a dead snake, its loose end raveled. Hatshepsut looked down at it, lying so frank and dark against the shining floor tiles. Then she straightened and pointed to one of Ahmose's wigs, waiting with its sisters on their ornate stands. Senenmut retrieved it, laid the linen padding on Hatshepsut's scalp, and set the heavy wig in place. It was worked in hundreds of small braids that brushed past her shoulders. Each braid was banded with gold and weighted with cinnabar beads like droplets of blood. The beads clattered as she turned her head this way and that, assessing. Finally she nodded. It would do.

Nehesi laid a collar of mother-of-pearl about her shoulders. He had chosen wisely. The collar was worked in the shape of two great vulture's wings: the wings of the goddess Nekhbet, the patroness of Egypt's Great Royal Wives. The tips of the wings came together in a point above Hatshepsut's small breasts, and from them hung a bright blue scarab cradling a golden sun-disc in its forelegs. The collar was heavy; she shifted her shoulders as if the skin beneath its weight itched, but the effect was stunning.

Quickly, Hatshepsut freshened the kohl around her eyes, dusted her lids with blue powder, and stained her lips crimson. Senenmut watched all these rituals of womanhood with a hot lump welling in his chest. She slid the rest of Nehesi's selections onto her graceless, girlish body: wide golden cuffs for her wrists and rings of red jasper for her fingers. She stood and gazed a moment at her image in the electrum mirror. The scarab belt and the wide collar did fool the eye; they gave the impression of a woman's curves. And the loose weave of the red gown both hid and revealed her small breasts with their pale nipples, the shadow of her navel, the clean-plucked juncture of her thighs. The dark slash of her wound was clearly visible. She frowned when her eyes fell upon its reflection. But painted as a woman, wigged and gemmed, she did lose much of her square inelegance; Senenmut was forced to concede that much within his pained heart. She was, in fact, very nearly pretty, ornate as she was now – a thing which was often said of the poor fierce girl by fawning courtiers, but never before said in truth.

"I am ready," she said. Then, "Wait. Senenmut, open that wardrobe there. Yes, that one, with the carvings of Mut on the doors."

Senenmut did as she commanded. Of course. He was always loyal, always devoted. Oh, how he would miss her! But a Great Royal Wife had no need of a tutor.

The opened wardrobe revealed row upon row of slender shelves, and on each one a different crown, gleaming in the light that streamed through the wall of columns.

"The cobra crown," she said.

Senenmut hesitated. "Please, Lady. I cannot touch the cobra crown. I am only a priest."

"You can," she told him. "I permit it. Bring me my crown."

Senenmut drew a deep breath. His shaking hands moved very slowly toward the simple golden circlet with its little rearing cobra. When his fingers closed on the crown and no gods appeared to strike him down, he moved with greater speed.

Hatshepsut took the crown from her tutor's hands and settled it firmly on her brow.

Senenmut let out a deep, tortured breath, a tearing sigh of loss. She looked into his eyes for a long moment, read the sadness there, and touched the side of his face with her cool hand.

A moment later she was striding away from him, raising a hand to summon Nehesi to her heels. Senenmut followed in her new and powerful wake, all the way back to the audience hall.

THE HOUR AWAY HAD DONE LITTLE TO COOL TEMPERS; Hatshepsut could tell that much as she approached. When the door guard admitted her the rage inside the chamber poured over Hatshepsut as hot and sharp as a wasp's sting.

Nehesi bellowed to be heard above the shouting. "The first princess, Daughter of the King, Hatshepsut, may she live!" His voice cut like a war drum. The arguing stopped.

Hatshepsut stepped around her bodyguard, revealing herself to the assembly. Voices, instantly subdued, riffled air still raw and bruised by shouting.

And then, the voice Hatshepsut had feared to hear. "Hatet. What have you done?"

Ahmose's face was pale with shock. Hatshepsut met her mother's red-rimmed eyes and held them for a long, sorrowful moment. To preserve maat, she must call her mother's visions false and break Ahmose's heart. *Forgive me, Mawat. All I do, I do for Egypt.*

"This fighting is a waste of words. I will not have my people squabble like carrion crows. If you cannot settle disputes civilly, I shall settle them for you."

Mutnofret stood, tense and wary. The braids of her wig were tangled about her face. "What trick is this, child?"

"I am no child. I stand before you a woman. Have you mislaid your eyes?"

"But you..." Ahmose took a few steps toward Hatshepsut and

faltered. Her eyes found the cobra crown on her daughter's brow, and her face hardened.

"I am fourteen years old: of marriageable age. I have come to inform this council that I will marry my brother Thutmose and be his Great Royal Wife. You are all witness to this proclamation."

Ahmose flinched as if Hatshepsut's words were a blow. "Hatshepsut, you cannot do this! You know of my visions. I told you what they mean! I am on the verge of securing the throne for you, the true Pharaoh, and you would spit in my eye?"

Mutnofret rounded on Ahmose. "You are on the verge of nothing. For hours you have squawked at us about visions and gods. But these good men and priests would see righteousness upheld! None of us will support a girl as king. The throne belongs to Thutmose."

Ahmose ignored Mutnofret, and the noises of assent from the men gathered around her. She stared steadily at her daughter, her eyes pleading, compelling. "What of the priests of Annu, Hatshepsut? The men who journeyed all this way to support your claim to the throne?"

"I know they made a great sacrifice in coming to my aid." She turned to Messuway and Nakht. "Your loyalty is like the breath of life to me. Like you, I know the importance of maat. Without order, Egypt is nothing. Without unity, we may as well surrender to the Heqa-Khasewet, who will come testing our borders again. My father taught me that much." She turned back to Ahmose, who trembled. "Mother, you have done so much to prepare the king's throne for me. I can only pray to all the gods that they will make me as good and as wise a Great Royal Wife as you."

"Great Royal Wife," Ahmose said, as if the title were a foul oath. Her lips twisted. She glanced back over her shoulder at Mutnofret, then, without another word, she left the hall.

CHAPTER TWELVE

HATSHEPSUT SAT QUIET AND STRAIGHT beneath the canopy of the royal barge. A strong wind blew down from the north, raising the surface of the Iteru to white-edged chop; the deck of the barge glimmered with spray. The ceaseless rocking of the great ship, stern raising before bow, jolting down again just as the bow lifted into the sky, made her feel distinctly ill. Or perhaps it was the presence of Thutmose beside her that sickened her so. He sat kicking his feet on his golden chair, shifting this way and that to watch the oarsmen bend and strain rhythmically at their task. Hatshepsut could feel Ahmose's silent, disapproving glare burning into the back of her head. Her mother had not spoken to her for a week – not since the council meeting, not a word during the planning of the wedding feast. The force of Ahmose's rage was a palpable thing, sharp-quilled and fire-hot.

Hatshepsut was robed in white, her gown overlaid with a heavy net of malachite and electrum beads. In her lap lay a bundle of fragrant lotuses. Her ornate woman's wig was stiff and restricting, its locks banded with tubes of lapis; her neck and shoulders ached.

"You look green," Thutmose observed.

"I think I may vomit," she said lightly, looking away from him.

"You'd better not. Mother would be angry."

Hatshepsut stared at him. "Mother? You're to be the king now, so *you'd* better not keep clinging to Mutnofret's hand."

"I'm to be the king now, so you'd better stop trying to provoke me. It's not working, anyhow."

"Oh, isn't it?"

The barge reached the midpoint of the river. Waset looked like a toy village on the green-brown bank, the kind children build of stones and sticks in the mud beside the fields. On the gentle rise to the east of the city, the miniature palace stood pale in the sun. Hatshepsut squinted at it resentfully as the High Priest of Amun made his way to the bow.

"Let the bridegroom approach!"

Thutmose, having rehearsed his part with his mother, slid out of his seat and sauntered to the priest's side. Hatshepsut admitted to herself that he did look as kingly as a boy of eleven could manage. He wore once again the long kilt of a grown man, neatly folded into dozens of pleats, and his belt was woven of thread-of-gold. He bore himself proudly beneath the weight of a colorful pectoral and the tall double crown of Egypt, its white pinnacle rising from a desert-red base. Of late he had grown. He would be a tall man one day, and not a torment to look upon, for all his plumpness and his smug pride. She would do her best to...not to love him; she could not see herself ever loving him. She would do her best to tolerate him.

"As Atum brought forth all things from the water, so do we bring forth this new union. Aakheperenre Thutmose, Lord of the Two Lands, king of all Egypt, stands forth to welcome his bride."

Hatshepsut sighed. She took up her lotuses. It was an effort to walk smoothly, the barge heaved so, and her feet dragged as though weighted with stones.

"Hatshepsut, king's daughter, do you consent to marry this man?"

"I consent." *Though he is no man.* She plucked a lotus from her bunch and offered it to Thutmose. She was pleased to see that some of its petals were wilted and brown around the edges. She bit the inside of her cheek to keep from smiling.

The High Priest offered Thutmose a little bowl of salt. As she opened her mouth, Hatshepsut closed her eyes, her will finally faltering. She could no longer bear to look on her half-brother's face. It was Senenmut she longed to stand with. If she had been crowned king she would have taken Senenmut for her own, made him Great Royal Husband, and kept him.... She choked at the sudden, overwhelming taste of salt on her tongue. Hatshepsut buried her face in her lotuses to hide her spluttering. Thutmose had dropped an enormous pinch of the stuff into her mouth; she spat into her flowers, hoping no one could see, and glared at him over the violet spikes of the petals.

Thutmose smirked back at her. Beneath the red edge of the double crown, his eyes glimmered with silent and cruel laughter.

"It is done," the High Priest intoned. "Joined before the gods, Aakheperenre Thutmose and Hatshepsut, the Great Royal Wife – may she be fruitful!"

As a troupe of musicians began to play at the rear of the jolting barge, Hatshepsut, swallowing hard, the taste of salt burning her tongue, risked a glance at her mother. Ahmose's eyes were downcast, her face still. Amid the celebrants clapping and swaying, the former queen regent was as defeated, as spent and wilted as a discarded lotus.

THEY FEASTED WELL INTO THE NIGHT. HATSHEPSUT AND Thutmose sat together at an ornate table upon the dais in the great hall of the palace, tasting and approving each dish as it was brought before them. Hatshepsut merely sampled the steaming cuts of roasted beef, the bowls of stewed kid, the fish baked in ornate casings of river clay, carved so deftly that they looked as live and fresh as if they had just been hauled onto the deck of a boat. Thutmose, though, had a hearty appetite. He gestured for portions from many dishes and enjoyed them noisily, chewing and slurping until Hatshepsut felt nearly as ill as she had on the barge.

Every wealthy house within a week's journey of Waset attended the feast. The wedding of the new Pharaoh was an unparalleled opportunity for currying favor with the courtiers and ambassadors who influenced trade; in high spirits, new friendships could be made, new promises extracted. She gazed down at them, at the hundreds of men and women seated around groups of tables, making merry over cups of wine and baskets of sweet bread. Had any of these women, dressed in their bright gowns, swaying and sparkling in their jewels, feel so uncertain at their own wedding feasts? She wondered.

The length of the hall stretched away below her feet. Bodies seemed to emerge from the shadows of the massive painted pillars as spirits appeared in the deep of night, then drifted into darkness again, the colors of their linens dimming. Where light fell about the lamps and braziers, laughter seemed to ring louder until it was almost mocking, the sound of carrion birds at a carcass. *My thoughts are too dark. I mustn't let them show on my face.* A servant bearing jellied fruits appeared at her elbow, bowing, offering up her tray. Hatshepsut took one and bit into it, and used its sweetness to conjure up a smile.

Acrobats – the most skilled group in Upper Egypt, Sitre-In had told her, trying to coax a bit of excitement – tumbled down the length of the chamber, their lean, hard bodies oiled and dusted with gold, flashing in and out of pools of lamplight as they went hand over foot, quick and lithe. They finished their performance in a pyramid, standing atop one another's shoulders; the smallest of them, a girl hardly older than Hatshepsut, naked but for a bit of linen tied around her loins, leapt from the pinnacle, her golden skin dazzling as she fell into the arms of two young men below. The girl posed for her applause; Hatshepsut joined her guests in acclaiming the troupe, resolved to play the part of the happy bride, for maat's sake if not for her own. She slipped a bracelet from her wrist and gestured to Sitre-In, who sat just below the dais with Hatshepsut's servants.

"Give the girl this, with the compliments of the Great Royal Wife."

"Yes, Great Lady." Sitre-In bowed. *My nurse has never bowed to me before. Must she always, now that I am the Pharaoh's wife, and will she ever call me Hatet again?* Maat demanded a nigh unrecognizable new world: she sat upon the dais, Sitre-In bowed at her smallest command, and she was Thutmose's wife. *What am I to make of it all?*

"A romance!" someone called from far down the hall. "Let us have a romance, to make the Pharaoh and his lovely bride smile!"

"Ah!" came another shout. "A romance to mirror the love of our king and his lady!"

"That promises a dull performance," Hatshepsut muttered.

"What?" Thutmose's mouth was full of the jellied fruits.

"I said, 'Yes, let us have another performance.'"

Thutmose waved to his chief steward; the players were admitted into the great hall. "You know what comes after the feast."

"Sleep."

"Not for you. I'll have some spear-work to do on you, wife."

Hatshepsut rolled her eyes. "Did you learn that language from your mawat? I'm sure she would be pleased to hear you

97

speak that way. And anyway, aren't you rather young to be throwing your little spear, Oh Mighty Bull?"

"I've been practicing."

"Your poor hand must be so tired."

He scowled at her as the actors took up their places and posed, waiting for their cue to begin. "Maybe I will save all the pleasure for the harem women, and you can sleep alone in your bed."

"How I will envy the harem."

Thutmose lapsed into resentful silence as the romance began. The crowd clapped hands and pounded tables; Hatshepsut grinned at her husband. It was the first genuine smile that had come to the bride's face the whole day through.

SENENMUT SAT TOGETHER WITH HATSHEPSUT'S PERSONAL servants in a place of great honor, a large round table not far from the royal dais. The women of the Great Royal Wife's chamber were full of wine and gossiped unashamedly – even Sitre-In, to Senenmut's surprise. He stole many furtive glances over Nehesi's shoulder up to the throne where his young lady was ensconced. Her posture was stiff; her cheeks were pale and resolutely unsmiling.

That she had planned to put herself forward as Pharaoh had been a surprise to Senenmut, but did not strike him as far-fetched. She was as intelligent a person as the throne could ever wish for, observant and astute, mindful of duty and of justice. She took to command as naturally as a bird takes to its wings or a child takes to laughter. She could be faulted in only one thing, and that beyond any mortal control: the true son of Thutmose the First had been placed into the wrong sort of body. What purpose had the gods in this? He watched young Thutmose smirking down the vast length of the great hall, gazing upon the hundreds gathered to honor him without a trace of comprehension or gratitude. Many times before had Senenmut despaired at the gods' designs, but never so intensely as now.

Some man called for a romance, and within moments the actors were ushered in, taking up their place unfortunately near to Senenmut's table. They acted out a rather foolish love story while a singer with somewhat too shrill a voice recited the tale. The girl fainted away from love-sickness when the boy touched her hand. Senenmut seized the tall flagon at the center of their table. The wine inside was cool; beads of water had gathered along the pretty, ornate lines scored along the flagon's belly. He filled his cup to the brim, then topped off Nehesi's as well.

The young acrobat had re-entered the feast – the one who had thrown herself from the height of the pyramid. Admirers had draped garlands of flowers about her neck and shoulders; there were so many that she was wreathed nearly to her chin.

Sitre-In sent a serving man scurrying after the girl, and when she approached the table, the nurse proffered a fine bracelet of gold and turquoise. "A gift from the Great Royal Wife, to honor your performance."

The acrobat took it between her delicate, slender hands. She had wiped the gold dust from her body, but traces of it remained in the lines of her knuckles and the edges of her henna-darkened nails. "The Great Lady is too kind. To perform before her eyes is the only reward I need." But she slid the cuff onto her arm and admired it against her skin. When her eyes flicked up from the bracelet, she caught Senenmut's eyes. "Hello," she said, sinking to kneel beside his ebony seat.

Senenmut flushed at the suggestiveness of her posture. He nodded a brusque greeting. Nehesi snorted into his wine cup.

"I am called Naparaye." The scent of her flower garlands overwhelmed his senses. Her slender body moved with an unconscious, liquid grace; her eyes were wide and dark, alight with promise.

"This is Senenmut, he of few words," Nehesi volunteered. "Once the tutor to the Great Royal Wife."

"Ah, a man of learning. Perhaps you could teach me."

Chuckling at his own discomfort, Senenmut turned his face away so the woman would not see his face flame red. He chanced to look up at Hatshepsut's throne. The Great Royal Wife was gazing down upon him. When she saw the color of his cheeks, his sheepish unease, she tilted her chin haughtily, turned to Thutmose with some tight-lipped comment. But in the flicking away of her dark stare he saw, too, the briefest flash of a desperate pain, ka-deep. All at once Senenmut was pierced by a cold stab of guilt. And something else, too. A terrible longing – for what, he knew not. For the way his life had been, perhaps; for the routine of their walks in Hatshepsut's garden, their discussions, the questions she knew were cheek, the answers he hoped were wise.

His silence had gone on too long. Naparaye was on her feet again, a movement faster than the flicker of a water strider's legs. She turned up her fine, straight nose and looked pointedly away from Senenmut, out into the great crowd of servants dodging between tables, of nobles' backs bent over conversation, ladies' shoulders swaying in merriment.

"Come, now," Nehesi laughed. "Don't be put off by my shy friend. You can see how he blushes – he is a maiden priest! Have mercy on the poor lad."

Senenmut gasped, mortified. He had, in fact, lain with several women, though he was not about to divulge the specifics of his private life to one such as Nehesi.

"If you need a lesson, beautiful Naparaye, there is much a soldier can teach you that a priest cannot."

Naparaye shot Nehesi a challenging glance.

"How to nock an arrow, for one. And how to peg a tent." He roared with appreciation for his own wit.

To Senenmut's surprise, Naparaye smiled. She brushed past

Senenmut; he was beneath her notice now, less than a servant. She plucked a flower from one of her garlands and tucked it behind Nehesi's ear, then leaned close to whisper. When she had drifted away again, Senenmut raised one eyebrow, a silent query.

"She is staying," Nehesi said, "with her troupe at the blue rest house at the high end of the fishermen's avenue. Though I do not suggest you go knocking on her chamber door tonight. She will be entertaining a guest." He stuffed bread into his mouth, grinning as he chewed.

Senenmut drowned his humiliation in wine, and schooled himself to keep his eyes off the dais. The suffering he had caught in Hatshepsut's eye was burned already onto his heart. He did not need to witness her sorrow again.

CHAPTER THIRTEEN

THEY WALKED TOGETHER FAR INTO the dry red valley, Hatshepsut and Senenmut, trailed by Nehesi and a contingent of guards bearing skins of beer, sacks of food, and swords – always swords, for Hatshepsut had never lost the caution Ahmose had raised her with. The evening was pleasantly warm, and the going was kind to their feet. Several days had passed since the wedding feast – days, ah, and nights, too, during which Thutmose had left Hatshepsut blessedly alone in her extravagant new apartments. She had spent those days absorbed in her rule, more often than not sitting the throne of the Great Royal Wife with the king's seat empty beside her. Thutmose frequently failed to return to his audiences from the mid-day meal, or sometimes begged off entirely, preferring to drive his chariot in the hills beyond Waset while Hatshepsut saw to the governing of Egypt alone. Nights she spent in an agony of loss, pacing in the dark through the private garden of the Great Royal Wife, its paths new and strange to her, a bewildering dream-world redolent with the scent of unfamiliar flowers and air salty as tears.

She had tormented herself with questions, and railed in her

heart against the gods. She would be a woman in truth one day soon, and would be of an age to take Senenmut as her lover. He was no longer her tutor; when the moon finally touched her loins she would be no longer a child, and her love for Senenmut would be as maat as it ever could be. But if she were to fall pregnant – ah, the gods would surely curse her for a sinner. For she would not allow Thutmose into her bed – of that she was certain – and any child she might bear could never be his. No – for the sake of maat, she would remain lonely, without a lover, without even a son to dote upon – with only her serving women and her pale night flowers for company. She had sacrificed her own ambitions and her mother's reputation as a prophetess, all for the sake of order. If she disrupted maat again, what was all this terrible sacrifice for? She had chosen her path, and Senenmut must not walk it with her.

They trekked deep into the ancient valley, to the place where the cliffs soared, red and glowing, into a brilliant sky. Against the cliff face the old temple of Mentuhotep crouched, the shoulders of its pyramid sagging above ruined porticoes and the crumbling slope of its ramp. The disuse of the place overwhelmed her with a sense of poignancy, sharp and sweet. She could think of no better place to cut Senenmut free.

A broken line of myrrh trunks, long-dead, stretched across the valley to the base of Mentuhotep's tomb. She paused and gazed down the remnant of the once-great avenue, imagining a time when it must have bustled with life, when priests came and went, when women sang the memory of the departed king, when the trees themselves dripped with beads of precious incense, sweet and soothing. Now there were only the pale bones of trees, a home for the vultures. She made her way to one and called her guards.

They laid a blanket out for her, and food. She took Senenmut by the hand – how little she had touched him, and how she would miss the warmth of his skin, that rare, precious treasure. Together they sat beneath the myrrh tree, in its latticed shadow, to eat.

"You quoted the Book of the Dead for me," she said, toying with a cone of soft white cheese wrapped in thick papyrus. "On the steps of the temple, that day when I stood against Mutnofret's men. You spoke of Re, and Sia and Hu." She watched as he swallowed hard, washing down bread and cold duck with a mouthful of beer.

"I saw that day what you intended to do. The moment I drove into the temple's courtyard I realized you would proclaim yourself Pharaoh. And it seemed the gods whispered in my heart that it was maat, that you should take the throne. I know you better than most. I wanted them to see, too, what you are."

"What am I to you, Senenmut?"

He stared at her with red-rimmed eyes. She would have taken his face in her hands and kissed him then, as she had kissed him before but longer, pouring her ka into his mouth as the gods had poured the ankh into his body and made him live for her – for her! But her guards were looking on, so she busied herself instead with the cheese.

"You standing there, the knife in your hands, facing down all those who spoke against you. Just a slip of a girl, but braver than any soldier I've ever known, and fiercer than a jackal. In that moment I wanted to protect you, not only from the men who would take away what is yours, but from the knife, too – from what you would do to yourself. And I saw, too, that I could not. I am only a man, and you are the child of the god."

She lowered her face, accepting his words. But the words heated and agitated her heart with a ferocity she did not understand, and could not name. *That is what I am to him. Half-god. Not even a woman. Untouchable.*

They sat in silence. A wind moved through the myrrh tree; its bleached, dry twigs clattered faintly, a small sound like holy rattles in a far-off temple.

"I doubt myself when you are near me, Senenmut."

He looked up, startled and wounded.

She smiled to relieve the sting of her words. "You were right to rebuff my affections, but you shook my certainty by turning away from me."

"I...I am sorry, Great Lady."

"There is no need to be sorry. You were right to do it. But I feel shaken and doubtful even now. You take something crucial from me, just by being near. I am the Great Royal Wife now, and soon I will go to the Temple of Amun to begin my duties as God's Wife. I cannot doubt myself. I can have no weakness."

He exhaled sharply, a sound very much like a sob. "Great Lady, do not...do not send me away. I know your mother has retreated to her own estates and has left you alone...."

"I have her stewards," Hatshepsut said, waving his concerns away with a languid turn of her wrist.

"A steward is not a regent. Nor is he a mother. You need people around you who are devoted to you, who will support you..."

"I have my women, and Nehesi."

"Please, Great Lady, do not do this. I can help you."

It chilled her skin, to speak to him as if he were nothing to her. "You will help me best by being far from my side." She gestured for Nehesi; the man blotted out the sun as he stood above her, passed to her hands the wool sack he carried. When her guard had withdrawn again to a respectful distance, Hatshepsut gave the bag to Senenmut. "It is not so bad as you think. Open the sack."

He did. Inside were two scrolls. The first was the deed to a house just north of Waset, a scenic farm high on a promontory overlooking the bend in the river. Its fields produced wine grapes and barley; Senenmut would live off the substantial wealth of his new estate for the rest of his life. The second scroll was addressed to the masters of the House of Imhotep, far to the north in the city of Ankh-Tawy. It was a guarantee of his expenses at the grandest school of architecture in all of Egypt.

"Great Lady," Senenmut said, his voice rough. "I cannot accept this. It is too much."

"It is nothing, compared to the love I have for you." She marveled at the lightness of her own voice. "There is more."

His hand went deep into the bottom of the bag. When his fingers found her final gift, she saw how he faltered, his mouth growing tight and pale as though he endured a terrible blow. He drew out her side-lock, tied with a red length of thread so it would not unravel.

"The gods gave me your wisdom," Hatshepsut said. "And gave you my heart in turn. I shall never forget you."

"Nor I you, Great Lady. Never, as long as the river rises. I am your most faithful servant, no matter how far from your side I may be."

PART II
HAND OF THE GOD

1485 B.C.E.

CHAPTER FOURTEEN

T HE SECOND DAY OF THE second month dawned in a
blue glory, filling the land with light, the sun's bright rays
sparkling across a valley of water. The Black Land slept beneath
the flood, gathering the Iteru's rich darkness into itself, making
ready to bring forth, when the river withdrew again, barley and
wheat, herb and fruit, green leaf and the flesh of game – all the
wealth of Egypt, her power everlasting. The avenue that led
from Ipet-Isut, from Amun's Temple at the very heart of the city
of temples, was thronged with people, nobles in their soft,
bright linen rubbing elbows with coarse rekhet in winter-wool
frocks. They raised great feather fans and waved bundles of
sweet grasses, their arms laden with dried flowers and herbs.
The morning was full of song.

Hatshepsut, seated easily beside Thutmose on a broad litter,
beamed at her people as a contingent of priest-guards carried
them down the avenue lined with seshep, statues of kings-as-
lions, their crowned heads rising stern and ancient above
outstretched feline paws. Even Thutmose managed a pleasant
demeanor today, raising his hand in acceptance of the crowd's
cheers. This was the beginning of the Beautiful Feast of Opet,

the festival to mark the annual rebirth of Waset's gods and confer on the Pharaoh long life, the power of Amun, and a continuation of his reign.

More than a year had passed since Thutmose had been crowned, since Hatshepsut had sent Senenmut away. During the course of that year she had immersed herself in the duties of God's Wife of Amun, glad for the comfort of ritual, the distraction of devotion. Though her voice was only serviceable at best, still she loved to lead the priestesses in song, loved to lift her iron sesheshet high and raise its clanging, rattling din, the sound so pleasing to the god, while the priests made their offerings. She loved, too, the moments when she would enter Amun's black sanctuary alone. By feel she would find the god seated on his throne in absolute darkness, and caress his cold, mysterious, male form, blind in the deep silence, whispering praises to him, knowing that he heard her and was pleased.

Because she was God's Wife, it was she who had led the priests this morning, well before the sun had risen, in washing and dressing Amun. They had draped about his shoulders garlands of flowers and braids of gold. They had tied about his wrists and ankles strings of precious stones and bells of electrum. And when he had been anointed until he was slippery and sweet with the oil of olives and myrrh, they had carried him through the darkness to his waiting barque, and under her direction the priests had set him gently inside. They drew blue veils about him – blue for the color of his skin. At last Thutmose had arrived, trailed by the attendants who bore the king's little ka-statue. Her husband had propped his statue before the god – before Hatshepsut, for she stood beside Amun within his veiled alcove, one hand on the god's golden shoulder. Thutmose begged for blessing, for long life and wisdom. She had liked that – ah, she had! – the sight of this boy who called himself a man, who called himself a king, kneeling before her.

Little, though, had she liked the sharpness in Nebseny's eyes.

Months before, the old High Priest had gone to join the gods at last, and the priesthood had raised Nebseny to take his place, with the blessing of the Pharaoh – and of the Pharaoh's mother, no doubt. Imperious as ever, missing nothing, Nebseny had squinted at the tableau – Thutmose in supplication, pushing forward his ka-statue, Hatshepsut standing proud and satisfied behind the blue veil at the side of the god himself. Nebseny disliked what he saw; she was certain of that. He never had cared for her, not since that day on the temple steps.

Outside Amun's temple they had mounted their litter and watched as the god's barque, borne on the backs of priests draped in leopard skins, preceded them. Before they left Ipet-Isut to pass before the crowd, two other barques joined them – Mut, mother of the gods, shrouded in red, her bright white vulture wings barely visible through the mist of her veils; and Khonsu, the moon-god, the son, whose white draperies showed his silhouette plainly in the morning light.

Along the avenue the celebrants shouted their questions to the gods, and as bow or stern of their barques dipped the questions were answered, yes or no. *Will my crops be plentiful this year? Will my trade with Hatti be good? Mut, will you give me sons? Khonsu, will the girl I love consent to marry me?*

Hatshepsut eyed Mut's barque, watched the gilded form of the goddess inside her house of veils, and whispered, "Holy Mother, will my blood ever come?" But at the moment she asked her question, neither bow nor stern dipped, and Hatshepsut was left unknowing.

Troops of soldiers joined them, their breastplates and shields decorated with falcons' feathers of smoke-blue and pale clay. At the first small chapel the sacrificial cattle were driven onto the avenue. The cattle's horns had been dyed blue, and their thick dark necks bore wreaths of woven papyrus leaves. Musicians thronged behind the royal litter. The reedy voices of pipes rose and broke through the shouts of the crowd.

Thutmose turned to smile at her, and Hatshepsut smiled lightly back, even though Mut had left her question unanswered. It was rare that her husband acknowledged her. She did not mind his absence from her life, but it was pleasant to receive his good graces today.

"It will be a good festival," he said.

"Ah, the river is high. The fields will be as fertile as ever."

"My own field grows more fertile."

"What do you mean?"

"I received a letter from the king of Hatti. He sends a daughter for my harem. She should arrive a few days from now. And the noble house of Ankhhor, governor of the sepat of Ka-Khem, sends a daughter as well. She is said to be very beautiful, and sweet-tempered, which is more than I can say for you."

He said it not unfondly, and Hatshepsut tossed her head in good-natured protest. The long ribbons adorning her God's Wife crown fluttered about her. She would not argue with him today. The Feast of Opet was a time of joy.

"Ankhhor. Is he not the brother of our new High Priest of Amun?"

"Nebseny? I don't know. It's not for the king to concern himself with the lineage of every citizen; leave that to the scribes. Why should I care about Ankhhor's brother? It's his daughter concerns me."

Hatshepsut shrugged. "I wish you well of them both – Ankhhor's daughter and the Hittite princess. May they give you hundreds and hundreds of sons." From all Hatshepsut had heard from the harem women, the great king Thutmose did nothing more than eat and boast when he visited his concubines. She suspected he was still uncertain of those particular kingly duties. He was, after all, still shy of twelve years old. A man's desires would be upon him in a year or two, and woe to the harem when that day dawned. "Will you give the women a feast when their new sisters arrive? They'll be expecting it."

112

"I must leave that to you. The campaign in Ta-Seti is finally concluded; the Kushites have ceased raiding my southern border and have scattered back into their rocky ditches like dogs with their tails between their legs. I leave tomorrow. I will make a display of the men we captured."

"Thutmose the Second is a great warrior," she said wryly.

He spoke of the southern army's victory as if he had actually effected some influence in the matter. It was not uncommon for one or another of Egypt's enemies to make war when a new king took the throne. Indeed, it was all but tradition for the strength of the Two Lands to be tested whenever the reign of a new Pharaoh dawned. This time Kush had descended in a flurry of small, fast raiding parties, attacking outposts and farming villages, herders and traveling merchants. Like demons they came seemingly from nowhere, raping and killing and thieving, then vanished again into the ravines and bluffs of their rocky, desolate land. Thutmose was too young and altogether too useless to lead the defense himself, and so Hatshepsut had sent in his place three generals to see to the campaign on the king's behalf. As good as they were, Ta-Seti, Egypt's southernmost sepat, was a difficult defense. It lay in a hard land where the river itself broke into wild cataracts. The going was difficult, she had been told. Chariots were all but useless beyond the river's banks. Soldiers were often obliged to chase down raiders sitting astride their horses, as drovers' children sat astride cattle. The fact that it had taken fully a year to throw off the Kushite raids troubled her.

"I shall be glad to see to the women's feast, then," she said, wondering how she might take some active part in strengthening Egypt's southern border. It was all well and good for Thutmose to sail upstream to Ta-Seti and count severed hands and strut about like a puffed-up he-goose. The real work of protecting Egypt would fall, as it always did, into her hands.

CHAPTER FIFTEEN

T HE DISHES HAD LONG BEEN cleared away and the
feasting tables carried back into the House of Women.
Serving girls moved about the twilit garden bearing pitchers of
sweet wine and bitter beer, and water scented with the petals of
roses or the tart rinds of fruits. They bore dates, too, and balls
of honey-cake rolled in dried flowers. It had been a fine feast, a
gesture of welcome to the new concubines as well as a continuation of the Opet festival. Hatshepsut felt in a celebratory mood,
with Thutmose away. Alone in the great hall, hearing audiences
and dictating her proclamations, she could almost imagine that
she was the Pharaoh.

She walked arm-in-arm with her dear friend, named Opet
like the festival. Opet was two years older than Hatshepsut and
a half-sister by blood, sired by her own royal father on a woman
of the harem. She had grown up in the House of Women and,
though her mother had never pledged her to the Pharaoh's
service – she could leave and marry a nobleman or even a tjati if
she chose – she had elected to stay.

"Where else could I ever live in such luxury?" she had once
said, when Hatshepsut had asked her why she remained. "Surely

not in some backwater sepat. Can you imagine? The lowing of cattle would be all the music I'd ever hear. No, I will stay here in Waset, sister. It suits me."

"But you may be required to lie with Thutmose, once he starts showing an interest in women."

Opet had shuddered elaborately. "By the time that happens I will be stooped and covered in warts, with my breasts hanging down to my knees. I have nothing to fear."

But now, as they drifted from one group of chattering women to the next, Opet confided that Thutmose's dreaded awakening may be approaching faster than either had thought.

"Last night before he left for his ships he visited to bid us all farewell. He pinched me on my bottom, and when Hentumire bowed to him he cupped her breast in his hand, right in front of everybody!"

Hatshepsut groaned. "He is insufferable. I must find some nursemaid to crack him with a stick until he learns his manners."

"You cannot beat a Pharaoh, sister. It will take subtlety, if he is to learn the right way to treat a woman. You'll forgive me, Great Lady, but you do not have subtlety. We shall all of us work together to train him, or the House of Women will become as rowdy as a brothel."

"I wish you all the gods' blessings on that endeavor. Amun knows it's a task too great for one woman alone."

They came to the raised stone shore of the garden lake. The water stretched out into the dusk, its surface deep violet, reflecting a silver moon that danced as a breeze rippled the water. A few women gathered there, sipping from golden cups as they sat idly on the stone wall. Some dangled toes in the water, squealing at the cold, while others, well into their wine, made a game of trying to count the bats that dropped to the lake's surface. The women broke off again and again, laughing as they lost their numbers.

Seated a little apart were the two newcomers. Hatshepsut approached them, and inclined her head to the princess of Hatti, a lovely young woman with an unshaven head of thick, dark-brown hair. It fell in waves about her shoulders, though she had knotted a few beads into the locks, no doubt in deference to Egyptian style. She wore an Egyptian-style dress, too – a green gown that hugged her shape and left her arms bare.

"Are you not cold?" Hatshepsut asked. "It is winter, after all. Shall I send a servant for a shawl to cover up your arms?"

"No, Great Lady," the princess said. She spoke Egyptian readily, if with a heavy accent. "Winters are much colder in Hatti. I think perhaps I will find the heat of Egyptian summer too great."

"What is your name?"

"Astartakhepa, Great Lady."

Hatshepsut tried to repeat the name. Her tongue tripped over the unfamiliar sounds; Opet laughed behind her hand.

"I think perhaps we shall have to call you something simpler," Hatshepsut said. "You are beautiful; until we learn to say your name correctly we may as well call you Nefer. I hope you do not mind a pet name. We are fond of such things in Egypt."

"I am honored to be named by the Great Royal Wife," she said, bowing.

The Great Royal Wife, Hatshepsut mused. *I will never grow used to hearing it. I will never think of myself that way – as Thutmose's wife.*

"And you," she said, turning to the other, the daughter of Ankhhor. "I hope your name comes easier to my tongue."

"As do I." The girl bowed smoothly, raising pale, delicate hands to Hatshepsut. "I am Iset, Great Lady, and beneath the notice of the God's Wife."

What a perfect blend of confidence and humility. This one is from a noble house, and no mistake. "Named for the goddess. I can see it is a name that suits you." Iset was slender, graceful, perhaps seventeen years old. She wore a fashionable gown, tight through the waist and hips, halting in a beaded band that left her breasts bare to peek through her shawl as she moved. She was lovely and light, all harmonious curves like an ibis bird, and her eyes shone with a happy complacency that Hatshepsut liked at once.

"The Great Royal Wife is too kind. Beside her beauty I am as dust."

Hatshepsut barked a laugh. "Men and women say many things of the Great Royal Wife, Iset, but seldom do they praise her beauty. No, I am not offended. I would rather be strong and wise than beautiful. Beauty seldom lasts long."

Iset smiled. Her wig was scented with benzoin and myrrh; as she tilted her head in a coy, conspiratorial gesture the rich, spicy perfume came powerfully to Hatshepsut's senses, set a thrill racing under her skin.

"The Great Royal Wife is wise indeed, then," the girl said. "It is good to have at least one wise ruler on the throne."

"I think I shall like you very much."

"I hope you shall."

"I can see your father prepared you well for life in a royal court. What else did he teach you?"

"I can sing, Great Lady, and dance."

Opet clapped her hands. "Let's have a song!"

Some of the women gathered nearby heard the suggestion and agreed. "Yes, a song!" "Ah, it's a good night for music."

Iset remained gazing at Hatshepsut, awaiting her command. Hatshepsut nodded, and the newcomer moved a little apart to stand facing the gathering of women. She smoothed her gown over her hips, eyes fixed distantly on the darkness of the garden, rapt and isolated, as if listening to the falling notes of a harp that only she could hear. At last she raised her voice, wine-sweet and water-pure.

My soul will not sleep
> *For want of my sister.*
> *The river runs between us,*
> *And I am sick with loss.*
> *My pool is broken*
> *By ripples unending,*
> *For the wind has blown her far away,*
> *The wind has blown her far away.*

Oh sister, your perfume
> *Is like honey dropped in water.*
> *Like spices and pomegranates,*
> *You stain my mouth with longing.*
> *My pool is broken*
> *By ripples unending;*
> *The wind has blown your odor far away,*
> *The wind has blown your odor far away.*

The gods have made your love
> *Like the advance of flames in straw,*
> *My longing like the downward stoop*
> *Of the falcon in bright flight.*
> *My pool is broken*
> *By ripples unending.*
> *I will fly to you on wind far away,*
> *I will fly to you on wind far away.*

I am a wild goose, a hunted one;
> *The beauty of your shining hair*
> *Is a bait to trap me in your net;*
> *Your eyes, a snare of meryu-wood.*
> *Gratefully I fall*
> *Into ripples unending.*
> *Hunt me, sister, far away.*

Hunt me, sister, far away.

Hatshepsut stood still as the women applauded. Iset's song had pierced her deep, raising memories of Senenmut, of their last day together, his red-eyed stare in the jagged shade of the myrrh tree. She wondered whether he still remembered her. Perhaps he was the only man who ever would. She knew she was not beautiful – she was too blocky, too coarse, and she had inherited from her father his curved beak of a nose, his bold front teeth. For all her brave words to Iset, she knew that it was beauty, not strength or wisdom, that made men fall in love.

"Great Lady?" Iset's brow was pinched with worry. "Did my singing offend?"

"No," she said quickly. "You sang beautifully, Iset. Beautifully. You must come to me one day and sing in my apartments; I would be glad of you." Mornings she attended Amun and by day she kept her court. But nights were long and quiet, and heavy with the absence of Senenmut. Music would be a balm to her lonesome kas; Iset's singing was as sweet and soothing as the smoke of myrrh.

The girl bowed again. "As you wish, Great Lady. I am yours to command."

CHAPTER SIXTEEN

"THOU ART THE LORD OF the silent, who comes at the cry of the poor!"

The chorus of priestesses repeated Hatshepsut's chant, lifting their sesheshet high above their heads. The iron rods were strung with bells, so black they drank the light of the braziers as the darkness of Amun's sanctuary swallowed fear and doubt.

When their voices and the clatter of their sacred rattles died away, she lifted her own sesheshet and cried, "Thou art Amun-Re, Lord of Waset!"

Again the rattles raised, again the voices chanted. She looked down upon her priestesses from where she stood on a small golden dais. The ribbons of the God's Wife crown fell over her shoulders. Her scalp was bare of any wig, freshly shaven; the diadem of electrum lay cold upon her forehead. To her right was the door to Amun's shrine, closed and guarded by four priests.

"Thee, who rescues him who is in the netherworld!"

The sun had nearly risen to reveal the god's morning aspect, Amun-Re. Beyond the group of priestesses, through the temple's great, high entrance, Hatshepsut could see how the sky lightened, tending, barely perceptible, from the cold blue of night to the golden hues of blessed day.

"For thou art merciful when man appeals to thee!"

The light fell now through the open doorway, a lance of gold in which cold motes rose and shimmered, swirling in the gathering warmth. Hatshepsut lifted her sesheshet for the final line of the devotion, and as she called it out to her priestesses, her voice brimmed with the joy of the breaking day. "Thou art he who comes from afar!"

The priests swung wide the doors to Amun's sanctuary. With a collective murmur, the gathered worshipers lowered their faces, none daring to look inside. The beam of light moved across the floor of the sanctuary. Hatshepsut stepped into it, pacing toward the still-hidden god with slow, deliberate steps.

The fifteen days of the Beautiful Feast of Opet had come, at last, to a close. The dream-readers and magicians had all agreed: Amun was well pleased, renewed and invigorated; the young Pharaoh's reign would be long and prosperous; and the God's Wife was a pleasure to the Lord of Waset. Hatshepsut had taken to her duties with a zeal seldom seen before in the history of her exalted station, often spending half the day tending to the god, when the demands of the court allowed. Nowhere did she feel as light of heart than in Amun's presence. She felt a kinship here at the god's side. And why not? Was she not in fact the kin of Amun-Re, his own daughter in flesh and in ka? In the black of the sanctuary she felt not only the presence of the god, but of her earthly father, too. When all the light was shut from her eyes she could feel Thutmose the First smiling upon her, as he had so many times in life, holding her upon his lap when she was just a small thing, walking with her in the gardens, listening to her recite her childish lessons.

You were right, Father, she whispered in her heart. *Maat is all.*

She paused with her sandals touching the edge of the

sunbeam. The light moved beyond her, stretching her shadow into the shrine. It crept by degrees up the god's electrum dais, fell lightly upon his golden feet, moved up his legs. Hatshepsut's heart beat harder, as it did whenever she looked upon Amun in the light. Such moments were rare, for the god preferred secrecy and dark, so that his brilliance, once revealed, might shine all the brighter. The shrine's interior slowly filled with morning light. Baskets and platters heaped with offerings resolved out of darkness, dozens of bread-loaves, strings of lotus blossoms, jars of oil both sweet and bitter, figs and melons and the tart, oily-skinned fruits brought in trade from far to the east. And of course, offered upon fine dishes of lapis lazuli and gold, heaps of myrrh, the resinous incense which was the god's favorite scent. Amun, glimmering, wrought all in gold, sat upon his throne and smiled down at his offerings, at Hatshepsut herself, who in her very flesh was his most sincere offering. His face was at once peaceful, haughty, amused – the very face of royalty, stern and eternal beneath the twin golden plumes of his crown, each one as tall as a man.

Hatshepsut moved toward him, shy as a girl with her first lover. She was God's Wife, God's Hand. It was her duty and privilege to please him in all things. She touched his arms gently, slid her fingers along them to his hands where they lay on his lap. Outside the shrine, the priestesses took up their hymn, singing loud of Amun's virility, of the force that had created all things.

Renew, renew thy creation, Lord of Waset! Thine is the life of the land!

As she caressed his chest, his face, his neck, as she knelt to kiss his feet, Hatshepsut could feel his approving presence in the chamber. It was the feeling of warm sun upon her back. *Thou art pleased, Lord Amun. I know it. Thou are pleased, even with me as Great Royal Wife. Thy will is maat, and maat is all.*

Bring forth the crops, fill the land with light! The priestesses were dancing now. Their skirts of red and white lifted and flattened as they whirled past the door to the sanctuary, swayed to the music of horns and drums. *The land is fertile! Sow thy seed, Lord of Waset, from the God's Hand!*

When the ceremony was over, Hatshepsut moved among the god's servants, sharing with them bread and honey, dates and wine spread upon tables in the temple's forecourt. The sun was well up now, sweet in a pale blue sky. She accepted the praises of priests and priestesses alike, dipping her head demurely when they spoke of her devotion. "You are so young, and yet so dedicated to the god. This is a blessing upon Waset – upon Egypt, in truth." "You have taken your station entirely to heart, Great Lady, and Amun's blessings will overflow onto the throne."

She separated from one small crowd of priestesses and wandered along a line of myrrh trees, breathing in the subtle, spicy scent of their winter slumber. Their branches lay bare against the sky, sharp, but beginning to swell with the promise of leaf buds. Nebseny leaned against one tree, wine cup in hand. The leopard-skin mantle of the High Priest fell over his shoulder to his waist. His golden leopard mask hung from a thong around his neck, glowering at her from his chest.

"A good morning to you, High Priest."

He half-bowed, formal but chill. "God's Wife. Your devotions today were...pure."

"I try to please the god in all things," she said, ruing the defensive tone in her voice.

"I am sure you do." He was stiff, mildly offended by her presence. She recalled the way he had looked the day she'd cut herself on the temple steps, how he had crouched, suspended somewhere between admiration and horror. She blushed at the memory of her impulsiveness, then turned sharply away, furious that her emotions could show so readily upon her face.

"Have I offended the Great Lady?" Nebseny's tone said he did not much care if he had.

His insolence angered her, but there was nothing she could do. Only two people in all the world stood above the station of the God's Wife: the Pharaoh and the High Priest of Amun. She had no choice but to suffer his disdain. "The sun is in my eyes; that is all. If you will excuse me, High Priest, I shall find a shadier spot."

Near the feast tables she saw three or four priestesses laughing merrily, bumping their hips together. Their company seemed infinitely preferable to Nebseny's. She made her way toward them, and sighed in relief when they bowed at her approach. Here, at least, she would find no scorn.

Nedjmet was plump and kindly, a happy, gossipy woman of perhaps twenty years with a protruding belly that proclaimed her a mother three times over at least. She welcomed Hatshepsut with a smile and a measure of sticky dates, which she poured into her hands. "Something sweet for the Hand of the God!"

"Oh – Nedjmet, I cannot eat another bite. Here." Hatshepsut held the dates out, and the priestesses each took a few, nibbling, until at last Hatshepsut's hands were empty. Her heart, though, filled. She loved the company of her priestesses. They understood her devotion to the god as no one else did.

"We saw you speaking to Lord Highborn," said Bakmut, an older priestess and thin, but still with a pretty face despite the lines of age beginning to show around her mouth.

"You should not speak of the High Priest so," Hatshepsut said.

"If the God's Wife commands," Bakmut said, her voice laden with amusement.

Nedjmet shook her head. "Great Lady, it might do you some

good to speak of the High Priest so, if you will forgive my saying it. What a strutter that one is. He's worse than a whole flock of geese."

Wiay, the newest priestess, laughed. She was hardly older than Hatshepsut herself, but already she had found her feet among the temple servants. Hatshepsut envied her a little, the ease with which she forged her friendships. *"Hahnk, hahnk!"* Wiay waddled like a goose and made as if to peck at the date in Nedjmet's fingers. "Count up the measures of grain! What is the wealth of Amun? *Hahnk!* Stop that laughing, priestesses! Amun demands solemnity!"

"Oh, Wiay, stop! The God's Wife will think us wicked."

Hatshepsut smiled. She knew their ease in her presence was due to her youth, but their camaraderie was such a relief that she could not feel indignant. "No, it is good to see you laughing. I wish I could be as free as you. It doesn't help to have Nebseny glaring at me and turning his shoulder every time I approach him. Why does he dislike me so? I have been absolutely devoted in my duties. I can't think what I may have done to anger him."

Dimly she realized that a woman of her station should not pour out her heart to the priestesses she led. But their friendly manner was such a relief after a year of marriage to Thutmose, of serving maat, of loneliness – a year without Senenmut. Their sympathy was more than she could resist.

Nedjmet and Bakmut shared a glance.

"Walk with us, Great Lady." Bakmut offered her arm. They wandered away from the feast tables, the priestesses talking of incidental things until they were well away from the gathering in the forecourt.

Near the great soaring wall of Ipet-Isut, where they could be sure of their privacy, Bakmut broke off her chatter and turned abruptly to Hatshepsut, her face solemn. "The truth is, Great Lady, Nebseny thinks you unnatural."

"Unnatural? Why ever would he think that? I've done everything according to maat."

"Is it true, Great Lady, that you have never bled?"

Hatshepsut's gaze dropped from Bakmut's kindly face to her own feet, which looked very timid and small to her, the gleam of her gold sandals obscured by the dust in which she scuffled.

Nedjmet spoke up. "The priestesses whisper – concerned, you see. We would never speak maliciously of our God's Wife. Everyone in the temple knows you have a male ka..."

"Eight," Hatshepsut muttered.

"Well, there you have it, then. Male kas. Your mother Lady Ahmose made it known among the servants of Amun. Some say it's your kas that have stopped your blood – that a female body cannot do – well, the things a female body must do, with so many princely kas inside."

"And that is why Nebseny spurns me? For my kas? For something I cannot help?"

Nedjmet clasped her hands. "Don't let that prancing goat intimidate you. Your priestesses back you in all things. We will never allow you to be replaced."

Bakmut hissed, and Nedjmet flushed deep red.

"Replaced?" Hatshepsut stammered.

Bakmut sighed. "There have been whispers about the temple – from only a few minor priests, you see – that if you are barren then you cannot be the God's Hand. Your role is to ensure the fertility of Amun, and, well...." She trailed off, but at the look of anger on Hatshepsut's face she said quickly, "Don't listen to any of it. It's never going to happen, anyhow. As Nedjmet said, all the priestesses love and support you. Nebseny and his hangers-on could never succeed in replacing the God's Wife without our consent. And we do not consent." She narrowed her eyes at Nedjmet, a look that fired arrows. "And that is why it is not worth mentioning such laughable rumors to the God's Wife."

Hatshepsut furrowed her brow. "The High Priest of Amun

would need the consent of the king, too, if he hoped to replace me. He could never do it without my husband's approval."

Wiay cocked her head. The locks of her wig fell across her pale, soft shoulder. "Great Lady, perhaps you can make a good show before the court, but your priestesses know that the king does not love you. And if you are unable to bear him children, might Thutmose be even more eager to set you aside?"

A chill settled into Hatshepsut's heart.

"Oh, stop this talk!" Bakmut said. "You are upsetting her needlessly. Great Lady, these are all rumors and nothing more. You must not listen. All you need know is that the priestesses are devoted to you, and your position is secure."

Hatshepsut turned back to Wiay. "The Pharaoh is still a child and incapable of siring children himself. He may as well be barren, young as he is."

"He will not be young forever," Nedjmet said. "But in any case, this is less about children – an heir can always come from the harem – and more about the power of the priesthood. If you ask me what I think..."

"No one asked what you think," Bakmut snapped.

"*If* you ask me what I think, I would tell you that Nebseny would prefer a more biddable God's Wife – a woman he feels he can control."

And all at once, Hatshepsut understood. She saw again the look of mingled fascination and revulsion on Nebseny's face that day on the temple steps when she had taken the knife to her own loins. Hatshepsut was devoted to her duties, yes – but also hot as an untrained horse, and falcon-fierce when roused. She was the blood of a king, the blood of a god, and Nebseny must know – as she herself knew, she now realized – that such blood might be capable of anything when stirred. As God's Wife, she held nearly as much power as Nebseny himself. He must feel that she was a bundle of kindle-sticks waiting for a spark. The High Priest would be pleased for any excuse he could find to remove her from office, to set in her place a woman more predictable, less ambitious, less strange.

"These are only rumors, founded on foul air," Bakmut insisted. "You should not trouble yourself, Great Lady. And my sisters should mind their wagging tongues."

AS HER LITTER-BEARERS CARRIED HER BACK TO WASET'S GREAT palace, Hatshepsut sat lost in her troubled thoughts, never hearing the hails of the rekhet she passed. She had drawn the litter's curtains, thick blue wool to keep out winter's lingering chill. Sunlight filtered in to her cushioned chair only dimly. In the mild blue light she turned this puzzle over and over in her heart, seeking a solution. She must find a means of securing her place as God's Wife, for she would not give that up along with the king's throne.

She ached for Ahmose's company. Immediately after the wedding feast, her mother had left her most trusted stewards at the palace to advise and assist Hatshepsut, then retreated to her estate on the bluffs south of the city. She had hardly said two words to Hatshepsut since, and her few words were always by letter, and always terse. Hatshepsut had wounded her mother deeply, she knew, by overturning her plans at the council meeting. She had withdrawn her loyalty from her mother's cause, and had, in effect, declared false Ahmose's visions, Ahmose's reputation as a god-chosen dream-reader, Ahmose's very purpose and identity. There, too, her wild rashness had overcome her, and she had made her own mother suffer for it. She was ashamed. And she was certain she would do it all again, if faced with the choice. *I would sooner tear Egypt apart with my own hands and give it to the Heqa-Khasewet brick by brick than see the false heir on the throne.*

No – Hatshepsut had done right. She had sacrificed her relationship with her mother for Egypt's sake. But she had acted in service to maat. *I have to believe that, or I will go mad from sorrow.*

She longed, too, for Senenmut. He would know the right question to pose, the right way to tilt his thoughtful face, to make the answer reveal itself within her heart. She closed her eyes, delving into sweetly pained memory for the sound of his voice.

You cannot act rashly, Hatshepsut. Not in this. There he was – ah, her tutor, her heart's brother! As the litter swayed up the hill toward the palace, she listened gratefully to his words. *Each time you flare up like wine tossed on a fire, you suffer for it later. Think this through.*

Her litter bumped down in the palace courtyard. She straightened the God's Wife crown upon her head, and waited for her litter-bearers to draw back the woolen curtains. As she made to rise from her seat, she paused. Across the courtyard, beneath the pale blue shadow of a massive painted pillar, another litter had just arrived. She watched in disbelief as its curtains, too, were pulled aside, and Nebseny emerged, smoothing his leopard mantle as he straightened. He caught her eye and smiled lightly, inclined his head toward her. Quickly she stood, shaking out her skirts. She chewed the inside of her cheek, admonishing herself to think, to observe, to keep the wine well away from the flames. She went to him, fixing a peaceful, confident smile upon her lips.

"High Priest. What an honor, that you would grace the palace."

"Great Royal Wife. His Majesty summoned me. We often talk together, afternoons."

"My husband has grown devout. I am glad to see this."

"Thutmose is most devout. He seeks Amun's blessing on his plans."

"His plans?"

"Surely the Great Royal Wife knows of the king's plans."

Their litter-bearers were still nearby, and Hatshepsut's guards had drawn near. Nebseny was careful to keep his tone free from mockery, but Hatshepsut read it clearly in his voice.

"Of course. I know more of his plans than you might think. I will leave you to the king, High Priest. The gods' blessings on your day."

She turned from him and made her way to her apartments. Nehesi trailed her as always; she felt the urge to send him after Nebseny, to cut the High Priest down. But it was a passing thought, a child's tantrum, instantly quelled. No. There was a better way, a cleaner way – a way that would secure her station indefinitely, put Nebseny in her own control, and bring all the priests of Amun to stand behind her as a body united. A way that would elevate her until none but the Pharaoh stood above her. By the time she reached her apartments, she saw her path as plain and secure as if it stretched, smooth-paved and brightly shining, into a secure and brilliant future.

CHAPTER SEVENTEEN

T HAT NIGHT HATSHEPSUT BURNED NO incense. Smoke of myrrh would only lull her, and she knew she must remain alert. The early night was rich with the scent of damp foliage. The perfume of evening crept in past the thick wool curtains hung over her chamber's windcatchers; the curtains stirred and flapped now and then as a strong breeze moved off the river. When her supper arrived she laid across her couch, gestured for a table. Her servants brought it with their usual alacrity, and with a flourish set before her a whole roasted goose, fragrant with the bouquets of herbs wedged behind its wings; cakes flavored with honey and milk; a stew of barley kernels and great black hunks of charred beef; a large jar of deep red wine, cool and inviting. It was far more food than she could eat on her own.

The musicians arrived precisely on time. She directed them to a corner of the room, well lit and warmed by braziers. They tuned their instruments as she sucked on the goose's wing bone, waiting.

At last she heard Sitre-In's sharp clap outside her door.

"Come."

Sitre-In led in the daughter of Ankhhor, dressed in a fine blue gown of a hundred pleats, her throat and wrists jeweled with turquoise and gold. Iset bowed low before Hatshepsut, her delicate, soft hands outstretched. "How may I serve the pleasure of the Great Royal Wife?"

Hatshepsut dismissed her nurse. Sitre-In could not resist a skeptical frown at the great heap of food on the table.

"I told you once that you must sing for me in my chambers, Iset. My heart craves for music."

Iset smiled. Her features were fine as a carver's masterwork, and took to expressions of pleasure as readily as though the gods had made her to feel only joy. The prospect of singing for the Great Royal Wife seemed to delight her quite sincerely.

"You honor me greatly." Iset peered around the room, taking in the high ceiling with its cycles of the stars laid in gold, the depiction of winged Mut upon the floor, picked out in tiny enameled glass tiles and twice the size of a mortal woman. The musicians stroked their harps; along the walls long, fine tapestries of goddesses seemed to sway in response to the soft music.

Hatshepsut lifted her bowl of stew to her lips and motioned for Iset to begin. She took up a place several paces from the musicians, clasped her hands beneath her breasts, and at once the room filled with her sweet, lilting voice. She began with a simple hymn to Amun – appropriate, for the last night of the Feast of Opet. The musicians took it up easily, and Hatshepsut could not tell whether Iset followed the music or the music followed her song. It did not matter. Voice and harp, flute and timbrel wove together, wreathed Hatshepsut in a rich pleasure so intense she could almost feel the music stroke her skin.

When the hymn to Amun was done, Iset bent her head to consult the musicians. They soon began a rollicking sailor's song; Iset clapped as she sang, stamped her fine, narrow feet, swayed with the words like a boat on the river. An epic was next, the Song of Sinuhe, the man who fled Egypt for fear of his life but returned again as an old man, for the Two Lands pulled so at his heart that he could not die in peace so far from its beauty and its gods. She sang ballads, war songs, hymns to all the gods of Waset. She sang lullabies and children's chants. She danced the quaint dances of the farming districts. The musicians were as tireless as she.

At last, when she had performed for nearly two hours, Hatshepsut raised a hand to stop her. Iset's face and collarbones flushed a pretty shade of pink. She stood, panting a little, waiting on Hatshepsut's word.

"Are you hungry, Iset?" She surely was, after so much activity.

Iset smiled timidly.

"Come, share my meal." There was more than enough for both of them. In truth, the meat and stew had gone cold, but the honey cakes were as sweet as ever.

Iset bowed her head. "Thank you, Great Lady. I am honored."

Tem brought a small, three-legged stool; Iset sank down upon it gracefully and accepted with a nod the platter of goose that Hatshepsut pushed toward her. The singer ate with delicate restraint, but Hatshepsut could tell by the way she did not balk at the cold roast that her exertions had left her famished. When the girl was engrossed in the food, Hatshepsut began to speak.

"You are from Ka-Khem."

"Ah, Great Lady."

"I sailed past Ka-Khem once, when I was a little child. Though in truth, every boat sails past your home. It is bound on all sides by the river, is it not? It must be very beautiful. Tell me of it."

"It is mostly a wild place, all marshes with great flocks of ducks and herons. There are crocodiles in the reeds, and at night deby come up from the river to graze. I could hear them barking at one another from my bed chamber in my father's house."

"I hear your father Ankhhor governs Ka-Khem well."

Iset's features stilled for one heartbeat. Then she beamed. "Father will be pleased to know that the Great Royal Wife knows his name, and is satisfied with his work. I shall write to tell him."

"Your district has always been important to Egypt's prosperity. Grain, flax, oxen...we cannot do without the wealth of Ka-Khem. I am grateful to Ankhhor for his wisdom and loyalty."

"Ka-Khem was not always so fertile. My father has worked hard; he improved the planting and harvesting methods and increased his lands' yields threefold. It was his success as a land-owner that led your royal father to name him tjati, and he has taught all the lords of Ka-Khem how to improve their lands, too. He has been a good ruler."

"Who ruled Ka-Khem before Ankhhor?"

Iset shrugged. "Some old man. Hapi...Hebi...I cannot recall his name. Father was glad to replace him, and glad for your royal father's blessing. In a stroke of Pharaoh's writing-brush our family became the highest in the district. Father was much impressed by how quickly a man's fortunes can change for the better, if one is in the good graces of the royal family."

"Does your father love this? The wealth, the power?"

"He is very fond of power."

Iset seemed to stare for a moment into a dark and forbidding distance. The sudden change in her sweet demeanor clutched at Hatshepsut's belly with a clawed hand. She pushed forward the plate of little honey cakes to distract the girl.

"What man does not love power, after all?" Hatshepsut said airily. "Men spend all their lives climbing the highest hill, don't they? But I have let this supper go cold. Tem, pour the lady Iset some wine. We must warm her up."

Hatshepsut sipped sparingly at her own wine, barely wetting

her lips as Iset told her all about the charms of Ka-Khem, the games she played as a child with her brother and sisters, the barley fields shining silver under the waters of the Inundation. When Iset had finished one cup of wine, Hatshepsut called Tem to pour another, but Iset placed her hand upon the rim. "Wine dizzies my heart quickly, and it would never do for me to lose my manners in the presence of the Great Royal Wife."

Hatshepsut ground her teeth. She had planned to rely on the wine to loosen Iset's tongue. She would need to try another angle. She sat up and gestured Iset to join her on the couch. The girl seemed to hold her breath a moment; her wide, expressive eyes brimmed with delight as she paused, clutching her neck-laces with one trembling hand. Then she stood slowly and crept to the Great Royal Wife's couch, sank onto it with tentative, breathless care.

Hatshepsut leaned toward Iset until her face nearly rested on the girl's shoulder. "The High Priest Nebseny. He is your father's brother, is he not?"

"He is, though I confess I do not know him well. He left for Waset to join the Amun priesthood when I was still a little girl. Father was furious. He..." Iset trailed off, uncertain, but Hatshepsut coaxed her words with a friendly touch, brushing the girl's shoulder with an encouraging hand. "My father Ankhhor has unusual ideas, Great Lady. They are not popular with everyone."

"Unusual ideas? About what?"

"About the gods."

"Oh?"

"He is a follower of the Aten."

Hatshepsut drew back, an involuntary twitch of suspicion. The Aten could hardly be said to be a god. It was merely the roundness and brightness of the sun – a golden disc without will, without thought, without word or intent.

Iset turned toward her, raised her hands in swift conciliation. "I am devoted to Amun and Mut, Great Lady. Do not think that all of my father's house share his views."

Hatshepsut shrugged. "It was only a moment's surprise. The Aten is a small god, and his influence is nothing beside Amun's power. I am not offended."

"At any rate, Father was furious that Nebseny was leaving to serve Amun. Nebseny was Father's favorite brother, and before my own brother was born, he planned to make Nebseny his heir. So you can understand why he was so angry."

"Certainly."

"Well, eventually Nebseny wrote to father from Waset to beg for vouchers and gold, for he had found trouble getting into the Temple of Amun – something about the Temple allowing the young men of Waset in first, before immigrants to the city – and he could find neither bread nor beer. He was living above a poor fruit-seller's shop, earning his very small keep by killing rats. Father decided he could not have Nebseny living in such a state, even if he had turned his back on the Aten. Word might get back to Ka-Khem and all the district would laugh at the house of Ankhhor. So he sent plenty of gold to Nebseny, enough to set him up with a home worthy of our family until he could convince the Temple of Amun to accept him. All it took was a few rats to reconcile them." Iset gave off a quick burst of shrill, nervous laughter.

It afforded Hatshepsut some comfort to know that Nebseny once killed rats to earn his keep. But it also inspired in her a grudging respect. The High Priest was indeed devoted to Amun; that could not be denied.

"In fact it was probably Father's support that helped him attain his station. He came to Waset a beggar, but thanks to Father, he rose to become a lord. And see where he is now!"

"It is a tale to sing of," Hatshepsut said, musing. "And you, Iset? What does your father think of you?"

"Oh...Father has always been good to me."

"How so?"

"I wanted for nothing growing up in his house."

"Did he dote on you?" Hatshepsut reached for the wine jar, but Iset's hand was there before her own. She allowed the girl to fill her cup. Serving her wine seemed to distract Iset from the question; once Hatshepsut raised the cup to her lips, Iset reluctantly went on.

"Father? Oh, no. He provided all we could want, but he is not a man to dote." Her voice sank, barely more than a whisper. Anxiety widened her eyes. "He is very stern. He does not approve of families that spoil their daughters."

"But even so, you must be his most beloved daughter. Why else would he send you to Pharaoh's harem, unless he wanted you to have a life of great leisure and beauty?"

"It has all been so beautiful," Iset agreed. "I suppose Father thinks highly of me, yes. He taught me the value of obedience when I was very young, and I have always been quick to do his will. My sisters are sometimes rebellious, but not I. And now here I am, living in a splendid palace, with everything I could wish for at my fingertips. Ah – and I am far from Ka-Khem. I miss it sometimes, but on the whole it is better to be in Waset."

It was not the beauty and ease of harem life that Ankhhor wanted for his favorite daughter. Now that she had some measure of the man, Hatshepsut was sure of that.

"I know the king was pleased when your father made a gift of you. News of your beauty and sweetness sailed up the river before you, and you have not disappointed."

She blushed. Her smile was shy and tremulous. "I do my best not to disappoint, Great Lady."

"Has the king favored you?"

Iset's mouth tightened. A certain hesitancy came over her, stilling her features and widening her eyes. "He has not yet. The king favors few women, and when they emerge from his chamber all they speak of are his wandering hands and crass jokes." She flushed again, realizing she had spoken ill of the Pharaoh. "Oh! Begging your pardon, Great Lady. I did not mean...."

Hatshepsut barked a laugh. "Never apologize to me for telling the truth, Iset. The king is still a boy. He will figure out how to get his sons one day."

Only half of Iset's pretty mouth curved into a smile. Hatshepsut thought she could see distaste there. It was not the opportunity to lie with the king that stirred Iset's enthusiasm for the harem life.

When their conversation had run its course, Hatshepsut called Ita and Tem to show Iset back to the courtyard and her litter. Iset bade her farewell with a charming bow, shy and flustered and appealingly meek.

Sitre-In arrived with more serving women, who at once set about clearing away the remains of the meal. She stood a moment, eying Hatshepsut with a skeptical stare that bordered on insolence. "What in the name of the green grass was all that about?"

"Pharaoh sails north in two days, does he not?"

"You know he does. He goes to bless the temples of the Delta, and to meet with the builders Ankh-Tawy. He desires monuments, or some such; perhaps a tomb. I don't know all the details. Why?"

"I shall sail with him. Send for my stewards in the morning. They will manage the court while I am away."

Sitre-In narrowed her eyes. "What are you planning, Hatet?"

Hatshepsut leaned back on her couch, letting her shoulders droop, her chin fall. She hoped she looked innocent. "Isn't it time the Great Royal Wife accompanied her husband on his travels? The court will think us strange if we are always apart. Perhaps I wish to build some monuments of my own. Oh, don't scowl at me, Mawat. I am itching for adventure, that's all. Life is so boring here. I have not been out of Waset since I was four years old."

"Whatever you are plotting, I know you well enough to know that you won't tell me until it's too late to stop you." Sitre-In dusted her hands together, brushing her own misgivings to the floor. "Very well; I will gather the Great Lady's stewards in the morning, as she commands."

CHAPTER EIGHTEEN

HATSHEPSUT SHIFTED ON HER THRONE, willing herself not to swing her feet or fidget with her hands. The day's court session brought an endless stream of nobles with petty gripes, merchants complaining of taxes, ladies begging favors of the throne.

The king's throne beside her was empty, as it so often was. Thutmose was habitually here and gone, sailing to and from Waset's harbor like a desert rat popping in and out of its burrow. He had left for his trip northward a day early with no word of it to Hatshepsut except by one of his stewards. By the time the news had reached her it was too late to join the Pharaoh on his ship. *No matter. I shall take a boat of my own.* It would be more pleasant by far to sail without Thutmose. She imagined how he would react to the sight of her ship chasing him up the Iteru, overtaking him, sliding past and far beyond as she waved sweetly to him from her deck. The prospect obliged her to suck in her cheeks to chase the smile from her face.

On the morrow she would turn the court over to her most trusted administrator, Wadjetefni, her mother's former steward, and begin her journey north. Wadjetefni was a man well-versed in the running of the kingdom; she placed the throne in his hands with full confidence and considerable relief. But the man had not assumed the burden yet, and the day taunted her with its slowness.

The Overseer of the Granaries of Amun was reading, in his flat, droning voice, figure after figure from a sheaf of papyrus. Hatshepsut squinted her eyes to keep her mind focused on his tallies and predictions for the harvest. This year should see a record reaping of grain. Egypt's wealth would increase many-fold; the stores would overflow.

The gods were well pleased with Thutmose on the throne. That truth could not be denied, and still made her sorrowful at times, when she was alone in her apartments and no one, not even her servants, could see her grief. She felt now and then a distant, distracting stab, a thin sense of betrayal and confusion, most prevalent when thoughts turned to her father. She had been so sure, reading over the scroll of Waser-hat. She had felt so powerful on the steps of Amun's temple with the knife in her hand. It had all felt so *maat*. But Thutmose the First had not named her heir after all. It had all been an illusion, that trip to Annu, the memories of the old priests. *This* was maat: Thutmose as king, and Hatshepsut his Great Royal Wife. It must be true, or the land would not fare so well.

The Overseer concluded his presentation. Hatshepsut made the appropriate signs of approval – a nod, a wave of the hand – and he was led away.

Wadjetefni came forward, bowed with a scroll in his hand. "An envoy from Retjenu, Great Lady, seeking the succor of Pharaoh."

Retjenu lay far to the north and east of Egypt's borders. It was a land of blighted desert; its people were prideful and diffi-cult; they never shaved and clothed themselves in coarse, inele-gant wool, and seemed to take yet more pride in their uncivilized appearance. Even their kings dwelt in tents among their flocks of sheep, as dirty as rekhet children, as arrogant as falcons. She braced herself, putting on a stern expression to forestall the presumptions this Retjenu man was certain to make, as the crowd in the great hall parted to admit the envoy to her presence. But the man who stepped forward was haggard beneath his tangled, unkempt hair and beard. His skin was sickly pale. And his eyes stared hollowly, vacant as if his ka had half-fled. He carried with him a letter for the Pharaoh and an air of great strain, the like of which she had never before seen on a Retjenu. Wadjetefni accepted the letter and read it aloud for her as she sat, still and regal on her gilded seat, gazing down upon the wretched man.

"To Mighty Pharaoh, lord of the great life-giving river, from all the chieftains of this land which you call Retjenu, which we call Canaan. We are your humblest servants. We proclaim your strength! Ever has our land been a friend to Egypt. We send this man to you in our direst despair. The rains were insufficient. Our herds already grow weak. We send him now, praying to God that he reaches Mighty Pharaoh in time. By the time he stands before you a drought most terrible will have befallen us. Never in hundreds of years have we suffered so. We beg grain from Egypt, that our children and wives will not starve. Take pity on us, Mighty Pharaoh! All know that Pharaoh's heart is as kind as his arm is strong. Be moved by the suffering of our little ones. Without your aid they will surely starve. We beg this of you as your most dedicated servants."

Hatshepsut watched the envoy as Wadjetefni read. His bleak eyes roamed over the foot of the throne, seeing nothing. She wondered if he had left a wife and little ones at home, in his rough desert tent, surrounded by his starving, dying herds – all of his wealth on mortal hoof, dropping into the harsh dust of his savage land. The man, for all his foreign ways, for his strange wool garb and his long, goatish beard, had eyes like Senenmut's on their last day together, stricken and pained.

"Does the envoy have aught to add to his letter?" She spoke the words in the man's own tongue. It had been long since she had used the language, but Senenmut had taught her well. She still retained enough words to be understood.

The Retjenu blinked. His eyes lifted to her own, just for a moment, before he realized his audacity and dropped them to the ground again. He seemed to brace himself against a great weight as he spoke. "Lady of Mighty Pharaoh, I had seven children and two wives. Each one of them is gone now, dead of illness or starvation. You cannot imagine the suffering, Lady of Mighty Pharaoh. It is a terrible thing, to see a child die."

Hatshepsut shivered. She had seen a child die. Half her life-time ago, she had clutched her baby sister Neferubity as fever took her life away. She had fought her servants, fought Sitre-In, even her father, all of whom had sought to restrain her. But she had run to Neferubity's bed to hold the hot, limp, small body, to weep over her as the frail little girl breathed her last. They had all feared that Hatshepsut, too, would sicken and die. All of them had feared it but Ahmose. Ahmose had always been so certain of Hatshepsut; no threat could touch her eldest daughter, not even that terrible fever. She had joined Hatshepsut in Neferubity's bed. She had drawn both her daughters to her chest and rocked them, the living and the dead, and Hatshepsut yearned all at once for the comfort of Ahmose's embrace. *Why now? Why should I remember now? Neferubity, and my mother's arms....*

"On behalf of King Thutmose, the second of his name, I speak to the people of Retjenu." Wadjetefni bent over the chief scribe, seated below her dais, to translate her Retjenu words into Egyptian; the scribe dipped his brush and set to work. "Egypt has heard your cry. Mighty Pharaoh weeps for the loss of a single Retjenu child. I send this man home to you with sufficient grain to see your people through until the season of rain. Do not forget the good that Thutmose the Second has done you."

Tears welled in the envoy's eyes. "Retjenu will not forget. Praises to the Pharaoh, and to his wise Lady."

She looked round for Wadjetefni. "I trust you to select the right man for this work. Send him to me tonight. He will share supper with me, for we have many details to discuss, and in the morning I will be gone."

"It will be as you say, Great Lady."

HER SERVANTS HAD PACKED HER CHESTS AS WELL AS THEIR OWN, and were bustling here and there in fits of excitement. Ita seemed nearly beside herself with anticipation, wringing her hands and muttering, "Oh! Oh!" as she went about her duties. Hatshepsut had never realized before how dull the life of a palace servant must be. She was glad to give her women a reprieve. A lengthy trip to the northern districts was exactly what they all needed to renew their spirits. Hatshepsut was bent over one chest, inspecting the contents and debating whether she ought to add two more gowns to what Tem had already packed for her, when Sitre-In cleared her throat.

"The steward is here – the man who will bring the grain to Retjenu."

"Very good. Has the food arrived?"

"Ah, it's waiting in your anteroom."

The steward was clad in a simple white kilt, head wigless and clean-shaven, as was the custom for a man of his work. He wore about his hips a simple woven belt made of thread-of-gold, and his sandals were plain; but for all his lack of grand airs, he carried himself with the quiet, austere confidence that only men of great works possess. By the lines of his face, he was of a middle age. The man's eyes gleamed with the merest hint of glad familiarity, though Hatshepsut was certain she had never seen him – or never noticed him, at any rate – in all her life. The steward bowed low, palms out. When he straightened she noted something else in his face, a brief, warm flash. Was it affection? Impossible.

"Share my supper, good man."

"The Great Royal Wife offers more honor than I deserve." But he moved toward the table eagerly. "In truth, Great Lady, I have eaten nothing since this morning's court. I have been hard at work on your plans for Retjenu."

"Tell me of them."

He talked while they ate. She grasped at once that his mind was exceedingly sharp. He had fixed the finest detail into place, and outlined several alternate plans in case of unforeseen difficulties.

"I am pleased," Hatshepsut said at length. "You are the right man for the work; that's plain. What is your name?"

"Ineni, Great Lady." He paused, and his demeanor became suddenly shy. "I...I served your mother, as well. Perhaps she has spoken of me."

Even with his eyes on a platter of figs, Hatshepsut saw the desperate hope that filled his expression. *Oh, gods! This is the steward Ahmose took as her lover!* But she could see no useful purpose to admitting she knew his secret. "I do not believe so. I am sure you served her well, though, as you will serve me well. I leave at sunrise to sail north; I will travel in peace, knowing this duty is in such capable hands."

Ineni ducked his head. "Yes, Great Lady. I shall do my best for you. To honor you, and your royal mother."

CHAPTER NINETEEN

A T DAWN, HATSHEPSUT AND HER women boarded the ship *Biddable Mare*, followed closely by Nehesi and a scattering of strong men who bore her chests of clothing and amusements. They would sail north with the current for nearly half a month, calling on temples along the way where the people could witness the God's Wife of Amun making her offerings to their local deities. Amidst her ladies' excitement, Hatshepsut held herself still, wrapped in a fine wool shawl to keep the chill of morning river mist from her chest. Her face was a mask of calm expectation, though she felt as if all nine of her kas danced, clapping their hands within her hammering heart.

Biddable Mare was a fast ship, built by the same wright who fashioned racing boats for many of Waset's nobles. Long and lean with a single, low-roofed cabin behind the mast, Hatshepsut would call it home as they journeyed to Ka-Khem. She gave her final instructions to Wadjetefni, admonished him to keep Thutmose in check when he returned from his current foray down the river. As the eastern sky warmed with the coming day, she watched the steward retreat down the ship's ramp.

She nodded to the captain, a broad, loud man with skin so tanned by the sun he was nearly as dark as *Biddable Mare's* wooden flanks. The captain barked his orders; the crew cast off their lines, and the ship swung away from the quay with its odors of old fish and dry lime. As the oarsmen began to row, Hatshepsut moved to the bow with her women gathered around her, allowing a smile of triumph. The crisp air of the river lifted and tossed the strands of her wig. The bow rocked down into the trough of a wave; spray fell upon her face and she braced herself as Ita and Tem clutched one another and squealed. Her heart was as light as the leaves of a great tree, fluttering and shimmering. But still she maintained her air of possession.

As the ship turned its nose east toward the great bend of the river, Sitre-In leaned toward Hatshepsut's ear. "I wish you would tell me what this is all about, Hatet. It is my duty to help you, but how can I do my duty if you keep me in the dark?"

"I am sailing north to catch my husband," Hatshepsut replied lightly, "so that I might stand at his side as he dedicates temples."

"Oh, don't give me that rotten old fruit. You loathe your husband."

"What an awful thing to say. The gods hear you, Mawat."

"You take your duties too seriously for this to be a lark. I might believe a flighty young queen would chase off after her husband for the sake of adventure – even a husband despised as Thutmose. But for you to leave the administration of the throne in the hands of a steward..."

"I trust Wadjetefni. Ahmose gave him to me; he is practically as good as Ahmose herself."

"The throne in the hands of a steward," Sitre-In went on firmly, "for an entire month. It is a long time – anything may happen. You know that. You have considered that. Whatever this is about, you deem it more important than sitting the throne."

"My divine backside sits the throne no matter where I go."

147

She narrowed her eyes at the glare of morning light on waves and resolved to paint thicker lines of kohl around her eyes the next morning. "I suppose the same is true of Thutmose."

"No matter where you go! Figs! You are too intelligent to believe that."

Hatshepsut sobered. She stared levelly at her nurse. "I once thought, Mawat, that I was born to rule."

"You were."

"Not as Great Royal Wife. As Pharaoh. But it can never be. The closest I may come is to reign as God's Wife of Amun. And I will do anything to preserve my power."

Sitre-In bowed her head, her deference tinged with a note of matronly impatience. "I do not see how leaving Waset for a month will preserve your power. Waset is the very home of Amun."

"And Ka-Khem," Hatshepsut replied, "is the home of Amun's High Priest."

By evening they had cleared the river's bend. *Biddable Mare* put in at the quays of Iunet. A messenger boat had raced along before them to announce the coming of the God's Wife; the shore was lined with people who cheered her as she followed Nehesi down the ramp. Iunet, she knew, was dedicated to the worship of Hathor, the Mistress of the West, Lady of Seven Faces. When the tjati and his family approached to offer a ring of sweet lotuses for her neck, she waved Ita and Tem to her side. They bore baskets of dried fruit and grain; Hatshepsut said to the governor, "Take me at once to the temple of Hathor. I have brought these gifts for the Mistress of the West, and my heart will never rest until I have done my duty to the goddess."

The people of Hathor's city led her to the great temple amid a clangor of drums and sesheshet. The ecstatic calls of reedy pipes blared from the head of the procession. She rode in a simple chariot with Nehesi and the governor's own driver; in lieu of gilding and bright paint, its sides were draped with early-blooming lotuses, its rails wound with fragrant herbs. They drove slowly, apace with the throng. Beyond the last shops and houses of Iunet, from the roofs of which children shouted and women raised their palms in salute, a broad roadway stretched across several spans of flooded field. In the distance, where the green water of farmland gave way to red desert hills, Hatshepsut could see a brick ramp rising onto the shoulder of a yellow stone promontory. The rocky hill wore the walls of Hathor's temple like a proud crown. When at last they reached the foot of the ramp, the procession broke up, the citizens of Iunet scattering to wait all about the temple's outer wall.

Hatshepsut gazed up the ramp. The entrance to the temple gaped violet in the gathering dusk, a hungry mouth. She pulled her shawl more closely about her shoulders.

"Help me down, Nehesi. Ita? Tem?" Her women stepped to her side, the baskets of goods clutched in their arms.

"God's Wife of Amun." Hatshepsut turned quickly. At the top of the ramp, two priestesses stood side by side in the temple's mouth. The shorter of the two gestured with her hands and arms; after a heartbeat the other, thin as a twig with the high voice of girlhood, spoke again. "Be welcome to the House of Hathor, the Mistress of the West, the Sovereign of Stars." The short woman moved her hands again with a fascinating preci-sion, each finger dancing. When the gesturing had finished, the thin girl spoke. "The goddess is eager to speak to her vessel."

Nehesi, Amun's man through and through, growled under his breath. Hatshepsut laid a hand on his arm. "She means no harm. I am the servant of all the gods, not only Amun. Come." She started up the ramp.

As she drew level with the two priestesses, her steps faltered. The short one was quite broad across the bridge of her nose, and her eyes were mismatched: one as dark-black as Hatshep-sut's own, the other a blue so intense it rivaled the color of a summer morning sky. Neither priestess wore a wig; their natural hair was done up in layers of fine plaits and gathered together into two symmetrical locks that fell over their ears in imitation of Hathor's own style. Hatshepsut was startled to see that although the short woman was still rather young, her hair was shot with white at the fore; several of her tiny braids were as pale as sun-bleached bone. The short woman raised her hands and gestured, picking at the air delicately, her wrists swaying this way and that.

The young priestess spoke as if in response to the other's movements. "The Hand of Amun, who brings pleasure to the god. I see a grove of myrrh trees; I smell their sap; it is a cloud of joy, and Amun rejoices in your name. But will you remember Hathor? She is jealous, and she has marked your flesh with her lion's claw, that you will not forget her."

Hatshepsut arrested her hands before they could fly to the scar at her groin. "I marked my own flesh."

Once more the gesturing, and once more the girl-priestess's response: "It is enough, for now, that you bring the Lady gifts." The short one with the unsettling eyes turned away, into the dimness of the temple's interior. "Imer will take you to the Lady."

Following, Hatshepsut stepped into a forecourt of deep indigo shadows. Pillars stood in orderly rows, rank upon rank. She gazed upward; the pillars held up a cedarwood roof, lost in black shadow. But the pathway Imer walked, a direct line that ran between the ranks of pillars to a high stone sanctuary, was left unroofed. Stars began to emerge in the visible strip of night, cold white fires in a violet distance. The light of a sickle moon, its points as sharp as a cow's horns, fell wanly into the forecourt to light the priestess' steps. Nehesi, too, stared up into the deep-shadowed heights, eying with a singular suspicion the faces of

Hathor that crowned each pillar. In his carelessness he blundered into one pillar; the hilt of his dagger clanged against the stone. The young priestess checked and glanced back at him, amusement curving her lips. But Imer continued on, unaware, and Hatshepsut realized that the priestess heard nothing.

"You are her voice," she said to the thin girl.

"Yes. Several of us who serve the Mistress of the West have learned to read Imer's hand-signs. She was born into a poor farmer's family. When it was discovered she could not hear, she was put out for the beasts to take. But it was Hathor took her instead. I have heard it whispered that a she-cow found Imer lying in the fields, and lifted the babe upon her horns, and carried her here to the temple."

The roof of sky ended at a great facade, the heart of Hathor's domain. Women in the simple white linen of priestesses moved along the temple's face, lighting a long row of braziers. As the oil inside caught and flamed to life, a golden light reached upward to illumine six of Hathor's seven faces, the crowns of great pillars staring down at Hatshepsut and her servants. The light wavered and danced. Each face of the goddess appeared to changed, flickering from benevolence to rage to indifference to motherly adoration as rapid and regular, as mutable as sun on water.

Imer had turned in the doorway to Hathor's sanctuary. Her hands spoke, and the young priestess gave voice to their meaning. "You must carry your offerings with your own hands, God's Wife. Before Hathor, it is you who are the servant, not your women."

"Yes. Of course." Hatshepsut took a basket in each arm. "Wait for me here," she said to Nehesi and her maids.

Inside, lamps revealed a cacophony of color. The walls of Hathor's temple were more brilliantly painted than any dwelling of Amun. The lapis-blue bodies of gods seemed to leap out from walls the color of fine turquoise stone. Imer led her across a massive sun-disk painted on the floor in the ripe red shade of pomegranates. Amid the confusion of color she could identify no single form of the goddess to worship, no statue in which the goddess could dwell. Instead, Hathor dwelt everywhere. Against one wall the goddess took the form of a pacing cow, adorned in jewels, lifting the sun-disc high between the great sweep of her horns. Against another she was a lioness, grinning with a terrible thirst for blood. Here she was the gentle midwife, urging a child from the womb of a squatting woman; there, she clutched a sinister flail to her breast and stared knowingly into an unfathomable distance.

"Hathor is all about you," the girl said. Beyond her shoulder Imer stared impassively at Hatshepsut. That unnerving blue eye saw everything, Hatshepsut was sure of it. Everything.

They ascended a staircase to the roof of the temple. The stars had come to brilliant life; they banded together in a great streak of white across the heavens. *The milk that flows from Hathor's udders. She is in the very night sky. I am in the presence of a goddess nearly as mighty as Amun.*

Hatshepsut set her offerings upon the bare rooftop and sank to her knees, pressed her forehead against the cold stone, facing the west. "Mistress of the West," she called to the night sky. "Lady who is all goddesses in one body. I offer to you, that you will be pleased with me, your servant."

When she lifted her face and clambered back to her feet she saw that Imer wore a slight smile, though her strange eyes were untouched by her pleasure. She signed, and the young priestess said, "How did you know that we leave our offerings here on the roof? We did not tell you to do it."

"It seemed right. The goddess is here; I feel her."

"The Pharaoh came this way not long ago – a week, perhaps. He is still a boy. He does not yet understand the importance of worship."

"He did not pay homage to Lady Hathor?"

"Oh, he did," the young priestess said. "He did the duty he thought was required, then left again to be feasted at the governor's house in Iunet. He gave only the smallest honor to our Lady, a cursory offering."

A swell of foreboding built queasily beneath her heart. "I am sorry. That was unjust."

"It was," Imer agreed, and Hatshepsut did not need to hear the words to read the offense in the woman's gesture.

"The Pharaoh's house must make amends to Hathor. When I return to Waset, I shall send girls here to Iunet, girls from fine houses to be raised by the goddess, to unite Amun's city with Hathor's. And I will build," she added, sensing the pledge of girl children was not enough. "A chapel to the goddess, in Ipet-Isut, among the chapels of Amun's own sacred family."

"It will suffice," Imer said. Her hands paused, clutched together at her breast, her face turned up to the broad white spray of stars as though she heard, after all, a voice speaking beyond the reach of Hatshepsut's own ears. "And remember the Mistress of the West, the Sovereign of Stars. If she asks any gift of you, you must not deny it, God's Wife."

The impossible breadth of the sky spread above her, and seemed to thrust at her body, to force her back to her knees, her forehead to the stones. Somehow Hatshepsut remained standing, though she swayed with the effort. She could not think what else any goddess could desire. Hathor was all but a stranger to her, but potent and present, here at the pinnacle of her own temple. She did not know how to appease the goddess's jealous desires. She wished for the presence of Amun. She knew, at least, what that god required of her: lead the chants, approve his offerings, caress him, bathe him, anoint him. She sensed that Hathor required something darker, something stranger, something infinitely more precious than anything Amun had ever demanded.

"I will deny her nothing," Hatshepsut promised. "Nothing."

"Good. Imer will take you back now. Go in peace."

It was only as she rode back toward Iunet, clutching the rail of the governor's chariot, that Hatshepsut realized what had unsettled her so about the Temple of Hathor.

I spoke. I spoke, and somehow Imer understood my words – heard my words – although she hears nothing. She recalled how the priestess had turned her face toward the heavens, receiving Hathor's word – and Hatshepsut had been the one who was deaf, plunged in a dark, star-studded silence. She shuddered.

That night the tjati if Iunet feasted Hatshepsut in his modest palace, and offered her his finest room for her rest. Maids had prepared it with music and sweet oils burning in shining lamps, with fine-spun linen to cover her. Her women lay upon soft mats on the floor, and when the lamps burned out one by one, dying with a gentle hiss, the room filled with the sounds of their slumbering breath. Hatshepsut lay awake for a long time, staring into the impenetrable dark. Her thoughts were all of Imer beneath the stars, demanding that Hathor not be forgotten. The way the woman knew Hatshepsut's words even as she spoke them was a torment; she rolled continually on the governor's bed, and rest evaded her.

All too soon, though, she fumbled into a harsh, unwelcoming sleep. She dreamed of squatting upon the birthing bricks, the Seven Hathors gathered in a half-moon before her to tell the fate of her child. Their voices raised in a gabble from which she could draw no words, and at last she heard nothing but a rushing, as if plunged beneath swift-moving water, and the pounding of her heart in her own ears. The Hathors' mouths continued to move, to twist upon their own black prophecies. And she could hear nothing! She struggled on the bricks; from between her thighs there came the form of a she-cow with the sun disc glowing between her horns, so bright Hatshepsut shut her eyes in fright. When she opened them again, the cow-child had changed form, and stood before her lion-headed: Sekhmet,

She Who Mauls. Hatshepsut screamed, a sound that tore at her throat but never reached her ears, and the Sekhmet child tore into her heart, drinking her blood, eating her kas until nothing was left of her. And when she had finished, she turned toward the solitary form that now advanced from the shadows: a man, long-faced and wise, his eyes downcast in shame. *Senenmut.* Hatshepsut tried to warn him, but the Sekhmet child leaped first, slashed his throat with her claws, lapped at his blood as it flowed upon the floor, a terrible satisfaction, a terrible grief in its eyes.

When dawn at last came, Hatshepsut was glad to board her ship and command the captain to cast off his lines. She left Iunet behind her with trembling relief.

CHAPTER TWENTY

"KA-KHEM! KA-KHEM SHORE AHEAD!" THE voice of the man high in the ship's rigging fell upon the deck thin and distorted. Hatshepsut had been sipping beer in her cabin, her women gossiping at her side; when she heard the man's words she leaped to her feet and strode into the open air. It was mid-day. The sky was bright, a high watery haze refracting the sun into a glow that made her blink tears from her eyes. The man in the rigging came shimmying down the mast. He had a dark cloth tied about his face; a small slit allowed his eyes to peek out at the bright world.

The captain came forward and slapped the man on the back. "Good! We'll moor before the sun is halfway to the horizon."

She sighed with relief. Adventure was more exhausting than she had imagined. She had slept in a different bed each night, and though the nobles and governors who hosted her were suitably gracious – even in the most rural of sepats – she suspected it was the unfamiliar beds which had allowed the dreams of Hathor and her strange priestesses to haunt her. She expected to stay in Ka-Khem for several days. The regular rest should do her some good.

As the afternoon progressed, the sepat of Ka-Khem appeared on the gray northern horizon. It was a blur of golden green distorted by the haze. As *Biddable Mare* drew closer, Hatshepsut could pick out the low, blocky forms of buildings and the individual plumes of smoke where farmers burned refuse in preparation for the sowing to come. Before long the scents of the shoreline – cattle dung and fish offal, the dry, harsh smell of caulking lime – came drifting over the water. Sounds, too, at last could be made out beyond the splash of water against the prow. Men laughed and shouted as they worked along the shore. Children sang their chanting games. Intermittent and faint, the high reedy call of a flute crested above the rest, a bird calling high in a far-off tree. She had reached her destination. Perhaps the hardest part was already done. In a few days Nebseny would be in her hand, and she would remain God's Wife, unchallenged.

The tjati and his family greeted her at the shoreline, as each governor had done at each sepat she had visited these two weeks past. This time, though, she sized Ankhhor up with a wary eye. He was as unassuming a man as Hatshepsut had ever seen. His face was thin and dry with age, but he looked sturdy enough despite his years, with an unbent back and a smoothness to his shoulders that spoke of a confident strength. His eyes were deep-set and calm, his mouth firm but not hard. He wore a fine, long kilt of the southern style, elaborately wrapped and pleated at the front: a subtle concession to courtly fashion, no doubt intended to emphasize his loyalty to the throne. His wife, the Lady Iah, wore the round-cut Nubian wig that was so stylish amongst Waset's well-to-do wives. After so many visits to so many districts, Hatshepsut was startled to see the fashions of her own city on display here in the far-flung north. Iah clasped her hands at her waist, smiling as she bowed. Hatshepsut could see where Iset had found her great beauty as well as her beguiling meekness. Age had not diminished Lady

Iah's loveliness but had rather elevated it, matured the youthful brilliance into a banked, warming glow. Behind Ankhhor his younger children stood with heads bowed: two girls who would soon outgrow their braids and a boy, perhaps eight or ten, who despite his downcast eyes carried himself with the childish arrogance that only the heir of a great and confident man can know.

She made her usual request to worship at the local temple, but Ankhhor seemed distinctly unimpressed. "On second thought," she said, "I am weary. Perhaps the gods will do me a kindness, and wait for me until the morning."

Hatshepsut joined Ankhhor for supper in his home – a palace, by rights, as fine as any Waset nobleman's. It was an impressive feast, spiced with the sweet-earthy flavors of the north. Hatshepsut ate readily. Her enthusiasm for the food did seem to please the tjati. He handled his wine cup carefully, watching her with inscrutable eyes.

In his wife Hatshepsut detected the faintest air of hesitancy, almost embarrassment. *There is your opening,* she told herself. *The Lady Iah is as kindly as her daughter. She is soft enough to feel shame over her husband's ambition. She is his weakness.*

When their supper concluded, Hatshepsut invited Iah to bathe with her, and the momentary flash of anxiety on the woman's face gave her a feeling of great satisfaction. Such a request from the Great Royal Wife could not be refused, and within the hour Lady Iah was clapping for admittance to her own chambers, which had been given over to the use of the Great Royal Wife for the duration of her visit to Ka-Khem. Ita and Tem, with the help of the tjati's servants, had prepared a steaming bath rich with the scent of crushed herbs. Hatshepsut held out her arms; her women undressed her. Iah's own women came forward, a bit hesitantly, to do the same. They stepped down together into Iah's recessed bath. Hatshepsut sank into the water with a grateful sigh.

THE CROOK AND FLAIL

"What a lovely home you have, Lady Iah."

"The Great Royal Wife is kind to say so. My husband's home is nothing compared to your own palace, I am sure."

Hatshepsut gazed up toward the windcatchers. Stars were beginning to emerge in the black sky. "This is a charming land. The lady Iset told me she could hear deby from the palace at night. Do you think I shall hear any this night?"

The water splashed a little as Iah shifted in sudden surprise. "You know my daughter, Great Lady?"

"Of course. A lovely girl, an excellent singer, and a very fine dancer. You taught her well."

"The Great Lady is good to say it."

"I spend much time talking to Iset. She tells me many things of her life here in Ka-Khem, of her family. I desired to see the place for myself, and to meet you."

"We are humbled." Despite the heat of the water and the perfume of the herbs, Iah's neck and shoulders were rigid.

"It must have been hard for you to let her go – to send her to the harem."

"I miss my daughter every day, Great Lady, it is true. But I have my other girls to cheer me, and my son."

"A daughter is a generous gift to the Pharaoh. And one as precious as Iset – it is plain that Ankhhor and Ka-Khem love Thutmose well."

"We...we have ever been friends to your royal family, Great Lady. Ankhhor owes much to Thutmose the First."

"Your husband is an ambitious man, yes?"

Iah hesitated. At last she said carefully, "I am lucky to be the wife of such a hard-working man, Great Lady. He puts the well-being of our family above all other concerns."

"He will make a great name for himself before he goes the Field of Reeds; I can see that. Oh, the things he will be able to paint on the walls of his tomb! Husband and father to beautiful women, tjati of a prosperous sepat, brother of the High Priest of

Amun. I wonder what else Ankhhor wishes to be remembered for."

Iah's face went pale. She busied herself with cupped hands, pouring water over her shoulders, her eyes turned shyly away. She shifted, reaching for a jar of soft soap perfumed with lotus oil; Hatshepsut stifled a gasp at the sight of three or four dark bruises on Iah's back. They were old, turning a sick shade of yellow around the edges.

Distantly, a rough, coughing bark sounded through the wind catchers. It repeated several times.

"A deby, Great Lady."

The sound recalled the sight of Iset's face, flushed, giggling over her wine. Hatshepsut smiled at the memory. "I will be sure to tell Lady Iset I heard her old friend singing."

Iah sighed. "I do miss my daughter. Is she well, Great Lady? Only tell me that she is happy. I know nothing of harem life. In truth, it was not the life I would have chosen for her, and I worry every day for her happiness."

"She has a very fine room in the House of Women, and she is surrounded by sisters. It is a good life, easy and beautiful. She wants for nothing."

"And in the harem does she see the king? My questions are impertinent, Great Lady, I know. But ease a mother's heart, I beg you. Iset is my first-born, and the dearest to my heart. I only wish to know that my sacrifice was not in vain."

"Would it warm your heart to know that she sees the king? That was the purpose, was it not, of sending her to Waset? Or was there some other reason Ankhhor wanted his daughter in Amun's city?" A look of panic flashed across Iah's face, and Hatshepsut laughed warmly to calm her. "Yes, Lady Iah. Iset sees the king. He is still young; he is not yet a man. But already he notes her beauty, and boasts of her sweetness to all who will listen. I have no doubt that she will be much favored by the Pharaoh when he grows into a man's appetites." She paused, considering the bruises on Iah's back. "I will see that he always treats her gently," she added, hoping her promise eased the lady's heart.

Hatshepsut stood, stepped from the basin, and held out her arms for her women to dry her. As they scraped the curved copper blade over her skin, flinging the water from her limbs to the bath's floor, she watched Iah rise from the bath to be similarly attended. There were more bruises on the woman's thighs, older and faint, but regular.

"I will retire to my bed now. It has been a long journey. Your company has been most pleasant, Lady Iah. I shall see you in the morning, yes?"

Long after Iah had bowed her way out of the bath, Hatshepsut lay awake in the lady's comfortable, roomy bed, listening to the deby argue in the dark marshes. Iah's words sounded again and again in her ears. *It was not the life I would have chosen for her.* The Pharaoh's harem was nearly the finest life any nobleman's wife could dream of for her favorite daughter. Nearly. Unless her ambitious husband had put other dreams into her heart. Unless his brother had dared to whisper of his designs for a new and docile God's Wife. Her thoughts raced a deep-rutted ring around her heart; her longing for Senenmut chased memories of Iset dancing, singing, laughing. Long after the deby had fallen silent and retreated to the depths of the river, the gods at last granted Hatshepsut the respite of sleep.

CHAPTER TWENTY-ONE

S HE HAD SPENT TWO DAYS in Ka-Khem, touring the countryside, approving in the Pharaoh's name of the clean, orderly towns, the fertile fields, the herds of cattle which produced the sacred black bulls of the north. Whenever she tried to raise the topic of Iset, Ankhhor would deftly turn her inquiries aside, his face unreadably placid, his words perfectly measured to give neither offense nor a hint of his designs. Hatshepsut allowed herself to be entertained with her usual courtly grace, fixing her regal smile on her lips, while inside her kas wailed in despair. Ankhhor was both too clever and too dangerous. The bruises on Lady Iah's body were proof of the man's hot temper. She had no fear for her own person, but she hesitated to say anything that may later cause Ankhhor to turn his wrath upon his wife or children. She could find no way to breach the subject of his plans for Iset without throwing wine upon the fire.

On the final evening of her stay, she paced about Lady Iah's room, grinding her teeth, while her women scuttled about packing her chests.

Nehesi entered and bowed. The bright, clear scent of the

waterfront drifted from his body; she longed for her ship, for an escape from the tension and frustration of Ka-Khem and the tjati's secrets. "Great Lady, the ship is ready to sail with the rising sun. I have seen to it."

She waved a hand, a curt acceptance of his news.

"Er – Great Lady, if I may be so bold to ask, what troubles you?"

She stopped her pacing and stared at Nehesi. If only she were a man – a tall, strong, imposing man like her guardsman, with a belt full of knives! She would have no fear of putting Ankhhor in his place then. But she was a woman – no, still a girl, by rights. Fifteen years old and female, for all her titles of power. She was well beyond her depth, ridden in her sleep by disturbing visions, unrested, weak, young…and female. "Nehesi, I came here for a purpose, yet now I find myself unable to act."

"What purpose, Great Lady?"

"Ankhhor sent his eldest daughter to Waset, not only as a gift for Pharaoh's harem, but to maneuver her into the position of God's Wife."

Tem gasped. "No, Great Lady! The station is yours."

"Of course it is mine. And it will stay mine."

Nehesi nodded, considering. "Have you proof of his designs, Great Lady?"

"The priestesses of Amun have heard whispers that Nebseny, the High Priest, wishes to replace me with a woman more easily controlled. Who would be easier for him to handle than his own niece – a woman as reliant on Ankhhor as Nebseny is himself? I tell you, Nebseny and Ankhhor plot to unseat me. Nebseny works his way into Thutmose's favors, too. Once they have ousted me from my station at the temple it will be easy for Thutmose to set me aside as Great Royal Wife. I am barren – he would need no more excuse than that, and with Nebseny complicit, the Temple of Amun would be quick to approve it, however my priestesses may protest."

Sitre-In clicked her tongue. "This is all too much of a tangle to be believed. You are seeing shadows."

"No, I have pondered over this for weeks while we sailed north. I know it is true. Thutmose does not love me; he would give nearly anything to set me aside, but he cannot do it without the backing of the Temple. Iset is the perfect replacement: quiet, sweet, malleable, and raised from birth to fear Ankhhor, and do his will. It all comes back to that man – to Ankhhor!" She pounded her fists against her hips, furious and helpless.

"I believe you, Great Lady. I see it." Nehesi edged close to her, talking low. "And why, Great Lady, can you not simply force Ankhhor to do your bidding? To back down, to withdraw his ambition?"

"I am a fifteen-year-old girl!" Her voice rose uncomfortably close to a shriek.

"You are the Great Royal Wife, the God's Wife of Amun. You are the daughter of Thutmose the First."

She caught her breath, about to protest, but Nehesi went on, his words a smoky whisper.

"You are the one who took the knife to your own flesh to silence those who cried out against you."

She slumped onto the bed in a misery. "That was the worst thing you could have said, Nehesi. What I did that day on the temple steps I did without thought, heedless of the effect I would have on Egypt. Senenmut would tell me, if he were here, that when I get myself into a passion it is like tossing wine onto a fire. I do more damage than good when I act so rashly. I must approach this carefully. I did not think Ankhhor would be so...unapproachable – implacable – dangerous to his family. I do not have the skill to talk my way into his heart and turn it. I am in far deeper water than I had ever thought to find."

Nehesi slapped his chest. "I've learned many things from battles, Great Lady. Sometimes it is good to avoid a fight with talk. Sometimes it is good to create a peace through negotiation and soft words. Sometimes, it is far better to dip one's arrows into the fire and shoot. If what you say is true of this Nebseny and this Iset, then your situation is dire. The time for soft words has passed. Now is the time to nock an arrow to the Great Lady's bow."

Hatshepsut rose slowly to her feet. "Perhaps you are correct."

"No," Sitre-In interjected. "I saw the bruises on Lady Iah's back. Do not put yourself in danger, Hatshepsut. Yes, you are the Great Royal Wife, but clearly this Ankhhor is violent and unpredictable. Let us return to Waset and leave this man far behind us. He cannot reach you there. The High Priest and his daughter are far away from the man himself; Ankhhor has no true influence in Waset. Leave it be."

Nehesi gazed at Hatshepsut levelly. The faintest smile curved his lips.

"I know the way to his chamber," she said.

Nehesi patted the hard planes of his belly, as if her words satisfied an insatiable craving. "Then let us go."

A LONE GUARDSMAN STOOD DUTY OUTSIDE THE DOOR TO THE tjati's private chamber. When he saw the great, dark form of Nehesi striding down the hall, his striped kilt flashing in the lamp-light, the hilts of his blades gleaming, the guard rushed away from his master's door with a wordless cry. Nehesi shoved the door open. It cracked against the interior wall so hard that Hatshepsut thought for one hopeful moment it might break away from its hinges. Nehesi's confidence had kindled a flame in her belly. She stormed into Ankhhor's chamber glowing with the heat of her rage.

The tjati's face betrayed one instant of shock. Then he rose from his couch, set aside the papyrus he had been studying, and bowed to her, calculating and flawless in his deference. "Great Lady. How may I be of service?"

"I know, Ankhhor, why you sent your daughter to Waset. She was never intended for the harem. Or not for long, at any rate."

Ankhhor stood unblinking and silent.

"You plotted with your brother Nebseny to raise Iset to God's Wife of Amun. With a God's Wife under Nebseny's control, the Amun priesthood would be even more in his grasp than it is already – all of its influence, all of its wealth. And because Nebseny is in your debt, the Amun priesthood would in fact be yours to command."

Ankhhor's eyebrows rose smoothly. "A pretty plot, Great Lady."

"Pretty indeed. Iset will not have my station. She will never be God's Wife. Your ambition has become an angry crocodile, and you have it grasped by the tail. You have overstepped yourself, Ankhhor."

His slow smile betrayed his amusement, but she read a grudging amount of respect in his eyes. No doubt he expected that the youth of the Pharaoh and his wife would blind them to his machinations. Coolly he said, "It is not for one such as I do deny the accusations of the God's Wife."

"Particularly since her accusations are true." She raised her finger, and Nehesi drew his sword. A bead of bronze fire ran along its edge as the Medjay held the blade at the ready, waiting on her command. "No one in all Egypt would stop me if I ordered my man to kill you, Ankhhor. The guard on your door ran when he saw me approach, like a rabbit under a hawk's shadow. It seems he has more sense than his master."

"I wonder, Great Lady," Ankhhor said, calm and collected, "what Pharaoh Thutmose would do if you did kill me. Ah, and the High Priest, my brother. How does the Great Lady imagine they would react to such an audacity from their volatile God's Wife?"

Hatshepsut smiled. "Let me show you how you have erred, Ankhhor. You knew the king is but a child, and that his Great Royal Wife is hardly older. You knew the God's Wife was young. You assumed she was like your Iset, soft and sweet, conditioned to do the bidding of the men who rule her. But now you see me for what I am. I am no Iset. Do you think any man can draw my reins, Ankhhor? How much less power does a boy have over Hatshepsut, the God's Wife of Amun?"

Ankhhor raised his chin, an arrogant acknowledgment of her words. "Then why do you not have me killed?" It was not a challenge, but an honest question.

"Because you are of more use to me alive than dead. I know you owe your wealth to my father's memory. You are in his debt, and so I know that you will give your service to me willingly. And because you will serve me willingly, you will be allowed to keep all the fine gifts Thutmose the First gave you. You will be allowed to keep your head, too."

Ankhhor's shoulders lost some of their tension. His mouth relaxed, almost imperceptibly; he was opening to her words, was perhaps even relieved. She thought she could even detect in his steady gaze some small measure of admiration.

"I could do away with Nebseny as easily as you, but maat means too much to me. A united priesthood serves my purposes. Nebseny runs the Temple well enough; I know that his devotion to Amun is pure. He is useful to me, but he is reluctant to bend to my will. He owes all he has to you, as you owe all you have to my father. I know, too, that I have said things to you which could be dangerous for me. We are in each other's confidence now, Ankhhor. You must trust me and serve me, or I will find it wiser after all to kill you."

"Trust you? In what, Great Lady?"

"Bring Nebseny to my side. Place him in my hands. Assure

his absolute loyalty to me, and in return I will give you something to boast of on your tomb wall. Iset will never be God's Wife, but give me your brother's obedience and I will ensure that she becomes King's Mother."

Ankhhor paused, considering. "Why did you not tell me all this in a letter, Great Lady? Why travel all this way to my sepat for such a message?"

"Letters can be intercepted, lost. I must be certain that Nebseny is mine; there can be no room for error. And, Ankhhor, you needed to look upon me with your own eyes to understand my power. You must know what the God's Wife is: no shrinking child, no weak, beaten woman. I am the daughter of Thutmose the First. I am the daughter of Amun himself. I am the Hand of the God. I will uphold any promise – or any threat. You know that now. You see me."

Slowly, Ankhhor nodded. A hot, rippling thrill of victory raced along Hatshepsut's veins, throbbed in her face, her limbs.

"I will do as you command, Great Lady."

"Swear it to me."

"I swear by Amun."

"Oh, no, Ankhhor. Do not think go deceive me. I know your heart. When the God's Wife commands you to swear an oath, you must do so solemnly."

Ankhhor hesitated only a moment. At last he said, "I swear it on the Aten, Great Lady. I will do as you command." Defeat dried his voice to a hoarse, grudging whisper.

THE SKY BRIGHTENED WITH THE APPROACHING DAWN. HATSHEPSUT saw her women safely aboard the ship, then turned at the rail to stare into Ankhhor's eyes. She held his gaze as the lines were cast off and the oars extended to push the ship away from the stone mooring. But it was the tjati who looked away first, turning to lead his wife and children back to his palace.

The sailors shouted their call-and-response song, heaving at a great line to raise the sail. The northerly wind was blowing; it caught the sail with a crack that bellied it out above the deck, above the lively gray water. *Biddable Mare* drove southward, kicking up a cold spray, an early flock of birds giving chase, crying. Flushed with the warmth of victory, Hatshepsut turned her face toward the rising sun.

CHAPTER TWENTY-TWO

S HE HAD BEEN IN THE palace only a few hours when one of the king's own men arrived at her apartments to summon her into the Pharaoh's presence. She had begged time to prepare herself, smiling as Ita freshened her cosmetics and chose for her a more ornate wig. So Thutmose had returned from his journey before she. He would be angry to learn that she had managed to venture from Waset in spite of his bid to leave her behind.

She greeted him sweetly in his magnificent room, far larger than her own and adorned without restraint. Thutmose was not one for subtlety. He had had the chamber repainted when he was crowned – a fact which pained Hatshepsut, for their father had revered the histories of the kings who had come before him and had kept their images and deeds on his walls to remind him always of a Pharaoh's duty. Thutmose's preference was not for duty, but for adventure. The brightness of new paint dazzled the eye, covering every brick of the interior with fanciful scenes of Thutmose driving chariots into war, hunting fanged lions and the mystical white deby, bringing down marsh birds by the brace with a single arrow.

The boy had done none of these things. He boasted of his fantasies as though the paint would make them fact. Spacious as the room was, it was crammed with the finest furniture, all of it ornately carved and glittering with gold. He would never entertain so many in his private rooms that four couches and eight tables would be required. It was thoughtless excess, and lent the Pharaoh's rooms an air of desperation rather than dignity.

"So," Thutmose said, reclining on one couch, glaring up at her. "You left Waset in the hands of your steward."

"Did I do wrong, husband? Has Waset flown to pieces in my brief absence?"

"That dreadful steward was forcing scrolls on me the moment I stepped from my boat!"

"Scrolls," Hatshepsut said in deepest sympathy. "You poor man."

"You are not to leave without my permission again. The palace runs better with you in charge." His voice dropped a note as he said it, as though the admission had to be forced from his mouth. "I like it better when I can relax on coming home, and not be made to turn my attention to this affair or that until I am ready."

"Let me make this up to you. Won't you dine with me tonight in my own rooms?"

Thutmose drew back on his couch, narrowing one eye in a sudden display of suspicion.

"Oh, don't be reticent, Thutmose. You are my husband, after all. Allow me to entertain you. It is my duty, is it not, as your wife."

The Pharaoh sat up. He braced his hands on his knees. "What are you plotting?"

"Nothing. Come, Thutmose. Let us put this animosity between us to rest. We have the Two Lands to rule, you and I. We ought not be so cruel to one another."

"Perhaps you are right. Yes, very well; I will join you for supper."

Hatshepsut bowed to him. She did not need to force the brilliant smile she gave him. But as she turned to go, he called after her. "Hatshepsut, do not think to seduce me. I know how the women of the harem clamor for my favor; I can have any of them I please, and any other woman in the world besides. I do not desire you. I would not have my wife make a fool of herself trying to trip me into her bed."

It was an effort to stifle her laugh. She lowered her eyes, hoping she looked despondent and defeated, like a woman spurned. "As you wish, my king."

HATSHEPSUT HAD ASKED ISET TO MAKE HERSELF ESPECIALLY beautiful tonight. When Sitre-In admitted the girl into the Great Royal Wife's apartments, she saw that Iset had taken the instructions well to heart. She entered with a quick, light step, eagerness trembling all along her slender body. A gown of blue linen so sheer it was hardly visible sheathed her form. About her hips she had tied a tiny, triangular apron of metallic scales, gold and electrum overlapping; it hid the clean-plucked fork of her thighs, shivering as she moved so that pale, warm skin revealed itself now and then through the glitter of cold metal. As Iset came forward with eyes downcast, Hatshepsut saw that the apron was tied not above but beneath the transparent gown; the clever inversion of courtly style was undeniably riveting. Hatshepsut found it difficult to keep her eyes from Iset's body. The gown was fastened at her throat by a simple, narrow collar of gold, and her wig bore a crown of fresh and fragrant lotuses.

Thutmose, seated beside Hatshepsut on her couch, jerked a little in surprise. "What is this?"

At the sound of his voice, Iset raised her eyes from the floor.

When she took in the sight of the Pharaoh seated beside his wife, she gasped and stepped backward, then recovered herself, her face burning red. "Mighty Horus," she murmured, bowing.

"It is a dancer," Hatshepsut said in answer to the Pharaoh's question. "Iset, the daughter of Ankhhor – a woman of your harem. You have seen her before. I thought you might enjoy some entertainment while you dine."

Thutmose's eyes rested on the apron beneath Iset's gown. "I might. Let us see how well she can dance."

"Very well, I assure you." Hatshepsut turned to her musicians, waiting in their corner with harp and horn. "Play something slow and soothing."

As they turned to their supper, Iset swayed with the sinuous, languid music. Her hips and breasts wove in counter rhythm; her arms reached and beckoned in a wordless expression of perfect, poignant yearning.

"She is one of the finest dancers I have ever seen, I think," Hatshepsut said. Iset flowed, water-smooth, across the floor, turned to display the easy, alluring rise and fall of her buttocks as her hips twisted this way and that.

"Mm," Thutmose said around a mouthful of roasted gazelle.

"How do you find the food?"

Thutmose nodded, reached for bread and cheese.

"I am glad you are pleased. It is maat, that a wife should please her husband."

He paused in his motion, glanced at her from the corner of his eye, then availed himself of the cheese without a word of response. Thutmose went on eating; she feared he was entirely unaware of Iset's presence, but when the song concluded and the girl held her pose – one knee raised, arms lifted above her head – Thutmose thumped his fist on the table in appreciation.

"Let us have another dance," Hatshepsut said. "A song of romance."

At the suggestion, Thutmose gave her a sharp glance. But the musicians took up an aching, wistful tune, and Iset at once moved into the rhythm, winding her arms about her own neck, caressing her breasts, her head thrown back in a posture of unfulfilled longing.

"By Mut's wings," Hatshepsut said in honest admiration. "What a treasure for the harem. Have you ever seen the like?" Iset caught her glance as she spun away from the couch and moved out across the floor, the hem of her dress floating in a languid circle about her ankles. The smile the girl gave her was somehow both secretive and direct; Hatshepsut heated with a sudden flush. "I think there is truly no woman half so beautiful in all of Egypt. The gods love you well, Thutmose, to give you such a gift."

Iset dipped her head as she danced, a shy and glad acknowledgment of Hatshepsut's words.

"Why, if I were you, dear brother, I could not restrain myself. I would take her to my chamber to dance for me alone, this very night."

Thutmose gave the girl a slow, considering leer. She faltered in her steps; her movements became graceless, rough, unappealing. Thutmose looked away, sighing, fidgeting with his wine cup.

Hatshepsut called for another tune – one of the fishermen's songs. Iset had been so charming when she had performed the rekhet tune the night of their private supper, but now she stamped and clapped with as much appeal as a beleaguered cow trying to rid itself of flies. When the song had finished, Thutmose neglected to applaud Iset's efforts, and yawned into his hand.

"What other entertainment have you brought?"

"The dancer is all, I am afraid."

"Not even a juggler? You don't plan well, sister."

She ducked her head in acceptance of his criticism.

"This has hardly made amends for your impertinence."

"I shall send one of my servants to the city and bring back a juggler. And a magician, if you like."

"No; now I am too bored to stay with you. Your rooms are not as beautiful as mine, anyway; I feel as if I am dining in a rekhet's hut." He flicked a hand at his guardsman who stood waiting by the door. The man swung the door wide and held it open for the Pharaoh. Thutmose stood and stared at her a moment down his nose, then bid her a curt good evening and left without another glance at her or at Iset, who had shrunk back against the wall and stood blushing with eyes on the floor.

When he had gone, Iset peered up through the locks of her wig, cringing and sheepish.

"You did that on purpose," Hatshepsut said.

"Great Lady?"

"You turned into a wooden doll – you danced like a moon-struck deby!"

Iset's lips pressed together; the laugh she tried to suppress snorted out indelicately through her nose.

"Oh, come here, Iset." Hatshepsut patted the couch beside her; Iset came willingly enough – ah, and gracefully, too, swaying as she walked, her hands clasped at her navel.

"By all the gods, I can't blame you for throwing it."

"Throwing it?"

"The seduction. Don't pretend you did not know what I intended. I cannot blame you. I wouldn't like to lie with him, either."

"Surely the Pharaoh is still too young to father children."

"I know he is boorish now, but he is a handsome boy at least."

Iset shrugged as if she had never noticed.

"One day, when he is a man, you will not feel so much reluctance. It would be wise to make him love you now, Iset. There are many women in his harem, but you could be his favorite."

Iset considered her words. Her knees were drawn up, her

feet tucked to one side. She toyed with the gauzy fabric of her dress, plucking at a wrinkle that had formed on her thigh. "Great Lady, you speak as if you will never lie with the king yourself. Do you...do you not desire him?"

Hatshepsut sighed. "For all my talk of his handsome face, I know what a trial he can be."

"Would it...would it please you if I were to lie with the king?"

"Very much, Iset. The king needs heirs, and I fear he will never get them from me."

Iset's face paled; her eyes seemed to turn inward, so that she looked upon a strange and painful place within her own heart. Hatshepsut, afraid she had somehow wounded the girl, laid a hand on her shoulder, reached beneath the girl's wig to caress the back of her neck. It was a touch Sitre-In had often used to soothe her when Hatshepsut's heart was in turmoil.

Iset closed her eyes. "I will do whatever the Great Royal Wife requires of me," she said, her voice sad and soft. "Always."

Hatshepsut withdrew her hand from Iset's nape. She could still feel the smoothness of the girl's skin singing along the length of her fingers, whispering in the tingle of her palm.

CHAPTER TWENTY-THREE

"YOU LOOK WELL," THUTMOSE SAID from his throne. "I haven't seen you without a scowl on your face for months."

Hatshepsut came to a halt at the foot of the dais. All about her, stewards moved in their characteristic flurry, a proficient and unceasing restlessness, the shuffling of scrolls organized and re-organized, the murmur of their voices directing scribes, the bustling preparation of the great hall for the morning's audiences. She smiled up at her husband. Today would be a good day. Wadjetefni had informed her as she took a light morning meal that Ineni had returned, and that he bore many fine gifts from Retjenu in thanks for her intervention. She climbed the steps to her throne and settled herself, neatening the pleats of her white gown.

Thutmose looked well himself, if truth be told. His skin was pleasingly dark from so much time spent on the river. He had shed a little of his accustomed weight. His face was still boyishly round, but his shoulders were beginning to broaden, his back beginning to harden with a hint of muscle.

"Have you been hauling lines on your ship? You look stronger than when I saw you last."

"It's the bow," he said. "I have been hunting whenever I can. I always find the time for a hunt, between visiting this sepat or that, or seeing to the garrisons."

Scurrying about Egypt, avoiding the great hall, the scrolls to be signed, the appointments to be made. No matter. Today would bring riches from Retjenu. She would not allow Thutmose's ignorance to rile her on such a fine and auspicious morning.

"Have you heard the news, husband? Your envoy returns today from his mission."

"What envoy? What mission?"

"The famine in Retjenu. I sent grain in your name. Surely you heard."

"Oh – that. I still do not understand why you bothered. Retjenu is full of filthy herders and I cannot see how it benefits Egypt to keep them fed. They are poor and arrogant, and too disorganized to stop the Heqa-Khasewet marching right through their country and into ours. It seems a waste of grain to me."

Hatshepsut swallowed a sigh. "I am sure Mighty Horus is right. All the same, it is no harm to keep Retjenu on friendly terms."

The morning session began. Overseers brought their tallies before the throne; messengers from far-flung sepats carried announcements of important marriages and deaths; and within minutes, Thutmose was fidgeting and sighing. Hatshepsut quietly offered, here and there, a crucial addendum to the decrees he dictated to his troop of scribes: more genteel wording, the softening of his edicts with appropriate sops to this noble's imagined importance or that noble's true influence. At last, just as she was beginning to feel every bit as restless as the Pharaoh, Wadjetefni bowed Ineni into the hall.

He made his way down the length of the great hall with a stately confidence, trailing six or seven men who bore heaps of orange- and dun-colored skins across their arms. At the foot of the throne he bowed low. His men stacked the skins neatly before Thutmose, who eyed them skeptically for a moment, then gestured to a steward to count and record the gift.

"Mighty Horus," Ineni said. "Fine pelts of leopard from Retjenu, and the pelts of great fierce cats from far to the north. See, they are striped, gold and black – very rare. The Retjenu kings acquire these pelts in trade, Majesty, with the Greeks, who in turn get them from savage tribes far to the east of their lands. The kings of Retjenu gave every last one of their valuable pelts to Mighty Horus in thanks for his intervention. A costly gift, but offered gratefully. Your timely aid saved their children from starvation."

"Skins," Thutmose said, sounding vague and confused. "What in Amun's name does Egypt need with cat skins?"

Hatshepsut cleared her throat. "The throne recognizes what a dear gift the Retjenu have sent, though the Pharaoh would gladly feed their children again without repayment." She blinked at the heap of pelts. It rather confused her, too. As rare as the striped skins were, they still seemed a paltry show of thanks. She felt the breeze had fallen right out of her ship's sail.

Thutmose turned to her. "I told you there was no use in helping Retjenu. They lack the comprehension of civilized men. Is there any other business for the throne? No? Then we shall retire. Wadjetefni, send the leopard skins to the Temple of Amun. The priests are fond of dressing like leopards. The striped skins shall go to my own rooms. I shall have my Overseer of the Needle turn them into carpets for my bed chamber. I'll recall the gratitude of Retjenu every time I walk across them." The Pharaoh sprang from his throne eager as a schoolboy set free from lessons, and descended the dais two steps at a time. His personal guard crowded behind him, blocking his retreating back from Hatshepsut's view.

She made her way back to her own apartments, pondering the Retjenu, Nehesi beside her. "I meant what I said," she told him. "I would gladly have fed the Retjenu without any repayment. But a few armfuls of skins seems a strange gift of thanks."

"Perhaps Thutmose is right. There is no accounting for a people like those – desert dwellers, sheep herders. Pah!"

"Don't ever say those words in my hearing again," she said lightly, teasing. "'Thutmose is right.' I ought to have you flogged!"

They had reached her chamber door. She could hear her ladies within: a chorus of delighted squeals, disbelieving laughter, the astonished clapping of hands. She hesitated, glanced up at Nehesi.

Ineni's smooth voice carried across an open courtyard. "Great Lady! A moment, if you please." The steward hurried toward them, his hands outstretched in supplication. "Forgive me, Great Lady. I was not truthful in the great hall. But I would not have risked embarrassing the Pharaoh; I am sure you understand."

"I do not understand," she said, a bit sharply. "What is this all about?"

"I had it all delivered to your personal chambers, seeing as how the Retjenu meant it for you especially, and no one else."

Nehesi frowned, wary, but opened the door at her gesture.

Never before had she seen such a tribute of riches. It was spread all across her anteroom: bolts of fine-woven wool, dyed in every color she could imagine, including the deep, evening-sky violet so prized by the people of Retjenu; boxes of polished stones, turquoise, lapis, quartz, jasper, winking in the light that fell in even golden shafts from the windcatchers; sacks of precious resins, their scent rich and alluring; exotic spices, necklaces, rings, musical instruments she could not name. And casks – stacks of them – filled with silver in every form: discs strung on leather thongs, statuettes of gods and animals, the bowls of lamps and incense burners. Her women giggled as they sorted through the goods, trying on the jewelry, draping themselves in fine cloth.

"The kings of Retjenu instructed me most sternly," Ineni said, "to deliver these goods to the Great Royal Wife. The man they sent – the envoy; you recall him – was quick to sing your praises to his leaders, Great Lady. I did not feel it necessary to force Thutmose's name into the matter, though I did find it prudent, you will understand, to separate a portion of the gift for His Majesty."

"Yes," Hatshepsut said, somewhat dazzled by the silver. She approached an open cask and lifted a fist-sized statue of a bull. It was heavy for its size – solid silver, not plated wood. "Retjenu has certainly demonstrated its gratitude."

Ineni glanced at her women, at Nehesi, and his mouth closed tightly.

She stepped well away from her servants and beckoned him near. "You took a great risk in – how did you put it? Not forcing Thutmose's name in the matter. Why?"

"In truth, I obeyed the instincts of my own loyalties. You know I served your mother. I was...her most faithful servant, Great Lady. Because I feel such affection for her, I also feel it for you. I hope I do not step out of my place in admitting as much. I am a steward to the throne and bound to serve the king, and I will ever be his faithful man. But that is duty. For you, I will go beyond duty."

For Ahmose, he will go beyond duty. No matter; I will take my allies wherever I may find them. She nodded. "I am grateful, for more than you know. This wealth was sorely needed, Master Ineni. Amun's granaries overflow, but grain is not as useful a currency as silver. Months ago I wished for a way to strengthen the southern border against the Kushites. My husband did nothing while a weak garrison struggled to throw back Kushite raiders. The gods have answered my wish – the gods and you, Ineni. I have more work for you, it seems. You will take the better part of this treasure and go south, to the garrison at the fourth cataract of the river. It is a poor fortress from all I hear, and Thutmose has shown no urgency to improve it. Trade these goods as you go south. Get what goods and workers you will need to shore up the garrison. Use the silver to tempt young men into joining the army, if you must. But our outpost in Kush must be improved. I will not allow another spate of raids – not the sort we had last year."

Ineni bowed. "It will be as you say, Great Lady."

NEHESI HAD FOUND A STORE-ROOM TO PROTECT RETJENU'S fulsome gratitude, and chosen his own loyal men to stand guard over its doors until Ineni was prepared to move south. When the last cask of silver and bolt of cloth were cleared away, she sent an invitation to Thutmose to dine with her once more. It had been well over a week since her last attempt to maneuver Iset into Thutmose's bed. She reasoned that the tribute from Retjenu was a sign of the gods' favor; tonight her plans would come to fruition, and with Mut's blessing, Iset would soon be with child.

But Ita returned flustered and alone, and dropped to her knees to beg forgiveness from her mistress.

"The king will not come, Great Lady. He is in a foul temper. He threw a goblet at me to chase me from his room! Oh, do not be angry; I tried."

"Calm yourself, Ita. It is none of your fault." *No doubt Mighty Horus is still pouting over his pile of cat skins.*

"Shall I send to the House of Women to tell them the dancer is not needed?"

"No," Hatshepsut said. "I shall dine alone tonight, if that is what the gods decree. But Iset is always a delight to me. Let her come and dance."

The girl arrived on the heels of the food. She was dressed as beautifully as ever: a red gown of the old-fashioned style, its skirt flowing loose and rippling from a tight, beaded band just beneath her breasts. The straps that ran over her narrow shoulders squeezed her breasts slightly from either side, so that they stood round and high and close upon her chest. She had painted her nipples with gold dust; they shone brightly against the soft-sand paleness of her skin.

Iset took up her accustomed position to dance and waited for Hatshepsut's signal to begin. But Hatshepsut considered the girl a moment, then beckoned her to the couch.

"You are a friend tonight, Iset, not a dancer. Share my supper."

"Great Lady, you honor me."

"I heard the deby barking in the night, when I was in Ka-Khem."

"You went all the way to Ka-Khem, Great Lady? I wondered where you disappeared to; I missed dancing for you. Did you see my family?"

"They send their love. Your mother misses you terribly."

"I write her letters, but it is not the same as being with her, holding her hand."

"Has the Pharaoh visited the harem since I saw you last?"

"Ah, here and there. I have looked for an opportunity to do as you want me to do, Great Lady, but he chose other women."

Hatshepsut's brow furrowed in spite of her resolve to remain impassive. She changed the subject, relating the story of her journey up the Iteru. The change put Iset at ease. As Hatshepsut talked she admired the simple comfort evident on the girl's face, the way her hands toyed with the beads of her dress. She should have felt rivalry with Iset, she knew. Word from Ankhhor had certainly not reached Waset yet, and Nebseny still believed he would use his niece to usurp Hatshepsut's station. But she was such a sweet girl, such a soothing presence, and so unknowing. She would be so harmless and pure if not for the plotting of the men of her house. Hatshepsut realized, startled, that she had been craving for Iset's company, for the simplicity of her conversation and the lovely, unconscious grace of her movements.

Lost in her thoughts, in the sight of Iset's fingers playing below her breast, Hatshepsut stumbled over her story and could not find her words again.

Iset lowered her eyes. "If it is not too bold to say it, I missed you while you were on this journey."

That pleased Hatshepsut more than it ought to have done. She laughed, a happy and foolish sound, then scolded herself for her transparency.

Iset glanced at her face, then away again, blushing. The girl's soft passivity stirred Hatshepsut's kas. In the face of Iset's yielding sweetness she felt a surge of power; her heart flooded with the knowledge of her own burgeoning might. She had discerned Nebseny's plan, had traveled to Ka-Khem herself, and intimidated this girl's noble father into doing her bidding. She had seen the need of Retjenu, and responded herself with great wisdom: not two hours ago this very room had been heaped with the proof of it. She had never felt so confident before.

"Come, Iset. My bed is much more comfortable than this couch."

Iset rose. The eagerness in her eyes was so intense that Hatshepsut looked away, an unaccountable flush rising to her cheeks. They walked together to her bed chamber, and Hatshepsut sent her women away. Sitre-In's disbelieving stare only fueled Hatshepsut's sense of power.

The two girls climbed onto the bed together. Iset stretched herself along the mattress, her hands clasped demurely across her belly. The girl's warm pressure on the bed seemed to pull at Hatshepsut; her body longed to roll against Iset's, to fall against her as a child's ball falls to the earth. She resisted, propping herself up on an elbow, gazing down at Iset's closed eyes, their lids painted with shimmering green paint. Her face was so serene, so lovely in repose. Her lips curled, a gentle smile of unfeigned joy. Hatshepsut thought of Lady Iah, worrying over her daughter's happiness. Could there be a better life for a woman than in the Pharaoh's harem? Surely not. Staring at Iset's beauty, she was aware of her own shortcomings. The gods were good to have made her who she was, the daughter of a king and born to great power. For had she been born the daughter of a nobleman, she would not be thought pretty enough to give to any man.

Hatshepsut had kept back a part of the Retjenu treasure for herself. Sitre-In had left the small cask on the table beside her bed. She lifted its lid and took out a long, jointed chain of silver; she draped it across Iset's throat.

Iset's eyes flicked open; she squealed. "Cold!" She plucked at the chain, lifted it to where she could see. "Oh! How lovely."

Hatshepsut drew another trinket from the box, a silver cuff set with a clear, red stone cut into sparkling facets. She lifted Iset's hand and slid the cuff onto her wrist. Iset lay giggling while Hatshepsut adorned her, wrapped her arms and ankles and neck in the riches of her own great power. Soon the girl was breathless, clutching her stomach to quell her laughter, tears of merriment shining in her eyes. Those eyes were as dark as ebony, though bright flecks of copper within their depths caught the light of Hatshepsut's lamps. She stared down a Iset's face, musing about Ankhhor, about Thutmose, about Senenmut.

"Great Lady? You seem so pensive."

"I was just thinking about the harem. Do you like it? Is it a good life?"

"Oh, ah, Great Lady. My room is not so grand as yours, of

course, but it is beautiful, and the gardens are lovely, and the women there are all very kind. Well – mostly. Some of them quarrel, you know, but they are kind to me. They treat me like a sister, even new as I am."

"I am glad to hear it. Would you ever wish to leave the harem?"

"Great Lady?"

"Would you wish to serve me, to wait on me here in my chambers, become one of my ladies?"

"Oh." Iset's eyes darkened, a sudden shadow of worry. "But how could I lie with the Pharaoh if I were your woman? I will do whatever the Great Lady asks, only..."

"Only you have a duty to your father's house. I understand. Think nothing of it; it was only an impulse. I would not ask you to shame yourself before your family, Iset."

The girl nodded in grateful relief. Then her eyes narrowed, peered at Hatshepsut through a sparkle of mischief. "Although, if I were to serve the Great Lady, I would learn the truth at last."

"The truth?" The shine of power coursing along her limbs dimmed and faltered.

Iset hesitated. The air vibrated with words she was reluctant to say, or perhaps was too eager to say; Hatshepsut could not quite tell, could not make out the meaning of the tremulous smile on Iset's lips, the strange, deep glimmer in her eyes.

"I have heard it whispered that you are not a woman at all." Her voice had lowered, a soft, rich murmur.

"What? Absurd."

"They say you were born with a man's parts."

Hatshepsut stared at Iset, incredulous, but when she saw the look of mischief crackling in the girl's eyes she blew through her lips and tapped Iset's shoulder. "You tease me! How unkind."

"Well," Iset said, sly and low, "how do I know it's not true? You often wear a man's kilt, after all. Are you hiding something beneath it?"

Hatshepsut found herself on her feet, though she did not recall standing. One moment she was lying beside Iset; the next she fumbled at the knot of her gown, quick as a flash of sun on water. With stiff fingers she worked the knot free; the gown dropped to her feet. The treasure of Retjenu chimed as Iset rolled to look at her. The curious intensity in the girl's eyes took Hatshepsut aback.

"Now you see: I am made like any other woman."

"What is that scar, Great Lady?"

"A reminder that I must never act rashly. See how well I heed it! Here I am, naked before a harem woman."

"It was wicked of me to taunt you. And it is not right that the Great Royal Wife should be at a disadvantage before a mere concubine, even one unused by the Pharaoh as I am." Iset stood, and with graceful hands she removed the straps at her shoulders. The beaded band slipped down her body; her breasts settled; clad only in the silver bangles, she faced Hatshepsut, her skin like polished ivory in the lamplight, pale, smooth, inviting a soft touch.

A roaring filled Hatshepsut's ears. She stood rooted to the spot. Every warning Senenmut had ever given her to think before she acted sounded all at once in her heart, a stern clamor from which she could draw no sense.

"You think me too bold, I am sure," Iset said, and at once Senenmut's voice fell silent. "But I was sent to Waset as a gift to the throne."

You were sent to Waset as your father's tool. You were sent to Waset to usurp me. You don't even know it, do you, Iset?

"I only wish to do my duty, Great Lady. You may think that because I am young, and only a dancer, that I do not see. But I see." Iset stepped toward her. Hatshepsut could not take her eyes from Iset's breasts, from the golden sun-discs of her nipples. She longed to press her palms against them, to feel their warmth. "Thutmose is a boy. He has a boy's mind. He is not the power of Egypt; it is not he who commands from the throne."

"No," Hatshepsut admitted, hoarse. And oh, the gratification she felt, to hear that truth spoken aloud! Her knees trembled from the force of it.

"My duty is to be pleasing to the one who commands from the throne." Iset drew so near that the warmth of her body raised the minute hairs of Hatshepsut's skin. Iset's arms wrapped about her; her hands moved slowly up Hatshepsut's back, and woke a shivering fire deep in her middle. It throbbed downward, past her scar, pulsing hot and insistent deep between her thighs. "Let me do my duty, Great Lady. I only wish..."

Hatshepsut cut her words short, swallowed them when her mouth fell upon Iset's. The kiss was sweeter than any she had stolen from Senenmut, for Iset's lips opened to welcome her tongue, and her teeth teased at Hatshepsut's lower lip until her breath came in short, desperate rasps. Their feet tangled in their fallen clothing; they staggered toward the bed. Iset giggled and tossed her wig to the floor, pulled Hatshepsut's own aside and ran her palms across the stubble of her scalp until hot shivers wracked her body.

Hatshepsut clutched Iset's breasts with both hands; the girl gasped, arched backward, and Hatshepsut kissed her there, pulled each nipple into her mouth, felt Iset's moan shiver through her own body. She returned to Iset's mouth, kissed her; when she pulled away she smiled at the golden paint smeared across Iset's lips. She had kissed the girl's breasts clean.

Iset dragged her thumb across Hatshepsut's own lips. Hatshepsut caught it and sucked; Iset's eyelids dropped, heavy with ecstasy; her surrendering sigh whispered in Hatshepsut's ear.

"I am yours. Gladly, Great Lady. Yours."

Hours later, Hatshepsut woke to find Iset murmuring in her sleep. Her fine, pale limbs lay angled across the bed linens. Her face turned toward the moonlight falling through the columned wall, and her lips, still smudged with gold dust, moved on half-formed, barely heard words. The tangle of silver chains about her neck returned a faint reflection of moonlight.

Hatshepsut wondered whether she dreamed of Ka-Khem, of her father's palace, the night song of the marshes. She pressed her face against Iset's bare shoulder, shuddered as a sob moved through her, silent but sharp, quelled deep in her belly. Her joy at touching and being touched, at the closeness of another body, was overwhelming in its strength. And her relief, too – an end to a loneliness so vast, so all-encompassing, that it could not be comprehended while she dwelt beneath its shadow. She could only see how isolated and miserable she had been before now that Iset's love shone upon her like a band of stars in a black sky.

And I must use her as my tool, the same way her father and uncle would use her. This sweet girl, dutiful and kind – he relief, the joy – the knowledge that even as she found her joy, she must keep herself aloof from it, must remain Great Royal Wife, God's Wife, the hand upon Egypt's reins – these were all too much to bear. She cried silently, her tears dampening Iset's skin. *I cannot even cry where she can see me. It is as Ahmose told me years ago when Father died. Iset has brought me love, this most precious gift, and yet with her I must still wear my mask. Even with her.*

Her hand drifted to her belly, and lower still. She traced the scar across her loins. She had a job to do with this girl. No matter how sweet Iset's company may be, she could not let herself forget.

CHAPTER TWENTY-FOUR

H ATSHEPSUT BACKED THROUGH THE DENSE
blackness of Amun's shrine. As she withdrew, the cool
golden skin of the god vanished beneath her outstretched
fingertips. She knew the distance to the shrine's door. Once
there had been a time when she had groped in fear along the
walls, certain the door had vanished through some unknowable
mystery of Amun-Re, certain she would dwell in darkness
forever, an unwitting sacrifice to her god. But she had been
God's Wife now for well over a year, and she moved with practiced confidence through the chamber, four, five, six steps backward and turn, and reach out with a palm, and – there! Her
hand rested on the door's familiar carvings. She swung it wide;
the light of day forced her eyes shut.

"God's Wife." She started at the sound of Nebseny's voice.
With a hand above her eyes as sun-shade, she squinted in the
direction of his voice. The sun at his back cast him with a brilliant halo. It had been two months since her journey to Ka-
Khem. She had waited for Ankhhor to keep his word, to send
his instructions to his brother. The High Priest bowed low to

her, lower than he had ever bowed before. "I would beg an audience with you, Great Lady."

She followed him to his private chamber, a large room for a priest's dwelling, appointed with a standing chest that was nearly as large as the one where she kept her own gowns and shawls, six chairs carved as fine as thrones, and a scattering of tables inlaid with fine stone. Nebseny offered her a cup of wine, but she shook her head. In truth, her throat was parched from her chanting, but her sudden apprehension would have prevented her from swallowing. She did not wish to choke and sputter before the High Priest's eyes.

"I have been instructed," Nebseny said with a careful emphasis on the word, "to tell you that I am your man to command. I am faithful to you, and deliver myself into your hands."

She held his gaze. Nebseny's stare was as flat and inscrutable as his brother's. At last she gathered herself. "I thank you for your loyalty. I reward those who are loyal to me. I keep my promises."

"My house waits to hear of its reward. I am sure you realize, Great Lady, that a powerful man cannot remain patient forever."

Hatshepsut narrowed her eyes. "A wise man remains patient as long as he must."

"Powerful men are not always wise."

"Then let me enlighten you, Nebseny. The Pharaoh is but a child. The day he shows a man's interest in his harem, I shall keep my promise to your house. Until then, I must counsel you and your family to patience, and to heed the pledge you have made to me."

Nebseny gave a single, abrupt nod. It was the most his stiff neck would ever bend, she knew.

"As you are my man, it would please me to see you leave off your habit of courting Thutmose's favor."

"I am the High Priest. It is maat that the Pharaoh should seek my advice."

She stepped around his protestations as surely as she moved through the darkness of Amun's shrine. "Then advise him in the presence of others, at court or at feasts. I will not have you closeted alone with him."

Nebseny's mouth tightened. But at last he agreed. "Very well. It shall be as you say."

"I thank you," she said, "for your loyalty. May Amun smile on you, High Priest."

A YEAR PASSED, AND THUTMOSE REMAINED DETACHED, preferring the deck of a ship to the seat of his throne, and in matters of the harem he remained a child. On her visits to the House of Women, Hatshepsut heard tales of his pinches, his lewd remarks, but no woman could yet say that she carried the Pharaoh's child. Hatshepsut sent frequent dispatches to Ka-Khem, reporting with all honesty that the Pharaoh had not yet come to appreciate the charms of his own concubines, and that Iset's womb remained empty. By the time the new year celebrations commenced, Hatshepsut found herself fretting. How long could she keep Ankhhor and Nebseny acquiescent?

At least her efforts in the south had borne sweet fruit. Ineni reported back frequently on the progress he had made. The old fortress at the fourth cataract had been completely rebuilt with walls twice their previous height; it was now spacious enough to house four times the previous capacity of men and horses. Kush already showed a marked reluctance to raid the southern sepats; the mere sight of the new fortress looming near the river seemed to deter their aggressions.

Hatshepsut's confidence waxed bright and full in the face of her successes. She sent for Iset more frequently, and often as not she started her days with her lover's spicy scent clinging to her fingers and lips. She did not fear angering the gods, for even had she a woman's blood, with Iset there was no chance she might carry a child who was not the Pharaoh's own. This, she reasoned, would keep the gods complicit.

But Sitre-In saw reason for concern. One hot day in Shemu, when the shimmer of flies in the garden made Hatshepsut feel languid and lonely and she had sent Tem to the House of Women for Iset, Sitre-In leaned close to her ear.

"Make that girl a servant, or the House of Women will positively burst from the burden of keeping your secret."

"Do you think they suspect?"

Sitre-In leveled such a look at Hatshepsut that she flushed at the obvious idiocy of the question.

"But I cannot force her out of the harem," she protested weakly. "It is her right to remain, to bear the king's heir if she can."

"The girl will jump at the opportunity to be nearer you. She is besotted with you; anyone can see it. Take that foolish grin off your face, Great Lady. You should not have lured her heart the way you did. Now she will be nothing but a body servant."

"Better than Thutmose's bed girl. I will give her the choice. Let Iset decide where she wishes to remain; I will not appoint her against her will."

She had hoped, for the sake of her secret purpose, that Iset would choose the harem, where Thutmose might eventually discover her beauty. But as Sitre-In predicted, Iset leapt upon the chance to serve as Hatshepsut's fan-bearer, her face alight with gratitude. The servant's room she would occupy was small and much meaner than her room in the harem, but Iset seemed not to care. She was near to Hatshepsut, and attended her daily: that fact alone was a fair trade for luxury, in Iset's reckoning. Hatshepsut worried over how she might now engineer the pregnancy she had promised to Ankhhor. But as more favorable reports of her fortress's progress reached her, as Nebseny continued to bow low to her whenever she attended the Temple of Amun, surety in her own might grew stronger. She forgot her concerns and spent nearly every night submerged in a deep ecstasy of Iset's body, Iset's hands, Iset's mouth.

She was jolted from her reverie in the season of Peret, at the Feast of the Emergence, as she visited the harem's celebration with her beautiful and eager fan-bearer in tow. Her half-sister Opet stole Hatshepsut away to a secluded corner of the House of Women. In the feasting hall the women had begun to clap and chant; a drinking game of some sort had captured their attention.

"I'm afraid," Opet said, coy and sly, "that the time we have long feared has come at last."

"Thutmose?"

"And I did not even have time to let my breasts sag, nor to grow any warts."

"Who?"

"Hentumire, Tabiry, and the girl you call Nefer – the Hittite princess."

Hatshepsut's limbs felt suddenly cold.

"Oh! What is it, sister? You are so pale."

She forced a laugh. "Only the pallor of fear. Now none of us are safe. Are any of the women with child?"

"It is too soon to tell. We all pray that Pharaoh will give us healthy sons, of course."

"Of course."

She found Iset clapping in a ring of women, stamping her lovely small feet and shouting. Inside the ring, two women linked arms and balanced cups of wine on their heads, bobbing and stepping in time to the chant. The cup toppled from one woman's head; the circle erupted in a jeer, and she snatched the cup from her partner's wig, raised it high, and drained it in one draft.

"Iset." Hatshepsut tugged at the girl's arm.

"What? Oh!" Iset's eyes were heavy with wine. She had apparently lost a few rounds of the game herself.

"We must get back to the palace." The House of Women seemed a forbidding place to her now, full of women praying for healthy sons, and all of them ripe to be visited by the king.

"Oh, must we, Great Lady? Come, go into the ring. It's an easy game. I will show you how." Iset draped her arm across Hatshepsut's shoulder, a too-familiar gesture. Hatshepsut stepped away from her abruptly, and Iset's eyes widened. Her mouth quivered on the verge of tears. "Hatet," she wailed.

The women nearest them turned tactfully away.

"Stop it," Hatshepsut hissed. Her hand itched to slap the girl; she knotted her fingers behind her back to keep herself still. "Where is my fan? Go get it. We are leaving now."

Iset wept bitterly in their litter. The return trip to the palace seemed to stretch on into a mortifying, fearful eternity. Thutmose might even now be passing in his own litter, making his way to the House of Women to sow his seed in half a dozen parched and eager fields. She parted the litter's curtains and peered out into the night. The road was empty, save for Hatshepsut's litter and the soldiers who guarded her.

"Get hold of yourself," Hatshepsut said when they were finally set down in the palace courtyard. "I won't have you sniveling all through the halls."

Iset pulled herself together enough to walk with quiet dignity past darkened hallways and porticoes, past servants drifting through the night-blue palace on their small errands. When they reached Hatshepsut's room she threw her fan down on the floor and stormed into the bed chamber.

Sitre-In's raised brows and pursed lips only angered Hatshepsut all the more. She went after the girl and found her face down on the bed, sobbing.

"What has come over you? Wine has never taken you so badly before. Talk to me; don't just lie there wailing."

"It is not the wine," Iset said, lifting a corner of Hatshepsut's fine blanket. She rubbed the ruined kohl from her face.

"Clearly not."

"Don't tease! It's cruel."

She sighed, lay down beside Iset, curled her body against her lover's. "All right. I will not tease. Tell me why you weep."

"Hentumire thinks she may be pregnant." Iset dissolved into choking, moaning sobs. Hatshepsut rubbed her shoulders, soothed her neck until Iset caught her breath and went on: "Oh, Hatet, I want a child – I want a baby! I want to hold a little one in my arms, and hear him call me Mawat. It's not fair. It's not fair!"

"Not fair?"

"I gave it all up," Iset said, suddenly quiet and rational. "Oh, I love you, Great Lady, but with you I can never be a mother. Since my father sent me to the harem, Thutmose became my only hope for a child. And I gave up all hope of a son...or a daughter...for love. Now I am only your fan-bearer, and I can never lie with the Pharaoh. What other man is there for me? My father intended me for the Pharaoh's harem; I cannot be married off to some soldier like a servant woman! Father would never allow me to see my mother or my sisters again. Oh, my heart will tear itself in two!" She buried her face in a cushion and wailed again.

"You want a child?"

"Oh – more than anything!"

Praises to Mut. A way forward, as sudden as that. "But I never knew, Iset. If you want a child so badly, why ever did you agree to serve as my woman?"

She rolled onto her side. She held Hatshepsut's gaze for a long moment, her dark, soft eyes all the more compelling and sweet for their shine of tears. "Because I love you, Hatet.

Because you are the sister of my heart. I want both. I want a child, and I want your heart." She huffed a sad little laugh, turned her face away again. "I acted like a foolish child. I never considered what I was losing, in gaining you."

"No. You are not foolish." She kissed Iset's shoulder. "Nothing would make me happier, Iset. You know I have never bled. The gods have cursed me with barrenness – I do not know why; it doesn't matter, for the gods have given me you."

Iset lay still. She breathed deep, two, three times, calming herself.

Hatshepsut went on: "Let us have a child together, Iset. You are my woman, and no longer a member of his harem. But I may do with my servants as I please. Let me send you to Thutmose's bed in my place."

"It would be a disgrace. The Pharaoh has his concubines, the most beautiful and well-bred women in all Egypt. He has no reason to bed a servant."

"There is no woman in all Egypt more beautiful than you, servant or no. He will not think it a disgrace. And I will send you to represent the Great Royal Wife, to do what I cannot do. In this, you will be honored above any concubine; you will be nearly as honored as I."

"And the baby..."

"He will be ours. Yours and mine. We will care for him together, raise him together. We will be his mawats, the two of us, and he will be Thutmose's heir. Do it for me, Iset. Say you will give me this gift."

In the garden, a little owl called *crick-crick-cree* into the night. The air was sweet with the odor of night-blooming flowers, and above that smell, the faint salt of Iset's tears. Hatshepsut held her breath, waiting for Iset's answer, in an agony of hopeful anxiety.

"I will do it," she said. "For you."

"And for you, King's Mother."

HATSHEPSUT LAY IN HER BATH, TRYING TO SOAK AWAY A NAGGING
dull pain in her back. It had gripped her suddenly early in the
day, had plagued her throughout the court session, coming and
going in regular, pinching waves. The pain had become a severe
annoyance; she had grown cross, and struck now at the surface
of her bath water with her palms. The water splashed into her
eyes; she spat in anger.

Six weeks had passed since her talk with Iset. In that time
she had sent Iset directly to Thutmose's rooms nearly every
night, first bearing notes of affection from the Great Royal
Wife, then baskets of his favorite sweets, and finally a troupe of
musicians who played while Iset danced for the Pharaoh's own
pleasure. At last, only a handful of days ago, Iset reported that
the Pharaoh had imposed himself upon her. Giggling with
embarrassment, squirming with disbelief at her own brazen-
ness, Iset had recounted the brief episode to Hatshepsut, thrust
for thrust. The two women had rolled in Hatshepsut's bed
laughing until they could scarce catch their breath, then made
plans for Iset to return the following day, and the day after, and
the day after.

With Iset so often occupied with the Pharaoh, there was no
one to rub the ache from Hatshepsut's back. Oh, she could have
made Sitre-In or Tem do the work, but neither could work the
pains from Hatshepsut's body half so well as her fan-bearer.
Another wave gripped her back; she wallowed in her basin,
groaning, clumsy as a carp in a shallow pool.

A light clap sounded outside the door to her bath. In a rustle
of linen, beaming, holding her breath with joy, Iset entered
before Hatshepsut could give her leave.

She lurched from the water. It sloshed up and onto the bath's
tiled floor; Iset lifted her skirts and stepped deftly backward.

"You cannot come in unless I say it!"

"Hatet..."

"I'm sorry. I have no cause to be angry. I feel unwell; that is all." She squinted at Iset, took in the triumphant flush of her cheeks, the brightness of her eyes. "You have news?"

But Iset's eyes dropped to Hatshepsut's groin. A curious stillness came over her face. The smile faded. Iset reached out a hand, gently brushed between Hatshepsut's thighs. She held up her fingers. The water that beaded there was dark as fertile earth.

"I have ceased to bleed," she said, placing her dry hand atop her belly, "while you have begun."

PART III
BANNER OF THE GOD

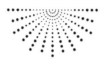

1483 B.C.E.

CHAPTER TWENTY-FIVE

THE SEASON OF THE INUNDATION would draw to a close in only a few short weeks. Already the waters of the fields receded. At the edge of every field, lines of tangled vegetation, of sun-bleached sticks and the refuse of southern towns washed downstream, marked the flood's highest point a muddy stride or two beyond the water's edge. Soon the men who farmed the Black Land would return to their crops, while the construction of monuments and tombs would grind to a near-halt for want of workers.

But there was time yet to build. Hatshepsut stepped from her litter a moment before Thutmose emerged from his own. The royal couple had arrived at Ipet-Isut to inspect and approve the progress of Thutmose's new monument.

Thutmose stretched in the sun; his fan-bearer scurried forward from among the ranks of their guardsmen to stretch his stem of ostrich plumes over the king's head. The Pharaoh had reached his fourteenth year. The promise of the man he would become was evident in his features: broadening shoulders, slender hips, stern if haughty gaze. He was taller than Hatshepsut now, a fact which seemed to please him greatly. He often lengthened himself a little when she was near, throwing out his chest, tilting his head back ever so slightly, as if to emphasize the difference to any who may be near enough to notice. As he lost the plumpness of youth, his face grew more handsome. His wide, angled eyes, full lips, and strong cheekbones favored his mother Mutnofret, still a great beauty, while the commanding sharp angle of his nose was entirely the contribution of their shared father. Thutmose had escaped, through the gods' blind luck, the large, somewhat jutting front teeth their father had graciously gifted to Hatshepsut. He was rapidly transforming into a young man of heroic good looks, as miraculously as the butterfly results from the hideous, squirming pupa and its uninteresting chrysalis. As he left his boyhood behind, Thutmose became a more appealing prospect to the women of the harem. A few already bore tiny new babes in arms, though none pleased Thutmose more than Iset's boy, his first.

Hatshepsut crossed the dusty avenue to her husband's side. Batiret scrambled to keep up. The skinny young girl was some ten or eleven years old, the child of a Waset noble house and a cousin to Wiay, the priestess of Amun. She had been sent to Hatshepsut to act as fan-bearer while Iset recovered from the birth of her son. Batiret had taken to the task naturally. Unlike her sharp-witted cousin, she was solemn and serious; her eyes shone with great intelligence, and she had a thoughtful, eager-to-please manner that Hatshepsut liked. She would wise to find some use for the girl in her personal chamber when Iset returned to her duties.

"My new gate will be a wonder," Thutmose declared, staring about him at the activity of the builders, hands on hips, as puffed with pride as though he had cut and set the great white stone blocks with his own hands.

He had commissioned a beautiful new entryway to Ipet-Isut, a flat-topped arch of pale limestone. The massive pylons to either side were be carved with scenes of the king's own glories. Whether these glories were to be filled in as they occurred, or whether they would be fabricated like the lion hunts of his bedchamber walls, Hatshepsut did not yet know.

"A wonder indeed," she said.

"Where is your usual fan-bearer?"

"Her name is Iset. She is back in the palace with our son, of course. Gods' sake, Thutmose, did you not notice that the girl I sent to your bed in my place was my fan-bearer?"

He did not respond to the taunt. He eyed Batiret, scowling, and said, "Your other fan-bearer pleases me more."

"So I hear." The shade on her face trembled; Hatshepsut laid a hand on Batiret's wrist to comfort the girl.

"And how is my son?"

"As strong as ever."

The boy was three months old now, plump and brown and sweet-smelling, with a quick, pink smile and a crackling little laugh. She had been relieved last year when Iset had confessed her desire for a child. There at last was a direct route to provide Ankhhor with the status he desired, and she had said whatever she deemed necessary to accustom Iset to the idea of going to the Pharaoh's bed as a servant, not as a true concubine. But once Iset's belly had begun to grow, once she had laid Hatshepsut's hand across its breadth to feel the child kicking within, the story she had spun for Iset became suddenly, irresistibly true. She did love this child even before she saw his face, for more than ever before, she loved Iset. By the time Iset entered the birthing pavilion, Hatshepsut thought of the babe as her own – as theirs, a treasure of a worth beyond measuring, a gift she and Iset would share all the days of their lives. And when the girl emerged from the pavilion triumphant, cradling their new son in her arms, Hatshepsut had wept with joy and gratitude. She had written to Ankhhor that very hour: *We have given the king a son, and his name is Thutmose, the third of his name.* Hatshepsut had insisted upon the name. She would have no uncertainty from any quarter that this was the Pharaoh's heir.

Thutmose led her to the nearest base of the gateway. It rose above them the height of two men, encased in a lashed-wood scaffolding. Men clung to the upper rungs, rasping the surfaces of the highest blocks; a drift of stone powder lifted on a breeze, blew from beneath their tools like plumes of offering smoke.

"Here is where I will make an image of my deeds in Kush," Thutmose said, pointing between rungs of scaffolding to the blank white stone.

"Your deeds in Kush? Those raids two years ago?"

"And more. I am going back to see to Kush myself. The fortress is finished at last; I will inspect it and lead an attack into my enemy's territory. I will make them pay for their audacity when I came to my throne." Thutmose crossed to the blocks on the far side of the avenue, detailing his plans for the carvings he would place there, fantasies of conquests to come, imagined campaigns to expand the new borders their father had forged for Egypt.

From behind her shoulder came Batiret's urgent whisper: "Great Lady!"

Hatshepsut glanced back. The girl's eyes were wide and staring. "There is a man, Great Lady, staring at you most impertinently!"

"Where?" Hatshepsut gazed past the thin brown shoulder to the shadow of the scaffolding they had left. Several men milled there, short-kilted in the heat of the day, their heads covered by the serviceable, cropped wigs of builders. They moved with heads down, some studying sheaves of papyrus, some toting reed baskets filled with tools, bread, wood scraps. One man balanced a great jug of water on his shoulder. She noted nothing unusual; it was the typical bustle of a building site. Then two builders who had been walking shoulder-by-shoulder parted,

THE CROOK AND FLAIL

one of them twisting his mouth in an angry oath, to pass around a figure that stood rooted to the spot.

The wig confounded her only for the briefest moment, for as a priest he had been bald-headed. It seemed her heart had eyes, and they opened wide in delight, took in the familiar stance, the narrowness of his shoulders, the thinness of his arms; his hands were folded at the knot of his kilt in that special way he had; his face was still long, still solemn, still beloved. His presence filled her like the breath of life, and woke the trembling of love along her limbs. In a bright chorus, a poignant quaver of rich, rising harmony, her nine kas sang his name.

Senenmut.

CHAPTER TWENTY-SIX

"I T IS GOOD TO SEE you again, man." Nehesi clapped Senenmut on the back hard enough to knock his short builder's wig askew.

"And you. My assignment to the Pharaoh's new gateway was something of a surprise to me. I never thought to be near Waset again, much less in the palace."

Nehesi led Senenmut from the courtyard where the chariot of a palace guard had deposited him. Two days had passed since he had seen Hatshepsut beneath the rising supports of the new limestone gateway. He had both feared and hoped he would encounter her there. She had glanced at him, then turned away while he stood useless as a felled ox. He had not been at all certain she had recognized him. Presently, though, the thin little girl who bore her fan had come running. "The Great Royal Wife would speak with you, builder. You will attend her the evening after next." He had spent those two days in a constant, vague discomfort, strung helplessly between eagerness and reluctance. An unsettling nausea had fallen over him, due no doubt to his lack of proper sleep.

Nehesi swung from an inner hall to lead Senenmut down

the outside length of the palace. A cedar roof extended from great supporting pillars to shade the route by day, though now the sun was low and dusk fast approaching. A lone man in the simple but well-made kilt of a palace servant moved along the walkway ahead, dipping his torch into the bowls of bronze lamps between pillars. As each lamp flared to life, it cast a yellow glow across the walkway; lamplight merged with the golden lingering light of sunset, which set the leaves of arbors and hedges in small private courtyards to shining.

Senenmut recalled walking this route once before with Nehesi. He remembered Hatshepsut sweeping down the pathway before him, the sight of her girlish back and shoulders pulling farther away, dauntless, while he struggled to keep up.

Nehesi nodded to the guards on her door. He clapped, his hands meeting precisely in time with two quick, painful beats of Senenmut's heart.

"Come," her voice said, its strength hardly diminished by the barrier of the carved double doors.

She lay across a couch of night-sky blue, robed in white linen, her wrists and ankles cuffed in gold. The room was more splendid than Senenmut had remembered, infused as it was now with the smoke of myrrh, with Hatshepsut's own languorous glow. The faience mosaic floor glittered in the lamplight; the walls bloomed with color, row on row of dancing goddesses, of queens, all proud women. But the sight that caught and held his heart was the curve of her body, the line from shoulder to hip that dipped and rose again like the path of the moon through a starry sky. That harsh, unlovely face, its awkward angles softened by a woman's careful paint, stared back at him. He recognized in the happy radiance of her eyes his own surprise, his own joy at their reunion.

Nehesi withdrew.

Senenmut recalled himself and bowed, murmuring some appropriate words of greeting.

She laughed at him. "Come here and eat."

He took the stool set across the table from her fine couch, and self-consciously attended to the meal. It was fine, rich food – three kinds of roasted fish, stewed fruits, and, Senenmut blushed to see, several of the peeled inner cores of lettuces, long and round-bodied, which were said to make a man tireless in love.

She plied him with questions of Ankh-Tawy, of life in the school of builders. He told her all he knew: of the man who had taken him as an apprentice only six months into his schooling, of the tomb he'd built for the headmaster of the school, so cleverly concealed among the natural features of the site that Senenmut had been released to his journeyman duties a full year ahead of schedule.

"I knew you would be a great architect," she said, and beamed at him.

"I would never have achieved any of this without you."

"Do you ever miss Waset? Your old duties here?"

He ducked his head, smiling. "Ah, Great Lady. I have missed you much, and often."

When they had finished their meal she led him out into a private garden, much larger and finer than the one she had enjoyed as a girl in the House of Women. This garden was four spans at least in width and breadth. It featured a shade sycamore much older and larger than any he had seen before, and beyond it, near the high protective wall gleaming pale in the moonlight, a small private lake. They walked its graveled paths, talking quietly of the years gone since they had seen each other last. No serving women trailed them now. In fact, Senenmut had seen no servants in her chamber or garden since Nehesi had withdrawn.

Hatshepsut carried a cup of dark wine; she sipped from it now and then, tilting her face to the moonlight, eyes closed, savoring the exceptional vintage. He stole glances at her face each time she did it. There was a compelling force in her presence, a might he could not name, and nor could he deny its power. So he surrendered, and turned his eyes on her narrow, angular face whenever she could not see his impropriety. The simple pleasure of the night, of the wine, perhaps even of his poor company brought a flush to her cheeks, a dreamy, wistful, feminine tenderness to the half-smile on her lips. Even the gap between her teeth looked elegant in the dusky garden, fashionable rather than coarse, and those large teeth themselves shone like ornaments of precious ivory. *If only the ladies of the court could see her this way, beautified by moonlight, graceful and happy as a goddess. Why, they would take files to their teeth in an effort to look like her.*

She left her empty cup on the rim of the lake, then led him toward the garden wall, recounting an amusing tale she had heard from a harem woman. He lost the thread of her words in a sudden cold wash of fear. His unreined thoughts had caught up at last to the more sensible portion of his heart. *Sake of Amun, Senenmut. You are a common man. You cannot fall in love with her.* There was no chance she loved him now, at any rate; that had been a girlhood folly. All noble girls felt a few heart-pangs for their tutors, provided their tutors were not too unbearably old and wrinkled. It was a common enough thing, quickly left behind with dolls and childhood games by the time womanhood arrived. No, she had summoned him here tonight to hear his stories, to pass an idle evening with a former servant who could perhaps be thought a distant friend. Senenmut clenched his fists, as though he might crush away his yearning with his hands.

They arrived at the garden wall; seeking some distraction, Senenmut ran his hands along it, noted the fine, flush joins of its blocks. The solidity of stone brought him back to his senses. He became aware once more of Hatshepsut's words.

"...but that is not what I think. What do you believe?"

"Er – pardon, Great Lady. What do I believe about...?"

"About men."

Senenmut hesitated. He shook his head helplessly, lost and light-headed.

Something canine, predatory – jackal – glittered through her smile. "I said, do you believe that men can really go two or three times with a woman?" She stepped close. He backed away instinctively until he made contact with the cold wall, then held himself very still. Hatshepsut drew even closer; he could smell the sweet wine on her breath, see the fierce amusement in her eyes. "I do not know what to believe; I have never lain with a man."

Senenmut could find no answer. He opened and closed his mouth, hoping the gods might supply some suitable response, but they granted him only a small, weak croak.

"I think you should show me," she said.

"Oh – oh, Great Lady." He caught her hands as they made their way to the knot of this kilt. Then he realized his brashness in touching the Great Royal Wife, and with a whimper he jerked his own hands away, pinned them to the wall.

Hatshepsut stepped back, laughing. "All right; I will stop being so cruel. I was only teasing you, Senenmut. Come away from that wall; I won't harm you."

She turned away and vanished into the dark garden. Senenmut stumbled after her, shaking with the twin forces of relief and bone-deep disappointment. He found her sitting on the wall of the lake. She had retrieved her cup and was idly dipping it into the water, pouring it out again to shatter her dark reflection. Tentatively, he sank onto the wall beside her.

"I have missed you," she said simply. "More than I can say." She watched his face for a long moment, holding his eyes with the same savor she had for the wine. At last she said, "It was true, what I told you: that I have never lain with a man."

"Not even the Pharaoh?"

"He will not have me. It is all one to me; he's a boaster and a lout, no matter how handsome he is. I have no time for him." But she turned her face away, her eyes downcast.

"Why will he not have you?"

She gave a small shrug of her shoulders. The beads in her wig clattered as she lifted her chin. "Because I am not as beautiful as other women. What does it matter? I am the God's Wife of Amun; even the High Priest does my bidding. Beauty is useless beside power."

After years apart, Senenmut was startled to realize how little she had changed. He read the lie in her voice, and saw that the lie was her shield.

"But you are beautiful, Hatshepsut." Senenmut's heart thudded; he did not know where his audacity to speak such words came from, unless they came from his knowledge of her heart, his desire that she should be happy.

She turned narrowed eyes to him, a familiar look of suspicion.

"I speak the truth. Beauty is not only a finely made face, or a slender, graceful body. No one would call a falcon beautiful – not set beside an ibis. But watch a falcon hunt – see its confidence, the power of its dive, the ferocity of its eye – and tell me, is that not a beauty all its own?" He swallowed hard, and like a fool he went on, heedless of the consequences. "You were beautiful to me, as a falcon is beautiful, when you stood on the temple steps with the knife in your hand."

She smiled, full and glowing, mouth open, nearly laughing with the pleasure of his words. And in a hot rush of madness, helpless before the loveliness of her smile, Senenmut cast himself on the mercy of her coarse beauty. Let the gods damn him if they would. The joy of her presence after so long apart was too much for a mortal man to resist. Senenmut gave voice to his heart, gladly, without regard for what was good and what was proper.

"And you are beautiful to me now. Your beauty is in your rarity; there is no woman like you in all the world. Flog me for saying it if you must, but I..."

She kissed him, long and deep. Senenmut did not push her away. The taste of her mouth, her tongue, eclipsed his senses, and he rocked helplessly in the embrace, until he lost his balance and broke from the kiss with a shout, catching himself on the lake's wall before he toppled sideways into the water.

She rose, laughing at his blunder. Her hands moved upon her own shoulder; before he could piece together the meaning of her movements the white gown fell away from her body and she stood naked in the starlight.

"Oh gods," he whispered, and would have backed away again, but the force of her presence pulled him near. She reached out her hands. This time when he grasped her wrists he pulled her fingers to the knot of his kilt. She worked at the white sash first, loosened the great loop of linen until it sagged around his hips. Something dark and heavy dropped from his sash into the garden grass. She gasped and stepped away. "Wait," he said, and bent to retrieve what had fallen. He offered the objects up to her in his palm: the bracelet of scarabs she had given him long ago, and the black braid of her side-lock.

"You kept these, all this time." She fingered the braid tentatively. Her face, downcast as she studied his treasures, held a youthful innocence that wracked him with desire, so startling was that pure, unconscious wonder set against her compelling force of presence, her frank, unashamed nudity.

"They are charms to me, magic spells."

She smiled up at him. "What kind of magic do architects use?" Her hands returned to his kilt, worked the second knot free. The linen unwound.

"We catch falcons," he said, and pulled her down into the grass.

CHAPTER TWENTY-SEVEN

H ATSHEPSUT WOKE EXHAUSTED FROM SLEEP, as she had done for half a month now. She lay pinching the bridge of her nose, groaning; her head pounded in the onslaught of morning's light. Yesterday when her duties at court and temple were finished, she had felt much too tired for entertainment and had retired with the sunset. She had not even kissed Iset or Little Tut good-night. The realization made her feel absurdly guilty; she dashed sudden tears from her eyes with rough fingers. In truth, she had not seen Iset for some time. Hatshepsut had brought Senenmut to her rooms most nights for weeks on end, as the girl was frequently closeted with the baby. She was absorbed with caring for him; she showed no interest in returning to her duties as fan-bearer. For Hatshepsut's part, it gladdened her heart to see Iset so joyful. If not for Senenmut's attentions she may have felt neglected. As it was, she was content to allow Iset her time as Mawat. But she missed the sister of her heart; there was no denying that truth. She wished for the girl's gentle hands to soothe away the headache.

Be sensible. Get out of this bed. Duty awaits.

She levered herself from her bed; a wave of nausea took her

and she gripped the headboard, choking and retching. Batiret pushed the bedchamber door open with one skinny hip. She balanced Hatshepsut's breakfast tray; Hatshepsut turned quickly from the sight, her stomach clenching.

"Go," she managed weakly. "Take it away."

Batiret sighed; she set the tray on a table and came to her mistress's aid. "Great Lady, you must eat to keep up your strength." The girl tugged at Hatshepsut's elbow, trying to lead her toward the food.

"I am fine. It was only the wine last night."

"Great Lady, you had no wine last night. You went to bed directly after your supper. You have slept many hours; you must eat, Great Lady."

"I do not want to eat. Draw my bath."

"I will do as my lady commands, after she has eaten. Look, I brought weak beer. There is beef stew if you crave savory, and honey cakes if you crave sweet."

The stew seemed strangely motivating. Hatshepsut took one faltering step toward the food, though her insides roiled. She stopped, swaying, swallowing the urge to retch.

Batiret placed her fists on her hips, for all the world like a tiny nurse. "Eat or the baby will be a weakling."

Hatshepsut stared at the girl. "I – I am not with child, Batiret."

She turned away, fetched the plate of cakes herself and offered the dish to her mistress.

"The stew," Hatshepsut said at once, squeezing her eyes closed to shut out the sight of the cloying, sticky cakes.

"My mother has many children," the girl said. "And I have many aunts, and they all have children. And two of my sisters are already mothers. I have seen eight babes born in my family already."

Hatshepsut accepted the bowl of stew from the girl's hands. She carried it back to her bed, huddled on the mattress while she sipped the thick broth. "But I cannot be with child."

Batiret had served as fan-bearer for an entire season now; Hatshepsut had come to know the girl's subtle expressions and moods well. Now she sat fussing with the breakfast tray with the raised brows and thinned, pale lips that said she had thought better of speaking her mind.

"Say what you will," Hatshepsut said warily.

"Why can you not be with child, when you spend so many evenings with the architect?"

"I hope you have never repeated that to anyone outside my chambers."

"Never, Great Lady." Batiret's answer was fiercely loyal; Hatshepsut trusted the girl. She was too intelligent to gossip.

"I am barren, Batiret. I cannot carry a child."

"I have washed your cloths myself, Great Lady. I know you have your blood." The child was too young herself for a moon's blood, and yet there she sat, scowling like a physician, speaking so matter-of-fact about washing cloths and architects.

"I have never had my blood regularly; it comes and goes without any regard for the moon. I have heard women say that such an affliction indicates barrenness."

Batiret rose, took the bowl from Hatshepsut's hands. She lifted one of her mistress's breasts; Hatshepsut winced, though the girl's touch was light.

"There; do you see? Your breasts are swollen and painful. And look how dark the nipple is."

Hatshepsut slapped her hand away. She crossed her arms over her bare chest. "You speak of the God's Wife as if she is a milk cow in the marketplace!"

Batiret shrugged. "It is the Great Lady's choice to believe her servant, or not. Either way, her belly will grow big."

It was the unshakable confidence in the girl's voice that convinced her. Hatshepsut crept from her bed again and stood before her great mirror. Batiret was right. Her breasts were noticeably fuller, and her nipples had gone astonishingly dark, the color of well-polished wood. "Amun's eyes," she swore.

Panic flooded her, erupted into her stomach to blot out all trace of nausea with an alarming tightness. "Oh – blessed Mut, what shall I do? The Pharaoh has never lain with me, Batiret. And he is in Kush, besides – far beyond my reach, even if I could seduce him. And I cannot – I cannot!"

"Peace, Great Lady. Peace."

"No – never! Thutmose despises me; he has always wanted me gone. And I have other enemies, too – the High Priest, and Ankhhor.... Now that Iset has had the child...."

Batiret clutched her hands at her own slender throat; Hatshepsut could see that her panic had terrified the girl. Perhaps she thought she was now responsible for the Great Lady's distress, having convinced her mistress of the truth of her condition. The girl's fear gave Hatshepsut a needed focus. With a great effort she smoothed her face, reached out to stroke Batiret's shoulder with a gentle, untrembling hand. "It's all right – I am all right now, good Batiret. Bring me that stew; I need to eat, as you say."

She forced the stew down her throat and into her unsteady gut. As she ate, she made Batiret recite for her the changes she could expect in her own body as the child grew. But she listened with only half her heart. The time had come for the Pharaoh to take the Great Royal Wife into his bed. More lives than her own depended upon it. Whether he would or no, Thutmose must lay with Hatshepsut.

CHAPTER TWENTY-EIGHT

HATSHEPSUT ARRIVED AT THE NEW fortress twelve days later, and never had she been so pleased to step from the deck of a ship. This had not been the stately procession she embarked upon two years ago, with ostentatious worship at every temple along the river's banks. The gods had granted her a strong, steady wind; her ship raced upstream as fast as a falcon's dive, nosing into every trough between waves along the way, jouncing upward and down a hundred times for every span it traveled forward. She slept aboard her ship when it moored at night, not at cities' quays, but in any sheltered cove or convenient eddy that presented itself. Her back was cramped and achy from the hardness of the deck's planks, and she had grown so used to the continual pitch and sway of river travel that now, on solid ground, she bobbed and stumbled on level footing, her body seeming to crave for that ever-present rocking.

Worst, though, had been the cataracts. She had watched from the prow one morning as the first came into view. The tension of the sail sent a deep, sonorous thrumming through the bones of the ship. Its vibration crept up her legs and shook her tender middle. On the horizon, the straight banks of the river seemed to fracture on many planes, ominous shards of stone surrounded by white foam. As the ship drew closer, the way ahead took on the look of two clawed hands unclasping, hard dark fingers unlacing, the river a wild chaos pouring from malevolent black palms. There was no way to sail past this obstacle; she was no sailor, yet even she could see it. Her crew furled the sail and rowed, an operation which took all day, for each stroke of the oars seemed to pull the ship ahead by only a hand's breadth, and often she had the sensation that they were slipping backward, that in a heartbeat they would be washed all the way back to Waset, in spite of the men rowing tirelessly against the current.

When at last they had cleared the cataract the sun was sinking in the western sky. The captain anchored early and doled out stronger beer than usual to the crew. Hatshepsut did not begrudge them their rest and their reward. The way the boat had shuddered and heeled as they passed between those terrible rocks, she found herself yearning for some strong beer herself.

They made their way past three more such treacherous passages. At the final two, the banks were level enough that most of the crew disembarked and towed the boat past the rapids on several thick lines. Hatshepsut, despite their insistence that the Great Lady remain aboard, had taken to the land to walk the length of the cataracts. That fearful frothing and hissing of the water, the smack of the chopping waves pummeling the boat's hull, the fountains of angry foam spraying onto the deck – it was all more than she cared to face a third and fourth time. Her stomach was still uncertain in the mornings, and she did not wish to give the sailors a show by vomiting over the rail while they towed her southward.

The fortress rose bright and strong on the western bank, situated on a rocky promontory with a commanding view of river, valley, and desert. New-quarried stone gleamed in the sun. It was magnificently built, three watch-towers, a high wall, and a low barracks and stable within, roomy enough to hold a hundred men and twice as many horses. Not quite half those numbers occupied it now, but as Thutmose came into his power and continued the work their father had begun, it would fill to capacity and make the southern border ever more secure, and ready the lands of Kush for Egypt's inevitable advance. And it was due to her own wisdom in dealing with Retjenu that this fortress had come to be. She nodded gravely toward its walls as if the fortress had saluted her, raised its stony palms to her presence in thanks. *Mine,* she thought, watching tiny dark men move along its walls, gesture from its towers. *I made this come to pass. It is mine.*

Beyond the fortress, in an open grassland a short distance to the south, the Pharaoh's camp stretched in the sun, lazy as a garden cat. The keening of pipes skirled above the din of quay and fortress. She followed the sound to the great tent at the heart of the encampment, a tall pavilion of blue and white cloth peaked by a massive cedar pole, its walls undulating lightly in the river wind. Around its edges clustered the tents of his guards, his advisors, his horse-keepers and huntsmen, the dancers and musicians and servants who entertained him. The grasses all about his camp lay flattened, crushed into mud, rutted by the wheels of chariots and hand-carts. Here in this rough country there were no litters to carry her, but she paid no mind to the mud that flecked her feet and dulled the brightness of her sandals.

The guards on Thutmose's pavilion bowed hastily when they saw her emerge from the mill of the camp crowd. She gestured them aside. When they hesitated, Nehesi shoved between them, held the flap of the tent wide for her to enter. From its cool, dark depths came the scent of roasted meat and onions. Her mouth watered. She had eaten sparingly that morning, fearing to vomit; now, as her eyes adjusted to the dimness she found the joint of beef on its bed of ruddy, wine-soaked onions as keenly as the hawk finds the hare. Beyond the food, Thutmose crouched on a gilded throne, gaping at her. She could practically hear the tiny child within her crying for the meat. Her hunger was suddenly terrible, driving. She pushed into the tent and made directly for Thutmose's table. Without a word of greeting to the king, she tore a piece of meat from the bone. It was tender, dripping with red juice, invitingly warm in her hand. She bit into it and eyed her husband, eyebrows raised in an ironic reflection of his own surprise.

"Good meat," she said, mouth full. "You surely took the best cooks out of Waset."

"What are you doing here?"

"I missed my husband. I craved for his company." She sucked her fingers, licked the savory juice from her palm, then helped herself to another piece. "Is that so difficult to believe?"

Thutmose said nothing, only watched in disgust as she ate through several handfuls of beef as quickly as she could. A serving woman appeared with a carved chair – not as beautiful as Thutmose's throne, to be sure, but suitable. Hatshepsut lowered herself into the seat and turned her attention to the onions. At last the ferocity of her hunger was somewhat tamed. "In truth, I wanted to see the new fortress. It was I who commissioned it, I who found the goods to pay for it. Why shouldn't I see it with my own eyes?"

"Then why didn't you sail south with me when I left Waset?"

"The moods and whims of women," she replied, shrugging. "What news in the south?"

Thutmose sighed. He plucked the linen towel from his own lap and flung it at her; she snatched it from the air, dabbed primly at her mouth. "Scouts have reported Kushite raiding parties in the hills to the west and south, but they seem intimidated by the activity here at the garrison. They have not attempted an advance. It's impossible for anyone to get a clear idea of their numbers, but these Kushite forces are always disorganized. Their numbers hardly matter. They could scarce stand against Egypt before the fortress. Now they may as well be a fly attacking a bull. How long are you planning to stay?"

"Why, my dear brother, I could almost believe that you are not happy to see me. No, don't fret. There is work that needs doing in Waset. The Hathor Festival needs planning, and the harvest will be in soon. I would hear the tallies from the overseers myself. If I do not see to these things, who will? Surely not you."

He scowled at her. "How is my son?"

Hatshepsut smiled. "Well. Strong. He grows faster than you would believe. He was crawling when I left Waset. His nurses say he will learn to stand before long, and if the gods smile on him he'll soon have a few words in his mouth, too."

She loved the boy. She could not hide the fact. To think the small shimmer of life inside her would soon be a baby as lively, as real as Little Tut. She resisted placing her hands upon her stomach. Instead she reached for more meat to feed the child. *It demands meat...he demands meat.* Surely a babe that craved for flesh so intensely must be male. She drew in an apprehensive breath. Never before had she considered what might become of Little Tut and Iset if she, Hatshepsut, bore a son. *I cannot think on that now. Not now. I must do the work set before me here, in this place, on this day. Protect the child first – protect Senenmut, protect myself. Once that is done, time enough to worry over the rest.* Heirs were not always chosen from the obvious stock of children. Had not her own father, a commonborn soldier, been raised up as Pharaoh in the face of great need?

Thutmose stood, stretched. A scurry of servants appeared from the tent's shadows and cleared away the remains of his meal. "I am going out riding with the fort's general. I'll tell my servants to see that you are given the finest bed in the harem tent."

"The harem tent?"

"Of course. You don't expect the Pharaoh to travel without a few of his favorite women to entertain him, do you?"

Since siring his son, the king had most definitely grown into a man's appetites. "I am the Great Royal Wife. I do not sleep in a harem tent."

"You do not sleep with me, either. I can only imagine you kick like a donkey in your sleep. I will not suffer it. Don't scowl so, sister. The harem tent is much finer than my own, believe me, and the women will be honored to entertain you. Now I must go. In a few hours the light will have faded too much for driving in the hills. I shall see you for the evening meal, I suppose."

Thutmose ducked through the tent's doorway. It rippled in the breeze of his passing while Hatshepsut sat wordless, staring at the place where the king had been.

THUTMOSE'S MOBILE HAREM CONSISTED OF SIX WOMEN HAND-picked by the king himself. Tabiry, dark-skinned with a full mouth, always smiling, was the most senior of the six, and she had taken on something of the role of leader. Dressed in a gauzy blue gown, belted and gemmed with baubles impractical for travel, she bowed Hatshepsut into the harem tent. It was, as Thutmose had said, far more pleasant than his own. Its walls of red cloth cast a warm, soothing glow upon the interior. A thin cedar pole held the peaked roof high; the circular smoke flap at its apex was drawn back, and a shaft of daylight fell into the pavilion, setting a column of motes to shining. In the center of the tent a great mattress of goose down lay upon a reed-woven platform. Cushions of silk and soft sheets of linen lay scattered across the mattress. Small braziers stood to either side, unlit at this hour but well blackened from the regular burning of oil for light and incense for mood. Hatshepsut could well imagine the frolics that took place between those braziers. Arrayed along the tent's rear wall were six modest beds and stacks of traveling chests, no doubt containing more wispy gowns, jewels, and other necessities of travel.

Each of the six women was hardly dressed at all, but wore the lightest, most open weaves, their young bodies on full display. Beside them, Hatshepsut felt rather a poor excuse for a Great Lady in her travel-rumpled dress of a sturdy, serviceable weight. *I am as plain as a servant compared to them.* But Tabiry and her women paid no heed to her dress, except to coax her out of it. They sent for a large basin of water, washed the grime of travel from her body with their own hands while she stood in the shaft of golden light at the tent's heart. Tabiry dressed her in one of her own fine gowns, and as the afternoon edged toward evening, Hatshepsut lay upon the great central mattress with the harem women, playing senet and laughing to the quiet accompaniment of a flute.

She cringed as Tabiry took two of her pawns. "You play a vicious game, Lady Tabiry. Do you ever challenge the Pharaoh to senet?"

"He hasn't much heart for senet, Great Lady." Tabiry's voice was rich and musical, reverberating in her lovely throat like two harp strings chiming together.

"We play other games with the king." Rekhetre was a pale girl, freckled, her face startlingly sharp beneath the fringe of her wig. Her body was lithe, almost boyish; Hatshepsut liked her small, impudent breasts with their pale pointed nipples.

"Does the Pharaoh always bring the six of you when he travels?"

"Usually," Tabiry said. "We have the heart for it – for living in tents, for being uprooted. Not all the women of the harem could be satisfied with such a life."

Rekhetre rolled onto her back, stretched her thin arms above her head. "And we get along well with each other."

"The Pharaoh is lucky in you; I can see that." She studied the senet board, making as if she were musing over her next move. But her thoughts were all for the confinement of this tent. She must not spend the night here, lovely and welcoming as it may be. "Do you suppose he will visit us tonight?"

The women seemed to hold their breath as she skipped her pawn across the board. At last Tabiry cleared her throat. "I do not think so, Great Lady. No doubt he will be tired from his ride in the hills."

Surely the gods themselves could not conceive of a chariot ride taxing enough to keep a fourteen-year-old king from enjoying six women at once. Hatshepsut did not need to hear the real reason. Tabiry was too tactful by half to speak it aloud. *The king does not love you. He would rather stay far away.*

So she must contrive her own way into his bed. Very well. Thutmose may have no stomach for the senet board, but Hatshepsut was rather a keen player. She claimed two of Tabiry's pawns herself and waited for the woman's next move, smiling.

CHAPTER TWENTY-NINE

HATSHEPSUT LET HERSELF INTO THUTMOSE'S tent while the last red glow of the evening still lingered on the western horizon. The Pharaoh was just finishing to tie on a fresh kilt; the old one, dulled with the dust of the surrounding hills, lay draped over one of the carved chests at the foot of his bed.

"How was your ride, husband?"

He looked up sharply at the sound of her voice, but when he saw her, standing in the light of an oil lamp, his mouth relaxed from its habitual scowl. She stood wrapped in Tabiry's delicate gown, a fall of open blue linen as light as eastern silk, through which her breasts and navel showed plainly. The harem women had adorned her with their gems, singing love songs as they slid golden cuffs onto her arms, rings onto each finger, a stylish wig of long, thin braids onto her head. They had painted her face and scented her body with an air of happy conspiracy, whispering advice on how best to please the Pharaoh. It had been easy to secure their complicity once she had admitted to them how she suffered in her loneliness, how her heart longed day and night for the love of her brave and handsome husband, but alas, the duties of his reign kept them always apart, and she remained a virgin, heartbroken and untouched. Finally, unable to sleep for the torment of her ceaseless yearning, she had sailed south to the Pharaoh's bed.

One of them, Keminub, much given to dreamy sighs and fits of wistfulness, had tears in her wide, earnest eyes by the time Hatshepsut finished confiding her tragic tale. "He will be unable to resist you, Great Lady." Keminub had fastened the necklace at Hatshepsut's throat and stood back to appraise her virginal beauty. "Go to him; you will see. You will fall into his arms and be a maiden no more!"

Thutmose stared at her, and did not answer. Neither did he smile to see her, dressed as beautifully as any of his six pets. But he did not frown, and she took that for a small victory. She came toward him, walking slowly to make her hips sway, as Tabiry had shown her. "Your ride – it was good, I trust?"

"Er – yes. The general is a good man, very wise and brave. We talked...we talked of the garrison's capabilities, and its needs. We shall need to find fifty more men at least before the general is satisfied, but I still say the Kushites are no real danger here." He stared at her breasts as he spoke.

"You said you would see me for supper, and here I am."

"My servants will be along with the food shortly." He looked thoughtful, considering her hips, her thighs through the sheer blue mist of her dress. "Why are you dressed that way? I have never seen you wear the like before."

"I wanted to make your evening pleasant; that is all. Shouldn't a wife do these things for her husband?"

Thutmose raised his eyes to her own, squinting warily as if he might discern her true purpose in her face.

"Look, Thutmose. You and I have been at odds since we were children. But we are not children anymore; we are the Pharaoh and the Great Royal Wife. We have a land to rule together." She reached out, made herself touch his arm, run her fingers down the soft skin on the inside until his shoulders tensed. "It is time we set our quarrels aside. Don't you agree?"

He waited, considering her words. "You do look nicer than usual. The color suits you. And when you paint your face like that, it's softer and more appealing."

She forced a smile. "Thank you."

"I have never noticed your body before, but it's..." he lifted his hands, made a rapid gesture, empty palms fluttering as thought he juggled words, searching for the right one. "...It's womanly."

"I am a maiden," she said, unable to keep a touch of irony from her voice, "beautiful and blooming."

The voice of one of Thutmose's guards carried into the tent. A moment later the doorway opened. A line of servants entered bearing the Pharaoh's supper. On their heels came Hatshepsut's contribution to the night's pleasures: the musicians Thutmose had brought from Waset, carrying their harps and drums, bowing to the royal couple as they passed, and behind them, Thutmose's six pets. Tabiry gave Hatshepsut a knowing, smoky-eyed smile. She took up her place near the musicians, and as the meal began she danced.

She lacked Iset's natural, pristine grace, but Tabiry's dancing held a coarse sensuality that Hatshepsut found alluring. The music seemed to twist around her body, to interweave with the brush of her thighs, the sway of her breasts. Her arms lifted, open, inviting, gleaming with gold; her glistening lips were parted as if she must catch her breath. She moved from one pool of lamplight to another, her dark skin sparkling and dimming, and as she crossed the pavilion, turning and rocking, Thutmose's eyes followed where she went. Hatshepsut filled his cup with wine.

When Tabiry's dance was done, Rekhetre and Keminub took her place, executing an intricate performance in which they spun a colorful veil between them, passed it hand to hand, linking arms so that it became impossible to follow, in the blur of the fabric, which woman held it at any given moment. As they whipped the veil about their bodies, stepping this way and that, they often drew so close together that their buttocks or breasts touched. Each time, Thutmose leaned toward them eagerly.

As the women took their turns entertaining the Pharaoh, Hatshepsut encouraged his arousal with a hand laid on his arm, her thigh pressed against his, her fingers trailing for a moment along the back of his neck. And she kept his wine cup in his hand. He warmed to her caresses; she stroked him more the more he drank, and withheld her hand when he ceased his drinking to eat or to make some snide remark about Hatshepsut's own inadequacy as a dancer. She paid no mind to his returning belligerence. It was a sign of his intoxication. She let her hand creep to the hem of his kilt, pushed it back to stroke along the length of his thigh. It could hardly be simpler to train a hound to hunt.

Thutmose raised his cup in salute to pale-eyed Itaweret, who had just finished singing; he giggled when the wine sloshed onto the tabletop. Tabiry leaned close to Hatshepsut. She whispered, "Too much wine, Great Lady, and he'll drop his spear and find himself unable to pick it up again."

The sight of Tabiry leaning into Hatshepsut's ear sparked a sly flame in Thutmose's eye. He gestured to Rekhetre and Itaweret. They seemed to know exactly what the Pharaoh desired; they hurried into a pool of lamplight and immediately began to kiss, twining their arms about one another, their hips and breasts pressing together in a show of urgency that made Hatshepsut's eyebrows raise in spite of herself. She watched with near as much avidity as the Pharaoh as Rekhetre pulled Itaweret to the pavilion floor and pressed her mouth between the other woman's thighs. Itaweret's hips rose from the floor; her back arched and she cried out, a song of pleasure so intense that Hatshepsut caught her breath. The sudden throb of her pulse pounded in her own loins. The other women joined, one by one, until the pavilion floor was a tangle of smooth limbs, of backs curving with the tension of desire. The scent of the women's bodies filled the tent, a warm spice that eclipsed the deep, lulling odor of myrrh and the tang of spilled wine. Thutmose looked down on the show and laughed, the triumph of command on his face. Hatshepsut could see, in his glinting, wine-glazed eyes, that more than the show itself, it was his power that inflamed him – his unquestioned ability to demand this performance from the women, the certainty that they would give him anything he pleased – and all because of the crown he wore.

She stood and removed his hand from the wine cup. Thutmose looked up at her, his face still slightly rounded by youth, reddened by wine. His expression clouded for a moment with boyish uncertainty. Then he seemed to recall himself, his crown, his power. He lurched to his feet. His kilt could not conceal his eagerness.

"I knew you'd come around," he said, the words indistinct. "Grew up thinking you were a boy, sister, but now you will see what a real man can do!"

"No doubt I will." She pulled him toward his bed.

"Ready, aren't you? Finally ready for me to make you a woman?"

Hatshepsut snapped her fingers; Tabiry looked up from the floor, looked up from between Keminub's breasts. At Hatshepsut's gesture she shook the women apart, led them toward the Pharaoh's bed.

Hatshepsut let Thutmose fall onto his linens. She stood back, watching with some amusement as the women gathered around him, bending to their task. Keminub was the last to approach the bed, and Hatshepsut seized her by the arm, making a show of sudden innocent terror.

"Oh, Keminub! I cannot do it. My poor heart – I am only a wilting girl inside. I saw his manhood through his kilt. He will wound me; I'll never stop bleeding!"

"No, no, sister," Keminub said. "You sailed all the way from Waset for this moment. It doesn't hurt – believe me."

"I'll be braver if I can watch first. You do it first, and later, when he is roused again, I will do what you do."

Keminub glanced at Thutmose, doubtful. He clasped Rekhetre to him, his mouth wet and insistent on her breast. "I do not know whether he will rouse again. He's had so much wine..."

"He will. I will see to it. You must go first, I beg you! It is all so new to me; I don't know what to do. Oh, please!"

The women surrounded the bed now, embracing one another, stooping to kiss the Pharaoh where he lay. "Where is my sister?" came Thutmose's voice from among the tangle of their bodies. She could see nothing of him but two feet and part of an arm; now and then his arm raised as he cupped a breast or pinched this woman or that, eliciting a squeal. "She wants me. She wants me to show her what a man can do! Bring my sister!"

"What a man can do...do you hear?" Hatshepsut clasped trembling hands at her throat. "I must learn first, Keminub, or I'll be wounded! I am the Great Royal Wife, and I command you. You must!"

"Very well, Great Lady. I will do as you command."

Keminub pushed past the fray. Hatshepsut watched as her head and shoulders rose above the other women. Thutmose's visible feet jerked and quivered; his shouts for Hatshepsut were cut off at once. Keminub bounced two, three times, and Thutmose grunted, sighed. The women stopped their work and stood back. Tabiry looked around at Hatshepsut, her eyes wide and questioning. But Hatshepsut nodded her approval, and Keminub slid from the bed. She wiped between her legs with a corner of the Pharaoh's bed-sheet. Sprawled on the bed, Thutmose drifted into sleep.

"Leave us," Hatshepsut said.

When they had gone, bowing and murmuring, she undressed and climbed carefully into bed beside her husband. He grumbled and rolled, taking most of the sheets with him. Hatshepsut jerked them from his grasp and settled in, suddenly exhausted.

The sounds of the encampment woke them at daybreak: the voices of Thutmose's guards talking low as they paced the perimeter of his tent, the strike of flint and bronze to start the cook fires. At the eastern edge of the camp a horse whinnied, and from inside the fortress walls three more answered, distant and thin.

Thutmose stirred, sat up, and pressed hands to his temples. "Gods," he moaned.

"Good morning, husband."

He gasped, glared down at her. His eyes were red-rimmed.

"Last night," she said, "the Pharaoh showed me what a man can do."

CHAPTER THIRTY

HATSHEPSUT ENTERED THE HAREM TENT when the sun had just begun to climb free of the eastern hills. Dressed once more in her simple traveling frock, she held Tabiry's blue gown carefully. Wrapped in its folds were the jewels and wig she had worn the night before.

"I came to say my farewell," she told the women. "And to thank you – especially you, Keminub. Thanks to your example, I am a virgin no more, and my heart is full, knowing that my husband loves me well."

Tabiry took the bundle from her hands. She chuckled with relief. "Then it worked. I wasn't sure, when I saw Keminub climb aboard him. I wasn't sure he would even wake again, as much wine as he'd drunk, much less rise. I am glad to hear it, Great Lady."

"Won't you stay a few days more?" Rekhetre held out a bowl of figs, but Hatshepsut waved them away. Her stomach was tender again.

"I cannot. There is much to be done in Waset – the Hathor Festival, you know. I hope the lot of you will return by then. I should like to see you again soon. You have been good to me, and I am pleased."

"Oh, certainly," Tabiry said. "I am sure the Pharaoh would not miss the festival. He loves..."

The sound of men shouting rang outside the tent walls, a sudden, clamoring urgency. Nehesi burst through the tent door, his sword half-drawn.

"With me, Great Lady. Now!"

"Nehesi, what is it?"

"Follow me to the ship. I'll put you aboard and the captain will take you out into the river where you'll be safe."

"Safe from what?" She followed him outside. The rising sun shone bright; she squinted into a confusion of white kilts flashing as men ran from tent to tent, fumbling sword belts about their hips. She glanced toward the fortress. A line of men stood along the top of the nearest wall, spears at the ready. From one of the towers a horn blared.

"Oh gods," Keminub wailed. The women gathered behind her, clutching one another. "It's the Kushites. Look!"

A band of men scurried down the face of the nearest hill; a sheet of pallid dust rose behind them. The soldiers of Thutmose's camp ranged to meet them. The gate of the fortress opened, but the fortress was a half mile or more from the encampment, and Thutmose's soldiers were few. The Kushite troop would be on them long before the garrison could intervene. She spun on her heel, looking for the Pharaoh. *There* – before his blue-and-white pavilion! He clambered into a chariot and took up the reins while two men still worked to secure the horses' trappings.

"Nehesi, take these women to the boat. Put it out into the river, well beyond bow-shot."

"You're coming with me." He made as if to seize her arm, but she stepped back, her eyes cold with command.

"I gave you an order, Nehesi!"

"Great Lady," he said, a note of pleading in his voice. But she sprinted for the Pharaoh's chariot before he could say more.

When her weight landed on the platform beside him, Thutmose yelped, then glared when he recognized his sister. "Get out of here, Hatshepsut."

"And go where? Wait inside your tent for a Kushite blade to come cut me from it? I think not."

Thutmose shouted to his horses; they lurched for the eastern edge of camp, toward the river, spraying mud from their hooves. Hatshepsut grabbed the rail with both hands. The wheels slammed into the rut of a cart-track and her wig flew from her head, into the crowd of servants who leapt from the chariot's path.

"You're going the wrong way!"

"Shut your mouth!"

"Name of Amun, Thutmose, where is your sword?" She saw now that he wore nothing at his belt, not even a dagger. "I thought you were going to drive out with your men, fight the raiders!"

Thutmose did not answer. He made the edge of the camp where the ground firmed, unchurned by so many feet, and slapped the reins against the horses' flanks. They lengthened their stride, speeding along the river bank.

"You coward! Turn this chariot and fight!"

Thutmose drove intently for the southern edge of the plain. He said nothing, did not so much as glance around at her admonishment. She reached for the reins and managed to lay hold of one; she tore it from his hand, struggled to turn the horses. Thutmose slapped at her, shoved her shoulder, struck her face until she nearly lost her balance. She let go of the rein and resumed her grip on the rail.

"Thutmose! Listen to me – *listen!* You are the king. What will it do to your men to see you fleeing from a fight? You will lose it all, Thutmose – their loyalty, and mine. Turn this chariot now and fight!"

The grass of the plain gave way to the dry, stony earth of the hills. The horses grunted and snorted as they struggled up the incline. Thorny brush hissed along the sides of the chariot, snicked in the spokes of its wheels.

"You know why they've attacked. They saw your tent. They knew you were here. They mean to kill you. Men will die defending you while you hide like a child."

"I am the Pharaoh; it is their duty to die in my defense."

"Are you? Even this woman would stay and fight, and yet the *Pharaoh* flees."

He dropped the rein again and hit her in the mouth. She shouted, wordless, full of rage, tasting the blood from her split lip but never feeling the pain.

At the crown of the hill he slowed the horses to pick his way behind a crest of exposed red rock. They were high above the valley now. The tents were spots of color against the open wound of muddied land, and the fortress's walls seemed too low, too fragile from this distance. She could see the army advancing from the fortress's gates, crawling across the plain to where the Pharaoh's few soldiers met the Kushite force in a ragged, straggling line. In the river, her ship crept under oar to the safety of the open water. She hoped the harem women were aboard. Her heart beat painfully in her ears, throbbed in her head, wigless and exposed as it was to the strengthening sun. Her pulse pounded a hot rhythm in her swollen lip. She stared about desperately, trying to find something to inspire her brother to return and fight.

Below the hill to the east, a dry gully leveled out at the edge of the plain. She followed the scar of it into the heart of the hills, to where its walls lengthened and darkened, exposing stern faces of the same sharp stone that had daunted her at the cataracts. From deep in the ravine a banner of dust wended up into the sky, thin at first, but growing larger, wider.

"Name of Amun," she said. "Thutmose, look! There's another Kushite force there – the ravine!"

Thutmose peered at the wall of dust, whimpering.

"We have to warn them! The garrison will close with the first group of Kushites and your camp and the garrison's rear will be exposed to the attack!"

Thutmose clutched at his belly. His face was pale.

"There's no time to be sick. Go! Back to the camp; warn them! Thutmose, you must!"

He shook his head.

"By the gods," she said, the words thick in her mouth, heavy with disgust. "Are you our father's son, or am I?" She raised her foot to his belly and thrust hard. He toppled backward from the chariot, grunting as he fell into the dust.

Hatshepsut seized the reins. It had been years since she had driven a chariot; she sent a brief prayer to Amun that the skill would return to her, and quickly. She hissed the horses down the slope, giving them their heads, trusting the gods to guide them past rocks, around the hidden burrows of desert rats. As she rode, the wind stealing her breath, the dust stinging tears into her eyes, she watched the betraying banner of the advancing Kushites. Their number must be great, to raise such a trail. But her horses were swift, and the gods were good. In a rattle of wheels, a tumult of hooves and the guttural grunts of her straining horses, he pulled ahead of the ambush, and ahead yet more. By the time she reached the level plain the ravine was well behind her. She whooped at the horses, sent them flying all the faster along the river, past the encampment, past the fearful din of the fight at its western edge. She did not draw rein until she had intercepted the first chariot from the fortress. Her horses stood blowing, lathered, trembling with the effort.

"General," she shouted. "A Kushite force from the south, from the heart of the hills!"

The general stared at her, startled, as his foot troops approached behind him. He seemed about to question her, but his eyes drifted beyond to the ravine in the southern hills.

"Sekhmet's teats," he swore. "Change course," he bellowed, gesturing with his spear to the south. "Ambush! Change course!"

The Egyptian force surged around her, past her. She fumbled the reins as her horses screamed and danced, and then the army rushed beyond her, charging to the exposed, vulnerable flank of Thutmose's camp.

A dark hand laid hold of her horse's bridle. "Nehesi!" His sword was drawn, his small shield slung over one shoulder. He pulled himself into the chariot.

"To the fortress," he said. "And this time, do not argue."

FROM THE NEAREST TOWER, SHE WATCHED AS THE GARRISON ringed the camp, met the raiders with a clash of bronze, a shout of anger and hatred, a sound that rang and carried across the distance to her ears. Nehesi tore linen from his kilt, soaked it with water from a soldier's discarded skin. He dabbed at her broken lip.

Hatshepsut stared beyond her guardsman's shoulder to the battle. A tent had caught fire; the smoke obscured the field, and she growled in her impotent fury, waving her hands in desperation as if she might clear the view, as if she could will the Egyptians to victory if only she could see.

"Easy," Nehesi said. "This lip is bad. Let me clean it."

She winced. Suddenly she could feel the pain of it, and she burned with hatred for Thutmose.

"We must go out to them. We must help."

"And what can you do for them, begging your pardon, Great Lady? You are seventeen, and a woman."

"I can fight." Tears flooded her eyes. The field obscured further, bled into a mess of smoke and brilliant color, the banners and blood of men. "I will fight! Give me a spear; I will kill them all, every last Kushite! I could do it. I could."

"I know."

The eerie brazen wail of a Kushite horn sounded. And again, a quavering call. Nehesi made an abrupt sound, part laugh, part grunt. "They're sounding the retreat. We have beaten them, Lady!"

Hatshepsut dashed the tears from her eyes. She leaned from the tower, across the parapet, the rough new stone pressing the breath from her lungs. A breeze lifted on the river, and the smoke moved into the hills, sluggish and dark. Several tents had collapsed and two had burned, but the Pharaoh's striped pavilion still stood. The Egyptian forces had drawn into a tight ring around the pavilion. Bodies lay scattered across the plain. And far beyond the remains of the encampment, a ragged band of men made for the mouth of the ravine, pursued by a handful of chariots.

She turned from the scene, her body tingling with relief. She shook violently as the madness of the battle left her, leaving in its place a watery, dizzy weakness. She laughed, threw herself into Nehesi's arms. He supported her down the tower steps, into the fortress's yard, through the gate. A lone chariot drove to meet them: the general, who reined his horses to a stop, leapt to the ground and raised both his palms to her in awed salute.

"Great Lady," he said. "The gods alone know how many men you saved today. At the pace we were moving, we would never have seen the ambush before it had taken our rear."

She did not know what to say. She stood leaning on her guardsman, blinking at the general. Suddenly aware that she had lost her wig, she raised a trembling hand to her head, self-conscious and overwhelmed.

"Come, Great Lady. This battle is yours."

Nehesi helped her into the chariot. Her knees felt on the verge of collapse; she held tight to the rail, swaying. The general drove at a trot toward the ring of Egyptians, toward the king's pavilion. She raised a pale hand to the army, and they shook their spears at the sky, roaring their acclaim. The sound invigorated her. When the general halted she stepped into the mud without his assistance. She raised both arms above her head, a salute to Egypt's brave men; they shouted her name. *Hatshepsut! Hatshepsut! The God's Wife, Hatshepsut!*

The general conferred with a few of his men. At his nod, the ring of soldiers parted. On the bare ground before the Pharaoh's tent a handful of Kushites knelt, their arms lashed behind their backs, their heads downcast, the points of Egyptian spears pressed to their backs.

"They are yours." The general leaned close to her ear. She could scarcely hear his words over the sound of her own name in half a hundred throats. "Your captives." He thrust the nearest Kushite onto his belly, face in the mud. Hatshepsut approached, watched the bound man at her feet as he struggled then lay still. The soldiers fell silent. Then she raised her foot and placed it upon the Kushite's head, the symbolic gesture of the king conquering his enemy.

Amidst the roar of her soldiers' approval, Hatshepsut glanced across the crowd. Thutmose had made his way out of the hills on foot, bedraggled and limping. He froze when their eyes met, tense and twitching, a lion in a crouch. Never before had Hatshepsut seen such a look of hatred on her brother's face.

CHAPTER THIRTY-ONE

S ENENMUT WAITED IN THE SHADOW of a great pillar. His lady's voice carried across the great hall, detailing her plans, her expectations for the Hathor Festival to come. From where he stood he could not see her seated on her small throne, the Pharaoh's own golden chair empty beside her. He preferred to lean there in the umber dimness, the cool carved stone against his skin, and listen to the music of her voice. It was an unlovely music, he knew. She lacked the refined timbre, the delicate inflection of a lady of the court. When she spoke it was with the brazen blare of a soldier's horn, sharp and command-ing. But was that not music all the same, surely as the sound of harp or pipe or flute? He liked this game of isolating her to but one of his senses. Gladly he worked at the task of her, memo-rizing each of her facets. This was the way her voice rose when she issued a decree, a sharp ascent, sure and swift, an arrow shot toward the sun; this the way it settled again as she pondered the advice of her stewards, their scrolls of tallies and sums. His lady's voice moved like a ship at full sail, taut with power, smooth and confident.

At last her business concluded and, anticipating the change

in her tone, he stepped from the shadows at the very moment she said, "And where is the Steward of the God's Wife?"

"Here, Great Lady." The sound of his new title was sweet in his ears. He walked to the foot of the dais, eyes on the floor. He did not need to look at her face to know that no hint of a smile showed there. None would, until they were alone together. He kept his own face humble, willing, as was proper for a steward.

"I have business with you, but the evening is growing late. Walk with me in my garden, and we will discuss what we must discuss."

He bowed, waited for her to descend the steps of her dais, sweep past him with an air of stern command. He followed her in silence, and the scent of myrrh and spice fell from her body. He walked in that intoxicating current all the way to her private chambers.

In her dusk-blue garden, when she had dismissed her women, he held his arms wide so that she might press herself into his embrace. The braids of her wig brushed his lips; she pulled back, exposing her big, bright teeth in a grin of triumph.

"I cannot tell you how I missed you, Senenmut. Oh, I wish you could have seen it."

"The new fortress?"

"Everything." And she led him to the red granite bench beneath the sycamore. Bats flitted among its sighing branches as she told him of her trek south, of Thutmose's camp, of her victory over the Kushite raiders.

He shook his head at her, laughing. "The gods never made a man as bold as you, I swear it."

"And you? How have you kept yourself occupied this past month, with me away? Not with the court ladies, I hope."

"Those wigs hanging on empty air? No. I have been overseeing the gateway at Ipet-Isut. It is nearly done now; I think you will be pleased. And I have been talking with tomb-builders, gathering information on a particular site across the river. You ought to have a tomb built, you know – a monument to your achievements."

"I am not planning to die any time soon."

"Nor is anybody. It will take a lifetime to build something worthy of your memory; best start now."

"And have you found a suitable place?"

"I may have. I need to survey it yet. The valley in the western cliffs, where you and I went years ago, when you sent me away..." He broke off. In the tree's dappled shadow and moonlight, he caught her expression of regret, of pensiveness bordering on sorrow. "You're not still upset about that, are you? I've forgotten it; you should, too."

"No – no, it's not that. I was only thinking." She looked away, out across her flower beds and hedges to the palace's outer wall. She stared at it with such intensity that he thought for a moment she could see through the stone. He waited for her to speak on. "Thutmose hates me, Senenmut. He would see me dead and in my tomb, if he could."

"The two of you have never been especially close, but surely he does not hate you. Not like that." *Not enough to kill her – no, gods, never.*

"You should have seen the way he looked at me, Senenmut, when I trampled the Kushites under my heel. He disliked me before, but now...."

Senenmut took her in his arms. Her breath warmed his shoulder. "You have nothing to fear. He is the Pharaoh, yes, but still a boy. You are the God's Wife of Amun. You have the priesthood behind you, the High Priest himself...."

"Nebseny. Yes, I have him, all right; I made sure of that."

"Thutmose is a child who runs from a fight. His soldiers saw him run, and they saw you ride to their salvation. They saw you take the Kushites under your heel. Even his men are with you, Hatshepsut. You have nothing to fear."

His words soothed her, he saw, though he knew she was too

bright to remain mollified for long. Soon she would begin turning his words over in her heart. She would ask herself the same question he pondered now. *What happens when the Pharaoh grows, and is no longer a boy? Can the priests of Amun protect her from a powerful man's hatred? Can I?*

Hatshepsut stood abruptly, a restless movement, a reined horse tossing its head, longing to run. "I think," she said, "that I was wrong after all, to give up my birthright and marry him. To be the Great Royal Wife, and not the Pharaoh."

Senenmut stilled himself, his thoughts, his heartbeat. How easy it would be to leap to his feet and agree with her. She was the true son of Thutmose the First, inheritor of his courage, his strength of will. Anyone could see it. And yet....

"Maat is maat," he said, apologetic, loathing the words, loathing their truth.

She looked back at him, held his gaze for a long moment. Her eyes were deep and black and sad. "Maat is all." She turned away, brushed past a hedge of night-blooming flowers, waxy and white. In a moment he heard her running footsteps receding into the night.

He followed, down paths blue in the moonlight. Always she was just ahead of him, turning, vanishing into the dark beyond a flower bed. Her flight troubled him, raised in his heart some unaccountable anxiety, as though she might run so far and so fast that he could never catch her again. Then he heard her laughter rise from the darkness, and suddenly they were children at play. He rounded a corner; his foot caught on some sudden obstacle; he fell onto the grass. As he rolled, groaning and chuckling, she sprang from the hedge where she had been hiding.

"You tripped me!"

She fell upon him, straddling his hips. When she leaned down to kiss him, her wig slipped, fell onto his face. She went weak with laughter; he rolled her onto her back and lay atop her.

"This is not maat," she said, serious and stern all at once. The note of the trumpet was in her voice again. Senenmut pulled away. He lay beside her on the grass, hands at his sides, staring hopelessly up at the stars. "But I do not care," she said at last.

He turned his face to look at her. Tears shone in her eyes.

"My father always told me that maat was everything, that it was the very soul of the sun, the essence that created life. What has maat given me – given us?"

"Us?"

"Not only you and me – all of Egypt. Thutmose on the throne – a Pharaoh who runs from his enemies. A child-king whose only cares to play with his harem pets. Maat has left me isolated – left me to fight for my station while some northern tjati plots to strip it from me. It has left me to fortify our borders when my husband cannot be bothered to even know where the borders lie! It has left me to see to the court, to worship, to justice – alone!" She knelt above him, took his face in cold, hard hands. "If I were Pharaoh – if I had had the strength to claim the throne when I should have, you would be my Great Royal Husband. Don't laugh! I would have made it so. Who would have dared stop me?"

"The priests of Amun, for one. And all the nobility for another. Even a Pharaoh cannot act without some restraint."

She sagged into the grass. "I know. I know it's hopeless even to think of it. It always was hopeless, no matter what my mother thought. Ahmose and her useless visions." They both lay silent, empty as forgotten vessels. Senenmut watched the moon slide in among the branches of the sycamore, a slow and inevitable sinking.

Hatshepsut reached for him. His hand moved to intercept hers; their fingers laced together. She whispered, "But I still do not care. About maat."

And in one quick movement she was atop him again, her face eclipsing the moon. Its light limned her in silver, and she hung for a moment poised among the stars. The glow around her seemed the presence of her ka itself – of all her kas, bursting from this body that could not contain them, could not house such greatness – by the gods, it was impossible, *she* was impossible, and maat was impossible, and Senenmut cared nothing for it, nothing. Reverent, he cupped her face in his hands, held her with trembling awe. She leaned, and slowly her eyes closed, and her mouth found his, and he could isolate her by facets no more. Every fire inside him woke at once. His senses brimmed, left him helpless beneath her, weakened, pinioned by her intensity, her shining. He panted, unmoving, as she pushed his kilt aside. He shut his eyes when she raised the skirts of her gown to her waist. As they came together, she moaning, he holding his breath, he thought perhaps the light of her kas would burn him away. It would burn maat itself away, and Senenmut would rejoice to see the flames.

CHAPTER THIRTY-TWO

T HE HATHOR FESTIVAL WAS OVER. Hatshepsut had performed all the rites of worship, presided with the Pharaoh over the great feast, her entire body tensed in anticipation of danger. Since falling pregnant, the terrifying dreams had returned, the nightmare of birthing the goddess who turned to Sekhmet before her eyes, who thirsted for her blood. Thutmose's coldness had only made the Hathor Festival a greater strain. He turned toward her only when ceremony or propriety demanded, and when he looked into her face it was with a force of loathing that chilled her from within. Yet no ill had befallen her. Hathor seemed appeased once more; the year would progress, fertile and pleasant. And perhaps her dreams would recede, too.

She lay in her bed watching the sun rise through her wall of pillars. Her heart reverberated with the feel of the nightmare's familiar impression: the dull, dense surprise as the cow-goddess drifted from between her bloodied thighs, light and airy; her rising horror as the form of Hathor stretched, lengthened, the lovable face distorting with a grimace of rage, the teeth turning to white daggers, the eyes to blind fire.

She rolled from her bed, stood warily. She was four months with child now. The morning illness had mostly left her, though some days she still felt dizzy and sick on rising. This morning she was lucky. Her legs were strong, her stomach without complaint. The morning air on her naked body felt fresh and bracing; she stretched; the dream recede into nothingness, and she shivered with relief and pleasure.

It was Iset who arrived to dress her. Hatshepsut greeted her with some surprise. "Are you to be the mistress of my bedchamber now?"

"No; only a dear friend who misses her lady. With the festival and the harvest, and all your travels, I have not seen you for so long – and Little Tut, of course. He keeps me well occupied. I paid Tem a silver bracelet to sleep late so that I could have the honor of dressing the Great Royal Wife."

Hatshepsut embraced her. "Iset. I have missed you; don't think I have not. These past months have been frantic, but you have been always with me, sister of my heart." She kissed her cheek. Iset's smile was as soft and lovely as the dawn light. "How is the boy?"

"Wonderful. He is so strong, so smart. He's beginning to talk, I think. At least, he tries. His nurse says he is the best baby she has ever cared for."

"I believe it."

Iset went to Hatshepsut's great free-standing chest and pawed inside, searching for her favorite gown. "Shall I give you some harem gossip, just like old times?"

"Have you been to the House of Women?"

"Ah, I like to take Tut there to play with the other babies. None of them are as adorable as he, though. I think the other mothers are envious."

"Surely your gossip is not of jealous mawats."

"Oh, no. It seems your husband has lost face among his soldiers."

"The only thing that surprises me about that news is that it took so long to reach Waset."

"Many of the concubines are from good Waset families, you know, and their mothers and sisters often come to visit. Apparently one can hear whispers in this wine house or that."

"What sort of whispers?"

Iset found the dress she sought, blue with golden thread at the hem. She held it to her cheek a moment, admiring the softness of the fabric. *You are two years older than I, and already a mother,* Hatshepsut thought, watching with some wistfulness. *And yet you are so innocent, you may as well be a child.* She felt a sudden urge to shelter Iset. But whether she needed protection from her family's plotting or from Hatshepsut's own, she could not say. The realization made her ashamed and angry, as it did whenever she allowed her heart to turn to thoughts of the girl.

"Whispers that say the Pharaoh is weaker than a woman."

"He cannot like that. Has he heard?"

"That I cannot say. But he has gathered up Tabiry and her girls – it seems he plans to leave Waset again. They say he plans to return to Kush and make war, to regain the respect of the southern garrison."

"How utterly ridiculous. Will he never learn?"

Iset draped the blue dress over Hatshepsut's shoulders, and bent to tie it just so at her waist. Her face came level with Hatshepsut's chest, and she halted, staring. Her breasts had grown yet more, she knew. They were certainly a good deal fuller than when Iset had seen her last. She waited, silent and still, for Iset to speak. The girl placed one hand on Hatshepsut's belly, felt the small rising swell. She jerked upright, and though she said nothing, her face was eloquent with fear.

"Yes," Hatshepsut said.

"Oh."

"When I went south to inspect the fortress, I lay with Thutmose, and I have conceived."

Iset nodded, looked down at her feet. The dress lay forgotten about Hatshepsut's shoulders; she knotted it herself, doing a poorer job than Iset would have done. It pulled across her stomach in a way that seemed to accent its slight roundness.

"Iset, I know what you are thinking. Here, sit with me." She took her by the hand, led her to the bed. Iset's skin was cold and pale. "Your son will remain the heir, Iset. I swear it. Even if I should bear a boy, he will wait in line behind Little Tut. My child will be his brother's heir, not our husband's."

"But you are the Great Royal Wife. Your sons come before any other's. It has always been the custom."

Only if they are sired by the Pharaoh. "Then I shall change the custom," she said lightly. "You and I have shared much. You are more than a friend to me, Iset; you are my heart's sister. When I think on Little Tut, I think on my own child. When I hold him, I hold my own son in my arms. We share him together. He was our idea, together; we created him. Do you remember how we decided, that night in Peret, with the owl calling in the garden?"

Iset nodded, then grinned ruefully. "Though I did all the work in making him."

"And that is why you are King's Mother, and ever will be. No one will take that from you." *For if they do, all I have will be taken from me. Oh, Iset, how I wish I could tell you everything – all of it: your father's plot for you, and Senenmut, and how I have used you, too, to protect my own interests. But I cannot. You would not understand. You are too innocent. You would never understand.*

Iset's eyes filled with tears; they spilled over to run down her smooth cheeks.

Hatshepsut gathered her to her chest. She could not tell whether the girl cried with relief or sorrow. *The gods damn this throne, and everything I have done to keep it. And the gods damn me, for wanting more.*

IT WAS ONLY IN THE AFTERNOON, WHEN HATSHEPSUT HAD SEEN to her courtly duties and was free to take her leisure in her garden, that she wondered how she would explain Little Tut to the nobles and priests. When she birthed her son, they would all expect him to be named the heir. And she would change the custom, as she had promised Iset, as she had promised Nebseny and Ankhhor, to set a harem girl's child above her own – no, not even a harem girl, but a servant. What excuse would her people believe? What could she possibly tell them to save herself, to save Senenmut, to save all of it? She felt a twisting in her belly. Perhaps the child had moved, or perhaps it was merely her own anxiety curling there, a fist beneath her heart.

"Hatshepsut?" Sitre-In's voice called from the direction of her chambers. She walked back steadily, slowly, resisting the childish urge to run to her mawat, to bury her face in her skirts and weep.

"What is it?"

"Your steward is here, Great Lady."

"Senenmut?"

"He has an urgent report for you, so he says."

The report was chilling. Senenmut recounted how, not an hour gone, the court magicians had begged an emergency council with the Pharaoh. They had consulted their charts of the stars, their lists of days, and had brought the dire news of a fire in the night sky.

"A fire? What in Amun's name does it mean?"

"I have read of such things," Senenmut said, talking low so his words would not carry to her women.

Hatshepsut stared vacantly at the thin, frail shape of Batiret; she watched the girl drop her spindle awkwardly in the shade, a stern furrow between her brows, while Ita and Tem spun deftly, their mouths moving on their incessant gossip.

"Fires hang among the stars at intervals of tens or of

hundreds of years. They are portents, Lady. They foretell great dangers or evils."

"What am I to do about this?"

"There is nothing you can do," Senenmut said. "I only wanted you to be prepared, for the people will surely make much of it. When fear runs through a city, there can be riots."

"This hanging fire – does it tell of a god's displeasure? Is it a sign of Amun's wrath?"

He held her eyes, steady and silent. At last he said, "You and I have nothing to fear."

"I hope you are right."

She dismissed him and returned to the solitude of her garden. The gods' displeasure – Hatshepsut shivered, though the afternoon was hot and buzzing with flies. The child twisted again in her belly; her heart lurched in response. *Great dangers or evils.* If indeed the gods were preparing to punish Egypt, it was due to their anger with the throne. It could be nothing else, for the Pharaoh's divine purpose was to act as conduit between gods and men. Responsibility fell upon the throne. But was it Thutmose's weakness that displeased them, or some other lack? *Is it his absence from the throne they abhor – or mine?*

She sat miserable in the brutal glare of the sun, slouched upon the grass where days before she had rolled with Senenmut. A wide and terrible vista opened before her, a scene of all her transgressions, all her failures in maat. She, the Great Royal Wife, carried a child that was not the king's. She had sworn to put her own son aside – the child of the Great Royal Wife's body, regardless of who sired him – in favor of Little Tut. And she had spurned the throne of the king when she knew it to be her birthright. Any of these, or all together, might be the cause of the hanging fire. But she felt, deep in the seat of her kas, that the coming fire would burn for her.

"It is me," she said, her face turned to the blazing sun. Its heat dried the tears as they welled from her eyes. "I have done wrong, O Amun-Re, my lord and my father! Only show me how to make it right again, and I shall!"

Amun gave no answer. He only sank into his western seat, pulling his light from the world with an inexorable slowness. Hatshepsut feared the coming night. When the first star appeared, hanging bright and silver above her lake, she shivered.

CHAPTER THIRTY-THREE

SHE MOVED ON A SMOOTH current. With the curtains of her litter drawn tight, shutting out the sight of the terrible night sky, she may as well have been sailing. *Upriver, to Ka-Khem.* She recalled the angry coughing of the deby far in the darkened marsh, the feel of Lady Iah's soft bed, its cool linens on her skin. She shut her eyes to push the images further away, the things she wished not to see, not to feel. Iset lying in her arms, gentle and trusting – Little Tut smiling upon her knee, reaching for her with his fat little hands, his skin as soft and sweet-smelling as down. Senenmut – that was most painful of all – Senenmut in the garden, moonlit and shadowed, his mouth open in a silent cry of pleasure.

Her hands were cold. They clutched a small bag, simple and unassuming, pure plain linen drawn with a string. She could feel the prickle of the herbs' stems poking through the cloth, digging into her fingers and palms.

Long before full darkness had come, the hanging fire had revealed itself, poised high above her garden, a silver slash of unmoving, unwinking light. It seemed to point directly down to where she sat huddled beside the lake's stone wall. It was the track of a fierce, bright claw scoring the flesh of the night; it was the scepter of Hathor, the Sovereign of Stars, and Hatshepsut did not know how to appease the goddess's rage.

The priestess Bakmut had provided the herbs. She had ever been loyal to Hatshepsut; she was sensible, old enough to spurn gossip, and had pledged herself to the confidence of the God's Wife. In Bakmut's small sleeping cell, Hatshepsut had made the priestess swear secrecy upon the very ka of Amun, then had whispered her need. Two days later, she had returned to the Temple as they agreed, and Bakmut had slipped the bag into her hands.

The placid sailing of her litter came to an abrupt halt. It lowered, and the curtain was drawn aside. She held up her hand as a sunshade although it was night, as if her hand might block Hathor's scepter from her sight. But its light was everywhere. It had intensified the past two nights, and now it added to the familiar cast of moon and stars a foreign, frightening glow. Nehesi pulled her to her feet. He escorted her back to the echoing solitude of her chamber. She kept her eyes fixed on the ground so she would not see the hanging fire.

Alone in her room, she took an offering bowl from her shrine box. She filled it with oil and myrrh, fanned a flame alight, wafted the smoke over the tiny figures of the holy family, Amun the father, Khonsu the son, Mut the mother. The sweet smoke wreathed Mut in a halo of white, and Hatshepsut crouched frozen, staring into the face of the goddess, staring through the goddess into a deep blackness where the air was thick and choking.

I do this for Egypt, she told Mut. *The child craves for flesh, for blood, and by night my dreams are of Sekhmet. Hathor hangs her scepter in the sky, and points to my shame. Would you have me unleash destruction upon my land?*

Mut did not answer. She only smiled, her eyes distant, her mouth enigmatic and still.

She shifted on her knees, bending under the weight of her duty. She remembered the sound of soldiers shouting her name. *They are mine. I raced with the news of the ambush; I came down from the hills to protect them. I am their guardian. They are my people, mine to protect.* She squeezed her eyes shut, for on the curling of the smoke she saw Senenmut at her wedding feast, turning away from the painted girl, the golden acrobat with the chains of flowers around her slender, beautiful neck. She saw his face turn up to hers, saw the ache of desire pulse through him. She trembled. *Amun, let this be right. My god, let this be all that is required of me. I cannot sacrifice more.*

When she stood, the alien silver light had fallen low through her pillared wall, coloring the floor of her bedchamber with patterns of blue and white. She did not know how long she knelt, how long she prayed. Her knees were tender; they would be bruised in the morning.

In her standing chest she found a tiny silver kettle, part of the treasure she had kept from Retjenu. She dipped it full of water from her ewer and set it among the glowing embers of myrrh in her offering bowl. The droplets on the outside hissed into steam. When the water was hot, she measured a quarter of the bag of herbs and let the dry, bitter leaves fall from her palm. They turned the water dark. A delicate, green scent rose with the steam. Carefully, with a corner of her blanket wrapped round her hand, she poured the brew into her wine cup. She offered one final plea to Amun for mercy, to Mut for forgiveness. She drank.

Hatshepsut huddled on the low wall of her lake. Hathor's scepter hung above, pointing its accusing, clawed finger. Its reflection sent a path of silver light from water to heavens. The brightness attracted moths; they spun in a column of luminous, flitting wings, revolving and tapering like the fingers of dust that sometimes grew up from the desert on especially hot days. She watched the image of the scepter shatter and reform as bats dipped to the lake's surface with a touch as light as Maat's feather, strafing for the insects.

Somewhere in the near darkness, Nehesi waited, tireless and alert, near enough to protect her but far enough to leave her to her thoughts. What few thoughts she had – what a relief it was, after these days of agonizing, to have come to a decision at last, and to cast her sacrifice at the gods' feet. What a relief to crouch on the cold stone and stare at the simple bats going about their business, to watch the soothing shimmer of moonlight on water. Cramping, distant and mild, clutched at her belly in intermittent waves. She must drink the herbs three more times, for three more nights, Bakmut had said. And then the pain would begin in earnest, but when it was done all her wrongs would be put to right, and no danger, no evil would befall the Two Lands. A pair of bats dove for the same fat moth and tumbled one over the other, righted themselves a hair's breadth above the water, parted ways. She smiled distractedly at the sight, as though it were a show at a feast, performed just for her amusement.

She looked around sharply at a rustle in the garden. Nehesi's bulk moved from one blue shadow to another, tense and alert. He paused, staring down a narrow pathway that wended around the edge of the lake to a distant stand of trees. Hatshepsut was filled with sudden terror, a cold tingling in her limbs. A cramp came upon her, stabbing into her middle, and she caught her breath, heart pounding.

A figure appeared from the path's bend, white and shining in the moonlight. It drifted toward her.

"Stop," Nehesi said. "Who is it?"

The figure did not respond, nor did it slow. Nehesi moved to protect Hatshepsut; he stood at the confluence of two paths, and the bulk of his shoulders and back blocked the figure from her view. His hand went to his blade hilt. And then, with a murmured apology, he bowed. Beyond his bent form, Hatshepsut looked into the face of her mother, knowing and sad.

"Ahmose." Hatshepsut came shaking to her feet.

"I know what you have done," Ahmose said. The sound of her voice, unheard after so many years, fell like a blow upon Hatshepsut's heart. "You must not go further. Do not cast out this child."

Hatshepsut's vision blurred. Her limbs seemed to float; she felt the catch and panic of falling, a sensation far away. When her senses cleared a heartbeat later, Nehesi's arms were around her, easing her back onto the lake's low wall.

"Great Lady? Are you well? Should I send for a physician?"

"She is well, guardsman." Ahmose sat beside her, took her hand in her own. "It is the touch of the god's hand she felt. It can come upon a person that way sometimes. It can take one's senses. But it is only a momentary effect. Leave us."

Nehesi hesitated, watching Hatshepsut's face warily. "Go," she told him, though her very kas seemed to quake. He retreated to his shadows.

"Mother." Hatshepsut could find no more words. Her voice broke with pain, with the emptiness of isolation, the weight of her duty.

"I know." Ahmose gathered her into her arms and rocked her. She sobbed against her chest, flooded Ahmose's white gown with tears. When her breathing steadied, Ahmose lifted Hatshepsut's face in her hands. "I know how you suffer. But, my child, you are doing the gods' work. They are pleased, Hatshepsut. They smile on you."

"No. Oh, Amun, blessed Mut, I have ruined it all. The hanging fire – it is a portent; Senenmut said! It foretells a great evil. It is my fault, my doing. I have destroyed maat with my selfishness, and now the very skies turn against Egypt."

Ahmose's laugh was low, gently chiding. She placed her hand on Hatshepsut's middle. "You have destroyed nothing. The fire is the sign of your child. This is a servant of the gods you carry, one who will bring them worship. Whatever you think you have undone, Hatshepsut, will be restored by this child."

She buried her face in her hands. "Oh, Mother. You do not understand. Thutmose is not the father."

"I know."

She clutched at Ahmose's hands, stared into her face, desperate and harried. "How?"

Ahmose smiled wryly. "I may be growing older. I may be only a lady now, and no longer the Great Royal Wife. But I am still god-chosen."

Hatshepsut remembered Mut's impassive smile, the smoke of myrrh surrounding her. She prodded at her bruised knees with tentative fingers. "I prayed to Mut tonight. Did the goddess send you to me?"

"You asked for understanding. I bring it."

"Mother, I have missed you. I have tried to rule well, but there is so much I do not know, and my heart fills with fire when I should be calm, and I make a mess of everything."

"I should not have removed myself from the court. I was wounded, but it is no excuse. I should have been stronger, should have put away my pride for you. I should have helped you."

"I made you a liar before the court. I am sorry. Truly, you can't know how sorry I am."

Ahmose lifted Hatshepsut's chin, made her look into her stern eyes as she had done so many times before, when Hatshepsut was a willful girl. "Do not apologize. It is your task to guide this land, your will that must be obeyed. You are the son of the god himself. He has shown me Egypt whole and thriving, unfettered by whatever unknown evil you fear. And he has shown me you upon the king's throne, with your baby in your arms. This star is your own scepter, Hatshepsut. It is the banner of your coming. Your triumph is written on the sky."

She thought of Little Tut then, of how it felt to cradle him. She longed to touch his soft hair, to blow her lips upon his warm, rounded belly until he squealed with laughter.

"I have secured Thutmose's boy as heir. I could never put him aside, not even for a son of my own body. I love him as though he were my own."

"There is no need to put him aside," Ahmose said. "Your child is a girl. You will bear a daughter of maat, whose dedication to the gods will be as vital to them as the breath of life is to man. She will restore all things that have been lost. She will shine as bright as your banner among the stars."

Hatshepsut's hands fell upon her belly. The child fluttered there, stirring minutely, as if in response to Ahmose's words. Tears washed afresh down Hatshepsut's cheeks – tears of gratitude, tears of relief.

CHAPTER THIRTY-FOUR

"THE GRAPES ARE THE BEST I've yet seen, master."
Paweraa plucked a stem from the nearest vine to hand.
He offered it to Senenmut.

Senenmut pulled a grape free, rubbed the glaucous bloom
from its skin, and bit. "Still quite tart," he said to his overseer.

"Indeed, but plump, and a greater yield than last year's. Last
year's harvest was, you recall, master, the best to date. We shall
do even better this season."

Senenmut nodded, placed a hand on Paweraa's shoulder.
The old man had come, part and parcel, with the estate
Hatshepsut had gifted him those years ago. Paweraa's family had
worked this land for generations; the fields of the estate were as
familiar to him as his own limbs and heart. It was Paweraa's
expertise that had kept Senenmut in his wealth – his knowledge, and the generosity of the God's Wife. Senenmut had much
to be thankful for, and as he toured his fertile fields, sampling
the produce of his land, he felt his gratitude as a surge of warm
contentment below his heart. The gods were good. As near as
Senenmut could tell, they had stayed completely whatever evil
they had promised with their hanging fire. The unsettling star

had burned for a week, a portent of nothing more than a few robberies within the city – then quietly faded away. Five months had passed, and the expected tribulations it seemed to foretell never materialized.

They came to the planting of barley, the season's second crop just beginning to ripen. The new-formed seed heads glowed a luminous, soft green in the sun. Paweraa pulled up a stem, held it up for Senenmut to see where some beetle or other had gnawed. He was detailing his plan for eradicating the pests – something about hiring local boys to run through the field, plucking the beetles and crushing them – when Senenmut became aware of a commotion at the far end of his fields. He shaded his eyes and peered down the line of a dry ditch to where the women of the estate worked, dipping water from the canal with tight-woven baskets dangling from the ends of great weighted levers. The women shouted, gestured toward the road. It ran along a causeway here, well above the level of the flood's high water. A chariot came from the south – from the direction of Waset. Nothing unusual in that; nothing to make the women stop their work and raise their voices. But in another moment he realized that the chariot was moving with great haste, and that it gleamed in the sun, banded in gold. *A messenger from the palace.*

Paweraa had forgotten his gnawing beetles; he, too, held his hand above his eyes. As they stood watching, the driver swung down the side road that led to Senenmut's estate. Senenmut's belly clenched in sudden apprehension. *Hatshepsut.*

He left Paweraa to make his own slow way back to the house and outbuildings. Senenmut sprinted to meet the chariot.

The driver was Hatshepsut's personal guard. He drew in his horses and stared down at Senenmut, his mouth tight with worry.

"What is it? What has happened to her?"

Nehesi put out his hand. Senenmut clasped it, allowed the

man to boost him into the chariot. "She is in the birthing pavilion."

"Early. At least half a month early, by what she told me."

"She will not stop crying for you. One moment she demands somebody fetch you, the next she pleads, and the next she simply wails your name. I have never seen her in such a state."

Nehesi turned his horses, hissed them back along the causeway. Ipet-Isut loomed in the distance, its towering walls a bright smudge on the horizon. Once past the city of temples, it was but one mile more to Waset and Hatshepsut's side.

"She cries for me, not for her husband?" Senenmut knew it was absurd, under such circumstances, to attempt a casual air. And yet he knew he must try all the same.

Nehesi pierced him with a dry, level look. He said nothing for a long while as the horses' hooves pounded, as the chariot rattled and jarred. At last the guardsman broke the silence. "No, not for her husband. He has gone south to make war on the Kushites."

Of course. It was a ridiculous question, Senenmut knew, but he was obligated to ask it all the same. He had been at court the day Thutmose announced he would trek to the border once more, this time to attack the Kushite king in his own territory and throw him into the dust. "For the glory of Egypt," Thutmose had pronounced. "To continue the great work my father started, to conquer every land until every place the sun touches belongs to Egypt, to our gods!" The courtiers had cheered and the Great Royal Wife had smiled upon her throne. But later, as Hatshepsut lay upon her couch, her ladies rubbing soothing oils into the skin of her swollen belly, she had sniggered over Thutmose's blustering. "He has no care for continuing my father's work, and no stomach for expanding Egypt's reach. Even had he, the boy would not know how to go about it. He only wants to put an end to the whispers at court, Senenmut." He had asked, "What whispers?" And Hatshepsut had been too pleased to supply the answer. "That he is weaker than a woman – weaker than me."

Senenmut fixed his eyes upon Ipet-Isut, willing it to come nearer, faster, faster.

"Even were the Pharaoh not gone away," Nehesi said quietly, barely audible above the relentless clangor of the wheels, "she would call for you still, I think."

Senenmut risked a glance at his companion. Nehesi caught his eye, said nothing. Then, with a force that nearly knocked Senenmut to his knees, he pounded him upon the shoulder. Senenmut stood stunned and fearful until Nehesi laughed, a grumbling cough of a sound, and Senenmut understood that the blow was not an attack, but a brotherly tap. *He knows. But we are safe in him, Hatshepsut and I.*

It took more than an hour to reach the palace. Nehesi tossed the reins of his blown horses to a guard and once more led the way through the maze of corridors, past pillars and porticoes, into the garden. Senenmut wanted to run, wanted to take up a sword and fight – something, someone, anything. He was afire with a terrible energy, a fear, a longing, a desperation that could not be contained. *She calls for me. Is it because I am her chief steward? Or because I am the father of her child?*

Was he? He had wondered, had agonized over not knowing. For so many nights, so many months, sleep had eluded him. He had lost uncountable hours watching the moon track across the sky, aching in his stomach and head, picturing the child growing within her, wondering. He dared not speak his fears – his hopes? – aloud. Since their return from the southern border, Thutmose hated Hatshepsut more than ever he had before. Hatshepsut had told Senenmut, of course, brimming with pride, how she had conquered the Kushite captives. And she had told him of the look on Thutmose's face when he saw her with her foot raised in victory – the naked loathing she had seen in her husband's eyes. Senenmut had seen it himself. The whole of the court had seen. There were times when, as the royal couple sat side by side upon their thrones, Hatshepsut would speak and Thutmose would turn upon her eyes black and clouded by hatred. He made no pretense at concealing his feelings for his sister. Thutmose hungered for a reason to tear Hatshepsut from her throne, put her aside, strip her of all rights and titles. To kill her. This child may be all the excuse the Pharaoh needed to be rid of his troublesome wife.

Nehesi guided him through the garden, turning down this pathway and that. They dashed through a cloud of swirling gnats toward a grove of slender shade trees. Over the sound of their own feet on gravel, Senenmut heard the ululating song of women, a clapping of hands. With a hot, tingling flood of relief he recognized joy in the sound, not sorrow, not mourning. They pushed through the grove; there before him stood the birthing pavilion, its thick linen walls painted with the images of the gods who protect women in travail: Tawaret the deby, her round snout open wide, tongue and breasts comically pendulous; Bes, the bearded dwarf, guardian of newborns; Iset and Hathor, Horus and Heket. A breeze stirred the pavilion's walls; the gods danced upon it as if in celebration.

A heavy-breasted woman stopped Senenmut at the pavilion's door. Her face was lined, though she wore a wig of youthful braids. "This is a place for women only, Chief Steward."

Hatshepsut's voice rose above the singing. "My steward is here? Midwife, let him in."

"Ah, lady, I am here." He tried to dodge around the formidable bulk of the midwife, but she stepped quickly this way and that, barring him.

"I said let him in. The birth is finished, thank the gods. A man can do no harm now."

The midwife narrowed her eyes at Senenmut, then, bowing toward Hatshepsut, she let him pass.

Hatshepsut lay naked upon a mattress. A shaft of light fell

through the pavilion's door, shimmering the drops of sweat on her bare brow. She breathed easily, but her eyelids were heavy with exhaustion when she gazed up into Senenmut's face. A servant knelt over her, wringing a wet cloth over her thighs, wiping away the last traces of the birthing blood.

Her arms were wrapped tightly around a tiny bundle swaddled in a length of fine purple wool. She clutched it to her chest. Wordless with awe and anxiety, he knelt beside her. *Gods, let the child not bear my face. It would mean the death of all three of us.* And yet he ached to look upon the baby. The need to see its face, to know it, welled in him with a sharp and beautiful poignancy.

Hatshepsut turned her arm, shifted aside to expose the child to his eyes. "My daughter," she said. "Neferure."

"Beautiful as the sun," he repeated. "A good name." She was red and creased, as all newborns were, her brow furrowed and angry. But even as small as she was, he could see in the shape of her face, the set of her eyes, the angle of her nose, nothing but Hatshepsut. She was her mother's daughter. No one who looked upon her could discern anything more than that. Senenmut's chest trembled with relief.

Hatshepsut stretched the bundle toward him. His heart stilled with reverence. He took the babe in his arms, marveling at her lightness and warmth. She stirred in protest, uttered a brief, shrill cry, then settled again. He could feel Hatshepsut's eyes upon him as he stared into Neferure's small, clenched face.

"You will be her Chief Steward, as you are mine," she said quietly. "And you will be her tutor, as you were mine when I was but a girl. You will be with her always, teaching her, protecting her. I have spoken it; it will be so."

He chuckled. "Another title, Great Lady? You honor me too much."

"This is your greatest honor. This is your greatest title. Cherish it, Senenmut."

He could not keep the tears from his eyes. With Neferure in

his arms he was helpless to wipe them away. One dropped from his lashes and pattered onto the baby's cheek. She flinched and grimaced, and the tear rolled to the crease beside her tiny round nose, trickled onto her lips. When she tasted it, she made a curious growling sound. Senenmut laughed. He pressed his forehead to the babe's, inhaled her strange, warm, thick-sweet odor. "I will cherish the honor, Great Lady. Thank you."

The women had continued their singing outside the pavilion, and now their song rose in pitch, broken here and there with the special delighted squeal that women will give when they see a small child and wish to pinch its cheeks or dandle it in the air. Senenmut looked up, expectant, and grinned in welcome as Iset entered the pavilion, beautiful and beaming. She carried Little Tut in her arms. The boy's eyes were wide and serious. When he saw Hatshepsut lying on her mattress he reached his hands toward her, whining.

"Look, Tut," Iset said, lowering herself beside Senenmut. "Look at your sister."

The boy surveyed the newborn, unimpressed, then squalled and squirmed from his mother's arms, clambering onto the mattress to cuddle into Hatshepsut's side.

Iset sighed. "He has been asking for you all day. I tried to explain to him that you were busy getting him a sister, but he did not understand. I think..."

The singing outside cut off abruptly. The buzz of many voices talking at once took its place, and the midwife at the door stuck her head outside, craning it this way and that. She drew back a step into the pavilion, turned and stared at Hatshepsut, her eyes wide and frightened.

"What is it?"

"Great Lady, a messenger," the midwife stammered.

"Let him in." Iset moved to cover Hatshepsut's nakedness with a sheet. She scooped Tut into her arms, her face pale.

Senenmut clutched the child to his chest. His heart raced.

A man ducked into the pavilion, bowing, his face haggard and shadowed. Senenmut recognized him from court: one of Thutmose's junior stewards, young but skilled and intelligent. He waited in a stoop for Hatshepsut's leave to speak.

"What is your message?"

"The Pharaoh, Great Lady." The man stared at his palms, searching. When he raised his face, it was stark with exhaustion and grief. "He is dead."

"Dead?"

The steward dropped to his knees as if expecting some blow from the God's Wife, some punishment. But she lay stunned beneath her sheet.

"Tell me how it happened," she said at last. "Midwife, bring a cushion for this man, and a jar of cool water. He is near as worn out as I am; anyone can see it."

The steward transferred himself heavily onto the cushion, drained the jar in a single, long draft. "You are kind, Great Lady. I have not slept for two nights. I took two men and a skiff from the Pharaoh's own ship, and we sailed ahead of his barge, back to Waset to tell you."

"Then tell me."

He paused, considering his words. "When the king reached the southern border, he was full of eagerness to begin his conquest. I was beside him all the while. I cautioned him to temper his eagerness – I and his other advisors, ah, and the general of the garrison. All his men. But he was hot as an untamed horse. With the dawn of the next day, he led an attack into the hills, and his men did find a small Kushite village. They killed some ten or fifteen men. It was a small victory, not worth the risk, we told him. And now the Kushites knew we were there.

"That night he returned to his encampment, and at dawn the next day a party of Kushites fell upon us. They were swift and used the land to their advantage. We lost too many men, but managed to throw them back, and even took a captive: a young man hardly older than the Pharaoh himself. He was brave and wild. He spat at us and cursed us in his own tongue and ours.

"I said to the king, 'How is it that this captive knows our language? He is a man of some import; he must be, to be so educated. Let us find out who he is.'

"The general, he..." The steward glanced at Iset, at Tut in her arms, obviously reluctant to expose the lady and the child to the details of his tale. "Well, he coaxed information from the Kushite, and he learned that the man was a prince, the son of the very Kushite king the Pharaoh had meant to kill. We counseled the Pharaoh to be sensible, to use this man to guide him to wherever the king now hid. But the Pharaoh, he was...very brave, as you know, Great Lady. He was full of his own youthful pride. He said, 'Let me send a message to this Kushite king, to strike fear into his heart before I fall upon him and take his hand as my trophy.'

"He approached the captive prince with his sword in hand. We urged him to stop, to hear our counsel, but the heat of war was in him, and he would not be persuaded. The Kushite's arms were bound behind his back, but he struggled to his feet when he saw the Pharaoh coming for him with death upon his blade. The Pharaoh struck and the Kushite danced aside. And then...then, Great Lady, before any of us could stop him, the Kushite kicked high, and caught the Pharaoh in the throat."

The steward dropped his head into his hands, trembling.

"Go on," Hatshepsut said, steady and cool.

"The king collapsed. We carried him to a tent and did all we could, but his throat had swollen; the firmness, here..." he touched his fingertips to his own throat to show the place, traced the protruding stone, "...the place felt broken beneath the fingers, shattered into pieces. The fortress has a physician, of course, and he did all any man could do, but the Pharaoh's breathing was labored, and before two hours had passed, his ka was fled."

He fell silent. Hatshepsut stared at the wall of the pavilion, softly undulating in the breeze. Senenmut followed her gaze. It rested upon the painted figure of Horus. The god's stern eye seemed to stare back at her.

"What happened to the Kushite?" Hatshepsut said at last.

The steward shook his head in some confusion. "The Kushite, Great Lady? Why, he was killed, of course. The general took his hand."

"A brave man."

"The general? Ah, he is..."

"The Kushite." She turned her face from Horus, considered the steward for a long moment. The man dropped his head under the strength of her stare. "And so you sailed before my husband's barge. Before his body."

"Ah. We put in at the first good-sized town we came to and requisitioned from the local House of the Dead enough salt to keep the Pharaoh's body for proper enbalming. He lies under the salt even now, two days out at the most, I would guess."

Hatshepsut returned her eyes to Horus. The god nodded as he moved in the wind. In the silence, Little Tut fussed in his mother's arms. At last Hatshepsut said, "You have done well. Go and rest. My Chief Steward has heard you; he will spread your news to my court."

The man bowed his way from the pavilion. When he had gone, Hatshepsut turned her face to Senenmut. He was startled to see sorrow there – a genuine mourning, when all he could feel was relief covering him, body and ka, like a glorious, soft mantle of gold.

CHAPTER THIRTY-FIVE

THE BOY KING THUTMOSE HAD lain beneath the enbalming salts for two months and ten days. His body had been emptied of its vital parts, the parts stored in jars. He was wrapped, finger by finger and toe by toe, in the most delicate of linen, spun from the straightest stems of flax. His coffins were carved and gilded, painted, inscribed with prayers and dedications from his sister-wife. A mask of gold was laid atop the still, hard form of the king's body, which looked small now, even for a boy not yet fifteen, bound in his wrappings like a goose trussed for roasting. The eyes of the mask were wide and smiling, boyish, kind, as Thutmose's had never been. Senenmut looked the mask, and turned away from that childish, almost pleading gaze. He turned and walked from the king's bedchamber as the final stars faded from a blue-black sky. He arrived at the gates of Ipet-Isut as dawn broke, spilling a pure light upon the crown of the high wall. The light ran along the wall's crest eagerly, as fire runs down a trail of spilled oil, snake-quick and flickering. It was the first hour of the day of the Pharaoh's funeral.

By the time the pale morning sun reached its hands over the

wall to touch the inner courtyards, patched with their chapels and shrines, the priests of Amun had all gathered at the water steps to await their barge. It would ferry them across the river to the valley where Thutmose's tomb waited. The boy had been so young; the tomb had belonged, in truth, to an older noble, some loyal man of the court. He had proffered it to Hatshepsut and she had accepted, set painters to work modifying, recarving, brushing over the grown man's life with the tale of the departed Pharaoh, his lineage, the sum of his few accomplishments.

Senenmut stood for a moment and watched the priests as they clustered about the mooring, hugging themselves in the brisk dawn air. He remembered his own days as a priest, when he was not quite fifteen himself. He remembered the funeral of the last king. He remembered Hatshepsut, a small girl in a sidelock, resolute and staring and very small on the great litter that bore her above a river of wailing mourners.

He tried to picture Neferure at that age – eight or nine, the age must have been. But all he could picture of the girl was a warm weight in his hands. Already she had grown too fast. The women all said it was an ill thing when a child was born too soon, that they seldom lived to weaning, and when they did they were stunted in body or in mind. Hatshepsut would grow quiet when the women said such things, withdraw into herself, her fond motherly smile freezing into a mask as strange and ill-fitting as Thutmose's. "You did nothing to cause it," Senenmut told her one day, when the talk of Neferure's early arrival caused Hatshepsut to frown. She had shaken her head. "I wonder."

And yet in spite of the bad omen of her early birth, in spite of the hanging fire that had preceded her, the girl showed every sign of thriving. She suckled at her nurse's breast like a hungry little calf. Her cry was strong and musical. Already she lifted her head on a wobbling neck, a feat which never failed to make

Senenmut sigh in admiration. The years would pass before he knew it – eight, nine, and more, and all too soon Neferure would be wed to Tut. Thutmose, they must call him now that his father was gone. Thutmose the Pharaoh, the third of his name. *May he be a better husband to Neferure than his father was to her mother.* That was the plea Senenmut would set before Amun's seat this morning, before he, too, made the crossing to the Pharaoh's tomb. The plea, and an expression of thanks. They were safe now, all three of them. A father could ask for nothing more.

He paused outside the shuttered chamber of Amun's dark sanctuary. He dared not enter without the leave of a Temple official, but there was not a priest to be found. He turned for the long hall of dormitories where the young priests had their tiny sleeping cells. His intent was to find a straggling priest and beg leave to visit with the god, but a warm nostalgia for his younger days came over him as he passed door after simple door, pacing the worn stones of the familiar hallway. He found the cell that had been his and hesitated, his hand on the door. But no – it was his no longer. Whichever young man lived there now would not appreciate the intrusion.

All at once he longed to see the rooftop where he and his friends had lounged on hot afternoons, doing their best to catch the breezes from the river, holding mats of woven reeds above their bare heads. His feet found the path to the stairway of their own accord. From the rooftop he could see the knot of priests milling like ducks in a shallows. A mile upriver, a bright linear slash detached from the pale quay: the massive funeral barge, and behind it, several more to carry the priests and mourners. Hatshepsut would be aboard, standing vigil over her brother's mummy. He moved down the length of the roof, drawn toward the distant barge where his lady waited. Birds in the myrrh trees below sang lustily. His ka felt freer than it had in months. He felt he might run down the whole long stretch of the building, but he was too dignified now for such boyish antics. The weight of the titles Hatshepsut had piled upon him kept his pace slow and even.

"...this is the time."

He arrested at the sudden voice from somewhere below, caught himself lightly on the balls of his feet so that his sandals did not so much as scuff on the stone rooftop. Senenmut held his breath. A murmur sounded, a low vibration of masculine voices, barely audible, nearly beneath his feet. A few more words rose into the range of his hearing, then died away again. "...could hardly be a better moment to..." To his right, along the lip of the rooftop, a wedge of stone stood up from the neat flush of masonry by a finger's breadth. It indicated a windcatcher set into the wall below, narrow bars of granite in a gap three hands high, oriented to filter the river breezes downward, cooling the room within. Being above the dormitories once more roused in him a spirit of mischief. He crept to the lip of stone and lowered himself silently to stretch along the rooftop, listening.

"I did not come all this way for nothing. I will see it done before my ship sails for home."

"And here I thought you came all this way for the king's funeral." It was Nebseny, the High Priest. A note of amusement colored his smooth voice.

"To pay my respects, ah." The other chuckled, said something low and mocking that Senenmut could not discern.

"It is too bad, though," said Nebseny. "The boy had come to like and trust me. Another week or so, and I might have easily convinced him to displace his wife and raise Iset in her place. His hatred for that abomination of a woman had grown so, he would hardly have needed a reason to do it. Since their little adventure in Kush he could not even stand to look upon her. It's a wonder he could bring himself to sire a child on her. Gods know I would not be able to rise to such a task. The woman is as unattractive as she is unnatural."

"It makes no difference now. We will have it done and see Iset on the throne. The rest will be simple." There was a pause, a faint sound of shuffling, the scrape of chair legs on stone. "You already sent word to your people? They are ready to do their work?"

An agonizing silence, while Nebseny gave an unseen gesture of an answer.

With intricate care, Senenmut pushed himself up from where he lay. He did not make a sound, though the pounding of his heart in his own ears was painfully loud, and a thousand desperate thoughts shrieked at once within his heart. On shaking legs he stood and checked that the barge was still moving, making its stately progress toward Ipet-Isut. Hatshepsut was safely aboard, he reasoned. The barge would not have sailed without her. For the moment, he could be certain that she was well. He rocked on his heels in an agony of desperation. He did not know whether to board the ship to protect her with his own unarmed hands, or run to the palace and warn her guards. *Of what?* He had heard only enough to know she was under threat, and not enough to save her.

Ah, that sorted his thoughts quickly enough. He crept along the rooftop until he found the staircase, then rushed headlong for the water steps. In his nobleman's wig and long kilt, all could see that he was no priest. The young men of the temple eyed him, jostled him, muttered about intruders into the god's business. When at last the barges arrived, Senenmut joined the first file of priests to board. The line of men moved too slowly and complained too much of his inexplicable presence. But once on the deck of their boat, he could see Hatshepsut standing, solitary and unharmed, at the head of Thutmose's coffin, which lay as final a felled tree beneath its canopy of blue linen.

She is unharmed. For now, that is all I need to know.

CHAPTER THIRTY-SIX

W HEN THE BOATS REACHED THE western shore, Senenmut was the first onto land. He leaped from the ship's rail to the uneven stones of the quay before the sailors could even jump from the deck, their lines in hand. "Here," one of them called after him, "if you're going to risk your neck, at least help us tie up, you fool!"

He paced in the hot red dust of the landing as the ships let out their ramps, as priests and mourners picked their way slowly to the shore. They gathered about him, their voices raising, shouting to one another, a few women already beginning to wail. He kept his eyes on Hatshepsut's great barge, watched, avid and frantic, as she was carried from its deck on an ornate litter. She held Little Tut on her lap. The child clapped his hands.

Senenmut surged against the crush of bodies, but he could not make his way to her side. The mourners moved like a great flight of birds, rippling this way and that, carrying him farther from the litter on stumbling, unwilling feet. He craned his neck, but the High Priest was not to be seen.

The coffin was borne from the ship on a golden platform. It

fell in behind Hatshepsut's litter, and with a raucous surge of sound the mourning began in earnest. Senenmut, no matter how he turned and pushed, could not free himself from the crowd. All around him women stooped as they walked, cupped dust in their hands, threw it upon their foreheads. His eyes filled with grit, ran with tears. The mourners tore their dresses, clawed at the sky with desperate hands, and on every side they cried out in a din that might have woken Thutmose's very ka, had it not already fled the living world.

Senenmut saw the broad, dark back of Nehesi appear for a moment beside his lady's litter. Then the man was obscured by a cloud of thrown dust. "Nehesi!" he shouted. The name was lost in the keening.

They pressed into the dry valley, between two upthrust faces of red stone. Senenmut slowed, let himself fall to the rear of the procession so he might make his way to the edge. From there he would run alongside the column until he was abreast of the litter. And all at once Nebseny was there, his face impassive above a drape of leopard skin.

Senenmut gasped to see him. Nebseny turned to gaze at him with simple curiosity.

"I know," Senenmut said. "I know what you plan to do."

Nebseny tilted his head.

Senenmut tried again, bellowing this time over the wailing. "I know what you plan."

Nebseny's smile was cold, joyless, pale-lipped. "Do you?" He lifted a bright object from his chest. It threw a great glint of sunlight into Senenmut's eyes; he shut them under the assault of the glare and the mourning dust. When he forced them open again, the golden face of a leopard stared back at him. Nebseny's eyes blazed through the mask's slits with a terrible triumph. Senenmut surged toward the High Priest, but a mourner's shoulder caught him; he staggered, spun, and Nebseny was gone.

AT THE MOUTH OF THE TOMB, SENENMUT FREED HIMSELF AT LAST from the press of the crowd. Hatshepsut was lowered from her litter. She carried the boy toward his father's coffin as priests lifted away its outer and inner lids. When they stood the wrapped and gilded body of her husband upright, Hatshepsut gazed at the golden face without a flicker of emotion. As she raised her voice, clear and strong, to recite the rites in the name of Thutmose the Third, Senenmut edged through the listening crowd until he had managed to creep as near to Nehesi as propriety would allow. He had to hiss the man's name several times before Nehesi glanced around, recognized Senenmut through the red grit that coated him, and gestured him near.

"I overheard a threat to the Great Lady," Senenmut said at once into Nehesi's ear. "The High Priest."

Nehesi's hand flashed to his sword, but Senenmut stayed it. "Not here, man! Use sense. You cannot kill him in cold blood, before Hatshepsut even knows the reason why. The people will tear you apart."

"Right. The moment the ceremony is done I shall be at her side." He caught the eyes of two of his guardsmen; his hands flashed in a series of signs. The guardsmen tensed, then turned to work their way through the crowd. By the time Hatshepsut raised the hook of black metal to Thutmose's gilded lips, opening his mouth to breathe in the sweet air of the afterlife, a contingent of guards had drawn up around Nehesi, poised for his signal. Hatshepsut lifted Tut high; the boy sucked on his fingers, his round face puzzled by the crowd that shouted his name.

Nehesi barked an order. His men dashed to surround the God's Wife and the new king. Hatshepsut pulled Tut against her chest, cupping his head with one protective hand. She glowered in confusion. He saw her mouth moving, shouting a demand.

But over the cries of *Thutmose! Thutmose the Third!* Senenmut could hear nothing of her voice.

He stared past the mummy into the cold black mouth of the tomb, where Nebseny the leopard stood waiting. Below the leopard's downpointed muzzle the mouth of the priest curved in a mocking smile.

The threat was never here – not from Nebseny himself, not from anyone in this crowd. The palace, then – it must be the palace.

There was nothing Senenmut could do that Nehesi could not – not when it came to strength or to blades. Reluctantly, Senenmut reconciled himself to leaving her in the Medjay's hands. He would better serve his lady as he always had done: with quick and careful thought.

The boats returned to the eastern bank, Hatshepsut still ringed tightly by her guards. At Ipet-Isut, Senenmut lost himself among the crowd, deliberately this time, letting the flow of priests carry him back toward the Temple of Amun. He peered around for Nebseny, and saw to his right the yellow of a leopard's pelt moving between two priests, darting like an ibis among the reeds. He dodged to follow. Always Nebseny evaded him, peeling further from the crowd, making his way into a secluded corner of the city of temples. Senenmut wondered where the High Priest's path led, who he was hurrying to meet. His assassins, no doubt; the ones who would do his work for him so that his hands stayed clean.

Senenmut halted in the shaded forecourt of a small royal shrine. Afternoon was advancing. Long shadows lay across the courtyard, converging in disorienting angles. He had lost sight of Nebseny. He held his breath and listened for some voice, some betraying scuffle, but here at the outer edge of the complex Ipet-Isut was eerily still. He moved uncertainly toward the shrine. It was a modest building as shrines went, walled in white granite. Two small pillars framed the entryway, above which the name of some nigh-forgotten prince was carved.

Senenmut took one step toward the shrine, hesitated, took another. A wind moved through Ipet-Isut; it rattled the distant leaves of the myrrh trees before Amun's gate; a few dry leaves scuttled past Senenmut's feet. He moved toward the shrine more boldly. As he passed the pillars, a blow fell on him from behind. He grunted, stumbled, fell to his knees in the dark entryway. Senenmut clapped a hand to the back of his head, feeling for blood, and turned to see Nebseny standing over him with his fist still raised.

Senenmut lurched, half-crouched, launching himself into Nebseny's gut. The priest sprawled backward into the court-yard; Senenmut followed, rolling. Nebseny was on him again in a moment. He raised a fist high but Senenmut threw himself aside; Nebseny's knuckles cracked against paving stones. He choked back a gurgling scream and rolled away from Senenmut. His breath hissed between his teeth as he fought against the pain.

Senenmut staggered to his feet. A streak of blood glowed darkly on the paving stones between his feet.

"So," Senenmut panted.

Nebseny clambered upright, clutching the bleeding hand against his leopard skin. The glaring mask hung from a cord around his neck. It watched the blood drip from the priest's hand with an expression of implacable hunger.

"If not at the tomb, then at the palace. You have sent killers to my lady. But they will not reach her. Nehesi and his men...."

"You fool. Can a guardsman stop a god? Can a dozen, a hundred? The will of the gods shall be done this very night."

"No one will come near her. No blade will have a chance."

"Confine her to her chambers until she is a withered old woman if you like." Nebseny smiled. "She must eat and drink eventually."

Senenmut's heart thrashed, reared like a panicked horse. *Gods damn me, why didn't I see it?*

"If I had a knife I would kill you right now, Master Senen-mut, favorite of the Great Royal Wife." His words were thick with mockery. "But even knowing what you know, you cannot stop it. No man can stop the will of Amun. Once she is buried beside her husband, I will find you and kill you myself. I promise you that."

Senenmut lunged, intending to strike Nebseny in the face, but the High Priest danced backward. His fingers closed on the leopard mask. He tore at it savagely; Nebseny shouted in pain as the cord snapped, welting the skin of his neck.

Then the High Priest laughed. His grinning mouth seemed poised to rend. "Run, Chief Steward! Your lady needs you."

He did run. He pelted from Ipet-Isut's towering gate, sprinted toward Waset. In the sky above the city he seemed to see a faded echo of the hanging fire. His thighs and his lungs burned, but he never stopped, never slowed. Long before he gained the road to the palace he feared his heart might burst and drop him in the dust. He implored Amun to carry him, to lend him enough strength, at least, to reach his lady before it was too late, and then he could die, choking for breath, his legs consumed by flames. The sound of celebration rose from Waset, improbable in the face of his desperation. His ears roared with the clamor of drums. The gateway. The guards shouting his name, waving him on. The courtyard, the porticoes...he flashed past them, thanks be to Amun, only let it not be too late! The hall that led to her door. The mask hard and cold in his hand. The door thrown open, a sickly light spilling into the pillared hall, the moving shadow of guards.

And above the roaring in his ears, the sound of a woman's agonized screams.

He fell against her doorway, legs collapsing, useless from the effort, breath a torment of red fire and sand in his throat, his chest.

Hatshepsut crouched on the floor of her antechamber, bent

over a still, pale form. She rocked under the blow of her grief, threw back her head and keened again. She cradled Iset's head in her lap. The girl's lips were blue. Her eyes were open, shallow and cold and dead.

The leopard mask fell from Senenmut's hand.

CHAPTER THIRTY-SEVEN

"IT WAS MEANT FOR ME."

Guards had come to remove Iset's body. They had been obliged to pry her from Hatshepsut's arms, while a pair of insistent hands pulled at her shoulders, took her away from the woman she loved. They were Senenmut's hands. She allowed him to wrap his arms about her, shield her eyes against his chest. His skin was hot from some great exertion, slick with sweat and with her own tears.

Senenmut led her to her bedchamber. She fell onto her great bed and curled there, sobbing and beating her hands against the mattress. When she had exhausted herself she lay calm, wondering with a blank, fuzzy curiosity whether the suffocating pressure in her chest would stop her breathing.

"It was meant for me – the poisoned wine."

Senenmut said nothing. He sat at her feet, his shadowed, sad eyes tracing patterns in the tile floor.

"It was the wine. I saw a trace of it on her lips." It did no good to announce these things, the few small pieces of the broken puzzle which she had fitted into place. None of it would not make Iset live again. But she kept talking, as though by reasoning it out she might build some wall of protection around herself. "He could not have known that Iset was so familiar with me that she would be in my rooms when I was not there, that she would think nothing of helping herself to my wine."

"He?"

"The one who wishes me dead." The words were cold and hard in her mouth.

Senenmut took something from the knot of his kilt. At first she thought it was a plate or an offering bowl. He turned it in his hand, and the leopard's face scowled at her.

"Nebseny," she said. "I thought I had secured him. I thought Ankhhor..."

"Ankhhor – his brother. So his was the other voice I heard." And Senenmut told her of his visit to the Temple, the conversation he had heard through the windcatcher, his struggle to warn her or her men during the procession. He told her how he'd fought with Nebseny in the shadows of Ipet-Isut. It was only then that she noticed the bruises beginning to ripen on his face, his arms.

"You are right enough," she said dully. "It must have been Ankhhor. I was a fool – a child – to think I had brought him under my control. Nehesi saw it true: I should have killed him in his own home. It was for Iset's sake I spared him, and now she is dead. Oh, gods, she is dead." She wept again for some long time, until Senenmut lowered himself to lie beside her. "Her father used her as a pawn, Senenmut. And I did, too. She loved me. I took her affections greedily. I was alone, but that is no excuse. I wielded her like a knife against my enemies. I came to love her, too, for she was sweeter than honey to me. And yet I never told her. She died not knowing."

They lay in silence until Hatshepsut's weeping once more passed. A fierce resolve came over her. Fear, too, but greater than her fear, the conviction that no one should be in a position to take anything from her again. Not her station, not her lover, not her power. She sat up slowly. Her head throbbed. "Go and fetch Nehesi," she said. "The three of us are going to the Temple."

THE PRIESTS FELL BACK BEFORE HER, BOWING, TREMBLING AT THE ferocity of her glare. Dark tracks of kohl trailed from her eyes, stained her face. She stalked through the avenues of Ipet-Isut, speaking to no one. Senenmut and Nehesi girded her to either side, attuned to her rage, filling themselves with the overflow of her awakened power. She caught a boy by the arm as he tried to scuttle from her path – an apprentice, no more than fourteen. He shrank from her, gulping, but when she held out the mask of the High Priest he took her meaning at once, and stammered, "In the shrine of Amun, Great Lady." When she freed him from her grip he sprinted into the dormitories with a quavering whimper.

The guards on the shrine doors fell away from her approach. And how not? Was she not the God's Wife, the very hand that pleased Amun, that spilled Amun's righteousness upon the land? She did not wait for Nehesi or Senenmut to swing wide the heavy, smoke-blackened doors. She opened the way herself, and strode into the darkness.

A remnant of starlight, faint and gray, fell into the shrine. It limned with a pale sheen the edge of a white linen kilt, a bare shoulder; it set a dusky halo upon the tips of a leopardskin mantle. Nebseny crouched, bowing, before the god. He turned sharply at her entrance, a rebuke ready on his lips – and froze at the sight of her. His eyes flicked to Senenmut, then back once more to the fire that burned on Hatshepsut's face.

"Your poisoner killed Iset." All her kas shivered at the words, the impossibility of loss. But her voice did not shake.

Disbelief lengthened his face. He drew in a rattling breath. In the dull shimmer of starlight Hatshepsut saw all of Nebseny's self-possession, all his arrogant assurance drain away like water from a cracked jar. "How?"

Hatshepsut clenched her teeth. She would not tell him. He did not deserve to hear of any sweet or good thing. She would never tell him of her love for his niece, how she had opened her life to the girl, had shared with her everything that was hers – even the dangers of power, it seemed. Even the wine in its jar, cool and dark and bitter.

Nebseny turned his back on the three of them, faced the god. Amun's golden skin glinted in the starlight. "I was sure," he muttered. "My god, how could I have misread thee? Thy will was explicit..."

"You saw me proclaim myself on the steps of this very temple years ago. And you barred my way. You kept me from my god; you kept me from my father. Amun's will was explicit then, and yet you did not listen."

He whirled to face her; the clawed feet of his mantle lifted and seemed to reach for her as he spun. "I am the High Priest of Amun. It is given to *me*, to hear the god, to understand."

"You served your brother, never the god. You served your family's name. Ah, I know how you suffered for the privilege, how you caught rats until Ankhhor raised you up, paid your way to the power you now hold. And for what purpose? To maneuver his daughter into the temple and onto the throne. To place Ankhhor's hands upon the crook and flail. And now she is dead, by your own doing. See how the god defies your will. Amun knows your iniquities, High Priest. His wrath is greater than Ankhhor's, Nebseny, I promise you. His wrath is greater even than mine."

"My devotion to the god is beyond question," he said, but doubt tinged his words.

"For all your devotion, you never could see the truth. I am

not merely the God's Wife. I am the son of the god, and the throne is mine."

Nebseny's ragged breathing filled the chamber.

"Where is Ankhhor?" she demanded.

"I do not know." The response was simple, flat. Hatshepsut saw at once that he told the truth. "I assume he took his lady wife and sailed for Ka-Khem when the funerary barge returned to the eastern shore. He – he will not know of Iset until he returns to his estate."

"I will find him later, and put an end to him, as I should have done when I had him under my heel in his own bedchamber." She jerked her head toward Nehesi; the great bull of a man drew his sword.

Nebseny scuttled backward until he collided with Amun's legs. "No! Great Lady, do not profane the shrine by killing in Amun's sight."

She tilted her head. "I wonder, is that Amun's will, or your brother's? You seem unable to tell the difference. You shall not set foot from this temple. I swear that on Iset's tomb. You shall die in the presence of the god you claim to serve. His son decrees it; his son will make it so."

Nehesi swung his arm; a wet crunch rang out, the sickening, jolting sound of sharp bronze cleaving flesh and bone. A black rain fell across Amun's visage, spattered hot onto Hatshepsut's face. It ran in trickles down the god's body; a thick black river pooled at his feet. The high-pitched, bubbling cry of Nebseny's fleeing ka echoed, bleak and already damned, from the unseen walls of the chamber. The god drank the blood, but it was his son who was quenched. Her belly was sated with vengeance; her mouth tingled with the taste of maat.

CHAPTER THIRTY-EIGHT

HATSHEPSUT SAT POISED UPON HER throne. Her hands gripped the arms, steadying herself. A queer dizziness had settled upon her, a swimming of her vision if she turned her head too fast. She reasoned with herself calmly that she could not have been poisoned. It was simply impossible. She had sent Senenmut to dip a jar full of water with his own hands, from a well deep in the city, not within the palace grounds. Sitre-In was sent to gather fruit and eggs from the market at dawn. Her nurse boiled the eggs herself, brought them to Hatshepsut still in the shell. She was not hungry; her stomach protested at the thought of food, so wracked was she with grief. But she knew she must eat something before her day's work began. Fruit in the rind and egg in the shell: she could think of no safer food, though even the sweet melon choked her with bitterness.

No, there was no possibility of poison. Not this morning, at least. It was exhaustion that made her head swim and her body tremble. Below her, the great hall clamored with the shouts of angry men, nobles and stewards, senior priests and politicians. She had summoned them, and they had come at once: all the great men of Waset, and some from nearby sepats, too, who had not yet returned home after yesterday's funeral. Judging by their red eyes and disheveled garb, none had slept any more than she had. Word spread quickly throughout the city. *Faster than a gazelle.* Before he set foot into the great hall, every man knew that an attempt had been made on Hatshepsut's life. Every man knew that the King's Mother was dead.

"Who is responsible?" one man shouted. "Who is the coward that murders with poison?"

Hatshepsut raised her hand; Senenmut, seated on the floor beside her throne cross-legged like a scribe, placed the leopard mask in it. "The High Priest, Nebseny." At the sound of her voice, all shouting died away. A few men recalled themselves and bowed, but she was past caring for such proprieties. She threw the mask from the dais. The men gathered at its foot drew back as if she had tossed a scorpion into their midst. The mask clanged upon the floor, rolled along its rim, shivered as it settled with a rising metallic reverberation.

"We must find him. This insult to the gods will not stand."

"He has been found." Hatshepsut said. "I spilled his blood myself. It's his cats-paws I want now: the scum inside my own palace who would dare to harm me."

The Overseer of Kitchens crept forward, bowing. "Great Lady, two of the poisoner's accomplices have been found already. I was most hasty in rooting them out when I heard of the death of our good King's Mother."

Hatshepsut glanced at Senenmut. He nodded fractionally. She saw her own thoughts confirmed in the dark glint of his eyes: *Hold the two who were taken. Question them. And detain the Overseer of Kitchens for questioning, too.* No amount of caution was excessive. Senenmut would see to it without being told.

"I am pleased, Overseer. But this is not enough. Nebseny did not act of his own accord. He moved under the direction of his brother Ankhhor, the tjati of Ka-Khem. Where is that man?"

Heads came together to confer; the assembly buzzed, but none stepped forward with an answer. She cut off the murmurs with a raised hand. "Find him. I do not care where he is, where he flees to. He will be found. I am prepared to give a great reward to the man who brings me Ankhhor's hand. Scribes, make it so." The line of scribes bent over their lap-desks, brushing her words into writ. Within the hour, Ankhhor's sentence would go out to the people of Waset, and beyond, up river and down, until every man in Egypt sharpened his blade on Ankhhor's name.

A man with the bare head of a priest raised his palm, moved through the crowd until he stood before the throne. Hatshepsut knew him: Hapuseneb, a senior priest of Amun, intelligent, quiet, and devout. He was a friend to her priestesses, she knew. She gestured for him to speak.

"In the living memory of Egypt, there has never been an attempt to murder one of the blood royal. It is an act audacious beyond belief; it flies in the face of the gods!" He opened his arms, addressing the whole of the great hall. "The Pharaoh and his family are the very conduits between heaven and earth, my good men. And the God's Wife – she is sacred to Amun! The Great Lady says Nebseny and Ankhhor are to blame, and I believe her word. But we must consider carefully what this means to Egypt. Is it enough merely to bring these men to justice? What does their act itself speak to? Is Egypt now a place where divinity means nothing, where a High Priest may spit into the eye of the very god he serves?"

"I know Ankhhor to be a devotee of the Aten," Hatshepsut said. "Indeed Amun's divinity means nothing to him, nor any other god's. He cares only for the physical aspect of the sun: that which he can see, a soulless fire without will or intent. His family – his daughter, his brother – they were pawns to him, tools of his will, and he intended their use to glorify not only himself, but his god, who is bereft of all good things, even of life.

"I take your meaning, Hapuseneb. My husband was a child under Nebseny's influence, and had Ankhhor succeeded in killing me, Iset would now be Great Royal Wife, and God's Wife, too. It would all have gone to Ankhhor, and to the Aten.

"The throne of Egypt must never again be so easily manipulated. Amun must not be so threatened. I will not see maat come under a godless man's assault, not so long as I draw breath."

She stood. Her head spun with the effort, but she held herself proud and straight. "My father was crowned Pharaoh though he was not a king's son. Why? Because the Heqa-Khasewet champed at our borders, waiting for a king to fall, waiting for a weakened Egypt to topple into their grasp. Instead, Thutmose the First fell upon them, and slaughtered them like dogs. He taught them the truth of Egypt's strength. Now, it seems, another enemy clamors for Egypt's weakness. But neither Ankhhor nor any other ambitious man shall sink his claws into the throne and claim it for his own self.

"My son Thutmose is an infant. He will grow into a great man; by the gods, I swear it. But now he hardly walks two steps under his own power. When I see Ankhhor's hand laid at my feet, which man will rise up next to try to seize the throne of Thutmose the Third?"

"Begging your pardon, Great Lady," said Sikhepri, old and fat, but deft in his politics, "you must marry again. Take a new man as king, and young Thutmose may be his heir, to rule when your new husband goes to the Field of Reeds. A grown man on the throne, sure of himself, formidable – that would put an end to schemers such as Ankhhor."

"I performed the funerary rites in Thutmose's name," she said. "I opened his father's mouth, and my hand was my son's. No; by law – by the will of the gods – Thutmose the Third is already your king, and no man's heir. That shall not change. But the Pharaoh needs a co-regent."

"You, of course, Great Lady," Hapuseneb said. "You are the

wife of his dead father, and you have accounted yourself well as queen."

She inclined her head in acceptance of the praise, but she said, "No. Put Egypt in the hands of a queen regent, and Egypt still has only a child for Pharaoh. A child will be a target for any man of Ankhhor's stripe: a temptation too great to ignore. As Sikhepri said, it is a formidable man Thutmose needs beside him: another Pharaoh. A joint kingship: that is what I propose. A leader who will guide him as he grows, and share the throne equally when he is of age. Not a queen whom every man in Egypt knows will be retired to some estate the moment the Pharaoh is strong enough to draw a bow."

"You will marry, then, Great Lady?" someone ventured. A few noblemen glanced doubtfully at Senenmut where he sat upon the floor.

She lifted her chin, gazed down the length of the great hall, and met no man's eye. "In my blood is the right to the throne. In three days' time I shall present to you – shall present to all of Waset – my son's co-regent, your new king."

CHAPTER THIRTY-NINE

DAWN HAD NOT YET COME. The promise of it hung in the air, a shimmer of expectation. Hatshepsut parted the draperies that hid from her the great railed balcony known as the Window of Appearances. From that balcony she would look down from the palace's height, through the sun's morning rays onto a crowd of waiting citizens. But the plaza was empty yet, still grayed by the memory of the retreating night. The darkness lessened to the east, but the sky was still colorless. She wondered, what hue would this morning's sunrise be? Red and pink and gold, like any other, no doubt. The thought soothed her somewhat, but still her belly was a knot of tension.

She turned back to her women. In this unfamiliar room, situated at the palace's highest point, they fumbled here and there, tripping over the chests they had brought up from her chambers. A guard clapped outside. She nodded to Tem; the woman demanded to know who sought entry to the presence of the God's Wife. There was a time when she trusted any guard, and would have ordered the doors opened at once. *Never again.*

Tem swung the doors wide to admit Senenmut, then shut them quickly again. Her Chief Steward bore the outline of a long, flat box across his forearms, concealed by a drape of linen. She plucked the cloth aside. The box was very fine, leafed in gold, lined along its edges in brilliant cabochons of carnelian and turquoise. The lid was carved with the image of the winged scarab bearing the sun-disk upon its outstretched forelegs. Her eyes rose from the lid of the box to meet Senenmut's. They shared a conspiratorial smile.

"Dress me," she commanded her women. They took her gown from her, the simple linen traveling dress she had worn on that fateful journey south. The pre-dawn air raised a chill on her skin, and all at once she ached for the feel of Iset's warmth beneath her bed-linens. But she turned, faced Senenmut, her limbs trembling. He did not avert her eyes from her nakedness.

Ita and Tem bent over the chests. They withdrew a man's long kilt, folded and pleated. She held out her arms as they wound it about her hips, secured it with an intricate knot. Ita lifted from the chest a golden belt, and fastened it, too, around Hatshepsut's waist. It featured a long apron beaded with the image of the cobra goddess, Wadjet, the protector of the king. They painted her eyes simply, lining them in kohl, forgoing the bright colors and intricate wings of a courtly lady. Her chest they left bare, except to blow a sheen of golden dust upon her nipples.

Another clap at the door. Senenmut turned to give the challenge, and Hatshepsut's eyes watered when Ahmose's voice answered.

"Admit her."

Ahmose stepped into the chamber behind the Window of Appearances with the quick movements of trepidation. But when she looked upon her daughter, a smile chased the worry from her face.

Tem opened a second chest. Her hands hung suspended over its contents, fearing to touch.

"Dress me," Hatshepsut said again. With trembling awe, the

woman withdrew the blue-and-white banded cloth of the Nemes crown, the symbol of the Pharaoh's power. It had taken some doing to procure it. The men whose duty it was to guard the sacred vestments of the Pharaoh did not take their work lightly. She had been obliged to send for a scribe and put into writing her proclamation that Senenmut was now the Steward of the Diadem, outranking the guards. They had given way quick enough when they saw the scroll, marked with the symbol of the king: for did she not speak in Thutmose's name, and enact all of his desires? "He desires nothing but his nurse's breast," Senenmut had muttered. "Ah, well, you have already given me more titles than I can count. What is one more?"

Tem affixed the cobra circlet to Hatshepsut's brow, and reverently tied the crown into place, folding and draping its long arms over her shoulders, gathering it with golden bands at her nape.

"Yes," Ahmose said. It was a word weighted with the fulfill-ment of a lifetime's longing.

Hatshepsut considered her mother for a long moment. Her eyes rested on the lines of Ahmose's brow.

"Leave us, all except Nehesi," she said to her servants. They departed; even Senenmut. When she was alone with her mother, she allowed her lips, her chin to tremble with the force of her doubt. "Will this work, Mawat?"

Ahmose took her hand. "You know it is the will of Amun. You feel it in your heart."

Hatshepsut nodded, though all she felt in her heart was the terrible ache for Iset, the same pain that had plagued her these three days past. It would never leave her, she knew.

"Besides," Ahmose said, smiling, "your steward has worked hard, I think, to ensure that it will."

Hatshepsut laughed, looked away, abashed. Senenmut had hardly slept for the span of those three days. He had formed up a contingent of loyal men, and in the name of the Great Lady they had gone from house to house, blessing each with vouchers for bread and beer, with baubles confiscated from the High Priest's own storehouse. "If this does not bring the people to your cause," Senenmut had said, "not even an act of the gods could do it." "I only need to buy their loyalty until they grow used to the idea." "One good flood will convince them. And if it does not, I will think of something else."

A murmur sounded outside the door. Hatshepsut glanced around for Nehesi, but he was already moving, one hand on his dagger.

"Who is it?"

The door guard's answer was hesitant, muffled. "Er – the Lady Iah of Ka-Khem."

"No; send her away," Ahmose said. Her grip tightened on Hatshepsut's hand.

"Admit her."

"Hatshepsut!"

"What can she do against my guard? I say admit her, Nehesi."

He did as he was commanded.

Iah tottered into the room, her fine dress soiled with some ugly, oily stain. Her face was dark with smudged kohl, the locks of her wig matted. She stared at Hatshepsut for a long, silent moment, uncomprehending. Then with a cry she threw herself to the floor, her palms stretched along the ground. A fine-woven bag lay where she had dropped it; a brown stain marred its corner.

"Rise."

"God's Wife. Great Lady," Iah sobbed, her face still pressed to the floor. Hatshepsut bent to her, guided her upright, folded her in an embrace. "Oh, gods, my daughter, my child!"

Iah's tears fell upon her shoulder, left their mark on the cloth of the Nemes crown.

"He brought you to Waset after all."

"Yes, Great Lady. He made me come. He promised me that I would see Iset again, see her..." she faltered. "See her crowned."

"I know."

Nehesi stooped, lifted the bag. He raised an eyebrow, a grim, unspoken question.

"You brought me a gift, I see," Hatshepsut said. "How did you do it? Tell me, if the telling isn't too much for you."

"We stayed at Nebseny's fine home – the one at the edge of the city, with the fountain in the courtyard. The day after...after the funeral, I was sitting beside the fountain cooling myself when I heard the criers in the street. I heard Ankhhor's name, and held my breath to listen. The criers were moving from home to home, you know how they do. They stood outside Nebseny's gateway and shouted that Ankhhor's life was forfeit. They did not know we were there; they only shouted their business and moved on. But they said Ankhhor had attempted to poison the Great Royal Wife, and that the King's...the King's Mother...."

"Yes, all right; go on."

"I turned to run into the house, for I was frightened, and suddenly Ankhhor was there beside me. He had no remorse, Great Lady. I saw it on his face. His only thought was how he could get out of the city alive. I knew, looking at him, watching the thoughts churning within his heart, that he had no care for my Iset, nor even for me; that he would leave me behind if it came to that, and I would never see my living children again."

She buried her face in her hands, drawing wild, panicked breaths. Ahmose moved to her side, stroked her arms until she calmed.

"I vowed inside my heart that he would not separate me from another of my children, that none of us would be his pawns again. I faced him calmly – the gods know how I found the strength to do it, for inside, my ka screamed Iset's name. But I faced him, and told him, 'We must prepare to leave. Come inside with me; we will disguise ourselves, and when night falls we will make our way to the quay and hire a different ship. We will be gone with the sunrise.'

"The gods blessed me, for he came along willingly. He was like a black bull going to the slaughter, arrogant and unknowing. I opened my chest and began holding up garments, suggesting how to hide our identities. And when he came close, I looped my shawl around his neck and tightened it. He fought; he was strong. But the gods gave me their strength. They did it for Iset's sake. I was stronger."

Nehesi opened the bag. Hatshepsut glanced inside; the hand was pale, curled like a leopard's claw.

"What reward do you seek, Lady Iah?"

"None," she replied, eyes downcast. "It is enough to be free of him. It is enough to know that he will take no more of my children for his own ends, and discard their lives like so much meaningless refuse."

"All the same, I will see you rewarded."

"Then grant me, Great Lady, my husband's wealth. I would use it to restore the temples of Waser and Iset in Ka-Khem, those he allowed to fall into disrepair. I will re-dedicate them in my daughter's name."

"It will be as you say. And this thing more: there will always be a place for you at court, Lady Iah – for you and your children. Whenever you wish to stay in Waset, to see your grandson grow, you will have an honored place by my side."

"My grandson."

"He has Iset's face. Would you see him?"

Iah's eyes brimmed with tears. She could not speak. Ahmose moved to the door, summoned Little Tut and his nurse. Iah took the Pharaoh into her arms with a cry that tore at Hatshepsut's heart. It was a sound of immeasurable loss and love.

Senenmut crept back into the chamber. "Great Lady? It is time."

She turned to stare at the drapery, suddenly overwhelmed with fear. The hair's-breadth crack between the heavy curtains glowed with light, a forceful red that struck tears into her eyes.

"Senenmut. I cannot do it."

"Certainly you can." He pulled the final kingly trapping from its chest: the ceremonial false beard, one great lock of braided lapis and gold. He tied it below her chin. She flinched from its stiff, unwieldy weight.

Iah's pained cry settled into silence, and Hatshepsut heard the voices of scores of people – hundreds of people, gathered in the plaza below the Window. The nobles and priests were there, waiting to see the man she had chosen to reign beside Thutmose.

"When they look on me they will jeer and spit."

"Trust in the work of your steward," Senenmut said. "You did not choose him because he is a fool."

No. I chose him because I love him. Because he is as the breath of life to me, the brother of my heart. And in the great hall I spoke from my heart's pain, because my sister is dead. Gods save me, I am a fool. "I am acting on my heart's whim," she said, protesting. "Wine on a fire. Is this maat? I do not know; I cannot see."

"And you do not care," Senenmut whispered.

Gently, Ahmose took Little Tut from Iah's arms. With the babe on her shoulder she drew the curtain aside. Tut gazed at Hatshepsut with Iset's eyes, trusting and loving. The morning light burst into the room. The crowd cheered, chanted. Their voices pulled her out onto the balcony, into the warm, golden dawn.

She looked down from a great height; the balcony seemed to rise beneath her, to stretch her higher into the clear new sky. She saw the faces of the nobles clustered below, their eyes and mouths round with shock. The crowd's cheer faltered to a murmur of confusion. Her throat went tight.

Ahmose stepped to her right, Thutmose riding on her hip.

Senenmut appeared to her left, the long gilded box in his arms. He lifted the scarab lid away. Inside, lying on a red silken cushion, lay the dual staffs of the Pharaoh's divine office.

Amun, if I am your son in truth, turn their hearts to me.

She took the crook and flail in her trembling hands. She crossed them at her chest, held them before her bared breasts for her people to see.

Hapuseneb was the first to shout his acclaim, his palms raised high. But quickly the crowd, their hands full of Senenmut's gifts, took up his chant, until the nobles, too, were forced to raise hands and voices in salute.

The light of the god spilled upon her face, warmed her hands. A ribbon of light ran across the river, touched the distant red cliffs, set them aglow. The god heard their voices as he ascended to the height of heaven. Her name rebounded from the fiery heart of Amun-Re, and the sound of it filled the whole of the Two Lands.

So said Amun, lord of the Two Lands, before his daughter Hatshepsut: Come to me in peace, daughter of my loins, beloved Maatkare. Thou art the king who takes possession of the diadem on the Throne of Horus of the Living, eternally.

-inscription from Djeser-Djeseru, mortuary temple of Hatshepsut, fifth king of the Eighteenth Dynasty

HISTORICAL NOTES

And here is the part of the novel where I make amends for all the liberties I took with history – or try to, at least.

It's a funny thing, being a historical novelist. My job is to find some kind of credible balance between truth – or what we may reasonably call "truth" as it applies to events 3500 years gone – and creative, entertaining lies. There are some things known about Hatshepsut and her family and courtiers and many things not known, but reasonably suspected based on the things known of other Pharaohs, other times, other politicians. I am a great lover of history, but also a great lover of story, and it is the responsibility and privilege of the historical novelist to bring long-dead people back to life in order to excite and inspire the reader. This is often a difficult task. Many decisions must be made, many options considered. Often fact must be delicately discarded in favor of entertainment – because, after all, who wants to read a novel without dramatic conflict? Palace intrigue, political peril, battlefield drama, and sexual tension – these are the reasons why a modern reader picks up a historical novel.

Faithful students of Egyptology no doubt rolled their eyes at the very mention of Senenmut's name. *Oh, brother,* I could hear them saying as I wrote the Senenmut scenes. *Another Hatshepsut novel where she has an affair with her steward.* Well, yes. Another one. A forbidden romance between the ruler of the mightiest empire in the world and her humble, common-born servant is quite exciting and romantic, even if in actual history Senenmut was almost certainly not Hatshepsut's lover – although I imagine, based on his astounding list of titles, responsibilities, and honors, that he was quite a fascinating and intelligent man, and all sorts of women probably found themselves in great admiration of his talents, even the She-King. That old "Senenmut and Hatshepsut sitting in a tree, K-I-S-S-I-N-G" trope doesn't appear in Egyptian historical fiction without good reason. Various inscriptions, including in Senenmut's own tomb, describe him as one who variously "gladdened daily the king's [Hatshepsut's] heart," and even "served in the palace of her heart," and "saw to all the pleasures of the king." In a modern western context, this sounds rather romantic – even somewhat racy. However, I doubt very much that the ancient Egyptians used such phrases in the same context as we.

Somewhat more indicative (but not by much) of the possible historicity of a Senenmut-Hatshepsut love connection was the especially close relationship Senenmut had with Neferure, and the intriguing lack of any mention of wife or children in Senenmut's tomb. He was careful to include a tribute to his favorite horse in his tomb, but no word on women or children other than his mother, Hatshesput, and Neferure. Virtually every other known Egyptian man's tomb made much of all the people who loved the departed, including spouse and offspring. Senenmut apparently never married. (Either that, or he was a great misogynist to whom women simply did not matter. That seems an unlikely stance for any ancient Egyptian, but especially for one who served the female Pharaoh so devotedly.) These facts have led to casual speculation that perhaps he was the real father of Neferure – and while I find this highly unlikely as real history (Hatshepsut and Senenmut both strike me as too professional and political-minded to engage in such dangerous tomfoolery; adultery was not smiled upon by the Egyptians) it does lend just enough plausibility to make it work quite well as an exciting fictional device. I am the faithful servant of story, as Senenmut was the faithful servant of the king's pleasure.

Fans of Egyptology will also note my use of Atenism as a plot device. The Aten – the physical, impersonal aspect of the sun, as opposed to the various personal aspects which included Amun, Amun-Re, Re-Horakhty, and more – is best known as the central god and the catalyst for the dramatic if brief political and social revolution known as the Amarna period, which followed the events in The Crook and Flail by some four or five generations. Because the Aten's popularity seems to have surged out of nowhere and then vanished again during the rule of Akhenaten and Nefertiti, it's easy to assume that the Aten was the original creation of Akhenaten. But in fact it was an old but minor god, definitely documented early in the 18th Dynasty and possibly referenced as far back as the 12th. The Aten had been around for quite some time, garnering its few followers here and there. I turned to its minor cult when I realized that Ankhhor needed some plausible motivation that would make him heedless of how he offended Amun and the other principal gods of Hatshepsut's time. If he didn't believe in the power of those other gods, he would not balk at attempting any atrocity against the divine royal family. Making Ankhhor an Atenist was the closest I could plausibly come to making him an atheist. (And I feel compelled to point out here that I do not think atheists are any more likely to attempt a royal assassination than anybody else.) And *perhaps* I have other motivations for establishing the presence of the Aten early in my body of work.

Iset's song in the garden of the House of Women is a mishmash of two real works of ancient Egyptian poetry: "Your Love Has Penetrated All Within Me" and "I Am a Wild Goose." A surprising amount of literature from ancient Egypt has been found, including several touching love poems or ballads. The Egyptians were passionate and expressive people; I encourage curious readers to seek out translations of their various stories and songs.

For all my transgressions against the truth of history, I hope the reader will forgive me, as I hope Hatshepsut, Senenmut, and the rest of her entourage forgive, looking down from their golden barque.

NOTES ON THE LANGUAGE USED

This novel is set in historical Egypt, about 1500 years before the common era and roughly 1200 years before Alexander the Great conquered the Nile. With the dawning of the Greek period, a shift in the old Egyptian language began. Proper nouns (and, we can assume, other parts of the language) took on a decidedly Greek bent, which today most historians use when referring to ancient Egyptians and their world.

This presents a bit of a tangle for a historical novelist like myself. Culturally, we are familiar with Greek-influenced names like Thebes, Rameses, and Isis. In fact, even the name Egypt is not Egyptian; it has a long chain of derivations through Greek, Latin, and French. However, the historic people in my novel would have scratched their heads over such foreign words for their various places, people, and gods. And linguistically, the modern English-speaking reader will probably have a difficult time wrapping her head and tongue around such tricky names as Djhtms – an authentic and very common man's name for the time and place where The Crook and Flail is set (rather the equivalent of a Mike or Tom or Jim).

On the balance, cultural authenticity is important to me, and so I've reverted to ancient Egyptian versions of various proper nouns and other words in the majority of cases. A glossary of ancient Egyptian words used in this book, and their more familiar Greco-English translations, follows.

In some cases, to avoid headaches and to preserve (I hope) the flow of the narrative, I have kept modernized versions of certain words in spite of their inauthentic nature. Notably, I use Egypt rather than the authentic Kmet. It is a word that instantly evokes the reader's own romantic perceptions of the land and time, whatever those may be, and its presence in the story can only aid my own attempts at world-building. I have opted for the fairly Greeky, English-friendly name Thutmose in place of Djhtms, which is simply a tongue-twister; and the word Pharaoh, which is French in origin (the French have always been enthusiastic Egyptologists) rather than the Egyptian pra'a, simply because Pharaoh is such a familiar word in the mind of a contemporary reader. Wherever possible, I have used "Pharaoh" sparingly, only to avoid repetitiveness, and have instead opted for the simple translation of "king." I've also decided, after much flip-flopping, to use the familiar Greek name Horus for the falcon-headed god, rather than the authentic name Horu. The two are close, but in every case reading Horu in my sentences interrupted the flow and tripped me up. Horus flies more smoothly on his falcon wings; ditto for Hathor, who should properly be called Hawet-Hor, but seems to prefer her modernized name.

As always, I hope the reader appreciates these concessions to historical accuracy and to comfort.

GLOSSARY

ankh – the breath of life; the animating spirit that makes humans live

Annu – Heliopolis

Anupu – Anubis

deby – hippopotamus

Heqa-Khasewet – Hyksos

Ipet-Isut – "Holy House"; the temple complex at Karnak

Iset – Isis

Iteru – Nile

Iunet – Dendera

ka – not quite in line with the Western concept of a "soul" or "spirit," a ka was an individual's vital essence, that which made him or her live.

maat – A concept difficult for modern Westerners to accurately define: something like righteousness, something like divine order, something like justice. It is to a sense of "God is in His Heaven and all is right with the world" as the native Hawai'ian word *aloha* is to an overall feeling of affection, pleasure, well-being, and joyful anticipation. It is also the name of the goddess of the concept – the goddess of "what is right."

mawat – mother; also used to refer to mother-figures such as nurses

Medjay – An Egyptian citizen of Nubian descent

rekhet – people of the common class; peasants

sepat – nome, or district

seshep – sphinx

sesheshet – sistrum; ceremonial rattle

tjati – vizier; governor of a sepat or district

Waser – Osiris, god of the afterlife, the underworld, and the dead

Waset – Thebes

ABOUT THE AUTHOR

Libbie Hawker writes historical and literary fiction featuring complex characters and rich details of time and place. She is the author of more than twenty books, including the international bestseller *The Ragged Edge of Night* (written under her pen name, Olivia Hawker.)

Libbie lives in the beautiful San Juan Islands with her husband Paul and several naughty cats. She spends her free time gardening, spinning wool, and knitting sweaters when she can keep her cats away from the yarn.